# DOOM OF STARS

By

## Martyn Rhys Vaughan

Published by
Llyfrau Cambria Books, Wales, United Kingdom.
*Cambria Books is a division of
Cambria Publishing.*
Discover our other books at: www.cambriabooks.co.uk

# REVIEWS
Other books by Martyn Rhys Vaughan

## *Domains of Darkness*

'The work of a highly creative mind, and also a perceptive mind. Using fiction to reflect the dark side of human nature e.g. the risk to humanity's future is not artificial intelligence but natural stupidity.' - **J. Gabb-Cousins** (from Facebook)

'Martyn Vaughan writes extremely well with a style harking back to the likes of Ray Bradbury and Isaac Asimov and the stories are finely crafted and well plotted.'- **R. Southall** (from Amazon)

## *Quantum Exile*

'A mind-bending mix of physics and environmentalism. Vaughan tells an exciting story and manages to weave important aspects of quantum theory into it. He also has an important message about what we are doing to damage the world's environment, in the bleak picture he paints of a planet which has gone past the tipping points and is sliding towards cataclysm. All in all, thoroughly recommended.' - **P. Brown** (from Amazon)

## *The Cave of Shadows*

'Martyn Rhys Vaughan's book is shot through with big ideas and big questions and in that sense it's a bold and brave undertaking. The book picks up pace throughout and is never less than entertaining, but the fact that the speculation is set squarely within the realms of possibility means that the book which at first seems like science fiction melding with fantasy might actually be a guidebook, a guidebook to chaotic times ahead.' – **J. Gower**, review in Nation Cymru.

*Dedicated to the men and women who preserve and protect the mystic mountain of Twmbarlwm, which lies not too far to the south of Arenig Fawr.*

Cover Design by **Terry C. Evans** (www.terry-evans.com)

The cover photo-montage includes images from
www.dreamstime.com
by Igor Borodin, Erectus, Jminso679, Patricia Marroquin, Wodthikorn Phutthasachathum and Aleksandar Blanusa.

And also images from www.alamy.com
by Steven J. Kazlowski and Ton Koene.

*Turning and turning in the widening gyre*
*The falcon cannot hear the falconer;*
*Things fall apart; the centre cannot hold;*
*Mere anarchy is loosed upon the world,*
*The blood-dimmed tide is loosed, and everywhere*
*The ceremony of innocence is drowned;*

From *The Second Coming*
By William Butler Yeats


*Should the term of our existence, which is but a moment, be the measure*
*for other durations?*
*Ought we to assert that what has lasted a hundred thousand times longer*
*than we, must last forever?*

From *Conversations on the Plurality of Worlds*
By Bernard de Fontanelle


*Portents will appear in sun, moon, and stars. On earth nations will stand*
*helpless, not knowing which way to turn from the roar and surge of the*
*sea; men will faint with terror at the thought of all that is coming upon the*
*world; for the celestial powers will be shaken.*

Luke, 25-27

# CONTENTS

# PROEM

As Fraschini looked out over the rolling yellow clouds, he hoped, as he had done so many times before, that they would break and yield a glimpse of the underlying land, but this time, as so many times before, there was no sign of a tear or rift in that undulating mass of ochre obscurity.

He gave an unconscious shrug of disappointment but continued to gaze out over the mass of roiling clouds, unaware that De Vries had joined him.

Both men stood silent for some time and when De Vries finally spoke, Fraschini gave a little start as he realised he was not alone.

'Still hoping for some change, something to see?' De Vries observed, in what was not really a question.

Fraschini shrugged. 'No harm in hoping.'

Both men fell silent again as they looked out over the slowly churning clouds.

In the brilliant sky, approaching the zenith, the last hope of humanity was glinting in the blaze of the fierce sun.

'What was that weird name you gave it?' De Vries asked, breaking the long pause.

Fraschini did not turn to look at his companion and in the thick plexiglass his reflection was impassive.

'*Spes Nostra*'

'Which means?'

Fraschini turned to De Vries, sighing as he did so..

'I've told you enough times. And it's not a weird name: it's a completely accurate, definite name.'

'OK, OK, calm down. I was just making conversation. I know you're under a lot of pressure, just take it easy. We all feel the same here.'

Fraschini gave a weak smile. 'Sorry. I know I'm jumpy, it's

1

just that we're so close now, so damn close.'

De Vries gave his friend a quick pat on the shoulder.

'You're worried that we're leaving too many behind, aren't you?'

'Of course. But we can't go on rescuing them. It's too energy-intensive. We can't go on doing it. It's just; it's just…'

De Vries waited, silent, immobile.

'It's just what I'm condemning them to. So many of them, people just like you and me. They don't deserve it.'

'No-one deserves it, no-one could possibly deserve it,' De Vries said slowly, and there was a great sadness behind his words.

He turned back to the window and the distant blaze of the object at which they had been looking.

'*Spes Nostra*', he said after a long pause, 'well named.'

Fraschini did not reply immediately; he continued gazing out over the empty yellow cloudscape but his mind was somewhere else: in a very different place and with very different people.

# BOOK ONE: Shards and Splinters

# One

Kalli stared up at the rising Moon and felt the cold hand of fear brush suddenly over her heart.

The Moon had risen silently behind her as she had struggled across the brittle ice and it now sat on the horizon, a mighty half-dome of pitiless red majesty.

Although she could not name any of the features on that massive quadrant, she could see many of them quite clearly, especially the dark ellipse of the crater Plato, staring contemptuously back at her from its station above the Mare Frigoris.

Familiar as she was with the sharp fangs of the biting cold, Kalli shivered involuntarily.

This was going to be a bad one—she knew it. Although not as well-versed in the lore of nature as any of the leaders of her Village, she knew, as any child would have known, that there was danger.

Were they near enough to the coast? They would find out soon.

Kalli glanced at her companions. They were still examining their fishing nets and harpoons and seemed unaware of the danger. She crossed to them, calling out Jansen's name as she hurried to him. He turned and stared at her with sealskin-grey eyes set in a face which seemingly had been constructed from old leather, a leather crisscrossed by a myriad spidery lines inscribed there by the savage climate.

'What is it now, girl?' he snapped in a voice which indicated that he had been disturbed once too often.

For answer, she half turned and pointed at the dull, crimson horn which had now risen noticeably above the ice crags since she had first seen it. Jansen looked beyond her at the rising satellite and shrugged.

'Plenty of time, girl,' he grunted, 'you've got a lot to learn. Instead of running around like a headless walrus, come and help us with these nets.'

'But the Moon…' she said, pointing again at the rising gibbous satellite.

Jansen was annoyed now.

'I said we had plenty of time. Now do you want to join in or shall I tell Tomlinson that you don't want to work?'

Kalli gave him a glare that in her mind should have burnt him to a smouldering cinder, but Jansen seemed unaware of that withering blast and gestured towards the nets.

He glanced at his fellow workers and shrugged.

'Young girls these days,' he observed, 'they don't know the meaning of hard work. They must think the fish will jump out of the water into their hands if they call them.'

One of the younger men gave a slight jerk of his head towards Kalli's slim form.

'I'd jump into her hands all right. And that's not all I'd jump into!'

The men laughed.

Jansen gave a quick smile to show he agreed with their appreciation but also quick enough to show that he wanted no more of this kind of banter.

'Right, enough of that,' he said briskly, 'let's get these nets done before we freeze our arses off.'

'Or anything else,' grinned the one who had commented on Kalli's charms.

'Enough,' Jansen said and raised a finger to show that he meant it.

Unabashed, the young man turned to the nets and for the next half an hour the entire hunting party worked on repairing them.

Finally, Jansen stood up and, brushing the powered ice from his breeches, said, 'That'll do. Let's get moving while there's still a chance of catching something.'

The entire band rose stiffly to their feet, their cold joints complaining at the sudden demand placed upon them.

Kalli came up to Jansen. 'Boss, don't you think we should

pull back rather than go further out onto the pack ice?'

Jansen's eyes, cold and harsh as the hummocked ice that surrounded the little group, gave her a stare that bored into her like the barbs of one of their harpoons.

'And why would that be, little girl?'

For answer Kalli turned so she was facing the way they had come and pointed.

'That's why.'

Behind her the Moon was now clear of the horizon, a vast semicircle of orange-red glory, but a glory smeared with black fungoid patches.

'Aren't you risking us all for a few fish when you know there's a Wave coming?'

'There's no need to worry about a Wave,' Jansen said, 'the Moon's got a way to go before it's full.'

'But I've never seen it this close,' Kalli pleaded, 'we don't know it'll follow the same pattern.'

' "Follow the same pattern"?' Jansen repeated mockingly, 'what kind of language is that? Why don't you speak like normal folk?'

Kalli stood her ground. 'It's not how I say it,' she responded, 'it's what I say. There's danger.'

For answer Jansen pointed farther out into the blue-white plane of the pack ice.

'Move.'

They trudged on while the swollen satellite rose steadily behind them. The cloudless sky slowly transitioned from an eggshell blue through aquamarine to a rich indigo-blue, as if an entire ocean was suspended above them. A few stars began to show; one in particular on the horizon opposite the Moon, shone with a fierce brilliance that flashed in fleeting tints of red, blue, and green. On very clear nights people as sharp-eyed as Kalli could discern much smaller stars that always appeared near to that particular star.

The men began to mutter: it seemed they were starting to share Kalli's unease.

6

*He's determined to bring something back to Tomlinson*, she thought, *even if it means killing some of us.*

But then the leading man of the hunters pointed and waved for them to stop. He rejoined the others and said, very quietly, 'There's a blowhole over there. Don't say anything!'

The rest of the men looked at each other, with excitement marked plainly on their frost-rimmed faces.

A blowhole.

Seals!

Proper, red meat for once!

They knew what to do. They all removed their spears from their straps and held them horizontally; all save Kalli, who had no spear.

'You stay back,' Jansen said to her, 'with your skin you stand out like a lump of coal. Watch out for danger. If you hear any sound that shouldn't be there—shout out!'

Kalli said nothing: she was used to comments about her skin tone. It was a great hurt to her that there was no one else in Tomlinson's group who shared her complexion.

The men gradually, silently, formed a circle around the blowhole and waited.

And waited.

'Keep your eyes and ears open, Kalli!' Jansen advised her quietly, indicating with movements of his hand that she should move away from the blowhole.

The great dome above them darkened to a fathomless violet in which more and more stars began to show through. The cold became so intense that it slipped razors of pain through Kalli's furs. She began to feel she was standing there naked, on the cruel pack ice.

Suddenly, without warning, a seal's head broke through the thin covering of ice over the blowhole. The men were ready and, equally suddenly, a ring of spears shot out and caught the seal in its fat neck. It had time to issue one short, surprised grunt before it died.

Hurriedly, before it could slip back into the freezing depths,

7

the men dragged it out onto the ice, its blood creating a little crimson rivulet on the hitherto pristine surface.

The men stood around in noisy triumph, slapping each other on the back and even hugging each other.

Kalli stood apart from them, not because she did not wish to share in their exultation but because she thought she had heard something and wanted to be sure.

She moved a little further away, her dark brown eyes scanning the gradually dimming ice fields, now lit a lurid ochre by the colossal Moon.

Abruptly there was no need to wonder for there was a great, deep-throated roar and a huge grey-white bulk emerged from behind an ice hummock, heading straight for the men and the seal.

An ice bear.

The men whipped their heads around when they heard that roar and fell back, lifting their spears as they did so.

'Don't take it on!' yelled Jansen, 'let it have the seal!'

Kalli heard one of the men respond with a shouted 'Like Hell!' and saw him dart forward, spear pointing at the creature's head. She could see that the bear was a male and a very large, very hungry male. As man and bear came together it suddenly reared up onto its hind legs and stood towering over him, jaws slavering, and with front legs spread wide, ready to descend and rip the human into bloody shreds.

The overbold man had the good sense to withdraw and the entire group were forced to watch impotently as the beast dragged the seal carcass away into the dim distance.

A silence fell, at first shot through with fear but a fear which was gradually replaced with anger.

Jansen turned to Kalli and beckoned her to come nearer.

'Why didn't you warn us about the bear?' was his bitter snarl, 'you had a chance to do something useful instead of whimpering about bloody waves!'

Kalli stared angrily back at him but found she had no retort. As she was too slight of physique to wield a harpoon, it was her

8

job to act as lookout and warn of dangers such as the bear. Jansen was not being entirely unfair in his raging disappointment.

It had all happened too quickly; she had heard the bear but only when it had almost been upon them. Almost against her will, she found herself saying, 'Sorry.' Desperately she added, 'It was in its winter coat so it was hard to see.'

The glares from Jansen and the other men made it all too clear that her apology was not accepted. But she understood their bitterness, for she felt it herself. She too had been looking forward to enjoying strong red meat; the lovely feeling of warm fat dripping from her chin, the feeling of fullness, of satiety that would follow the orgy of consumption.

And now it was not to be. Just the thin, bitter flesh of starving sea birds or skeletal fish.

Again.

The band looked around and even Jansen was forced to admit that it was now far too late in the day to attempt to catch another seal. And because of their struggle with the seal, they had not caught any fish either.

The whole expedition had been a disaster and Kalli glumly accepted that she was in part responsible.

They trudged back over the pack ice shelf to the permanent ice in total silence, with Kalli keeping a discreet distance behind the men.

Above them the sky-dome was now jet-black, shot through with brilliant, unblinking stars like dimensionless points of cold crystal, shining steadily with a pitiless silver radiance, while ahead of them the great half Moon was completely clear of the horizon. No longer coloured by atmospheric absorption, it too blazed in white majesty, casting the group's long weary shadows far behind them across the ice.

The trip back to the huts seemed much longer than the trip out.

9

# Two

Kalli sat slumped on the pile of furs in her corner of the main hut. She had tried all of yesterday and most of today to shake off the feeling that she alone was responsible for the disastrous end to the hunting expedition, but that was hard with everyone regularly throwing her unpleasant glances.

Would Jansen never stop talking about it? She took comfort in opening her box of treasures. She looked through, but without really seeing much detail, her brightly coloured science books. She stopped at one page which showed two circles on a black background. One was labelled "Earth", the other "The Moon." The "Earth" circle had two bulges on it, one on the side facing the Moon, but slightly ahead of an imaginary line connecting the centres of the objects, and had another bulge on the other side, similarly displaced, but in the opposite direction. She knew those bulges were the tides raised on the Earth by the pull of the Moon; she even thought that she understood why there were two bulges, rather than one. For some reason she was not like the mass of Tomlinson's group; they had to know many things about their environment in order to survive in it, but they were not interested in abstract knowledge, blaming it for the catastrophe that had overtaken the world, not too long ago.

Once when she had done something wrong or said something bad – she couldn't really remember – one of her books had been taken from her and thrown on the fire. She had cried for days until the threat of corporal punishment had finally silenced her.

She looked at her companions, huddled around the central fire of bits of coal and driftwood.

They were not bad people; she knew that. They felt bitter that their future had been stolen from them and that they had been left scrabbling for food on the edge of existence.

She put the books safely away in their box, placing a thin animal skin over them and then took out her real treasure.

It was a gleaming white ball, easily small enough to fit in the palm of her hand. It was opalescent with the nacreous sheen of tropical seashells – although she did not use that comparison, never having seen any tropical seashells. It felt oddly warm to the touch, even on the coldest nights, as if there was some small power source deep inside it. She remembered how her mother had given it to her, shortly before her disappearance, and warned her never to lose it.

'One day, you'll know its importance,' she had said. 'My father said I should look into it but I never found the courage. I didn't want to know. Perhaps you will.'

*One day.* When would that day be?

Where was her mother now? she wondered, was she even alive? She could still vaguely remember her appearance, her great fuzz of hair, the smile which seemed to hint at some great sadness in her past—but no more. Of her father, she had no memory at all. Just a father-shaped hole in her past.

Once or twice she had thought she had seen a kind of motion in the sphere's pearly depths, as if something was trying to rise to the surface. That had happened several times recently, with increasing frequency—but not tonight.

She gave one last look at her special treasure, put it in the box and stowed it safely behind the pile of furs that was her bed.

She became aware that there was an excited buzz in the air and that something other than her dereliction of duty had caught the attention of her companions. She could hear a faint crackling noise and then a steady hum and realised that they were preparing to listen to the broadcast from the Westranian Congress in Jacksonville, somewhere in far-off Florida.

She had heard of Florida but only as a magical land where snow never fell and water always stayed liquid and there were lots of tall trees and brightly-coloured birds and other wonderful things.

The President was speaking.

'My fellow Westranians,' came a deep, resonant voice, 'we have done well. All of my listeners can congratulate themselves on how they have faced the challenges which daily assault them. Life is not easy for any of us but you can rest assured that we form one strong community, one mighty race which will not be found wanting in these days of trial. We are one people, strong, united. We will not tolerate incursions from those less gifted than ourselves; those who are jealous of our achievements, jealous of our spirit of unity.

'No, we will not let rapacious Eastranians take what we have gathered by the sweat of our brow, our dedication, our refusal to let misfortune take away our birthright. You will be pleased to hear that I have refused to send any more shipments of wheat and soya to those ingrates.'

Some of Kalli's companions looked at each other at that point in the President's speech, apparently unsure what "ingrates" meant. Some appeared not to have heard of the hated Eastranians.

Unaware of the confusion he had generated, the President continued, 'And now we have just passed the half-point of Winter. Soon warmth will begin to return to our beautiful lands and the ice will retreat to its rightful place in the far North. Soon the soil will be warm enough for the sowing to begin, and you, my friends, will assuredly reap the bountiful harvests that you so richly deserve.

'I leave you with this message: Love one another just as I have loved you. Enjoy the returning sun and stay strong.'

With that exhortation, the radio went dead and was immediately switched off to conserve the batteries.

Kalli felt slightly puzzled: the President's closing words had sounded oddly familiar; she seemed to remember them from her early childhood.

She shook her head. She could not remember. Her entire childhood was a jumbled mass of memories; some of which seemed to be contradictory. She couldn't be sure how much her supposed past had been dreamt up in her own brain.

She was catapulted out of reverie by a strong hand descending on a shoulder and shaking her vigorously. Looking up, she found herself regarding a barrel-chested man with a salt-and-pepper beard that spilled over his chest, seemingly down to where his navel would be, if it had been visible.

Tomlinson. The group leader.

'Wake up, girlie,' he said in a basso profondo, 'time to do something useful for a change.'

Obediently, she sprang to her feet, anxious to do something that would help restore her status.

'We need more coal,' Tomlinson said, and with a wicked grin added, 'and don't fall over in there or we'll never be able to find you!'

Kalli smiled; she had learned that frowning at these jibes didn't help, they just made them more likely to be reiterated on an ascending scale of unpleasantness. If she smiled, the jibes would not be repeated for a while.

She went outside with a bag in her hand in which to carry the coal.

Despite the feral cold that nipped at her extremities with gnawing hunger, she still found time to stare at the sky.

A full day had passed since the incident with the bear, and the great Moon had not yet risen. But again she could see that brilliant star on the horizon, flashing in a myriad of colours as if it were a slowly rotating diamond. Some people said they could see two or three smaller stars in attendance on that big one, but Kalli knew that they were mistaken, or rather, had not seen all that could easily be seen. She could see four much dimmer stars around the bright one tonight, as she always had. And they moved: sometimes there would be three on one side and only one on the other. She had read of a world with four satellites but the books she had read as a child had said that those satellites were not visible to the unaided vision. So it couldn't be that world.

She shrugged and gave up; it was far too cold to stand and stare at the bitter sky and ponder questions that she would never be able to answer.

She opened the door of the little hut and gathered some coal in the darkness and when the bag was almost too heavy to lift without a grunting effort, she went back out into the frigid night.

The coal supply was getting very low, and that was a worry. There was a local branch of the Westranian Government in the nearby big city which offered occasional help, but the vital mineral was very hard to find. All of it had to be extracted from ancient mines that lay deep underground which needed to be pumped free of tonnes of stagnant, iron-polluted water before it could be reached. She did not envy the men and women who had that job. She'd rather face a starving bear.

The warmth of the hut was like the return of a much-loved friend, and she stood for a moment savouring the comforting embrace of the warm air, laden as it was with the smell of unwashed bodies and greasy scraps of old meals. That is, she stood there until a barrage of obscenities reminded her that she'd left the door open.

Another blunder. Would she never learn.

The fire was now banked until it was hardly alight but it would continue to provide essential warmth throughout the night. She had read that the nights were very long in the time of Winter, but she had noticed that some months ago that they had been longer than they were now.

And yet the cold had been increasing until very recently. How could that be?

Her companions settled down for the night and very soon the hut was filled with various levels of snoring, some soft and gentle, others loud and raucous.

But not quite loud enough to disguise the giggling and grunting that was coming from one corner of the hut which seemed to indicate that at least two people were still awake.

Kalli knew what they were doing and wondered if there would come a time when she would be doing it as well.

As yet, she felt no need, except occasionally she would wake after a particularly vivid dream and find herself breathing heavily with a warm wetness on her thighs.

She pushed those strange thoughts from her mind and

settled down for sleep.

But just as she was hovering on the edge of sweet unconsciousness, she was brought back to high alert by the sound of great crashing noises in the far distance, in the direction of the pack ice. It was as if great slabs of stone were being ripped apart by a giant's hands and then tossed aside, to crash thunderously to earth.

Others had heard it too, and heads poked out of their covering furs, turning to their neighbours who were as disturbed as themselves.

Kalli found herself staring at Jansen who had got up and was standing near the door.

He waited for a while until the mighty thunders slowly died away and then turned to return to his file of furs.

But Kalli knew what had caused the tumult and as he passed her to return to his bed, she saw concern in his eyes.

She said nothing but she could tell that he also knew what the sounds had been and was worried.

As well he might be, for the noises were caused by the pack ice splintering under the force of a great Wave.

# Three

The next morning dawned bright and clear—but then most mornings did around mid-Winter. Kalli slowly became aware of the yellow light from the sun through cracks in the hut's walls where the moss had fallen out. She snuggled further into the soft, warm furs that embraced her like a second womb.

No need to get up just yet.

There she was wrong, for the furs were abruptly pulled off her and a voice she knew only too well growled, 'Up you get, my little black bed bug. Up you get!'

Jansen was not one to be disobeyed, especially after her recent blunder.

Soon they were standing outside the hut, their breath rising in misty cloudlets as they waited for Jansen to give his orders. Kalli blinked at the rising sun, still half-hidden behind low vapours.

It looked very slightly bigger. Was that possible or was it a result of atmospheric distortion? The word "refraction" came from somewhere, although she wasn't quite sure what it meant.

She gave up on that issue and was startled when Jansen pushed something cold and heavy into her grasp. Looking down, she saw it was a rifle. That meant exactly one thing: they would not be going out onto the pack ice today. They would be going inland to hunt for things that one could not get close enough to harpoon, and that could only be red deer. Kalli knew that deer were roaming nearby, trying to find patches of snow thin enough so that they could get at the underlying vegetation.

Jansen looked at her, his features displaying a disquieting expression.

'You've had a bit of practice with firearms, haven't you Kalli. I'm giving you a second chance, though God knows why. Don't bugger this one up!'

Kalli looked at the rifle with some alarm; it was true she had had some practice, but not as much as she would have liked, as ammunition was in short supply and they had no blank rounds. But there was nothing she could say; she understood that she was being given a second chance at proving herself to be a valued member of the team, and she respected Jansen for doing that. She didn't dislike any of her fellows: she just wished she was more competent at the tasks they appeared to find so easy. Perhaps she had spent too much time in looking at pretty pictures of astronomical objects instead of learning more useful things, like the quickest way to gut a fish.

They set out, trudging through the old, brittle snow. Nothing fresh had fallen for some time, and much of the snow was on the point of becoming ice, which made progress difficult. She glanced up at the watery sun, now half-hidden by wispy cirrus. It definitely looked slightly larger, so the President must be right about it being more than halfway through the winter. She could just remember the previous Summer, and a vision flashed fleetingly through her adolescent mind. She remembered everything being green instead of this endless blue-white wilderness. She remembered being in the open air without being swaddled in thick layers of fur and animal skin and the feel of the sun beating gloriously down on her mahogany skin.

But there were also memories that were less welcome: memories of suffocating heat which had made it impossible to move around; of the green vegetation turning first yellow and then brown and becoming so dry that the leaves could be easily crumbled to dust in a youthful grasp.

If that was Summer, it was a place to which she did not wish to return.

Suddenly a man's palm was placed against her chest and she realised that she was meant to stop. In her daydreams, she hadn't realised that they had marched so far from the camp. She looked around, aware that Jansen had noticed her lack of attention. Ahead was a bare copse of black, twisted trees, long since slain by the merciless cold. And between the dead copse and her group was a small herd of red deer, their snouts bent down into the snow, which they were pushing aside in attempts to find some scraps of edible vegetation beneath, apparently with little success.

Jansen looked around at his company, finger to his lips; the excitement showing in the small amount of his face visible beneath his furry hood. He silently waved to his group to fan out so that there would be marksmen on either side of the deer; Kalli, he indicated, should stay with him.

Together they watched as the men silently spread out, so that there were a few on either side of the deer, rifles lowered and at the ready.

'This is your chance, girlie,' Jansen whispered, 'you know how to use that thing. Line up on the big boy in the middle and let him have it.'

Kalli felt a sudden burst of mixed emotions: she didn't want to kill the magnificent beast in front of her yet she knew her people needed good, red meat and she also felt a sudden surge of excitement; excitement in the knowledge that she now had the power of life and death and that she would soon receive the praise of her fellows.

And then the enormity of the situation hit her; she must not mess up this time!

The stag before her continued to push at the snow, his breath rising around him in great wispy clouds. She lined up her rifle on the vital spot and squinted along the barrel, as the gun had no sights. The stag, oblivious to the danger, continued to move forward and then, just as she was about to send the killing shot into it, abruptly turned to look back at his hinds.

If Kalli had known any swearwords she was prepared to say out loud, she would have used them then, because the animal turned away and she was confronted by its posterior. She decided to move in tandem with him to get a good side-on view again and slowly moved to the right, keeping her eye on her quarry all the time. Finally, she had a clear sight of him again and raised the rifle to her shoulder.

*Just a little bit more to the right*, she said to herself and began to adjust her position at the same time as she unwisely decided to fire.

Her foot caught in a root hidden in the snow and her arm jerked to the left just as the rifle fired.

Almost instantly, there was a man's voice giving a scream of pain as the deer scattered.

Jansen acted immediately. He swung his rifle up, fired, and brought the stag down with a single shot.

He then ran in the direction of the scream to find one of his men clutching his upper right arm, with blood seeping between the fingers.

'That stupid bitch shot me!' the wounded man yelled, nodding in Kalli's direction. She stood where she had been when she had fired the rifle, almost literally frozen to the spot, a look of horror etched on her face.

Jansen cut away the fur over the wound and then grunted when he got down to the flesh.

'You're in luck—superficial. She hasn't blown your muscle away. You'll live and work again.'

He then turned and motioned to Kalli to join them.

'Look at what you've done, you stupid, stupid child!' he roared at the cowering girl. 'I give you one chance to do better and this is how you repay by nearly killing one of my best men!'

'Sorry, sorry,' was all Kalli could offer in the way of an answer, 'I tripped. I'm so, so sorry.'

'I should shoot you, you useless cunt!' the wounded man roared but Jansen put up his hand to silence him.

'That's enough of that language here.' He turned back to Kalli, who quailed under his glare. 'I should kick you out of our group as you're just a troublesome hanger-on. I should.'

Kalli stared at the snow beneath her feet and muttered, 'I'm sorry.'

Jansen apparently had come to a decision, for he straightened his arthritic posture and said, 'I'll punish you when we get back. I'm not going to kick you out because we need every pair of hands during the winter. I'll lick you into shape if it kills me. Or you,' he added, seemingly in deadly earnest. 'We'll have to go to London to get more antibiotics. In the meantime, get one thing right and help the men carry that stag back to the camp. Thank Christ there's someone who can shoot in this band!'

The silent trek back to the camp felt endless; Kalli felt that she was at the centre of an invisible bubble blown from anger and contempt. Was there anything she could say? This was much worse than the bear incident; perhaps she just wasn't fit to be a member of Tomlinson's group.

Eventually, they reached the camp. The injured man was given into the care of the women who bathed and bound his injury and gave him the last of the antibiotics that the company had.

Jansen stopped Kalli just inside the hut and said in a calm, clear voice, 'Get your box of trinkets.'

Trembling, Kalli obeyed. Jansen opened it, took out every book and ripped each one into shreds, letting the torn pages flutter to the floor like dying butterflies. He then gestured to the girl to put the pieces onto the fire.

Then he gave the box a final shake and the shining ball fell out, to land at Kalli's feet.

'No!' she cried, 'that was my mother's last gift to me! Please let me keep it! Don't make me put in the fire!'

'No, I won't do that,' Jansen said impassively, 'it might burn the place down and I don't want to add that to your list of foul-ups. Follow me.'

He turned back to the hut entrance with the girl close behind him and, drawing his powerful arm back, he threw the ball as far as he could. With tears drawing lines on her cheeks, Kalli watched the sphere describe a low arc and plunge into the snowdrifts an impossible distance from the doorway.

'That's that,' he grunted and looked down at the sobbing girl. 'Don't cry, Kalli. It was either that, or I threw you out instead of that ball. You've had your head in the clouds for too long. Your priorities are all wrong, my girl. What good is looking at pictures of Saturn and Mars? Does that put meat on the table? Well, does it!' He reached down to shake her at that point.

'No,' Kalli sniffed, through her tears, 'No, it doesn't.'

Jansen smiled; the smile of a hard man who had been moulded by the harsh land he had been forced to live in, to endure. 'Well, let's say no more about it. We're all in this together. You're different to the rest of us, but that's not your fault. You'll get there in the end.'

And with that, he left her. She lay on her pile of furs, still sobbing. But gradually the sobs turned into sniffs and then snores and muffled grunts as she fell into an exhausted sleep.

*** 

She awoke, and it was deep night. She could hear the snores and the mutterings of those lost in dreams emanating from the rest of her people.

For some reason she could not understand, she threw off the furs and stood up. The hut was dimly lit by the sombre red glow of the banked fire but she was able to see that she was the only one awake. As if under some compulsion, she turned to the great door which kept the feral cold outside. Slowly, silently, she approached the door and swung up the great spar that held it shut.

She stepped outside and the cold hit like a great breaker of pain crashing over her. It seemed that stilettos of ice were being forced into every part of her body, cutting and slicing into every orifice.

The gigantic moon was resting on the far horizon, throwing amber light over the land. She remembered the direction and distance that Jansen had thrown her ball and as if under some outside control, she headed in that direction. Her feet were bare, but she seemed impervious to the pain that insidiously climbed her limbs as she walked out into the implacable night. Her glazed eyes looked only straight ahead and so she did not see a brilliant point of light, shining like a magnificent, resplendent star, rise in the north-west and pass directly overhead.

She reached the area where she thought the ball had landed

and mechanically began to brush the hard-packed snow away with freezing fingers. Her face was emotionless, as if she was not entirely aware of what was happening. She pushed snow away until a deep hole had formed, but still there was no sign of her treasure. Still she continued and then, without warning, a light shone with a soft, blue glow through the overlying ice. She lifted a fist and smashed it down, shattering the ice. Fingers that felt no pain reached through the shards and retrieved the sphere.

She stood up, straight and strong, in the dying amber light and returned silently to her bed, after replacing the ball in her box.

And after she had placed it in the box its light went out, as if the object had known it was home.

# Four

When she awoke, for a few moments, she did not remember her excursion into the night. Then when she did remember, she thought it must have been a dream. Furtively, she looked around and after confirming that there were no curious eyes studying her, stole a swift glance into her box. The sphere was there. Then she was frightened: if Jansen ever found it, real trouble would follow. She looked around, attempting to look innocent and unconcerned. Everything looked normal. Everybody seemed normal. Jansen ignored her until the time came to leave for their trip to the big city. Only there could the group stock up on antibiotics, ammunition, seeds and other domestic necessities.

The young adults of the community gathered together for the trek to London shortly after a meagre breakfast of cooked grain and seeds. As well as Jansen, there were two young men, Ethan and Craig, and three girls, all around the same age, one of whom was Kalli. She was the youngest by several years and the other two girls, Kiara and Sharon already had partners and would soon be pregnant. They usually ignored Kalli because she had not yet fully entered the realm of womenfolk. That was the way of things.

Jansen was present, of course, as the group leader. The rarely-seen Tomlinson was the head of the entire community, but hardly ever did he venture out into the ice and snow and was content to issue orders from his pile of furs, which naturally occupied the closest spot to the fire.

'How far is it to London?' Sharon said, after she had stopped giggling with her companion during their competition to catch the boys' attention.

'Half daylight to get there, some hours there, and another half day to get back,' was Jansen's gruff response.

Sharon nodded after receiving that information, but Kiara had realised something.

'Hey!' she blurted, 'that means we'll be coming back in the

dark! The days aren't that long!'

Jansen shrugged. 'I didn't know you were afraid of the dark. Shall I ask your mother to come instead?'

The young men burst out laughing and Kiara blushed, while her companion smiled a satisfied smile.

Kalli said nothing. She felt it was best not to draw attention to herself, and in any case she had already worked out the likely time of their return.

And so it was that they set out across the hard-packed snow, at first altogether, but soon their different rates of progress found them strung out in a line, each carrying a bag or sack containing dried fish or hunks of venison—the least desirable cuts, of course. Jansen led them but, as he was no longer a young man, this forced the entire line to slow down to his pace. Kalli gradually drifted to the end position, not because she could not keep up but because no-one was talking to her. Eventually, she began to feel a burning resentment at her isolation: was she the only one who had ever made a mistake? Had Jansen never blundered when he had been a young man – if ever he had been!

She decided that she was not going to remain in silence for the entire journey and caught up with the traveller immediately in front of her, who happened to be Ethan.

'Hello,' she said as she drew abreast, nervously gripping the handle of her knife, 'What time do you think we'll get there?'

Ethan looked startled as if she had just dropped from the sky.

'Oh, hello,' he finally managed to reply, 'around midday I guess.'

Silence fell. Kalli found herself experiencing a strange sensation as she strode along with the youth. A feeling as if she wanted to stay with him, to be close to him, to reach out and— perhaps—touch him. She struggled to break the intolerable silence.

'What's London like?' finally came to her lips.

He glanced at her. *He's very good-looking*, she thought.

'It's big. Very big,' he said, 'much, much bigger than our

24

camp. It's the biggest place in the world, some say. It's a city.'

A city. Kalli had seen that word in one of her books, below a picture of impossibly tall buildings either side of a big channel of a blue colouration, which was labelled river.

The thought excited her. To see such buildings—it must be wonderful!

She didn't realise for a moment that her vision had caused silence to fall again and was slightly startled to hear Ethan say, 'That was bad luck with the stag.'

His words brought her back to the here and now with a crash. She didn't want to remember that near tragedy.

'Yes,' she replied, after an awkward pause, 'I was very lucky not to kill someone.'

Ethan continued to look at her, which she liked at first but then began to make her uncomfortable.

'You're not happy here, are you.'

She tried to laugh. 'What! Of course, I'm happy here! Why wouldn't I be?'

'Because you're not like the rest of us.'

She twisted her smile into a frown. 'What, because of my skin? Because I look like a lump of coal!'

His smile remained a smile. 'No, not that. We're all used to that now. No, it's the way you talk, the things you're interested in. Like: "What happened to cause the bad Winters." Like: "Why does the Moon keep changing size." Nobody else asks those questions.'

She shrugged. 'I can't help it. The questions just come into my head and I ask them. I can't not ask them. I don't understand why no-one else does.'

Ethan's smile was gentle now, which she loved. 'There you are. That's it. You can't help it. And everybody else can't help *not* asking them!'

She smiled back, enjoying the mutual smiles. Then she stopped smiling. And stopped walking.

She turned her head to the north and cocked it, as if listening to some faint, far-off sound.

'Listen,' she said, 'do you hear it?'

Somehow Jansen was aware that someone in the train had stopped moving and he held up a hand to tell the others to stop. He walked rapidly down the line to Kalli.

'Why have you stopped?'

For reply, she pointed north and said, 'Can't you hear them?'

In the silence that followed, all Jansen and the others could hear was the sound of their breathing and the thin, mournful whine of the wind.

'No,' Jansen finally said, 'I hear nothing. What am I supposed to be hearing?'

She looked up at him, into penetrating grey eyes. 'A kind of howling. Very far off. A howling.'

Kiara gave a muffled cry and said, 'Wolves!'

Jansen spun around. 'Stop that right now! There are no wolves in this part of Westrania. None!'

The girl continued, in a kind of breathless voice, 'My mother told me about wolves. They look like big dogs, but they kill— and eat…'

Jansen went up to the girl and to Kalli's amazement slapped her across the face.

'There are no wolves in Westrania. None!'

Kiara burst into tears and put her hand to the spreading red patch on her face.

Jansen looked around at all of them in turn.

'Let's have no more of your nonsense or you'll have me to answer to. I don't want anybody coming up with stories like that or we'll all be frightened to go on. We're moving too slowly as it is.' He turned briefly to the crying girl. 'I'm sorry I hit you, Kiara. I shouldn't have done it but you were frightening the rest of them.' Then he looked at Kalli. 'And you. No more hearing things that aren't there. Got it?'

Kalli nodded. She'd had enough conflict.

She got it.

\*\*\*

26

The struggle over the icy snow seemed interminable, and Kalli gave up speaking shortly after the incident with Kiara. Much as she wanted to carry on talking with Ethan, she soon found that she had run out of things to say and glumly returned to her position as the final member of the wearily plodding line.

And despite the monotony, she was on high alert, straining her ears to see if she could again detect those worrying sounds she had heard earlier. And she was certain: she had heard them! Her books had contained no reference to wolves, but she guessed from the reaction that the girl had caused that they were things which it would be best to avoid.

Still they walked on. And on. Kalli found herself looking down at her feet and her entire world seemed to be reduced to hard, dirty snow. Then she heard noises coming from all directions, but this time the sounds were immediately comprehensible.

People.

She looked up. There were groups of people on either side of her, and groups beyond them in the distance. She was mildly startled; she had never seen so many human beings before; people who were not part of her community. Some were going in the same direction as her own group; some to other destinations. Those nearest seemed friendly, and many waved to Kalli's band as they passed. She tried talking to Ethan again.

'Who are all these people? I've never seen so many!'

Ethan gave one of his pleasing smiles again. 'People just like you and me, Kalli. Some are going to London and some are coming from London. London is where everything happens—I thought you knew that.'

Kalli nodded wisely, even though that thought had never occurred to her, and even managed to wave back at some of the other travellers. Then she heard Jansen call out: 'There she is! We're here!'

The group had stopped when Jansen had called out and gradually reformed into a side-by-side grouping. They all looked in the direction in which Jansen was pointing.

There was a slight haze of drifting ice crystals whipped up by a passing breeze, but in the vague distance there were the unmistakable shapes of huts.

And what huts! They were much bigger than those of Kalli's group and some were two stories! And she was almost sure she could see one that had three stories!

Jansen confirmed what everyone had presumed.

'London,' he said, in a voice which almost seemed tinged with awe, 'Here we are!'

'It's incredible!' Kalli breathed, 'so big!'

She saw Ethan grin at that. 'Yes,' he said, in the amused tones of the experienced man who has seen it all before, 'it takes a bit of getting used to. The first time I came here I was just like you.'

But London had not exhausted all her wonders. Kalli's keen ears picked up another mystery; a strange, whirring noise, unlike anything that she had heard before. She looked around, trying to find the source. Ethan noticed her puzzlement and, with yet another tolerant smile, tapped her on the shoulder and pointed upwards. She followed his gesture and saw a black shape moving against lead-grey clouds hiding the sun.

'What is that?' she whispered, not entirely certain that she shouldn't be frightened, 'It's too big to be a bird.'

'It's not a bird. It's a machine, a flying thing made by men. It's a helicopter.'

A helicopter! Kalli remembered in the picture of the city in one of her books there had been a thing drawn in its sky which had borne the title "Helicopter."

And here it was. They did exist!

For some time, she watched the strange machine circling, slowly descending as it did so. She concluded that it must be landing somewhere in the great city. But it was at this point that she realised that although she had been standing still no-one else in her party had, and she was in danger of being left behind—a frightening thought. Looking desperately around, she caught sight of one of the girls just about to disappear into the maze of streets. She ran after her, and, catching up, said almost tearfully, 'You could have waited!' Sharon gave her a disdainful look. 'What have you done for me lately?' was the reply and then she carried on walking.

Realising that she had not found an ally, Kalli hurried on until she had almost caught up with Jansen, who somehow knew she was behind him and said, 'You get lost in London, my girl, and you'll never be seen again. Got it?'

She nodded her acceptance in the direction of his shoulders as he marched on in front of her, knowing that Jansen seemed to be able to see things even when he wasn't looking directly at them. And this time—making sure she was staying with her companions—she was able to look around at the amazing place she found herself in.

She had never seen so many people! Who knew there were this many! The sound of them all was oppressive after the quiet of her home Village. Everybody seemed to be shouting and screaming, and people were continually bumping into her without the slightest indication that they were aware of her existence. There seemed to be no end to the buildings, and everywhere she looked there were streets and alleys leading off in all directions, with more buildings at the ends of them. She noticed that there wasn't so much snow in the streets or on the roofs as she was used to and concluded that the heat of this mass of people sufficed to keep the worst of the Winter out. This sudden blast of unfamiliar sensations was overwhelming and for an instant or two, a feeling of claustrophobia gripped her, coupled with a growing desire to run away, to run back to the empty ice-fields. But she fought those feelings back into the depths of her mind and calmed herself. She knew one thing, though—Jansen was right: if she did get separated from her companions, she really would be lost.

Fortunately, that did not seem to be a risk, because Jansen halted his group outside a particularly sizable building, constructed from well-carved timbers and displaying windows with clear glass in them. Over the wide doorway was a large panel bearing the words: GOVERNMENT OF THE WESTERN DEMOCRATIC REPUBLIC, below which was a circle with two shapes painted inside it. Kalli could recognise the shapes as representations of the continents of North and South America. Jansen motioned for them to enter and then followed.

The large room was at a temperature which its regular occupants presumably found pleasant but which, of course, was far too hot for the assembled party. Behind a desk sat two strongly-built men wearing slate-grey uniforms and peaked caps, which both bore the logo of the two Americas Kalli had seen outside. They looked incredibly bored.

Jansen walked up to the desk and stood waiting to be acknowledged. The two men behind the desk carried on writing, stopping at one point to have a brief conversation which caused one of them to burst out laughing. Finally, the one who had been laughing wiped the smile from his features and looked up at Jansen.

'What do you want?' he eventually said, in an accent new to Kalli.

Kalli watched Jansen as he began his request; strangely, he seemed to have shrunk somewhat as if the gaze of the two men was melting an ice carving. When he spoke, his voice had shrunk too; it had lost the ring of surety, of command.

'We need antibiotics. We need ammunition and seedstock as well.'

There was silence for a moment, broken by a small snigger from the other man.

The first leaned back in his chair, putting his arms behind his head.

'Yeah, you and all the other snowmen in this God-forsaken place. What you got to offer?'

Jansen beckoned some of his party and showed the officials some dried fish and venison steaks. The first one looked at them, turned one of the steaks over a few times and then slammed it down.

'Crap as usual. What do you assholes do out there all day?

30

Fuck penguins?'

Jansen looked puzzled. 'There are no penguins in Westrania.'

The other looked up. 'Don't be a wise-guy with us, fella.'

'No sir,' was all Jansen said. Kalli was astounded. She had never seen Jansen as a subordinate before. This London really was a strange place.

After what seemed forever, Jansen handed over twice as much as he had initially offered and was rewarded with some boxes; light ones which contained antibiotics and heavier ones, some of which contained ammunition and others which contained seed potatoes, amongst other hopes for the future.

With boxes safely stowed, the group returned to the welcome frigidity of the outdoors.

Jansen looked a little downcast for a few minutes but gradually his assertive manner returned as the memory of his humiliation faded.

'Come on,' he said, with a visible effort at regaining his swagger, 'let's go and get a few drinks inside us before we head back!'

# Five

As Kalli followed her group through the bustling streets of the big city, a thought which had lain only half-expressed finally opened up in her mind, now that the initial burst of awe had faded.

London was certainly an impressive conglomeration of people and structures, but it didn't look much like the city pictured in her book. Where were the tall towers and the streets filled with motorised vehicles? She understood that the world had changed much in recent times, but was this place truly worthy of the name "city"? She thought of asking her companions but realised that she would either be met with incomprehension or scorn and so she kept silent.

Without warning, the labyrinth of streets suddenly opened up into a great empty square. Empty, that is, except for a strange machine. The front of it was made from some transparent substance and it had four large, flat blades sprouting from its roof. And on its dull grey surface—the logo of Westrania.

And there was something else. Leaning against it was a man of about the same age as Ethan and wearing the same make of uniform as had the two unfriendly officers. He was taller than the two youths in Kalli's party, and his uniform seemed a little too small for him. He had a short, neatly trimmed auburn beard and eyes that seemed to lock on Kalli as she passed.

She realised that this must be the "helicopter" that she had seen in the sky. Somehow feeling oddly shy, she met the young man's gaze. He was too far away for Kalli to see the colour of his eyes, but his gaze seemed to penetrate her in a beam of brilliant sunlight. For an instant, she hesitated. She wanted to cross to this stranger and his strange machine. She wanted to ask him a torrent of questions; she wanted to listen to a torrent of answers. She wanted...

Then she realised that she was in danger of being left behind again, but for a few mysterious moments she could not break her gaze. Then he looked away and the spell was broken.

She hurried after her group.

They had not noticed the odd incident and she re-attached herself to the rear of the party. Before much longer, they came to a somewhat ramshackle building, which leaned out above an intersection of four meandering alleys. Loud, out of tune, singing was booming from the structure. The doors were wide open and a great flood of warm air was pouring out onto the street; warm air mixed with the various smells that only a mass of overheated people can produce, along with a sickly odour unfamiliar to Kalli.

'In we go!' Jansen announced, his spirits now fully restored it seemed, 'Only one drink, mind, and then we must be off.'

They all entered the building; a task which was more difficult than one might have thought as it involved elbowing people out of the way or forcing themselves through a throng of people who definitely did not wish to be parted from each other. Finally, they came to a long counter that occupied most of the rear of the sizable room behind which stood two women and a bulky, completely bald man. 'What do you want?' the latter demanded, in a tone which indicated that it might be wise not to want anything at all. Jansen was unabashed.

'Five beers,' he said.

'What you got?'

Jansen slapped a very small, very scrawny piece of venison on the counter which the man stared at for some time, held up to the light and then reluctantly grunted, 'OK.'

Kalli, in the meantime, had performed the minute amount of mental arithmetic necessary to realise that Jansen had not included her in his order. 'What am I having?' she asked, finally realising that she needed to raise her voice over the continuous rumble of the merged conversations behind her in order to attract Jansen's attention.

He looked at her with an expression which appeared to indicate that he had only just remembered that she was part of his group—which was probably the truth.

'Oh, you,' he said, 'well—nothing. You're too young.'

Ethan was standing behind him and said, 'That's not fair, Boss. She's not that young'

Jansen looked back at the bored barkeep. 'And a mineral water,' he added.

Kalli sipped at her mineral water; it was flat and like everything else in this bar, unpleasantly warm. Jansen wasn't enjoying his beer either. He pushed the glass towards the bald man.

'This beer is made from chemicals,' he grunted, 'it tastes like piss.'

'Is that right?' was the uninterested reply from the barkeep as he reached for the glass. 'OK, I'll pour this away and then I'll piss into it and you can see if you like that better.'

Jansen scowled and retrieved the greasy glass, took another sip with obvious distaste, and turned his back on the unconcerned bar staff.

Kalli looked around the room; still marvelling at the size of this crowd of chattering people. The noise level was so high that she began to think her ears must be bleeding. It was then she noticed that a man was silently staring at her from one of the tables in the centre of the room. He had the same skin tone as she, but his short, curly hair was as white as the pack ice.

Not knowing if this was normal behaviour, she raised her glass and essayed a smile.

He did not respond.

It was then she felt a peculiar sensation in her pubic region: a momentary sharp pang. She pulled at Jansen's sleeve, in increasing distress as he failed to respond. Finally, he turned and looked irritatedly down at her.

'What now?'

'I need to go pee. Where's the toilet?'

He pointed at a bare wooden door in the corner, and she hurried into the stinking room beyond. There was only one stall and mercifully it was unoccupied. As soon as she was inside, she pulled down her trousers and put her hand between her legs. And stared in horror at her hand when she lifted it.

Blood. Fresh, bright red blood.

She stared at it, her mind spinning. What had happened? Had she been stabbed? Was she dying? Desperately she tried to think.

She seemed to remember hearing muffled conversations between some of her female companions in the hut which might have been referring to this kind of thing.

She patted her crotch with the last remaining piece of toilet paper and, pulling her trousers up, returned to the bar. Kiara was deep in discussion with Sharon but Kalli could not wait. Ignoring Sharon, from whom she could expect no help, she tugged at Kiara's sleeve and managed to pull her away from her companion. Keeping her voice as low as possible without becoming inaudible she explained her predicament to the puzzled girl.

Slowly, as comprehension dawned, a broad smile spread across Kiara's features.

'No, you're not dying,' she said, shaking a little with suppressed laughter, 'you're just half-way to becoming a woman! Took you long enough; I thought maybe it had sewn itself shut!'

Kalli looked blank and then suddenly little overheard items clicked together and she understood.

'And what's the second part?' she said, in a strangely nervous voice.

Kiara's grin became even wider, so much so that it looked as if the bottom of her face was going to detach itself.

'You know!' was all she said.

And Kalli did know.

She let Kiara return to a bemused-looking Sharon.

Kalli stood there, feeling a mixture of relief and a growing sense of pride.

A woman! She was almost a woman! Everything was alright.

She leaned back against the bar, feeling a little weak in the knees in her relief.

It was then she saw that the black man was still staring at her with eyes that burned in a face twisted with a hungry longing.

In her new-found confidence, she was about to cross the room to demand why he was staring when Jansen suddenly said, 'That's it! Time to go!'

The group put down their glasses and followed Jansen out of the door. Kalli threw a backwards glance as she departed.

She was still being stared at.

The street felt cold after the moist fug of the bar, and for a few seconds everyone except Jansen seemed a little disoriented by the effect of the cold on their blood-alcohol levels. As the rest of them stood around in a slight haze, Jansen was looking at the sky.

'Hadn't we better get moving?' Sharon asked in a thick voice, 'I mean if we're going to get back by nightfall?'

Jansen shook his head. 'We're not going back yet.'

'Why? You said we had to.'

For reply, Jansen pointed behind them and upwards.

They turned as one. The sky was rapidly being filled by ominous black clouds whose interiors were occasionally illuminated by savage lightning flashes.

'That's a snowstorm. We're going nowhere.'

# Six

Jansen knew of a flophouse not too far away and, like ducklings following a parent, they trailed after him through the darkening streets.

By the time they got to the extremely dilapidated building which Jansen identified as their destination, snowflakes were already circling and swirling around them and a snarling wind was biting at their ankles.

In a state of high exhaustion, they piled in and after Jansen had handed over the last of their fish and venison in exchange for a meagre supper, they collapsed into their rooms; one for the males and one for the females.

The women's room was so unclean the surfaces felt greasy to the touch and smelled of sweat. What little light there was came over the top of some slats of wood, which were presumably hiding some damage to the glass beyond.

The women—of whom Kalli now regarded herself as a member—took little time to collapse on the beds. However, the next problem was that there were only two, and it was not long before the question of who slept where came to the fore.

'We can't share a bed,' Sharon said to Kiara, 'you stink like a fucking seal that's been dead for a week.'

'I love you too,' Kiara snapped, 'but I'd rather sleep with a dead seal than you.'

At which point, two heads turned in Kalli's direction. She shrugged. 'OK, one of you can sleep with me. Do I get to choose?'

'No!' was the unanimous reply.

The evening wore on: in total boredom as there was nothing to do. Kalli learned a bit more about her companions, although Sharon still seemed reluctant to talk to her.

They knew very little of the world beyond the isolated Village that was their home. They had no ambition other than to become mothers in the fairly near future. Like Kalli they knew that it wasn't always Winter but being somewhat older they had a clearer memory of the Summer; of how it started as a wonderful time, at first a lovely period of melting ice and retreating snow; then a miraculous time of green things springing up through the freshly revealed soil. There was first the time of sowing; then the time of guarding the maturing crops, with the added responsibility of keeping the plants free of the hordes of insects that came from nowhere to feast upon them; and then the harvesting and the revelry. Feasting and drunken kissing in the warm fields under a clear blue sky in which blazed a glorious sun.

And then the bad times. Times in which the sun swelled above them like the ripening of an evil fruit. Times in which the gentle warmth mutated into a sapping heat, and then a draining blast from the open maw of a terrible furnace. Then the greenery first wilted and then withered, finally blowing away in clouds of brown dust.

Kalli shuddered. She could remember the late stages of Summer and recognised their account as a terrible truth. What was wrong with this world so that it swung between fire and ice this way? Her books had not mentioned this state of affairs.

Eventually there was no more to say and they retired to bed, blowing out the feeble candle which had been their only light. Sharon had one bed to herself while Kalli and Kiara shared. It felt very odd to Kalli as she felt another body get under the sheet next to her, and after a few moments of wriggling that body lay so close that their hips were pressed together.

Both women said nothing for a moment and then Kiara said, 'Goodnight.'

'Goodnight,' said Kalli and lay there in the warm darkness, certain that she would not sleep.

During her sleep, she dreamed of charging red deer stags and terrible, ravenous, red-eyed bears rising out of the snow to attack her. But she also dreamed of a young man with a short beard and a gaze that had seemed to hold her captive.

\*\*\*

38

She woke in the early morning with a start. There was a heavy object lying on top of her, hampering her breathing. She was being attacked!

Then warm lips were pressing on hers, and she realised that her attacker was Kiara.

'What are you doing?' Kalli gasped as soon as the lips were temporarily withdrawn, 'Get off me!'

'Come on,' Kiara replied, in an odd, husky voice, 'there's more than one way to become a woman you know!'

Kalli put her hands against Kiara's shoulders and pushed. 'I don't want this. Get off me, please.'

Kiara raised herself slightly. 'Come on, Kalli. How do you know you don't like it if you don't try it?'

Kalli managed to extricate herself and slid out of the bed. 'Kiara, I like you. I've got nothing against you. But I just don't want this, OK?'

Kiara stared at her for a few moments, then shrugged. 'OK. Please yourself. But you don't know what you're missing.' And with that, she rolled on her side, presenting her back view to Kalli.

Kalli stood looking at Kiara's back for a short while, and then she was seized by a compulsion to get out of this place. She turned, put her shoes on and wrenched the stiff bedroom door open and marched out. No-one else was up and she had to unlock the front door herself.

After the almost airless womb of the bedroom, the cold air outside was like a knife. She gasped as it tore down into her lungs and had to hold on to the door frame for a few seconds. Then she strode out into the street, having to force her way through a thick carpet of snow that must have slid off the roof in the night. She wasn't sure why she was walking and she had no plan of where she wanted to go, except a dimly expressed idea that it might be nice to stumble upon the city square and its occupant.

A watery sun flashed through a gap in the cloud cover; a gap that rapidly widened until the cloud started to disappear like a thin cobweb held over a flame.

A few people began to appear in the snowy streets; with heads down, they took no notice of her as she trudged through the snow. They had their own business to attend to; the need to find ways of getting through another drear day, and a slim black girl held no interest for them.

Kalli walked on; her head full of whirling contradictory ideas. She had not found Kiara's attentions particularly unpleasant, but it was not what she felt she needed at this point in her life. Kalli thought again of the blood she had seen on her hands; that meant something important and she felt she now had a destiny that she had not glimpsed, only a few days ago.

It was then she became aware that someone might be following her.

She risked a quick glance over her shoulder, and then abruptly changed direction, darting into a side street. Another glance over her shoulder a few seconds later.

He was still there. A moderately-sized man in a heavy greatcoat.

She hurried on, and then an iron determination began to grow in her. She was a woman now; a woman who had dealt with deadly bears out on the pack ice. She would not run like a frightened mountain-hare. She turned a corner and waited.

As expected, he came around the corner, turning his head from side to side in his hunt.

Kalli leapt at him like a spring uncoiling and brought her knife up in a savage blur so that its wicked point rested on his throat. A small spot of blood appeared at the tip of the steel.

'Who are you? Why are you following me?' she hissed, 'Speak or I'll gut you like a herring!'

The man didn't move. 'You can put the knife away. I have no intention of hurting you.'

Kalli pressed the knife infinitesimally further in. 'That's not an answer. I repeat, why are you following me?'

In a somewhat strangulated voice, he said slowly, 'Put the knife away. I will tell you everything. But you must trust me.'

Kalli remained motionless for a few moments more. She

had no desire to kill a man.

Eventually she pulled the knife away and took a few steps back. The man turned to look directly at her.

It was the white-haired man from the bar.

'You!' she gasped, 'what do you want with me? How did you find me?'

'I followed you to the flophouse last night,' the man said, 'I have much to say to you.'

'You're mad,' she breathed, 'or a murderer. Get away from me now before I kill you!'

He spread his arms wide, and a look almost of pleading came into his eyes, 'Don't say that to me, Kalli. It is Kalli, isn't it?'

Now it was her turn to look frightened. 'How do you know my name? How!'

'Kalli, can't we go someplace where we can talk? It's too damn cold to just stand in this street.'

She stared up at him, not lowering the knife but keeping it at the bottom of an arc which could terminate in his throat. 'I'm not going anywhere with you.'

He pointed into the window of the building next to which they were standing. 'What, not even for a cup of coffee?'

She stepped back slightly before she allowed herself to glance into the building. She saw a counter and tables at which a few customers were seated. There was a machine behind the counter from which faint wisps of steam were rising.

'OK,' she said, 'after you.'

The man's craggy face relaxed into a smile. 'Thanks, Kalli.'

She did not smile. 'After you.'

After he had entered she continued standing outside, frozen by both cold and indecision. Should she take this opportunity to escape from this unwanted encounter? She looked again into the room—it looked safe enough. She went in.

He indicated an unoccupied table and she sat down, arranging the chair so she could still see the door. He went to the counter and came back with two mugs of a steaming brown liquid.

'You should like these,' he said, 'they only use the best chicory.'

She took a sip, found it too hot and put the mug back down. She fixed the stranger with a glare as cold as the street outside. 'I don't believe in wasting time. You know my name—tell me yours.'

He nodded to show he accepted the instruction. 'Charles. My name is Charles.'

'OK. We've got that sorted, Charles. Now the important stuff. How do you know my name?'

He slid his hand across the table, obviously intending to take Kalli's hand. She withdrew it. She tried the coffee again. It was still too hot.

He withdrew his hand and sat up straighter, fixing her in a stare which seemed to indicate that he was about to say something important.

'I should, Kalli, because it was I who gave it to you.'

She went rigid. 'What! What do you mean? How could you have done that!'

He leaned forward and once again she withdrew.

'Kalli, I named you because I am your father. Well, we both did; your mother suggested the name and I liked it.'

She found herself laughing. 'You're my father! The man who deserted my mother when I was just a kid! You'd better be lying because otherwise I really am going to kill you!'

A silence fell; a great silence that was so heavy she could feel it pressing down upon her in an almost tangible cloak of stillness. She watched the man's face, so close to hers on the other side of the table. So close that she could almost drive a fist into it as a punishment for this outrageous claim!

His eyes became slightly hooded. 'You shouldn't talk like that to your father,' was all he said.

She started to rise. 'That's enough. I've got to get back before they leave without me.'

He put out a hand. 'No, sit please, Kalli. I'm sorry – I've no

42

right to speak to you so harshly. I'm sorry.'

She sat back down. 'Talk. And quickly. I've got little time here and you're wasting it. Speak and speak quickly.'

He looked at the table as if unsure of what to say. 'I'm very sorry, Kalli. Sorry for what I did to you. It was a difficult time with your mother. But I did love her for a while.'

'You're not making the best of your time,' Kalli commented drily, 'Speed up.'

He raised his face so that he was looking directly at her. His eyes seemed misted with some unknown fluid. 'We met a few Summers ago in the camps. She was young and still grieving for her father. The world was going crazy, and we weren't sure whether we were going to survive. Maybe that's why we clung together, the last people to get on the lifeboat. You came along not long afterwards. You were an accident.'

'Thanks,' she said, 'that's nice to know.'

Charles shrugged. 'I didn't think it was right to bring a child into a world like this. I still don't. But we were young and strong, by today's wretched standards, and— and it just happened. And it couldn't be un-happened. So I took you in my arms, we named you and loved you.

'From then on we did our best to survive and for some time it looked like we were going to make it. As a Lecturer in English Literature I wasn't very practical—but I tried to learn fast. But gradually a change came over your mother as she saw what was happening to the world; a great depression seized her, and she lost all interest in me. I was like a ghost but still alive; one you could touch if you wanted to. But she didn't want to.'

'My heart is breaking.'

'Easy for you to mock, Kalli,' he said, 'as somebody once said: "*He jests at scars that never felt a wound.*" You're still young. You haven't been scarred.'

She leapt to her feet. 'Haven't I! A mother I hardly knew. A father who walked out and then has the nerve to ask me to forgive him—I guess that's what you're doing. And left to bring myself up amongst people who don't like the way I look! I'm

43

going!'

'No Kalli, don't go,' he said, 'I didn't walk out—I was thrown out.'

'Thrown out? My mother threw you out? Why would she do that?'

'She became sick, sick in the mind. It was the guilt—she couldn't handle it.'

'What guilt?'

'The guilt of what her mother—your grandmother—had done.'

'And what had she done that was so terrible?'

He looked directly at her again, and Kalli felt a worm of cold fear beginning to ascend her spine.

'Why ruin the world. Your grandmother ruined the world.'

# Seven

Kalli leapt up from her chair, which went crashing to the floor behind her. People in the coffee shop looked around, alarmed by the sudden noise.

'You're mad!' she yelled, 'how dare you say things like that about my grandmother! How dare you!'

The proprietor came from behind the counter and was heading for the source of the tumult, but Kalli was already exiting the door. It groaned on its hinges as she swept out, but even as she strode away she could hear Charles calling after her, 'Kalli, stop! You've got to hear the entire story and then you'll believe me!'

'I'll never believe you!' she shouted, without turning her head, 'my mother was a wonderful, kind woman. She couldn't have been like that if her own mother had been some kind of monster!'

She could hear Charles running after her; his breathing heavily laboured, as if running was an unwise exertion for him. She whirled to face him. 'Don't follow me!'

As Charles came running up to her, his feet slipped on the ice under the crust of snow and he slid into the wall of the nearest building, his head hitting the wood with some force.

She stopped her headlong flight and returned to him, putting out her arms to offer to help him to his feet.

'Are you hurt?'

'Of course, I'm hurt!' he snapped, 'This was your fault—if you'd only stop and listen!'

'I will never listen to your stories,' she said, 'However you cut it, it was you that walked out on me. And now you follow me around, trying to tell me lies about my family!'

'I'm your family,' he said plaintively.

'No, you're not! I don't owe you anything. You didn't help bring me up; you left my mother to do that. She taught me everything!'

He looked up at her, holding the side of his head that had hit the wall, and a strange look came into his dark eyes.

'No doubt she told you about the stars and planets and showed you those nicely coloured pictures in her books.'

'Yes. So?'

He staggered to his feet and looked down on her.

'Did she tell you about the Doom of Stars?'

'What?' Kalli looked confused. 'No. What does that mean?'

But he had finished. He turned and began to walk slowly away.

And then he stopped and turned.

'Never mind, ' he said, 'you'll find out soon enough.'

She watched him walk away, still holding the bruised side of his head. Thoughts tumbled over each other in her own head: could this peculiar man really be her father?

And what was the meaning of that sinister-sounding phrase—*Doom of Stars*?

She knew enough from the books that her mother had given her that stars were colossal orbs of energy and could not be snuffed out by any imaginable force.

Then she shrugged—there were enough problems in the world without strangers loading new and unintelligible ones on her. She had to get back to the Village.

It was then she felt a stab of fear: she had twisted and turned so much in her attempt to escape from Charles that she was no longer sure of the way back to the flophouse. Jansen     was notorious for his early rising: if she were not there at the appointed hour of leaving—they would leave without her.

She looked around in all directions in rapidly rising alarm. Each road looked the same: each contained almost identical grimy, weather-blasted buildings leaning towards each other; some so close they seemed on the point of touching. She turned completely around trying to determine which of the streets looked the most familiar, but it was no use—she did not know how to retrace her steps back to Jansen and her companions. Panic began to seize her—although the Village was only half a day's trek away, she had never been out of its immediate area by herself before. She had visions of a lonely death out in the white wastelands.

Eventually, she concluded that she had to make some attempt to get back to her companions; otherwise, the death by starvation that she feared would come to her in London's uncaring streets. Choosing a direction at random, she set off.

A few people passed her, heads down against the needle-like bites of the wind. She tried asking for help but received no replies; not even an acknowledgement of her existence. Still she trudged on until a loud noise broke in upon her churning thoughts. At first, she could not locate it until she realised it was coming from above. Looking up, she saw the helicopter emerge from the grey haze and pass directly above her, heading in approximately the same direction. It passed much closer to the ground than her previous aerial sighting, and she could make out the pilot in his canopy before it moved beyond her into the cold distance. *It must be landing*, she thought, *it's so low*. For an instant, she remembered the young pilot she had seen and an inexplicable warm tremor passed through her, but she shook the feeling off. He would not be able to help her—she must help herself!

And then, after what seemed an eternity, she turned a corner and there was the flophouse, only ten metres away. Hope broke upon her like a Summer sunrise and she ran to the door and burst in, causing the proprietor to look up in alarm from his newssheet.

'Who the hell are you?' he said in a bad-tempered growl, clearly not recognising her from the night before. 'Go back out and then come in like a normal person.'

She ignored the criticism. 'Jansen. An old man called Jansen. Two boys and two girls. Jansen. Are they here?' The flophouse felt warm to her after the icy streets, and she let her furs fall open.

The proprietor stared at her as if seeing her for the first time and, after an odd pause, said: 'They've gone. They looked for you, but no-one had seen you go. But Mr Jansen left a message for you. It's back here if you want to read it.' He raised the counter flap to allow access. Eagerly she went in and stood next to him.

He looked down at her and said in a slightly different voice, 'You know when I was younger, we used to have a little treat called chocolate. And I feel like a little chocolate treat now.' And in a swift movement he had her pinned against the wall of his cubicle and was bending down to kiss her.

Kalli knew enough about men to know she was in trouble. But she also knew a bit about male physiology and in a single swift movement drove her knee between his thighs. As he doubled up, she made her escape back into the bitter streets. But those streets were not as bitter as the roar which followed her: 'If I ever see you again, you little bitch! I'll...'

She ignored the predictions which the proprietor was yelling, detailing the various unpleasant things he was going to do to her: she knew he wouldn't be going anywhere for quite a while, and soon his bellows were lost among the labyrinthine highways of London.

What to do? Where to go? She knew she would have to find her way out of this sprawling monstrosity of a city and head out into the snow. She would have to remember the direction from which she had come, but the problem was that one part of that snow-mantled landscape looked much like another. Jansen had known what to look out for: she did not.

The terrible realisation that she was lost and alone hit her like a physical blow, and for a moment she felt her eyes mist in self-pity. But she shook it off; she had faced worse than this and with that realisation came the memory of seeing the terrible hunger displayed in the face of that starving bear out on the pack ice, and she smiled. Being lost in London was nothing compared to that horror—she would find a way back to the Village, however long it took. With renewed energy, she strode off down the compacted snow and ice which constituted the pavement, and she looked up at the sky. London was to the west of the Village; she knew that much. *Find the sun, determine which direction is east and keep heading that way.*

*Find the sun*—that was the problem: the entire sky was one

unbroken expanse of smooth, featureless grey. There was not even a slightly luminous patch to show where the sun might be hiding. As she walked, she cast increasingly despairing glances at that ceiling of grey clouds, which showed no signs of dispersing.

Keeping her gaze directed upward, she failed to notice a wide patch of exposed ice and went tumbling, her face hitting the ground with a sickening impact. She lay there in pain and humiliation and once again fought to stop salty moisture from filling her eyes. Perhaps it would be best just to lie there and gently drift away. Perhaps...

It was then she felt powerful arms grasp her own and pull her gently to her feet. Half-shed tears and melted ice crystals blurred her vision for a few moments. And then, as her sight returned, she found herself looking into the youthful face of a man with mesmerising gold-flecked green eyes, a short auburn beard, and with curls of similarly coloured hair protruding from the edges of his parka hood.

'You!' she said.

He looked puzzled, with a hint of amusement. 'Me? Yes, me! Have we met?'

She felt excited, flustered and embarrassed all at the same time. 'No, no, we haven't met. I—I saw you as we came in. You were standing next to the helicopter.'

He moved slightly to one side, revealing the very machine in the near distance. 'What? That helicopter, do you mean?'

She found herself laughing, without quite knowing why. 'Yes, yes! That helicopter!'

He looked at her with a smile in his eyes. 'I remember you now. You went past with an old guy and some other young people. And you stared at me for a long time.'

'Did I?' she said in what she hoped was a light-hearted manner, 'Did I? How rude!'

He touched her face, and she did not move away. 'You've got blood running down your face. You hit the ground pretty damn hard. Come on, I have antiseptics in the chopper.' Noting the slight look of alarm which had crossed her face, he added:

'The helicopter. It's an old slang term.'

Looking around, she realised she had blundered into the large square in which she had first seen the helicopter. She felt better; that must mean she had been heading in the right direction after all. Then, realising that her new companion had walked off without her, she hurried after him. He opened a small first-aid kit and dabbed her face with the stinging antiseptic.

'You're a brave girl,' he murmured as he applied the liquid, 'not wincing at all.'

'I'm used to worse,' was her only reply, as she gave an indifferent shrug.

'I'm sure you are,' was the approving response, 'and now that we've got this far I think I should know your name. I can't keep calling you "Girl-Who-Fell-Over", can I?'

She laughed, this time openly and unaffectedly. 'No, no. I'm Kalli.'

'Kalli,' he said, rolling the syllables on his tongue, 'Kalli. Nice name. I like it.'

She realised something. 'You've got the same type of voice as those awful men in the Government office.'

He grinned. 'Yeah, me and a couple of million others. I'm with the Government too. The great and glorious Western Democratic Republic a.k.a. "Westrania" for short. Look, let's sit inside the chopper. It's too freaking cold out here.' Kalli followed him in. The smell of the machine was totally unfamiliar to her: oil, plastic, leather in odd combinations. She looked around, staring at the banks of dials with no idea of what they were. She also noticed the rifle in its harness near his seat.

She wanted to go on talking with him. 'With the Government. So you're from Jacksonville?'

'Well almost, I am from Florida. But a little town called Pensacola. Not too far from Jacksonville: on a windy day you can spit over it.'

She looked at him, quizzically. 'You can spit over it?'

He burst out laughing and rocked back in his chair. 'God, you really are a country girl, aren't you!'

She half rose. 'You're making fun of me; I can see that now. I think I'd better go Mr—Mr…'

'Jason. My name is Jason. You were more interested in my accent than my name. So who's being rude again?'

She sat back down. 'Sorry. I'm all messed up today.' And she told him the story of getting lost and the incident at the flophouse. But she didn't mention the man who had claimed to be her father.

'Bastard,' he had muttered after the flophouse tale. 'What a jerk. Still I can't fault his taste in women.'

Women. She liked the sound of that word. She was a woman.

His next comment was not quite so flattering.

'Still, Kalli, you're awful young to be wandering around this pile of crap. Do you mind if I ask how old you are?'

She was silent for a moment, not wondering why he had asked a personal question. It was in fact something that she had not thought about.

'I can remember three Winters, so I must be three.'

He gave an odd smile. 'Yes, three. In the new way of reckoning. I prefer the old system. But I shouldn't have asked. Calendar age doesn't mean anything anymore; now that everything's messed up. And the bad diet round here makes people look less mature than they really are.'

She didn't want to leave Jason but she had to continue her return journey.

'I'm sorry—Jason—but I have to get back to my Village.'

He didn't reply directly. Instead, he said, 'Have you eaten today?'

Instantly she knew that she was desperately hungry. Her stomach appeared to have been stuffed with shards of broken glass.

'I thought not,' he replied, taking her look for his answer, and reached behind him. He opened a small plastic box and took out some small round things. 'Cookies,' he said, 'Enjoy!'

She did. The explosion of sugar and fat in her mouth was

wonderful beyond words. He offered another and smiled again when it was almost torn from his hands.

'Attagirl,' he said, 'there's a lot more like those back home.'

'Florida must be a wonderful place,' she mumbled between chews.

'I've seen worse,' he said, 'like this place. All this damn snow and ice.'

She removed a large crumb from her lips and transferred it into her mouth.

'It isn't always like this. But, Jason, I'm sorry but I really have to go. Back to my Village.'

'And how long will that take?'

'About half a day—if I can find the right way.'

'If you can find the right way? Half a day? Tell me more about the place.'

She described the surroundings of the Village and he gave a confident nod.

'The Thames estuary. I can get you there in twenty minutes.'

Her face filled with joy. He stared at it and for a moment he felt as if he was being drawn into her, merging, fusing, becoming one.

'You can! How?'

He leaned forward and thumped the control panel. 'Well, this baby can walk a lot faster than you can!'

Kalli's eyes opened wider than she had thought possible. 'What! You'll take me on this machine of yours!'

He shrugged. 'Why not? I've done my work for today. Flitting over to your neck of the woods is no big deal. Strap yourself in and let's go!'

She didn't know how to do that, of course, so he leaned across her and did it for her. Almost against her will, she found his closeness, the pressure of his body on hers exhilarating. Her heart seemed to beat a little faster as she absorbed his body odour; the smell of his hair just a few centimetres below her nostrils; the warmth of his body seeping through his heavy clothing.

All too soon it was over and he leaned back in his chair.

'Ready?' he said, with a quick smile. She nodded.

Abruptly there was a tremendous noise as the craft's motor came to life and the rotor blades shuddered. Slowly at first, but with rapidly increasing speed, the blades began to spin. Then the craft gave a sudden jerk and lifted from the icy ground.

Kalli's excitement swiftly turned to alarm. She had never been more than a few metres above sea level before and the reality of being really high quickly became alarming. In growing anxiety, she watched the icy city square become smaller and smaller and the other buildings rush in from the boundary of her field of view, also shrinking into abstract patterns as they did so.

And then it was too much—this was not how she imagined flight. Instead of a gentle floating through the air there was a shuddering vibration, the deep thrum of the engine, the clatter of the whirling rotor blades.

'No!' she cried, 'let me down! I can't do this! I'm frightened!'

He turned to look at her, and he reached out an arm and touched her shoulder.

'It's OK, Kalli. You'll get used to it. I've done this a thousand times. Look, we won't go straight to your village. I'll take you on a tour and if you're not loving it by the end, I'll buy you a condo in Pensacola with ice-cold Bud coming out of every tap, to go with the best fried chicken wings and American Cheese money can buy!'

Much of what he said was meaningless to her but she gave a taut smile, nodded and finally said, 'OK, Jason. I trust you. Let's go.' And she had a strange feeling that she had heard the name "Pensacola" before somewhere in her childhood, but she could not think how that could have happened.

He gave another cloud-piercing smile and said, 'Attagirl! Now the chopper will tilt as we turn, but that's just the way it should be. It's gonna be fine, real fine.'

She gave him a weak smile at which he just grinned and said, 'Hold on—here we go!'

The helicopter did indeed tilt as it banked onto its new

53

course. Kalli's fingers went white as she grasped the edges of the seat, but she said nothing.

'Take a look around,' he yelled, over the noise of the engine and the whirling blades, 'you won't see this again!'

She obeyed; unenthusiastically at first, but then the wonder of her aerial viewpoint began to replace the fear. She could see the myriad streets of London spread out below her like a map she had once seen in one of her mother's books. So many streets—no wonder she had got lost! And now that the tension had lifted, she was able to look into the far distance, a distance shrouded in a grey haze. And in that distance, she could see great shapes; shapes which looked like colossal pillars that were leaning at impossible angles. Two of those mighty pillars were actually resting against each other, as if giving each other mutual support.

'What are those?' she shouted, pointing into the grey distance.

She became aware that his smile had changed into one which conveyed an emotion which she could not identify.

'I'll take you there, Kalli,' he said, 'it's about time you learned more about this place you call home.'

'Yes,' she replied, 'I'd like that. But what are those huge things? They're gigantic!'

He looked at her, and somehow all levity had gone from his voice.

'Those things, Kalli, are all that remain of a great city.'

'What city?'

'That, Kalli, is London. The real London.'

# Eight

Kalli turned away from the icy landscape below and stared at Jason; not entirely satisfied she had heard him correctly.

'The real London?' she repeated blankly, 'what are you talking about?—there can't be two Londons!'

'There aren't,' he shouted, 'Look—I can't explain it in all this noise. Wait until we get down!'

The helicopter swept on, and the elongated shapes rapidly became clearer. Kalli could see that all of them were leaning at peculiar angles, with no two having the same orientation. They all had rectangular holes which she assumed were windows, but in the London she had just quitted the windows had been filled with clear glass: here they were just black and empty, like the fleshless eye sockets in a human skull. Some of the towers were not even attempting to stand but lay prone and shattered. They swept over one which stretched horizontally near a great frozen river. Jason pointed down at it as they flew over and he mouthed a word which looked like "Shard". The structure certainly looked like one, because its stupendous form tapered to what would have been a sharp-looking point—if the top portion had not been broken off.

Everywhere she looked there was ruin; remnants of what must have been majestic towering edifices; towers so tall that it would have seemed that they were scraping the sky.

As that phrase came into her mind, she remembered that picture of a city in her mother's book again. It had shown a scene much like this would have been when these once magnificent structures had stood erect.

This jumble of stone had been a true city!

But what had happened? What dreadful cataclysm had been visited upon it to lay it so low in broken, tumbled destruction? She turned to Jason, wanting to ask that very question, but he seemed engrossed in studying his controls. She returned her unwilling gaze to the vast desolation beneath her, seeing ruin after ruin, ruin piled high upon ruin. Although they had been built upon a Cyclopean scale, now there were very few of the devastated buildings which were much taller than those in the ersatz London behind her.

Her mind recoiled from the inevitable conclusion: something terrible had happened here; some destroying force had come upon a thriving city of magnificent lofty constructions and had contemptuously thrown them down and then ground a titanic heel into the resulting shards and splinters.

She became aware that Jason was looking at her with a sombre expression. She turned fully to face him and he said, 'Had enough?' She nodded, equally downcast, and the helicopter tilted as it banked onto its fresh course. This time she did not tightly grip her seat.

They left the real, ruined London to disappear back into the grey haze that had previously hidden it and flew on in silence. Jason threw her the occasional glance but the look on her face must have warned him to remain silent because he did not speak.

Then he shouted to her: 'I'm going to put her down for a while. Looks like you need to take five.'

She nodded silently, and the helicopter began a rapid descent. It came down on a featureless white plain with a small bank of drab conifer trees in the near distance.

He got out first, came around the front of the machine and opened her door. She climbed out carefully, and for a moment they stood there, forming a motionless, silent tableau.

Then, finally, she said, 'What happened to that beautiful place?'

He did not answer at once but directed his gaze up into the smooth, featureless grey sky. He turned. 'There was a great disaster that destroyed that city. And not just that city. All over the world. The world was changed from a place where life had been much easier than it is now; a time when summers were not so hot; when winters were not so cold. When things made sense.'

'*The world was changed*', she repeated, not understanding the dread import of those few words, 'how could that happen? Why did it happen?'

He continued looking at the sky. 'There was a woman. A very clever woman—but she did something bad, very bad.'

Kalli felt her heart jump—this sounded terribly, horribly familiar!

'What woman? What was her name?' she said, in a voice so strained and cracking with emotion that Jason immediately turned to look at her with something like alarm in his face.

'I don't know the details,' he said, seemingly choosing his words with care, 'I don't know her exact name. I think…'

Her face contorted then in a blaze of anger; an anger so fierce that he involuntarily took a step backwards.

'You don't know!' she hissed, 'what do you know! Why are you here, Jason? Why are you flying around in this machine? What is this Government of yours doing here?'

He faced her squarely, feeling embarrassed and foolish to be taken aback by a teenager, 'I'm a kind of collector.'

'A collector? What do you collect—young girls that you find in the streets?'

'Sometimes,' he said, trying to control his own rising anger at being interrogated like this, 'I collect R. I. F. people.'

'R. I. F.?' she said, 'Riff people? What are Riff people?'

'No, not "Riff". R. I. F.,' he said, spelling out each letter, 'R. I. F. people.'

'And who are they?'

'It stands for a phrase, not a very nice phrase, I guess.'

'And?'

He showed cleared signs of hesitation and for a second looked away. 'It stands for "Resourceful, Intelligent" and …'

She said nothing but folded her arms and stared at him.

'…and "Fertile",' he concluded.

She stared at him, the whites of her eyes momentarily showing around the pupils.

'Fertile!' She backed away. 'You collect women—to make them have babies?'

She turned.

'No, Kalli stop!' he yelled, 'it's not like that! I'm not collecting women for some kind of harem!'

She did not know that word but the urgent pleading in his voice made her stop and turn.

'Go on,' she said.

'The danger, Kalli. The thing that killed that city, that killed every city. It's not gone away, Kalli, things are going to get worse. Some people say that the world is ending. I…It…' He stopped: she was no longer listening. She had her head cocked and her face bore an intent expression as if she was striving to hear some sound at the limit of detection.

'Kalli, what is it?'

She waved him into silence. Then she turned. 'We've got to get out of here. Now!'

'What the fuck for, you stupid little…'

She pointed at the little cluster of fir trees and spoke one word.

'Wolves.'

Then he saw them. From the trees burst a grey mass of running carnivores, heading straight for them, baying as they came on. Instantly he ran back to his side of the helicopter and as he ran, he shouted, 'Kalli—get in!'

But as Kalli reached for the door, she heard a deep-throated growl from the other side of the machine and a scream from Jason. She ran to his side only to discover that the pack's leader had already circled around before the rest of the animals had burst from the wood and was now rearing up on its hind legs in front of Jason. It was a massive, grey-muzzled beast that stood as tall as its human prey and, unable to move, she saw the force of its onslaught as it crashed onto Jason, knocking the man to the ground like a doll. He battled to keep the snapping jaws from his throat, thrusting his arm sideways into that red maw as the alpha wolf tried to get close enough for the fatal bite.

'Kalli!' he screamed, 'the rifle! Get the rifle!'

She forced herself between the battling pair and flung the pilot's door wide, desperately reaching for the weapon. All the time the dreadful baying of the main pack grew swiftly louder as they neared. She pulled it out and pointed it at the wolf's head and pulled the trigger. Nothing happened.

'It doesn't fire!' she wailed, the memory of her failure in the deer hunt forcing its way into the turmoil of her thoughts.

'It's an auto-loader!' came the panting reply, 'there're three safety settings! Quick you dumb-ass—quick!'

Desperately she adjusted the safety catch. There was a click. Two. Three.

She fired at almost point-blank range into the wolf's massive head as it twisted and turned, working its way closer, closer to the soft flesh of Jason's throat. The recoil knocked her back, half into the cockpit, her legs dangling outside. But not before she had seen that evil head explode into red destruction.

Jason staggered to his feet. 'Get in! Get in!'

She obeyed. He struggled into the pilot's seat, his hands flying over the controls.

Just then, the whole machine rocked to one side as the main part of the pack hit it in a slavering tsunami. The noise of their frustrated rage was deafening and everywhere she looked she could see snapping jaws and terrible eyes blazing with the fire of hunger.

Would the motor never start? Then there was the roar of machinery springing into life, a great shudder and she felt the helicopter abruptly lift. Looking out on her side, she saw one wolf hanging onto the landing gear for a few metres of flight, before it accepted defeat and crashed to earth, landing violently on top of one of its fellows.

Her vision seemed to dance crazily for a few moments, and then she found that she was sobbing in relief. Then she remembered Jason and looking fearfully at him, said, 'Are you alright?'

He lifted his right arm. The fur of his parka had been torn away, and flesh stippled with dripping red streaks was visible.

Kalli gasped. 'Are you OK?' A terrifying thought struck her. 'Can you fly this machine?'

'I'm not too bad. I'll have to go and get some shots and a few stitches after I say goodbye to you. And yes—I can still fly the chopper.' He paused. 'Sorry I called you a dumb-ass back there.'

She smiled crookedly. 'That's alright. After all you didn't know then that I was about to save your life.'

He gave a short laugh which turned into a dry cough. 'Yeah, that's right.' He looked at her. 'You did save my life. You're quite a girl, Kalli.'

'Maybe I'm an R.I.F. girl,' she said, lifting her chin and speaking in a challenging manner.

'Yeah, maybe you are. Perhaps we should stay in touch.'

She said no more: conversation over the thunder of the motor was challenging enough.

He carried on speaking for a while. 'Deer must have moved west, looking for new pasture. Should have realised the wolves would move too. The big carnivores are using the ice sheets to cross over from Eastrania. Should have taken that into account—guess I'm the dumb-ass around here.'

He glanced at her, realised that she had stopped talking, and then returned to the controls. 'Let me know when you recognise the terrain.'

She nodded and looked out through the door pane. Below was the endless snow, occasionally dotted with the black forms of trees. Then she saw another block of black objects, which soon resolved into rectangular shapes which could only be huts. And not far beyond she could see where the land melded into a flat, featureless expanse which must be pack ice.

'There!' she cried, 'that's my Village!' The helicopter immediately banked and began to descend. As she stared at the land as it rose to meet her, she reflected on how much had happened in such a short time. Only a few hours ago she had met a man claiming to be her father and then thought she was lost in a collection of ramshackle buildings that had dared to call itself London! *And then I met Jason,* she reminded herself.

There was a bump and as silence washed over her, Kalli

knew that her adventure in the sky was over. She had flown! She turned to her pilot, suddenly realising that this amazing time was ending too soon. She wanted more! He was speaking. 'Kalli, I owe you a great deal.' He grinned. 'It's true that if I hadn't been such a nice guy and given you a lift, I wouldn't have landed there and been attacked by wolves, but that's no big deal. I did land and you did save my life. I'd like to stay in touch.'

'And how do we do that?' she said, feeling a sudden flurry of excitement. He handed her a small rectangular object made of a lustrous metal.

'Here. If you need me, press this big black button on the side and you'll be able to speak to me. I'll know where you are once you turn it on.' He tapped a small black dot near the object's top. 'If this flashes red, the battery's dead. Put the communicator in direct sunlight until the light goes out. Got that?'

She nodded.

'Attagirl. Now off you go.'

Kalli stared at him for a few moments and a sudden desire to kiss him exploded in her mind. She leaned forward slightly, but he was already turning away. Knowing the moment had passed, she said, 'Goodbye, Jason. Thanks for everything.'

He nodded. 'Stand well clear of the chopper before I take off. Don't want the rotors to chop you up. Off you go. Maybe we'll meet again.'

She smiled. 'Maybe we will.' And with that, she climbed out of the machine and walked in the direction of the Village. When she heard the motor cough into life, she turned and watched the helicopter ascend towards the grey ceiling of the sky. In seeming moments, it was just a moving dot. And then it was nothing at all.

It was then she realised that she had forgotten to ask any more questions about that mysterious woman and her terrible crime. She shrugged and carried on into her familiar surroundings.

The first person she met, an elderly woman of at least forty, stared at her in surprise and said, 'What are you doing back so soon? Where's the others?'

Kalli was puzzled for a second and then she realised that her aerial journey had been so swift that she had reached the Village long before Jansen and his party. They were still plodding through the snow, no doubt certain that they would never see her again.

'I took a shortcut,' she said to the bemused woman and hurried into her hut. She went straight to her corner, and, looking around to make sure she was not being watched, took out her secret box. To her relief, the last treasure was still there, still gleaming in opalescent splendour. She turned her back to the few occupants of the hut and ran her fingers over the lambent ball.

There seemed to be something different about it: she had felt a slight electric shock as her flesh had touched its smooth surface. For an instant she felt dizzy and her chin slumped onto her chest.

And then she saw something, a vision so powerful that the hut and all its tatterdemalion contents quivered and vanished, being replaced by sights and sounds as clear and real as if she had been magically transferred to another land. She saw strange, lofty buildings made of stone, steel and glass; she saw well-dressed, healthy, vibrant people. She saw...

So great was the shock that, instinctively, she dropped the glowing ball, causing the vision to vanish instantly. She was back in the dingy, gloomy hut. Instantly Kalli understood that something had changed in the sphere; somehow it had come alive and was sending pictures into her brain! She realised that now, more than ever before, it was imperative that no-one take the sphere from her. It must have many secrets she had not even begun to fathom. It must be hidden so that Jansen could never again throw it away.

With a steely determination, Kalli rose, looked around to see if that strange incident had been observed and, deciding that it had not, she placed her strange objects, the old and the new, in a small satchel and slipped back outside to find a secure hiding place for the mysterious sphere and Jason's communicator. She knew that there was an abandoned hut, set back some distance from the Village. Looking neither to the left nor the right, she strode off to find it; knowing that nothing and no-one would stop her.

# Nine

When Jansen and the rest finally arrived in the Village, they all gazed in stupefaction at Kalli.

'How in the name of all that's holy, did you get here?' Jansen said, looking her up and down as if checking to see if it were really her.

They all listened in wonder at the tale of her aerial experiences; of the dead city of London (although Kalli suspected Jansen knew of that necropolis by his lack of surprise); of the battle with the wolves. Kiara gave Jansen a very hard stare at that point in Kalli's story, but he managed to avoid noticing her glare.

'Anyway, you're back now,' he said, dismissing her experiences as of no value. 'There's a lot of work to do.'

But Kalli found Jansen no longer overawed her. 'What work?' she said.

He looked a little surprised at her confident tone. 'We got to go back on the ice,' he said, 'we're running short of good fresh meat. We need another seal—or,' he added, 'any seal at all if you remember.' If Kalli could have blushed, she would have done so, but she held her ground. 'The ice is getting thin,' she said.

'Then we'd better do it sooner rather than later,' he said, walking away.

Ethan came up to her after Jansen had left. 'It's good to see you again, Kalli,' he said, 'I was afraid we'd lost you; that something terrible had happened to you in London.' She smiled up at him but, to her surprise, found that she no longer felt that slight flutter in her insides as she had on their previous encounters. In the end, all she could say was: 'It's good to see you too, Ethan,' and then a silence fell. They looked at each other for a while and then Ethan nodded and said, 'Welcome back,' and walked away. Kalli watched him go, surprised at herself, at her lack of reaction. She remembered Jason and their life or death struggle with the wolves, and a sadness swept over her.

Had meeting Jason ruined her chance of happiness with her own people? Had she thrown away reality in the vain pursuit of a dream? Then she remembered the communicator: Jason, or his voice at least, was only the press of a button away. A frown crossed her face; he was nearby only until his obscure mission was over and he had harvested all the R.I.F people that he needed. When would that day come; how soon would he be winging his way back to exotic Florida?

Kalli threw off those thoughts: there was no end to them. Better to return to the workaday world that she was destined for. She looked around and considered the bare patches of ground that were beginning to show through the snow. It was unquestionably receding, which meant she was right to conclude that the ice would be thinning. Soon it would be unsafe to venture too far out on that treacherous surface. But would Jansen listen to her warning? She doubted it: he had shown no signs of heeding a girl who he obviously regarded as a liability.

She turned and looked inland. There, a twenty-minute walk away, was the ruined hut where she had hidden the communicator and, much more importantly, the eldritch sphere that promised to reveal so much. She knew she could not visit the hut very often; Jansen would undoubtedly notice her prolonged disappearances. Yet she must find out more from that sphere; she must see more. The brief vision she had been given had been of a marvellous city; a city which resembled what the true London must have been like in its glory.

How long before she would learn all the secrets of the sphere?

\*\*\*

'We must move further up the coast,' Jansen said to a selection of the able-bodied members of the Village, who were sitting in a rough circle on the floor of the main hut. Tomlinson, as usual, was asleep near the central fire. 'We're after seals?' Craig said. 'Yes,' Jansen said, 'Kalli's right—the ice is thinning.

65

Summer's coming.' That comment caused no flurry of excited pleasure in Jansen's audience. They knew of Summer; of disappearing rivers; of killing heat.

The older men in the group spoke up. 'We can't hang around. The seals will be moving out into deep water. Then we'll be left trying to catch those fucking fish. I hate fish!' The others laughed; but slightly uneasily. Most of them hated fish.

'You're right,' Jansen said and stood up. 'That's why we're moving out today. Get your rifles and harpoons.' The group looked a little unsure; unsure, that is, until Jansen barked: 'Now!'

It did not take long for the hunters to gather their equipment and assemble at the main door. To Kalli's surprise, Tomlinson shouted 'Good hunting!' as they trooped out; she had thought he was deep in sleep.

They began the long trudge to the unknown part of the coast. Kalli noticed almost as soon as their trek started that the air felt distinctly warmer than on her previous expeditions. She looked up at the sun as it slipped behind a thin bank of cloud. Its disc was a distinct whitish circle through the hazy covering.

There was no doubt. It was larger than when she had walked to London. Summer was coming.

The trek to the new part of the coast was long and wearisome. Conversation among the group members, desultory at first, faded away as the true length of the journey became apparent. Kalli managed a few sentences with Ethan and Craig before tiredness overtook them, but the older men she avoided completely, not having forgotten their earlier lascivious comments about her. One or two tried to engage her in banter but the quality of their stares at her warned her not to respond.

Eventually, they came to the coast. This part contained a deeply curving bay whose seaward arms were far out in the omnipresent grey haze. Midway between the land and the main part of the estuary was what looked like an old fishing trawler, its rust-streaked hull tilting over at about twenty degrees from the vertical. 'That's been there quite a while,' Ethan said and Kalli nodded, being too out of breath to speak.

The group began their hunting expedition, walking slowly out onto the pack ice, harpoons at the ready. Kalli could tell that the ice had thinned considerably since their last foray and for the first time she was aware that she was walking on a relatively thin crust over deep, cold water. The air felt different too: although still near freezing, it held the promise of warmth, and after that promise—heat.

They passed near the old trawler, and Kalli looked at it with some interest. This was only the second large machine she had ever seen, the first being Jason's helicopter. As she had thought, it was covered in brown-orange streaks of rust, and near where the hull dipped below the ice there was a long horizontal rent. *What had the world been like when that vessel had last sailed?*, she wondered, before Jansen's barked orders dragged her back to present.

The hours crawled by. They found a blowhole and first stood, and then sat, around it.

More time passed, and the sun crept down from its low zenith towards the dim horizon.

Nothing.

Eventually they were reduced to putting their lines down into the dark water and were rewarded—if that is the right word—with a few small fish. Jansen looked at them in disgust. 'Not good enough,' he muttered, apparently to himself, 'not good.'

One of the older men yelled to Kalli: 'Hey, Kalli—why don't you get us some tasty bear steaks?'

'Leave her alone!' Ethan said, 'can't you ever forget about that?' Kalli put a hand on his arm. 'It's OK, Ethan. I can look after myself.'

And somehow Kalli knew that she could; it was not that she believed she could take the men on physically, but she now had a deep belief of surety coursing through her. A feeling that she could handle whatever this world could throw at her. A feeling that she possessed as yet untapped resources.

During that vainglorious thought, she suddenly looked

67

around to see if another bear had approached to punish her for her overconfidence. But there was nothing other than the deepening blues of the early evening.

Eventually Jansen admitted defeat. 'We'll have to call it a day.' With audible relief, his team turned to begin their homeward march only for some to groan audibly when they heard Jansen add: 'We'll try again tomorrow.'

As they walked away Kalli found herself walking along with Ethan, who said to her, 'Kalli, did something happen to you in London? You seem different.'

'Wolves attacked me,' she replied, 'I told you about that.'

'But this Jason person. Did he say anything to you? Do anything to you?'

'No,' she said, in a tone which indicated finality.

They walked on. The clouds had dissipated and the cold seemed to be pouring down from the bitter sky in an invisible cascade. The bright, sparkling star with its four attendants was now higher in the sky than when she had first seen it. Ethan spoke again. 'You're not happy in this Village, are you Kalli.' It was not a question.

She carried on walking, not looking at him. 'No, I'm not. Why should I be? Let me ask you something. Have you realised that when Jansen takes us out on these hunting expeditions, I'm the only girl? Where's Sharon or Kiara?'

'He took them to London.'

'That's different. That's not the reason. He wasn't expecting trouble, and he wanted lots of hands to do the lifting and carrying. Why give me the job of looking out for bears?'

'Then what is the reason?'

She sighed. 'There's something about me he doesn't like.'

'What—you're not saying it's because you look a little different to the rest of us?'

'No. Well, maybe just a little, but that's not it. It's as if he resents me. As if I've done something terribly wicked.' And then a thought struck her. 'Or maybe he thinks someone in my family did.'

Charles' words came hurtling back upon her: *Your grandmother ruined the world. The Doom of Stars.*

Ethan shrugged; a gesture only just visible in the blue-grey gloom. 'He's hard on all of us. It's his job to lead us.'

But Kalli was no longer listening. She could not shake Charles' words from her mind.

*Doom of Stars.*

What was the "doom of stars"?

She did not speak again, and eventually Ethan left her and rejoined the rest of the band.

That night Kalli suddenly woke from a troubled sleep. She looked around but she was the only one awake. Then she realised what had awakened her.

In the distance, she could hear the dull rumble of ice snapping and rending under the power of a Great Wave.

*\*\*\**

The next day, Kalli had no chores to do in the morning and so she left the hut as unobtrusively as possible and set off for her secret place, glancing regularly behind her.

No-one seemed to be studying her or following, and so she increased her pace, all the time wondering what she would learn today from the sphere. It seemed a long journey to the ruined hut but eventually she pulled open the rotten, decaying door and hurried inside.

The roof was still mainly intact but there were great tears in the walls, and the upper floor had almost entirely collapsed onto the ground floor, leaving planks resting upon each other in crazy angles. There were broken boxes, harpoons without points, torn fishing nets and many quite unrecognisable and unidentifiable objects. She spent no time on any of the detritus and debris that choked the little building but strode directly to the corner of the room where she had piled wooden shards and fragments of nets to conceal her two vital objects. Underneath the last layer was the box she had earlier taken from the main hut and inside, resting inertly against each other, were the communicator from Jason and, more importantly, the enigmatic sphere.

She sat back against a mound of netting and placed the box upon her lap. A shaft of sunlight was pouring through the one hole in the roof in a golden shaft of brilliance. Motes and specks were whirling and dancing within that shaft. Amongst them was a particularly large blob of dust, which was lazily descending to the floor. Kalli watched its drifting fall for a while, afraid to pick up the sphere despite that being the sole reason for her being there. She wanted to see more, but the intensity of the vision she had been given on the previous occasion had been so intense, so vivid, that she wondered if she would ever be able to return to the world of reality if she entered its influence again. She looked down at the box, aware of its slight weight on her legs, seeing her brown hands gripping its sides.

Then she reached in and picked up the ball.

The hut vanished.

She felt warmth, a pleasing, gentle warmth such as she had only experienced a few times in her short life.

She was in a room, but an impossibly grand one with immense windows which must have been made from the finest glass possible because they appeared to contain no glass at all. And beyond each of those windows was a vista that made her mind swirl with wonder; a vista of mighty buildings, great towers reaching up into the sky, towers such as must have been in dead London before they had been overthrown. But all was not well in this place either: some of the colossal towers had gaping rents in them.

In the centre of the room was a miniature fountain throwing up sparkling waters which fell back in graceful parabolas into a small pool. The room contained exquisite chairs of colourful fabrics and polished wood; wood so fine that it seemed to glow with an internal radiance. On the walls were representations of landscapes in rectangular wooden frames, landscapes which changed as one moved about the room, showing different aspects of the scene.

70

And on one chair in the centre of the room was a man. A youngish man with a kindly face. But here again, something bad had happened: his face bore red marks, as if sharp fingernails had torn across it, and his clothes were ripped in places.

'Hello,' he said, 'you can see me but I cannot see you. All I know is that you are a descendant of mine. I don't know if you are my daughter or a child of my daughter. All I know is that a line of inheritance, of blood, links us. We cannot communicate, I'm afraid. You may ask questions but I cannot hear them, and so I cannot reply to them.

'You may wonder why the sphere that you are holding is showing these things to you. You must be wondering that, so I will assume that you have already asked the question. And it is a good question.'

The man stopped speaking and glanced toward the window; his manner showed concern, of worry, as if he were expecting to see something horrific outside. Then he turned back to where Kalli would have been, had she actually been in the room.

'The truth is that a great danger has come upon the world. A danger so great that we do not know who among us —if any— will survive. But I am recording my thoughts, my experiences so that if any of my line survives they will know what happened. I don't know if you are my daughter, my grandson or my granddaughter, or even someone even more remote. I only know that to be able to activate the sphere you must have recently come of age. This must be so, otherwise the knowledge that it will give you would destroy you. I don't know what kind of world you are living in. I only know that it will not resemble my world; it will be a despoiled, ruined world. That is why I need to let you know exactly what happened so that you will know the truth. What I have seen and experienced you will experience; the things that I have yet to see and yet to experience will also be stored in the sphere and you will experience them, almost as if you were me. I am not at all certain that the knowledge will be of use to you. Frankly, I doubt it. But I do not want the story of these days to be lost forever in the chaos that I am sure is now inevitable.

'So be patient. Do not try to absorb all the sphere's knowledge at once—that would surely destroy you. The sphere will remember what stage you were at when you return to it.

'Why am I doing this? Because whoever you are, you are of my lineage and your mother's. It is doubtful that we could have done much for you in our real lives. This is our testament to our posterity. A warning not to repeat the mistake which had brought such terror upon us.'

Kalli could take no more. She dropped the ball from her nerveless hands, and she was back in the ruined hut. The blob of dust was in exactly the same position as it had been when she had picked up the ball. She watched it continue its unhurried descent to the floor. No time had passed whatsoever. And yet she had seen so much!

She looked down at the box and its contents. She reached for the communicator. One press of a switch and she would be talking to Jason.

She put it back. No, she must learn more from the sphere and of this man who claimed to be an ancestor of hers. Only when she had gained all the knowledge contained within and learned its terrible secrets; only then would she seek companionship.

She became aware that her head was throbbing. Even though no time had passed in the exterior world her brain had been relentlessly active under the stimulation of the sphere. When she stood up, her legs felt weak. She had only just begun to explore the artefact's powers, and yet she felt that she had been walking for hours.

She would have to be careful.

But she looked down once again at the object. She would learn all that the sphere could tell her.

And then, when she had learned all that she could learn, she would know all about this world that she was trapped in.

And what could be done about it.

# Ten

Kalli felt strange for some time after she had put her secret box away. Her head ached and she felt weak in her limbs. As she left the hut, she had to support herself on the door frame for some time in order to avoid slumping to the floor. When, finally, she managed to leave the hut, she looked down the slope at her Village and for a few moments it seemed impossibly far away. Then her head cleared and she began the journey back to the communal building.

Although she had only been away for a short time, everything seemed different. She looked around in the smoky dimness and everywhere she looked she saw dissolution and squalor, whereas before she had only seen the signs of a simple lifestyle. Everything seemed, dirty, worn out, helpless, hopeless. This was not the world she had glimpsed through the powers of the sphere—or anything like it. She shook her head, trying to clear it: there was too much happening; too much change and flux. After her quiet life in the Village, in which indistinguishable day followed indistinguishable day, this change in her circumstances was dizzying—and more than a little frightening.

She lay on the furs in her corner and was instantly asleep.

She awoke to find a heavy, calloused hand shaking her. A deep, loud voice said, 'Come on! Do you want to sleep your whole life away?'

The voice belonged to Jansen, of course. As her eyes flickered open, she saw the familiar, weather-beaten face only a short distance away. For a moment, her newfound confidence instructed her to tell him to go away—or words to that effect. But that would be a step too far, she decided, and reluctantly stood up.

'More hunting?' she said in a weary voice.

'What do you think?' was the reply, 'did you think we were going to spend the day making snowmen? Get your harpoon— you might think I take you along for decoration, but I take you out there to learn, girl. Maybe one day you will!'

Jansen did not notice the cold fury in her face, a fury now barely hidden. Or if he did, he said nothing.

And so they began the long march to the newer part of the coast. Kalli noticed that the snow had receded even more than the last time she had looked, thinning in scattered patches like hair disappearing from a balding man's scalp. Bare, dark brown soil was gradually being revealed; a frozen soil which would not be warm enough for planting for some weeks yet.

Ethan joined her once again, and they made a halting, disconnected kind of conversation for some time until he finally decided that it wasn't worth the effort and rejoined Craig. Kalli watched them for a few moments, noticing how both young men were more animated when they were together; laughing as they shared the occasional joke. She felt a pang of sadness; she knew she had never been an integral part of the Village; she had always felt something of an outsider, and now she was drifting farther from them, and the drift was accelerating. Once again, she felt pity for the Villagers; and an almost maternal concern. Whatever had brought these people so low into a life of hardship and penury, so low that they lived permanently on the edge of starvation, could not possibly have been any fault of theirs. And they did not complain; they accepted their lives as normal and did their best to live and laugh and love.

But she was no longer a part of it. The sphere had destroyed that possibility. No-one else had anything like it. It was hers alone and it seemed to be promising a destiny far beyond this simple collection of huts. How exactly she was to claim that destiny, she did not yet know—but she would.

They arrived at the bay and looked out over the fissured pack ice. The air was clear of ice haze and they could see far across the great estuary. Kalli almost convinced herself that she could see its opposite shore. But she had other things to think about.

'Do you think it's safe?' she said to Jansen, 'the ice is getting thinner every day.'

Jansen swore under his breath and then turned to her. 'Not this again. Look girl, I decide whether or not it's safe! I've been doing this since before you were hatched. Before you were dumped on us.'

An electric shudder passed through Kalli. *Dumped on us? That must mean she hadn't been born in the Village, that someone had taken her there and arranged for her to be taken care of. That someone had to have been her mother, she could remember no-one else.*

Her childhood memories had always been vague and confused. She could remember little other than life in the Village, only a few stories her mother had told her as a very young infant, but that didn't mean...

'No more hanging about!' Jansen yelled, turning from Kalli to the rest of the group, 'Off we go! And this time we're going to bring something tasty back to cook!' As he said that, he turned back to her and with a twisted grin, said, 'And if we can't catch a seal, maybe I'll cook you!'

She made a wry face and he walked past her onto the ice, laughing.

They spent some time searching for a blowhole as the one they had seen yesterday had disappeared. They walked past the derelict trawler and went farther out than they had the previous time. Kalli looked behind her nervously; the shore seemed a long way back. She glanced down at her boots and pressed down with one foot. There was no cracking noise under her pressure and she looked up, feeling foolish to be so timid. Craig had seen her and came up with a big grin splitting his face. 'What's the matter, Kalli? Afraid you'll fall through?' To her horror, he leaned in and patted her belly. 'Maybe you could do with losing a little weight!'

She was about to say something, or do something—she was never quite sure—when Craig suddenly looked up at the sky with a puzzled expression.

'What is it?' she said, following his gaze.

'The light. There's something different about it. Something wrong.'

Knowing that Craig was usually a very stolid, unexcitable

75

youth, she scanned the sky. And then she noticed it too: a strange dimming of the light, as if a great candle were burning down. She looked across the cloudless sky in a rapidly growing alarm, trying to find an explanation. One by one the entire party came to a halt and began looking upwards. Even Jansen looked slightly concerned.

Then she saw it: the sun. One side of the sun looked flattened as if a black line had been drawn down it. And as she watched, that line ate away a larger fraction of the brilliant disc, and as it did so she noticed that it was very slightly curved.

And then she had it.

'It's OK,' she shouted, 'it's an eclipse! A solar eclipse!'

She saw them relax; eclipses were not unknown, and they must have seen several in their lifetimes. They stood there on the ice, watching in awe as a tremendous black disc began to cross the sun like a closing lid. A stiff wind began to whip up ice particles around their legs as more and more of the sun's radiance was cut off. Kalli glanced in the direction from which the black disc had come and saw a strange purplish twilight rushing upon them.

And then, suddenly, there was totality. The last sliver of incandescence was extinguished and a premature night was upon the darkened ice. But a night like no other. Above them was a black sky, sprinkled with stars. The coruscant star with its four companions shone fiercely just above the dark horizon. And above the stunned hunters was a colossal jet-black disc, completely blocking any sign of the sun, hiding any suggestion that there had ever been a sun. There was no corona, no pink prominences, just a great, black emptiness. Where there had been a strengthening sun, there was now just this horror, a black hole, a great cavern in the sky into which they all would fall and disappear. Kalli felt dizzy from staring into that ebon cavern and she turned away from it; wishing it would be over. The others had found it disturbing as well; there were no more awed cries of wonder, just nervous silence.

The totality seemed to last forever, and then she saw her

faint shadow on the ice and heard the others give cries of relief and approval. Looking up, she saw a blinding line of radiance on one side of the blackness and knew that the eclipse was ending.

Jansen was the first to recover.

'That's it! Show's over. Let's get some hunting done before we freeze our balls off!' He threw a mocking glance at Kalli. 'Or in your case…'

'Don't say it,' she warned him, and he shrugged and turned away.

They went a little further out as sunlight spilt over them in a great comforting cascade, and the last of the ominous dark disc winked out of existence. Just one thing refused to go away in Kalli's mind. She had noticed some time ago that the Moon had seemed bigger than she had ever remembered seeing it. What could that mean? What events could follow on from that size, that nearness?

They found a blowhole at last and took up their stations around it, harpoons at the ready. They stared into the dark water, eyes straining for the slightest movement in the depths. And then they saw it! A head broke clear of the water, a head with soulful brown eyes and a mouth fringed with a human-looking moustache.

'Now!' Jansen shouted and a ring of harpoons shot out, penetrating the seal's neck. All but Kalli's that is. At the moment of action she had found herself staring into the creature's eyes and for a moment compassion had seized her. By the time she had decided to strike, the animal was already slumping in its death throes, and her harpoon point passed harmlessly to one side.

Jansen hadn't noticed her latest blunder in the excitement, and he yelled, 'Kalli! Bear! Look for bear!'

She spun around, allowing her unbloodied harpoon to rest on the ice.

Bear. She must not fail this time. Her gaze swept over the ice field while her ears strained to hear the approach of heavy paws. She was on high alert for the faintest unusual noise.

And had there been a strange noise? A kind of rumbling.

One of the older men was standing next to her and was helping to drag the seal out of its hole. Pumping blood stained the whiteness of their surroundings in an ever-spreading scarlet patch.

'Did you hear that?' she said.

'What?' he said testily, 'keep your eyes looking for a bear, Goddammit. We don't want the bastard to jump us when he smells the blood.'

She did not comply but stood straight, eyes searching for the source of the noise which it seemed that only she could hear.

Then she felt a faint vibration in the ice, a jerking, throbbing tremor. A tremor that was growing.

In a sudden silent thunderclap of fear, she knew what it was. She pushed past the men on either side of her and rushed to Jansen. He was still tugging at the seal when she grabbed his arm, and with preternatural strength spun him around to face her.

'Get back!' she shouted, 'we've got to get back to the shore!'

'What the hell?' Jansen said, when he discovered the identity of who had spun him around like a top, 'what's the matter with you, you stupid girl!'

She stared up at him, her face a mask of cold resolution, 'We've got to get back! There's a Wave coming!'

The others heard the dread word and looked around anxiously.

'Wave?' Jansen repeated, 'what are you talking about?'

But there was no need for further discussion.

Now they all heard it; they all heard the distant roar of kilotonnes of water being driven up into mountainous fury; the terrible rumbling, groaning noise of ice being smashed into shards and splinters by the irresistible power of a furious tidal wave.

It was difficult for Jansen's weather-beaten skin to pale but to Kalli's desperate gaze it seemed briefly to attain that state. Then he said: 'Forget the seal! Run!'

As one, they turned and obeyed. 'Don't drop the harpoons

and rifles,' he said, 'we can't afford to lose them!' The seal slipped back into the cold waters, unnoticed, unconsidered.

Kalli found herself at the back of the stampeding Villagers, and, as she ran, she could hear the thunder of the enraged waters grow louder and louder behind her, as if a terrible beast was closing on her.

Which was the exact truth.

They were nearly at the trawler now.

She slipped and fell. She turned to look behind as she struggled to her feet.

And saw it. A vast grey-green wall that stretched from arm to arm of the bay and was rapidly becoming mightier and angrier as the land shelved upwards below it. It seemed as if a living mountain range was bearing down on her and even in the few seconds in which she stared at the Wave it grew noticeably more tremendous and terrifying. Already it was necessary to lift her head to see the foaming crest. The noise was incredible: it was a physical force, shaking her like a rat in the mouth of a terrier.

Turning away from the monster, she ran again, but suddenly the air was full of flying splinters of ice like a thousand airborne needles as the Wave destroyed the ice sheet between it and the fleeing Villagers. One splinter caught her in the back of the knee and she went down again. Bright blood stained the ice.

Suddenly someone was there, helping her to her feet. It was Ethan. 'We must take shelter in the ship!' he shouted, his voice hardly audible above the thunder of the approaching Wave, 'We'll never make it to the shore!' She nodded, and he guided her to the great rent in the side of the trawler. The air was now thick with flying ice particles of all sizes which formed a swirling white fog around the two figures. The ice beneath their feet shook and trembled as the titanic mass of water towered above them. With Ethan's help, Kalli hobbled to the gap in the metal hull, and gingerly stepped over the twisted blades of torn metal around it. She turned. 'Come on!'

As she reached out to help him over the lip of the hole, a flying spear of ice caught him in the neck and he disappeared into the ice fog. The next second the Wave hit.

She felt the trawler lift up like a cork in a whirlpool and hurtle towards the shore under the terrific impetus of the water. The vessel rolled on its side so that the hole in its hull was uppermost and she was tossed violently onto what had been a wall and was now the floor. Through the hole she could see the edge of a tremendous cliff of glaucous water, casting off streamers of spume and spray amidst a storm of shattered ice. Unable to move under her own volition, the shuddering trawler threw her up and down like thistledown.

And then the Wave broke. Cascades of icy green water crashed down through the gap as the trawler was slammed against the shore. Metal screamed as rivets gave way like wet paper, and the tear in the side widened before her terrified eyes. Certain of death, she closed her eyes and waited for the end. Water struck her in seemingly endless blows.

The trawler gave one last great shudder and stopped moving. A few seconds later the icy cataract ceased. There was an eerie silence.

Kalli lay there for some time, unable and unwilling to move. She waited for the ordeal to begin again, not daring to believe it was over. The hole through which she had entered was now some way above her, forming a ragged-edged skylight, and weak sunlight was streaming down on her. Finally, she accepted that the Wave had spent itself.

But she was now trapped inside the trawler. She could not reach the gap as it was now some distance above her. She smiled grimly. She had replaced death by drowning with death by starvation.

But no! That was not the fate which the sphere had promised—she would not die here today. She reached around to the back of her knee and felt the flesh. There were two flaps of torn skin, but the gash was not deep; she would not bleed to death. Slowly, carefully she began to move. Her entire body was bruised and sore under the pummelling she had received, and movement was painful.

Most of the water that had crashed into the hold had drained away through smaller rents in the hull, but a quick inspection proved that it was impossible for her to get through them. She tried to visualise the layout of the trawler. It felt like it was now lying on its side, which meant that the deck would now be vertical. To escape from this trap she had to get to that deck. She looked around, knowing somewhere in this hold there must be a door to other parts of the ship. In the gloom, she saw a horizontal rectangle in a far wall. A door—now on its side, of course. She struggled to it as fast as she could and was just able to reach the handle. She attempted to turn it but it did not budge. After looking around to see if there was anything she could use as a tool, she decided that there was not. Apart from a few small packing cases, the hold was empty. She returned to looking at the door. Beyond lay Life. On this side was only slow Death.

The choice was simple. The choice was stark. The door had to be opened.

She looked at the packing cases and it occurred to her that if she stood on one, she would be able to get a better purchase on the handle. Swiftly, she brought one over to the door and stood on it. It collapsed, throwing her to the floor.

Kalli sat there, rubbing her left arm, which now had bruises on top of bruises.

There was one more case. She brought it to the door and slowly, carefully, stood on it. It creaked alarmingly but did not break. She grasped the handle and flung all her meagre weight and meagre strength onto it. Veins stood out in her forehead and her arms as her face twisted into a mask of agony. For a few seconds, the weird tableau of the immobile young woman and the immobile steel door held and then there was the noise of groaning metal and the door opened outwards. The sudden release of effort flung Kalli onto the floor, giving her a fresh collection of bruises. Beyond lay a corridor clothed in darkness. She entered and began her search for a way out of the trawler, back to the outside world. Eventually, faint light in a passageway led her to an opening through which she could hear the raucous calls of gulls. As she thrust her head through the gap, she found herself looking down on the deck, which was indeed nearly vertical. She discovered that the trawler was lying sideways in a vast expanse of grey-black mud; the gift of the retreating water. She looked down the vertiginous wall that once had been the deck. Hesitation was not an option, she knew that. It was too far simply to fall to safety, so she was forced desperately to slide from one precarious handhold to another, down and down that dripping metal cliff, until it was finally safe to drop to the ground.

Or so it seemed. When Kalli did finally release her grip and fell to the mud below she sank up to her knees in grey gloop, and for a dizzying few seconds it seemed as if she were going to carry on sinking into a glutinous tomb. But soon her descent stopped and she was faced with the new ordeal of walking through clinging fingers of sucking slime in order to escape from the resting place of the trawler.

Progress was agonisingly difficult through the knee-high muck, and it was an exhausted Kalli that finally crawled out onto solid ground and collapsed upon it, bleeding and panting. She lay there looking up at a sky which was now cloudless and eggshell blue. The sun, long since freed from its encounter with the Moon, shone cheerfully down.

But when Kalli finally managed to stand upright again, it was no cheerful sight that confronted her. Out in the bay, the pack ice shelf had completely vanished and all that remained of it were a few, isolated floes, drifting upon the choppy grey water. Similarly, the last vestiges of snow upon the land had gone, either swept away by the might of the Wave or submerged under aprons of the mud. The land before this upheaval had been desolate; now it was ruined; despoiled. But she realised then that the delay in escaping from the trawler was one of the chance events that had saved her. Otherwise, she would have been sucked out to sea when the waters receded.

There was no more to say or do. She looked around for other survivors but saw none.

And so she began the long walk back to the Village; alone.

# Eleven

Evening was well advanced when she arrived at the Village and a cold wind had sprung up from the east, whipping the remaining loose snow into flakes and then lifting them to become dancing points of light in the dimness.

As she slowly limped into her hometown, she discovered that although not as totally destroyed as the area around the bay, it too had suffered. The Wave had been worse for her because of the funnelling effects of the topography, but the Village had not gone unscathed. Two of the smaller huts had been swept away and there had been casualties. But nothing to compare with the slaughter at the bay. She later discovered that one of the older men had also survived, riding a snapped-off tree trunk to safety; but Craig, Jansen, Ethan—all were gone.

She knew then that the Village was finished, now that it had lost its real leader and many of the younger generation. Tomlinson was revealed for what he truly was; an ineffectual old man who wandered in a daze among the ruins, asking what he could do to help but not actually providing any assistance. The survivors soon learned to ignore him, while Kalli required no learning time at all, and blanked him from the start.

She had looked up the slope and felt a surge of relief to see that the Wave had not reached her hut. Her two treasures should still be there. And so she spent the rest of the evening with her people. One of the women bound her wounds, and she helped bind the wounds of others. She hugged some of the younger women who sat in keening despair over the loss of the young men and thus the loss of their chance for children. It was now the final resting place of the middle-aged and old.

Tomlinson, disregarded and shunned, returned to the fireside and took no further part in the affairs of the Village, then or ever. Kalli found a few stinking pieces of fur to cover herself that night but lay there for some time, listening unwillingly to the sobs and moans all around her. The Village without Jansen. It seemed impossible. Irascible and stern though he had been, he alone had known what to do, what to plan for. And now the Village was a headless beast, conscious only of its pain.

As Kalli lay there in the cold darkness a realisation came to her; a realisation that made the darkness even colder: This world was dying. That was why everything looked ruined; that was why there were signs that the past had been better—even glorious; now there were only remnants which were simply burnt-out shells of what they had once been; why there was no progress; no hope.

A dying world. And one in which she was trapped. But that realisation had another meaning: it meant that there was no more time to waste. She must ignore its warnings and take everything from the sphere in one session; she must take all its purpose; all its knowledge.

And with that thought echoing in her mind, she finally slept.

***

The next morning, the survivors shared the remaining scraps of food amongst themselves. Kalli took less than her share because she no longer intended to stay in this place. She looked at the Villagers with great pity; there was no warming seal meat for them this morning and in all probability never would be again. She washed the few pieces of leathery pemmican down with cold water and then stood up. Should she say goodbye?

She decided against it and, turning, left the Village forever. She strode up the hill, her heart hammering with the thought that perhaps she had been too optimistic and her precious box had indeed been swept away.

It had not. This time there was no hesitation. She sat down on a pile of old nets and opened the box. There was a sudden gust of wind, and looking up, she saw two seagull feathers begin a slow, spiralling descent to the floor. She then looked back in the box and her face hardened with resolution as she picked up the ball and grasped it firmly between her hands.

Had there been observers in the hut they would have seen very little. Kalli's eyes closed and her face went blank. Her body went rigid and in her motionless grasp the sphere pulsed with a pleasant, warm, pearly light.

The first feather settled gently on the floor; then the second.

Kalli's eyes fluttered open and she stared at the sphere. It no longer glowed, and its surface was a dull, matte grey. Its work was over.

Had the observers stared at her face they would have seen a change. The musculature of the face was unchanged, and so was the underlying bone structure, and yet the face was different. It now was a face of granite determination; no longer the face of an inexperienced teenaged woman. It was the face of someone who had looked into a pit of nightmares, had seen all that it was necessary to see, and then turned away; sanity intact.

Kalli stood up and looked at the ball. She had drained every iota of information from it and her brain was still reeling from the impact of the great slabs of knowledge which had crashed in. All that had been in the sphere was now in her brain. Its job was over, and she knew if she were to have a child she would not need the sphere to teach it all she knew. She threw the ball away.

She now knew of at least part of the existential peril which faced them all. She now knew much of what constituted the Doom of Stars.

She picked up the communicator and activated it. For some time there was only a faint crackling, but that did not concern her. Very little concerned her now.

Then a voice said, 'Kalli? Is that you?'

With an emotionless face, she replied, 'Yes. Come and get me.'

# BOOK TWO: De Profundis

# One: Tamira Adekola

Tamira Adekola's eyes widened in amazement and she looked up at Idris Parry as he stood there, waiting for a response.

'It's considered impolite to stare at people with one's mouth half-open,' he said, mischievously.

'But it's incredible,' she breathed, 'I was there! I felt the ground beneath my feet, the wind in my hair, the smell of the sea. I was there!'

'Yes, so was I,' he said, 'that's my memory of a beach in South Carolina, two years ago. For a few minutes—you were me.'

'I don't think I like the sound of that,' she laughed, removing the headset, 'Two of you. One is bad enough!'

He pretended to look hurt, which was, of course, merely a ploy for her to make it up to him in the way they both liked. After they had finished kissing, she said, 'You wouldn't really want me to turn into you, would you?'

'I think I've just proved what I like,' he said, 'but the visualisation—it actually felt like reality? You really thought you were there?'

She nodded. 'It was incredible. It felt so real—perhaps a bit too real.'

'What do you mean?'

'It was weird. One second I'm sitting here ready to go to the party and the next I'm standing on a beach in South Carolina, watching the pelicans fly past. That sort of thing shouldn't be possible.'

He smiled. 'That's the physicist in you; you like things to follow simple cause and effect. You can't be in an apartment in Greater New York one second and on a beach in the Deep South the next. Why, that would mean travelling faster than light, wouldn't it?'

She waved a finger at him. 'You're stepping outside of your comfort zone now, Idris. Just because you're a good neurophysiologist doesn't mean you know everything.'

He pulled her to her feet and they kissed again. Then as he pulled away, he lifted one eyebrow and said, 'A *good* neurophysiologist? I'm a *great* neurophysiologist!'

'Whatever.' She adjusted the straps on her dress, checking her appearance in the 3D-mirror and turning to him, said, 'Do I look OK in this?'

'You look wonderful in that,' he replied, without turning around. Adekola frowned, but before she could criticise his immobility, he had turned to the apparatus on the chair she had recently quitted. It resembled nothing more than a hair-drying helmet from the mid-twentieth century—though neither of them would have known that resemblance. 'You know, I think I can shrink this damn thing down to a really manageable size. It'll never be much use if people have to lug a cabinet-sized thing around with them.'

He patted a lustrous, ebony-black unit which stood about a metre and a half high on four stubby legs. A single ruby light winked near the top of it.

'How are people to make sense of all those memories?' she asked, adjusting a strap for the fourth or maybe fifth time, 'it'll just be one confused mess of jumbled up memories, won't it?'

'No, the software allows you to imprint standard video clips into the stream. As long as we do the recordings while we're still compos the viewers shouldn't get lost.' He bent over the device. 'Now, if I could...'

She pulled him away and said, 'Now come on, Pasteur or Watson or whoever the hell you think you are, we have to go. I'm meeting Elizabeth tonight for the first time since I became an official member of her staff and I need to make a good impression on my new Boss.'

His brow wrinkled. 'Elizabeth Baldwin? She's got a fearsome reputation as a hard-faced lady who doesn't suffer fools gladly.'

She gave a brilliant smile, the ivory of her teeth contrasting with her skin's warm mahogany. 'Then I have nothing to worry about, do I? You, on the other hand…'

She left the playful insult unfinished and, returning to the mirror, touched it twice in quick succession.

Her image disappeared and was replaced by that of a plump, brown-skinned woman with black hair pulled into a tight bun and a small, frizzy-haired child, whose complexion was almost intermediate between that of Parry and Adekola. The image was indistinguishable from the view which would have obtained had the foursome all been in the same room together.

The child ran towards Adekola and for a second it looked like she was going to hug the woman, but she stopped—because she was only an image.

'Mommy, mommy!' the child said, 'Elena's been teaching me some lovely Mexican songs. I like the one about the little cricket and the cactus. Can I sing it to you now?'

Adekola smiled gently. 'Not now, Jahia. Daddy and I are going out now but I'll be spending all day with you tomorrow and you can sing me all the new songs you've learned.'

Jahia clapped her hands. 'You'll like the one about the little cricket. It's funny!'

'I'm sure it is, darling, but you'll have to sing it slowly because my Castilian isn't as good as yours.' Adekola looked at Elena. 'I hope she doesn't give you too much trouble tonight, Elena.'

The other woman smiled. 'No, Señora, she is a very good girls. And she love to sing.'

Adekola's smile became broader. 'Thank you, Elena, I'll see you both in the morning.'

Jahia and Elena waved and disappeared a second after Adekola touched the mirror again.

'You know,' Parry said, coming up behind Adekola and hugging her over her breasts, 'Having a Mexican maid in this day and age is very old fashioned. Some people would call it a cliché, demeaning even.'

She turned and placed a finger on his nose. 'Indeed they would—if Elena actually was a maid, instead of a good friend of mine who loves children. It's a little role-playing game. Sometimes I'm the maid.'

'That I've got to see! A French Maid, I hope!'

Still laughing, they left the room and took the elevator to the ground floor. From there a silent, AI-controlled taxi took them through the brightly lit streets of Greater New York.

From time to time, Parry glanced up at the colossal towers they were passing, lovely in glowing pastel shades. Adekola watched the colours change on his face as he looked up.

'You know,' she said softly, 'you act like you've just got here. No native New Yorker spends anytime looking at the buildings, day or night.'

He grinned. 'I'm a hick from the sticks. I can't help it!'

She leaned over so that their faces were almost touching. 'Well, I *am* a native so, cornball, if there's anything you need to know just ask me. I can even get you a good deal on the Brooklyn Bridge.'

They both laughed.

The autonomous taxi hummed gently to a stop below an incredible tower of steel, glass and synthetic stone which soared so high that its peak was lost in misty obscurity. They watched their transport shoot silently away into the night and then looked up at their destination. Above the huge, many-columned entrance a softy glowing sign read: "TransTerrestrial Solutions."

'Well, here we are. The taxi didn't get lost this time,' Adekola said, 'and so into the lions' den!'

He gave her hand a quick squeeze. 'They're the antelopes. You're the lioness.'

As the silent elevator whisked them past floor after floor, Parry stole a swift glance at his partner. She was definitely looking nervous. Then the doors opened and the buzzing hubbub of a myriad voices burst upon them, coupled with teasing aromatic scents and exotic smells, combined with a vision of dozens of gaily-costumed people, either in kaleidoscopic motion or earnestly arguing in tightly formed groups.

'Wow,' Parry said, 'quite a party.'

'Elizabeth would expect no less,' Adekola said through tightly compressed lips.

Feeling slightly like servants who were intruding on their employers' society ball, they entered the spacious room and for a few moments looked around wondering what they should do next. 'Look for the biggest crowd of people,' Adekola said *sotto voce*, 'that's where she'll be.'

Parry pointed to the centre of the room. 'There.'

Adekola followed her partner's gesture and saw that there was indeed a large grouping of people; a grouping which had naturally sorted itself into concentric rings, with the least valued members of the party occupying the outermost ring and doing their best to get themselves noticed. Parry and Adekola had no option other than to attach themselves to the periphery of the group. There they stood, like orphan members of the outmost regions of the Oort Cloud, doomed to spend an interminable time in obscurity.

That is, until the central sun of the grouping suddenly noticed Adekola and gestured to indicate that she could join the fortunate ones who occupied the innermost region. She and Parry squeezed themselves through the throng, uttering the occasional *'Excuse me'*, and *'I'm so sorry. Do you mind?'* before arriving at the much-coveted position near the party's hostess.

Elizabeth Baldwin.

Parry had only ever seen videos of her before but she was instantly recognisable.

She was stunning.

She was tall, elegant, and somehow managed to be both slim and curvaceous. When she moved, she was lithe and sinuous, and her movements were in a way which reminded Parry of how a Big Cat would have moved on the African savannahs—if there had been any left, that is. Her appearance was also reminiscent of a Big Cat, for she had a lustrous mane of hair which shone like spun gold; hair so rich and exuberant it seemed impossible for the human epidermis to carry so many hair follicles. And as he approached her, semi-mesmerised, he could see that her irises

91

were mainly the deep, cold blue of the finest sapphire but with an outer ring of the pale sky-blue of liquid oxygen.

But she was not looking at Parry. Instead, she extended a delicate hand, tipped with expertly-shaped pink nails, to Adekola and said, 'Tamira! Lovely of you to come! I was afraid you weren't going to make it.'

Parry was transfixed. Her voice matched the rest of her. It was mellifluous, sensual and sweet all at the same time. It was like liquid honey being poured over peaches.

Adekola was speaking. 'Yes, I'm sorry, Elizabeth. It took a little while to get Jahia settled. Sorry about that.'

Elizabeth smiled, showing teeth which were brilliantly white and perfectly formed, just as Parry had known they would be. 'Yes, children can be a drag, can't they? I'm always glad I chose not to be tied down like that.'

Adekola drew Baldwin's attention to Parry. 'Elizabeth, I don't think you've met my partner. This is Idris Parry.'

Baldwin extended her hand to him and as their flesh touched, he felt an electric thrill intoxicate his nervous system. Her flesh was so warm, so soft!

'*Idris?*' she said, as one perfectly shaped eyebrow arched, 'Strange. You don't look Arabic.'

For a moment Parry thought he'd lost the power of speech and then finally said, in a strangely dry voice, 'No, it's just one of those odd coincidences. It's a name which is found in Arabic and also in Welsh.'

The eyebrow arched infinitesimally higher. 'Welsh? I don't seem to recognise that word.'

'I'm from Wales; south Wales. My family is originally from the north, but...'

She gave him a smile as bright as burning magnesium. 'Of course. Australia. I should have known! Please forgive me. And what do you do for a living, Idris?'

'I work in neurophysiology,' he said, feeling oddly diffident.

'What—you help people with nervous complaints? Motor neuron, perhaps?'

He found his gaze held by Baldwin's as if it were held in an immaterial vice. 'No, I like to think I'm working on the frontiers of neurology. I'm doing advanced research in the foundations of memory.'

'How interesting,' she replied, with what seemed to be the hint of a smile hovering on full red lips, 'Personally, I've never seen the biological studies as genuine science.'

He wasn't sure what she had said for a moment and then, with an effort, broke free from his imprisonment in her gaze, 'I'm sorry, what did...'

'I mean,' she said, ignoring his attempt to break in, 'biological studies lack rigour, lack the techniques that could reduce them to the fundamentals of existence—the coulomb, the farad, the weak force, quantum gravity. The human brain is of no interest to me; it is simply a crude bag of simple chemicals in water. It has no significance in the universe as a whole; plays no part in the unfolding of the cosmos.'

And with that, she dropped Parry and turned back to Adekola.

'Now, Tamira, I take it you're looking forward to going up to Plato?'

Adekola gave a half-smile. 'Yes and no, I guess. I've been in space before, but only as far as Low Earth Orbit. The Moon, well, it's a different world!'

'Indeed it is, but from the point of view of our project it's just like taking the first step outside your own house; just like standing on the veranda. Why, if you turn around you can still touch the door to your house, feel its walls. You've hardly begun to walk away from home. That's why I've called it Project Independence—we're finally going to say goodbye to Mommy.'

Parry stared at his partner. She had somehow become diminished by being in the presence of Baldwin; as if she had shrunk; become juvenile. He heard her say: 'Well, I'm still in contact with my mother.'

Baldwin gave a tolerant smile. 'How sweet. I never cared for mine. I always felt that she was just a little bit jealous of me; that

I was doing things that she had wanted to do but had never had the courage.'

A silence fell. Parry felt that he should assert his presence and get back into the conversation but, before he could think of something to say, Baldwin indicated that their audience with her was over.

'Well, it's been lovely talking to you both but I really must see some of my other guests, or they'll think I'm ignoring them.' She turned to Parry. 'And Idris, it's been especially pleasant talking with you. You really must tell me more about Australia. I've never been, but perhaps one day you can show me how to throw one of your boomerangs.'

And with that, she had gone, leaving a cometary tail of fragrance behind her.

Parry watched her go until her laughing form was lost in the crowd which closed around her. Then he felt a sharp dig in the ribs.

'Hello?' Adekola said testily, 'Hello? I'm still here, you know!'

He turned and looked sheepishly at his partner. 'Sorry. It's just that I've met no-one like her before.'

'No *woman* like her before, you mean,' Adekola said, looking in the direction in which their hostess had last been seen, 'But I don't really blame you, I guess. She's a force of nature. Unfortunately.'

Feeling slightly guilty, Parry slid his arm under his partner's and whispered, 'You've got nothing to worry about. You graduated *cum laude*, remember.'

Adekola nodded. 'Indeed I did. Unfortunately for my ego, Elizabeth graduated *summa cum laude*.'

Parry gave a wry smile at that and after looking around noticed the robotic waiters were scurrying around and said, 'Dinner will soon be served, it seems.'

Adekola looked up at him and said, 'Why don't you mix and mingle for a spell? You might make some contacts.'

He shrugged. 'I doubt it. They're all mathematicians and

physicists, aren't they. They'll probably ask me to shine their shoes.'

She gave him a stern look under which he eventually wilted, said, 'OK, OK,' and disappeared into the crowd. After some time he returned with an exasperated expression corrugating his face and took up his station next to his partner, saying nothing.

Most of the other dinner-guests were now seated and were eagerly awaiting their meal. As Parry searched for his seat, he noticed that Baldwin's concentric bands of influence were still apparent even at the dinner table. Her gravitational influence on the diners was clearly evident, as most of them had their heads fixed in her direction. He and Adekola eventually found the cards bearing their names, and Parry was not in the least surprised to find that they were not amongst the innermost orbits around the human sun that was Baldwin. Still, that was the way he liked it, he reminded himself. Her gaze upon him had been a little too direct, a little too forensic, and had made him feel like a frog strapped to a dissection slab.

Freed from that laser-like inspection, he tried to relax and enjoy the evening but found Adekola someone detached.

'What is it?' he eventually asked, putting down his spoon.

'What? Oh, I don't know…' She looked at him and tried to smile. 'It's that woman. There's just something about her that gives me a kind of chill. A chill in my bones.'

He squeezed her silken thigh. 'I'll warm you up when we get back.'

She smiled, but he could see that the smile was too fleeting; too shallow.

The robotic waiters swept the starter plates away and, after a noticeable delay, the main course was delivered. As usual there was some swapping of plates due to the general incompetence that robots often displayed. Adekola was staring at her meal, apparently trying to remember whether or not she had ordered it. Parry had been wondering the same thing and whispered to her, 'So much for AI. And whatever happened to those Quantum Computers that were going to change the world?'

But Parry's musings were interrupted when the man next to him turned and spoke, causing Parry to have a little start of surprise because until that moment he had been ignored by all except his partner. 'This "Meet" stuff they're making now isn't too bad, is it?' the man said, 'Up until now it's come a poor second to cardboard. Almost tastes like real meat, doesn't it?'

'Yes, it does,' Parry replied, hoping the insincerity was not too apparent in his voice, because like many of his generation he had never tasted real meat. He knew that the synthetic material—unimaginatively called "Meet"—contained all the protein, fibre and vitamins that the original animal product had contained, plus many more trace nutrients, and that was enough for him. He looked down at the brown slab resting innocently among the vegetables and almost shuddered at the thought that once it could have been a piece of flesh carved from an animal. *Thank God those days have gone forever!* he thought to himself.

Suddenly he felt an elbow in his side and turned to face the dinner guest again and was surprised to see what could only be described as a leer on his face.

'You look like a real meat-lover to me,' the man said in slightly quieter tones and leaning uncomfortably close, 'How do you feel about getting your hands on the true stuff?'

Parry thought rapidly. Meat wasn't exactly illegal, but it was—what was the phrase – "frowned upon in polite society".

'I'm sorry,' he said, thinking rapidly, 'but—but my wife is allergic to it. Couldn't have it in the house, you see.'

The man looked both disappointed and annoyed. 'Hey, I thought you Australians were still frontier-types. I guess I was wrong.'

Parry wondered briefly if he should make another attempt to correct these misapprehensions about his nationality, but the man had turned away. He never spoke to Parry again.

The meal ended. Adekola engaged in a desultory conversation with the people nearest to her, and then Parry indicated with a nod of his head that they should go off together.

They walked through great, burgundy-coloured drapes and

stood on the balcony looking out over the great city. Cool evening air washed over them in a refreshing stream.

'You don't like them, do you?' Adekola said to her partner. He shrugged.

'Not terribly. It's not that I actively dislike them, it's just that they're all very wrapped up in their own projects. They all seem to think that only their field of research matters. No-one made any attempt to find out what I do. The one bloke who spoke to me was trying to flog me real animal meat.'

She smiled and put a hand on his shoulder. 'Darling, everyone's going to know you're a foreigner if you use words like "bloke" and "flog".'

He grinned. 'It's not easy being Australian in New York— believe me!'

They laughed and turned to look out over the metropolis, which stretched out below them in a softly-glowing kaleidoscope of pleasing shades that were slowly rotating through an extensive palette.

'What is this fascination you've developed with memory, Idris?' she said to him, 'Why memory, of all things?'

'*Of all things ?*' he repeated. 'Tamira, memory is what makes us who we are. You know that there are neurological conditions where the sufferer cannot remember the previous day? Terrible brain diseases where people can't remember who their children are? Well, just think if that was a condition which existed from birth. In the future, if people knew that they were at high risk of having one of those horrors, they could park their memories like women store their ova. Memory is what links all the instants of consciousness together like beads on a thread. Memory is what makes us individuals. Like all physicists, you think that only fields of force and subatomic particles really matter. But what if one morning you could not remember that you had made a great discovery about subatomics the day before?'

She nodded. 'Point taken. And you think that understanding memory will help unlock more secrets of the brain?'

'Indeed I do. But it's more than that. My research could help

97

individuals understand more about themselves. Memory plays tricks, is faulty, unreliable. Let me give you an example. For most of my adult life, I thought the family cat had been a Maine Coon. I was certain of that. I could even draw you a good picture of her. But one day I found an old video among my father's things and there was I hugging the family cat. And it was a delicate little Himalayan Colourpoint. Not a Maine Coon at all. How can we know who we are if we have false memories about our lives?'

'I see. I should have realised that it would be more than a passing interest. We are...'

She stopped, cocking her head towards the dining room. 'I think we'd better go back in. Sounds like Elizabeth is starting her speech.'

They returned to find the entire throng listening attentively to Baldwin. Adekola caught the other woman's glance and thought: *She knows I've missed the beginning and is not pleased!*

Baldwin returned her gaze to the massed guests and continued, 'As you all know, I am CEO of a department of the International Council for the Peaceful Exploration of ExtraSolar Space.' She paused and then gave a megawatt smile, 'Fortunately my department is called "TransTerrestrial Solutions" so you will be grateful if I just use that name from now on!'

The room broke into a riotous burst of laughter at what Adekola thought was a fairly obvious statement. Baldwin continued. 'My department—and I know you will forgive me when I add "under my direction"—is poised to make a great breakthrough in trans Solar exploration. I call it "Project Independence." Regrettably, this is not the place or time to go into details but the Council will soon be issuing an official communique on my...' She paused again and smiled again. 'On *our* breakthrough. However, I have arranged that all the guests present here tonight will receive a copy of the communique as a reward for your generous donations.'

Parry looked sharply at Adekola. 'Donations? Have you...'

She waved him into silence as Baldwin said, 'In the meantime, I would like to introduce you all to the senior members of my staff who will be taking the project forward.'

She read out a short list of names and Adekola was among them.

'Please could all those talented researchers come to the front so that everyone can see you.'

Adekola felt a warm flood of satisfaction suffuse her body as she rose from her chair and made her way to where Baldwin was standing. She recognised a few of the faces of those she was to be working with, though not all. But she was not really looking at her peers: she was looking at Baldwin with the same sensation of awe and respect that the acolyte feels for the master.

'Turn and face the room, dear,' Baldwin murmured, placing a very gentle hand on her shoulder. Adekola did so; feeling a glorious smile crease her face. She felt light-headed, as if she had drunk just enough to send her into a warm fug of tipsiness. This was it! All her hard work was going to be rewarded!

Under Baldwin's tutelage, she was going to become famous, renowned! Her name would be there in the annals of the science of this century!

Baldwin was standing next to her. Adekola inhaled the other woman's scented breath as the latter leaned nearer.

Then she heard Baldwin say, in a honey-sweet voice, 'My dear, your partner is simply delicious. I think I might like to get to know him better.'

## Two: Idris Parry

Adekola sat back in her chair, her fingers absent-mindedly playing with Jahia's hair. The child did not seem to mind and continued turning the pages of her book, revealing one brightly coloured image of an astronomical object after another.

Parry noticed Adekola's mood and gently disentangled her fingers from her daughter's hair.

'What's the matter?' he said, 'after last night's triumph I thought you'd be on top of the world.'

She looked up at him, uncertain of what to say. She felt somehow cheated. She should be feeling elated, triumphant even, after the ceremony, but she was still not sure of how to react to Baldwin's strange comment at the close of the evening. Had it just been an idle observation, a light-hearted, girlish comment between women of the world, after alcohol had worked its magic, making people say things that they would not otherwise say?

Yet she doubted it. Baldwin had not seemed even the slightest bit intoxicated; in fact, she strongly suspected that the woman never did let herself become that way. Adekola was sure that Baldwin liked being always in control and only revealed to the world what she chose to reveal—and not a nanometre more.

She decided to throw off this feeling that was eating away at her.

If Baldwin thought she could get anywhere with Idris, let her try. She'd soon find out that she wasn't the only strong-willed woman in town.

But no sooner had Adekola dismissed one concern then another rose to the surface. Was she actually up to this job for which she had been selected?

She realised that Parry was still looking at her, and she had not answered his question. She decided not to mention Baldwin's comment but instead to express her doubts about her own abilities. When she had revealed her worries to Parry, he rocked back in his chair and laughed.

'You! Not up to it! That's ridiculous! You're the sharpest, brightest woman I've ever met, ever heard of. If anyone's Baldwin's equal, it's you.'

She gave a brief smile of gratitude. 'That's a lovely thing to say, Idris, but I'm afraid you're not fully competent to judge me. Our disciplines are too far apart.'

He grinned. 'OK. I'm just a biologist, one step up from a monkey, according to Baldwin. I'll just take a few minutes to scratch my genitals.'

She brightened. 'That's my job!'

'OK,' he continued, 'why don't you try to explain your PhD thesis to me again. Just to prove how bright you really are. Black holes, I believe; the fate of all stars.'

She gave a mock groan. 'Not again! I hate to see you holding your head and moaning.'

'Try me,' he said, 'I've eaten a lot of Ffish today. Brain food, you see.'

'Ffish!' she tutted, 'why they have to give these protein bars such silly names I've no idea.'

'PhD,' he gently reminded her.

'You asked for it. Here we go.' She drew a deep breath and then began: 'Black holes are not the fate of *all* stars—it depends on the mass. My thesis was on the concept of a charged black hole; which of course are not likely to exist in nature.' Her voice slipped into an academic drone. 'Specifically, we will consider the case of Reissner-Nordström-de Sitter black holes. According to the solutions to the equations of general relativity produced by those gentlemen, a black hole that is electrically charged has a secondary boundary within the event horizon, known as the Cauchy Horizon. Here, spacetime is indeterminate. Now, what do we mean by that? Well, it means that it is impossible to construct a causal chain from a past time to the present time. This in turn means that it is impossible to predict any future state, or, to put it another way, there are an infinite number of possible futures which are all equally probable and which can not be shown to be causally connected to the present moment. This can be shown by invoking the Reissner-Nordström metric...'

She continued with her exposition for several minutes until Jahia tugged at her pants leg and said, 'Mommy, Daddy's asleep.'

She stopped and addressed Parry in a slightly threatening manner. 'Are you really asleep?'

He opened his eyes, yawned, stretched and said 'Who me? I was hanging on every word. Wonderful stuff and you explain it so clearly. I feel like I'd like to visit a Reissner-Whatchacallit black hole right now!'

She threw a cushion at him and that was the end of their discussion on Reissner-Nordström-de Sitter black holes.

*** 

The next day was the one which Adekola had both longed for and also dreaded: her interview with Baldwin. Obviously, she had spoken to that lady on several earlier occasions but this was the real deal; the time that she would be questioned and evaluated by her new superior.

She sat mutely in the room of Baldwin's secretary, who having welcomed Adekola, now proceeded to ignore her while she made sweeping motions with her fingers over the softly glowing screen of her AI interface.

Adekola looked around, seeing a plush office decorated to the highest standards with soft furnishings, hardwood furniture, and boasting a magnificent living mural of what could only have been the Amazon rainforest at the peak of its majesty. For a while she watched, as impossibly gorgeous birds, bedecked with Technicolor feathers, flew in and out of colossal tree canopies or performed elaborate mating rituals on slender branches. Once, the mural showed a jaguar thrusting its way through the undergrowth, its great muscles flexing under its speckled coat.

'Magnificent,' Adekola breathed, not realising that she had spoken aloud. The secretary looked up.

'That jungle, you mean?' she said, rather sharply, 'what a

waste of resources that was. The cities of Amazonia are a real joy. The nightlife is incredible. Have you been?'

Adekola pulled a face. 'Not on my salary.'

The secretary stared at her for a moment, with the expression that is usually reserved for the discovery of a squashed bug on the sole of one's shoe. But all she said was 'Oh' and then returned to her writing.

The minutes dragged by. Adekola stood up and walked to the great picture window. She found herself looking out over the tremendous towers of Greater New York, marvelling at how they thrust up like titanic stalagmites in some impossibly vast cavern. Although not now bedecked in their soothing, night-time colours they were still resplendent with the shining majesty of brilliant metal, sturdy synthetic stone and polished glass, many of which materials were now reflecting the yellow, early-morning sunlight straight into the room.

It was then she heard the voices. Having moved closer to the door of Baldwin's inner sanctum, she could definitely hear that Baldwin already had a visitor, a man with a deep powerful voice; a voice of one used to command, used to the wielding of authority.

And there was another voice, a much higher-pitched voice. This voice also carried authority but one modulated into beautiful tones; as if a harp had been given the power of speech.

Baldwin.

Suddenly both voices stopped and almost immediately the door swung violently open, catching Adekola with a glancing blow. She had not realised she had moved so close to the door.

The owner of the deep voice turned out to be a large, powerfully built man with broad shoulders, hands like shovels and an angular jaw bearing the black beginnings of stubble. He evidently needed to shave twice a day to prevent the development of a buccaneer type beard. His right hand carried a heavy, gaudy ring, bearing some kind of heraldic device

'What the hell...' he said testily, realising that his forcible opening of the door had caused Adekola to be struck. 'What are

103

you doing there? Eavesdropping?'

Adekola made no direct reply, as the accusation was true. Rubbing her arm, she tried to summon up righteous anger.

'You should be more careful. You could have hurt me.'

'So sue me,' he said, 'I think Solarian Technologies could stand the bill.'

He looked her up and down as if examining a mare at an auction. 'Or you could come and work for me—as long as you don't mind being paid in kind.'

Adekola had no idea what he was talking about and stood motionless, mouth slightly open as she struggled to think of a reply.

Then the man waved the huge hand bearing the ring. 'Forget it. You're not my type.' He turned to the secretary. 'Book me in with Her Highness in two days' time. Got it?'

The secretary nodded, and he was gone.

Adekola stood there, not sure if she'd been insulted or not. It was then she heard a sweet voice calling her from the room behind.

'Tamira, are you going to stand there all day? Please come in.'

Ignoring the cold stare that the secretary was giving her, she entered.

Baldwin was sitting behind a wide desk that looked as if it had been carved from mahogany—but surely in this modern age, that would be impossible? As usual, she was smiling.

'Tamira, wonderful to see you again. Please take a seat.'

Adekola obeyed, casting a quick glance at Baldwin as she did so. The woman was truly stunning, she thought reluctantly. She was made-up, of course, but in the expert way that makes the woman look like she is not wearing any make-up at all. Two incredibly blue eyes returned Adekola's glance.

'That man,' Adekola began, diffidently, 'he was very abrupt with me. He said he was from Solarian Technologies but I thought that your project was publicly funded. Solarian Technologies is a multinational combine, isn't it?'

'It is and it is,' Baldwin replied. She had the rare ability to speak clearly whilst displaying the broadest possible smiles. 'The private sector will be involved after we have demonstrated the validity of our approach and met all our obligations to the Council. All in good time.'

'But what was he doing here in such a foul mood?'

It seemed possible for a moment that Baldwin's smile had diminished slightly. 'He's a personal friend of mine. May I inquire as to why you are examining my private life?'

Adekola's heart missed a beat. She had not started this interview in the best possible way. She had let her annoyance with the man take her into dangerous waters. Time to retreat— and fast.

'I'm sorry, Elizabeth. I'm a bit edgy today. It's the excitement of being part of your team, I guess. I'm used to a quiet life. It seems I don't handle excitement too well.'

Baldwin waved a perfectly manicured hand. 'Forget it. You've every reason to be excited, my dear. I am going to achieve momentous things and you are going to be part of it. Our names will be writ large in the history of this century.'

Adekola relaxed as once again delicious, warm thoughts of fame flashed through her veins. She leaned forward in her excitement. 'Can you give me a more detailed outline of the project? If I'm to become famous I'd like to know how!'

'Of course.' Baldwin leaned backwards in her deep synthetic leather chair as if compensating for Adekola's movement towards her. 'I can tell you it involves the creation and manipulation of negative matter.'

Adekola's brow furrowed. 'Negative matter? You mean "antimatter."'

Baldwin raised a scarlet-tipped finger. 'Let's establish some ground rules here, Tamira. Never, never, ever tell me what I am thinking or what I mean. When I say something, I mean every word I utter. Take affairs of the heart, for instance. Your partner, for instance, the one with the Arabic name who isn't Arabic. He's very attractive. I must really plan a trip to—what's the phrase?—

"Down Under".'

Adekola wondered if she should make another attempt to correct the misapprehensions surrounding Parry's nationality, but decided that to contradict Baldwin again would not be wise. But Baldwin's next words chilled her to the marrow.

'One of the more rewarding things about being me is, I can have any man I want. If I want your man, I will take him.'

Adekola sat, incapable of the slightest movement, staring at Baldwin, who for once was not smiling. Then the other woman burst into melodious laughter.

'Tamira, Tamira, you're priceless. That's another thing you must learn about me—I have a wicked sense of humour. I said that to shock into paying attention to every word I say. Understood?'

Adekola nodded, feeling relief turning her muscles to water.

'Now, back to business,' Baldwin continued briskly, 'we were discussing negative matter, I believe. No, not antimatter but matter which is negative to the force of gravity.'

'Negative to the sign of gravity? But negative matter is just a daydream. It can't possibly exist!'

Adekola found that a finger was pointing at her again. 'Tamira, you're not doing very well this morning. Perhaps you should stick to mineral water in the evenings. If I say I am investigating negative matter that is exactly what I mean. No more. No less. If I say I am going to take your partner as my sexual plaything, that is exactly what I mean. Do we understand each other?'

Adekola nodded, her shoulders slumping. She had made a complete hash of her first formal meeting with her Boss. Perhaps she should hand her resignation in right now. She was so used to being in command, to making pronouncements that everyone had to listen to, that she found being in the opposite position very unnerving. Looking at Baldwin she felt that somehow she had been returned to the status of a juvenile girl being corrected by her mother. It seemed that an invisible force was flowing from the other woman, sweeping away all her self-assurance.

*Goddammit!* she said to herself, *Why do you have to be so beautiful!*

She became aware that Baldwin was smiling at her again. 'Tamira, I can tell you're very het-up this morning. I simply meant this to be a friendly chat; all girls together if you know what I mean. I think we'll leave it here and meet again at the formal briefing meeting with all my staff. That's in two days, of course.'

Adekola nodded. 'Yes, I've received the memo.' And then to her horror, she found herself saying, 'Can I go now?'

If the room had been in darkness, Baldwin's smile would have illuminated it. 'Yes, my dear. Off you go.'

Baldwin watched the other woman leave, head slightly bowed.

She smiled again, but this time it was a somewhat different kind of smile.

And she thought to herself: *I can have any man I want. If I want your man, I will take him.*

\*\*\*

Later that evening Adekola sat in her usual chair, staring into space, oblivious to Jahia playing at her feet.

Parry looked up from his workpad and said, 'Snap out of it for God's sake. It wasn't that bad. She didn't fire you. You didn't kill anybody.'

Adekola raised dull eyes to him. 'You weren't there. I felt a complete fool. I annoyed her, I know. What she must think of me…'

Parry tried to smile. 'Look, stop thinking of her like some kind of goddess. She shits and cleans her nose just like everybody else. Now listen, I think I've made a breakthrough in miniaturisation of my interface device.'

Adekola stood up, almost knocking Jahia over. 'Oh stop it, will you. Who cares about whether your cat was a pedigree or some street moggy? What does it matter? How's knowing whether your bedroom was blue, or green with little pink spots, going to change the world? It's all so trivial!'

Parry crossed to her and, grabbing her shoulders, turned her to face him.

'Stop that! Snap out of it and stop feeling sorry for yourself! And kindly stop belittling my work just because I don't mention Schrödinger's Cat rather than my own!'

She pulled away from him, feeling hot tears beginning to flood her eyes.

'Oh, listen to yourself!' she snapped, 'you're such a genius! Baldwin would have you for breakfast!'

'Mommy, stop shouting,' Jahia said in a frightened voice.

That stopped her. She sat down again, pulling the child towards her and stroking her hair. 'It's all right, darling,' she said, 'Mommy won't do it again.' Then she looked up at Parry. 'And I'm sorry to you as well. You see, I'm used to having authority; used to people coming to me for answers, solutions. But Baldwin just brushes me aside. It's like being a schoolgirl again! That woman's got under my skin like a tropical disease. I don't think I want to work for her. I really don't. And your work…I guess I don't understand it.'

He smiled a smile of relief, knowing that the storm was over.

Sitting next to her, he put an arm around her, and she rested her head on his shoulder.

'My work isn't just about memory,' he began, 'that's just a spin-off. It's about the question of identity, the hard problem of consciousness. Consciousness is the most wonderful, but also the strangest, thing in the universe. How is thought, desire, volition related to simple matter? Where do these things come from? And as I said before, memory is what fixes a person in reality, creates an unbroken line through time. Without memory, we are nothing.'

She gave a weak smile as she looked up at him. 'That's wonderful. One day I'll ask you to remove all memories of that woman from my mind!'

They both laughed and then kissed.

# Three: Elizabeth Baldwin

Elizabeth Baldwin rose from her chair. A shaft of sunlight from the enormous windows was shining on the dais, near to where she stood. She moved into it and the mellow light fell full onto her shoulder-length hair, turning it into a cope of lustrous gold. Momentarily, she seemed wrapped in a lambent nimbus. She was already smiling but somehow managed to extend her smile so it was even broader; leaving her audience wanting more of this visual narcotic.

'Esteemed colleagues,' Baldwin said, turning her head so that eventually she could be seen full-face by everyone in the great hall. 'We are gathered here to celebrate the beginning of a new, great episode in the magnificent story of human achievement.'

Adekola looked up from her workpad, as yet inert. She did not direct her gaze at Baldwin: she knew that person's appearance well enough. She glanced around at the others who filled the great hall; her peers, her colleagues. *All gathered there to worship at the shrine of Professor Elizabeth Baldwin*, she thought, and then was a little shocked with herself for being so bitter. After all, Baldwin had done nothing to her except extend the opportunity of working on this grand project (whatever it was). And yet...

No more time for bitterness: Baldwin was speaking again. Behind her was an enormous screen which at the moment was dark and inactive.

'For decades now we have been moving tentatively out into the Solar system, after the false start of the mid-twentieth century. And why are we doing this? To collect rocks to be studied by a handful of elderly gentlemen in dusty universities no-one has ever heard of? To measure the concentration of frozen carbon dioxide on the surface of Rhea?'

She looked around at the throng of faces below her; none of those faces was older than early middle-age and all were looking up at her with signs of deference, verging on adulation.

If she was expecting an answer none was forthcoming, and she continued: 'It is a question of survival, of course. I'm sure you know that as well as I. The environmental ravages of the twentieth and twenty-first century did great harm to our mother world; so much harm that we must now look beyond her plundered resources in order to heal her. Science will enable us to do the things that we now must do, but we are not doing them for the sake of pure research. Any ivory tower divertissements are a luxury that we cannot afford. Ever since the early days of interplanetary probes, we have known that none of the other worlds of this system can provide a home for humanity. They are too arid, too radiation-blasted or both. No, we must look beyond these lumps of rock or gas for the materials we truly need and in so doing, perhaps, find a second home for our species. An ark, if you will, which could grant us a better chance of survival in a hostile, lifeless galaxy.'

She paused at this point, and once again scanned her rapt audience.

'Any questions? If you wish to speak, press the red button on your desk.'

Adekola stared at her fingers, head down as if trying to avoid Baldwin's gaze.

Twenty seconds ticked by.

Forty.

Nobody spoke.

Suddenly, Adekola thought she must say something, anything, to make some kind of impression; to stand out; to get herself noticed.

Just as Baldwin was turning to face the screen, Adekola pressed her button.

There was a melodious chime and the material of her desk switched from what had looked like fine-grained wood to a softly glowing green glass. The identity of the person who wished to speak could not be mistaken.

Baldwin turned back to the audience, and her face

seemed to light up when she saw who it was who wished to speak.

'Tamira!' she said, 'It's lovely to see you again. I should have known that someone like you would want to question me.'

Adekola wasn't sure if that comment was genuine or sarcastic, but she decided to press on.

'Professor Baldwin...' she began, giving a little start of surprise at how her amplified voice boomed out through the hall.

Baldwin raised a delicate finger. 'No, no, while we're still in the preparatory phase of our mission, I insist on "Elizabeth".'

Adekola gave a quick smile and continued: 'You said that the galaxy was hostile and lifeless, but surely life, and therefore intelligence, must arise anywhere there are the necessary conditions. And those conditions must be commonplace. Look how life has thrived on Earth and actually moulded the planet to fit its needs.'

Baldwin made a small gesture to someone at the side of the dais, and a young man came from the wings, carrying a chair. She sat on it, directly facing Adekola, smoothed her skirt with a few deft movements and then spoke.

'Tamira, even if I didn't know and respect you, I would be able to guess that you have been keeping company with biologists. This idea that intelligent life is inevitable and widespread is very old-fashioned and comes from the fallacy of arguing from a sample of one. Please allow me to show you how that fallacy operates by telling you a little story; a parable—if I may use that expression.

'Imagine that you are a uranium atom in a block of that metal, an atom that is sentient but cannot observe or communicate with all the other trillions of uranium atoms.

'After each half-life period there are only half as many uranium atoms as there were at the start. This goes on and on, and at the end there is only one uranium atom left. That atom is aware of the vast amount of time which has passed and of the fact that it is still around, alive and well, hale and hearty.

'And it says to itself, "Wow, what a nice place the universe

111

is! Here am I alive and well, hale and hearty after all these years. What a peaceful, kind, loving universe I inhabit!"

'But that atom does not know the history of all the other atoms, the ones that started out just as happy and optimistic as it did, and how one by one they were winnowed away and fell silent.

'And we are that atom: we think we live in a universe that cherishes life, that encourages life, that *wants* life. We look back on our long history, devoid of world-destroying events, and congratulate ourselves for having the wisdom to live in a lovely garden; not realising that we could not have done so *unless* there had been no such events.

'Therefore we are not living in a lovely garden that nurtures and cherishes; in a garden overflowing with vigorous, abundant life. We are here purely because of blind chance; we are the incredibly lucky one that somehow escaped all the cataclysms that overwhelmed and destroyed our fellows out in the wider universe. They were like us and they were destroyed.

'And one day, just like that last atom, our little life will end. At long last, one of the myriads of fatal possibilities that could have happened at any time before, will finally happen.

'And that will be that.

'And that is why we have to fight for what we want; to claw our way up against all the forces that hate us and want to drag us back down again to nothingness.'

She seemed to be on the point of panting out her words as if inadvertently revealing more of her nature than was usual but stopped and then appeared to be looking directly into Adekola's eyes and through them into her core of being.

'Do you understand now, dear?'

Adekola found she could not speak and simply nodded. She felt completely deflated but still sure that somewhere in her inner mind, in her subconscious, there must be arguments which she could wield against Baldwin's bleak view.

But they did not come to her, so she nodded again and pressed the button to end the conversation.

Baldwin stood up, gave a curt signal to the man who had brought the chair, waited for him to move it to the side, and then turned to the great screen behind her. She gave a swift hand motion and the screen flashed into full-colour life.

It showed a stubby, wingless vehicle against a background of a few scattered stars.

'As we all know,' Baldwin said, 'this is the standard space tug which at present is the summit of our achievements in space travel. A very low summit, I'm sure you'll agree. A standard Thermal Nuclear drive using hydrogen as reaction mass, which regrettably means it is nothing more than a glorified steam engine. Robert Louis Stevenson—or whatever his name was—would recognise the principle.

'With this kind of engine, we can travel back and forth between the space stations and the Moon and the Lagrange Points, and just about make fly-bys of Venus. There is some wishful thinking about building "Cloud Cities" there, I believe. But even Mars remains problematic, due to the lengthy exposure to cosmic radiation. For decades, we have talked about more powerful engines. I won't bore you with an exhaustive list but I'm sure you'll recognise hoary old terms like Plasma Magnet drive, EM drives, various types of ion drive; Bussard Ramjets. I could go on but I don't want to lose you all on the first day.'

There was a ripple of laughter across the room, at what she had said.

*They love her!* thought Adekola.

Baldwin put up her hand, palm towards her researchers. 'Thank you for your appreciation. But I must warn you that what I am about to say is not meant to be humorous or satirical.'

She turned back to the screen and made another gesture. A stylised representation of astronomical objects replaced the space tug. Adekola saw that in one corner of the screen was a small yellowish point and at the other corner there were two more points of a similar colour, so close that they were almost touching, and also a more distant reddish point. Adekola recognised the objects: the Sun and the Centauri system.

113

'We all know what this schematic is representing,' Baldwin continued, 'the nearest system to our own but totally out of our reach. Even with our most powerful rockets it would take thousands of years to get there. But we need to get there; we know the Centauri twins have a world which could be terraformed to provide the second home for our species, a home we cannot find in our system of planets.' There was a theatrical pause. 'But what if...'

Another gesture, and a glowing vermillion line suddenly appeared, bridging the gap between the two star systems. Baldwin admired it for a few seconds and then turned to her audience and there was a new look on her face; a look that Adekola could not immediately interpret. It was a strange expression, one moulded from triumph and—and something else. A hunger. Yes, that was it.

*A hunger.*

'I won't insult you by asking you to guess what that line represents. It is obviously a wormhole.'

There was a susurration in the room; a rustling, whispering noise as people turned to each other and in quiet voices exchanged their expressions of wonder and excitement.

Baldwin stood on the dais, surveying her scientists with a look of tolerant pleasure at their reactions.

'Yes, an Einstein-Rosen bridge, popularly known as a wormhole,' she eventually said, 'I am sure there are questions. Let's have them.'

A dozen desks flickered in shades of green but only one person, milliseconds ahead of the others, was chosen to speak.

'Professor Baldwin...'

'Elizabeth.'

The young man who had spoken looked slightly embarrassed but continued, 'Elizabeth, wormholes are only a theoretical concept. The conditions necessary to create them do not obtain in the real world.'

Adekola nodded. She had been one of those who had not reacted swiftly enough. When she looked back at Baldwin that lady was seated again, obviously prepared for a long discussion.

'Eduardo, isn't it? Yes, thank you for that comment, but surely you must understand that if a phenomenon is permitted in physics, then somewhere and somewhen that phenomenon will be actualised. And we have known since the early twentieth century that wormholes are permitted by relativity. Recent work has shown that in order for them to occur in nature, regions of vast energy flux are required. Obviously, that is not what I am talking about here. Some also have speculated that extra spatial dimensions are needed for wormholes to both exist and be stable. I have shown that those unlikely conditions are not required, at least not for the wormhole itself.'

She stopped and her face became less welcoming and amicable, although still smiling. But for once the smile looked forced.

'But enough of this moonshine. Project Independence will not create itself. Activate your pads and look at the derivations on the first page. Now, please.'

Adekola obeyed, and a dense series of equations appeared before her. Panic struck her for a moment as she stared at the thicket of symbols that unrolled before her. For a sickening instant she thought she was completely out of her area of expertise.

Then she recognised an equation, and then another.

But as she ploughed slowly through the proofs, proofs that were both hypercomplex and elegantly presented with an incredible parsimony of assumptions, she gradually realised what kind of intelligence was possessed by Professor Elizabeth Baldwin.

# Four: Mr Wójcik

Parry stared at the robot concierge.

'The name is Parry, Idris Parry,' he said as slowly and clearly as possible, trying, rather unsuccessfully, to keep the mounting irritation out of his voice.

The machine stared back at him, its optic lenses catching the westering sun and sending reflected beams into Parry's eyes. He moved slightly so he could see it better.

'Harry, Idris Harry,' the robot said, 'No-one of that name lives here.'

'Parry! Idris *Parry!*' Parry knew there was no point in losing his temper, but it was impossible not to. He was hungry and he wanted to have a rest before Adekola returned from her meeting and Jahia was brought back from nursery.

The robot stood up from behind the desk. It had a silvery exterior and was basically humanoid, with a cylindrical torso, two legs, two arms and a gleaming ovoid head with those two bluish eyes that had held Parry in their unemotional gaze. Parry wondered momentarily whether he would be able better to deal with the thing if it had greater similarity to a human, but soon realised his mistake. The manufacturers had tried some decades earlier to produce robots that looked like people, but the population had rejected them. Robots that looked almost—but not quite—like people stirred deep, inchoate fears in the human unconscious.

'Mr Harry,' it said, in a voice which reassuringly held no hint of a threat, 'I must ask you to leave this establishment. I apologise for any inconvenience.'

Parry had had enough. 'Override code AK72-Alpha,' he said, as unemotionally as the robot.

The robot immediately sat down again and became motionless. A smartly dressed, middle-aged man came out of the office behind the robot.

'I'm terribly sorry, Mr Parry,' he said, looking somewhat

flustered, 'I'll override security for you.'

Parry thought of himself as an easy-going man, but he was tired and hungry. Working on the miniaturisation of the device had not been easy.

'This is the third time this month, Mr Korzinski. The third time.'

The tone was angrier than he had intended, but it had the desired effect.

'Yes, I must apologise, yet again. I'll have this one recycled. And if you'll accept a small gesture from us, tonight's meal will be on the house.' He gave a quick smile. 'Within reason, of course.'

Parry returned a perfunctory nod of gratitude, being only too aware of the limits to the generosity of the management.

The elevator whisked him silently up to his apartment. As he travelled, he pondered the fact that Artificial Intelligence had failed to live up to its early promises. Quantum computing had also stalled due to the lack of materials which would hold the entanglements. Great blocks of machinery the size of buildings worked reasonably efficiently within classical limitations and had helped with some fields of research and economic management, but the technology had not translated well to smaller dimensions. And robots were notoriously liable to breakdowns, both physical and mental. Fortunately, the lurid predictions in horror stories of robot rebellions, when the metal slaves turned on their masters, had not come to pass.

At least, not yet.

What had come to pass were minor irritations like the one he had just experienced.

Whoever managed to turn today's clumsy marionettes into the sleek and efficient creatures of science-fiction would make a fortune, he thought.

Unfortunately, that wasn't his field.

In his room, he flung himself into the armchair that looked out over the mighty cityscape, dropping his briefcase as he sank into the chair. Parry stared at the little fountain that sparkled and tinkled in the centre of the room. He touched a control on his chair and each parabolic curve of water became a different colour, shifting from shade in an order that he had never been able to predict.

He activated the vision screen in the far wall and studied what delights the management in its infinite generosity had decided to offer in compensation for his dealings with the incompetent robot. It was slightly better than he had expected, and he chose something that he knew Adekola would like.

Having set up their evening meal, Parry stood up and pressed his hands into the small of his back and winced. Too much sitting in front of computer monitors. He had a gym membership but never seemed to have the time to go there. He crossed to the wall opposite the great picture window through which the gargantuan towers of Greater New York were visible and smiled as he studied the painting on that wall. It showed a range of hills, the highest of which was dusted with snow. Above its peak, grey clouds were moving slowly, occasionally revealing strips of blue sky as they briefly thinned. In the valley below there was the twisting line of a distant river. He gazed at the scene with a wistful expression.

*Under Arenig Fawr.*

Would he ever see it again, ever stand upon its heights and look out over the austere crags of Eryri, the ancestral home of the Parry's?

The smile became more wistful. Probably not. He had to go where the work was.

He sat back in the armchair and gradually his eyelids fluttered as he drifted into a light doze.

It was shattered when a brown hand descended on his shoulders and shook him awake.

'Wakey wakey, sleepy-head. Had a hard day?'

He smiled up at Adekola. 'You could say that.'

She laughed and sat in her own chair, kicking off her shoes.

'Not as hard as mine, I'll bet. Trans-Dimensional analysis. I thought I understood it, but now I'm not so sure. There were

118

times today when I felt like a chimp that's been taught a few tricks.'

She looked around. 'What's for dinner?'

'All sorted. Your favourite.'

She sighed. 'Just as well. That damn robot at the door. Insisted that I was a strange man. Me, a man!'

He grinned. 'You don't look like a man from where I'm sitting!'

She smiled. 'Thanks. But I'm too tired for any fun and games tonight.'

'Was it that silver robot again?'

'No, a new blue one. At least I hadn't seen it before.'

Parry groaned. Even the replacement wasn't any good. He decided to change the conversation to what he really wanted to talk about.

'Do you remember me talking about miniaturising my device?'

She looked up from massaging her toes.

'Vaguely. What about it?'

He opened his briefcase with a theatrical flourish.

'Well, I have succeeded.'

He brought out two devices that looked like wristwatches. 'Voila!'

She stared at them, clearly unimpressed.

'Old-fashioned wristwatches. Please pick me off the floor.'

'Now, now,' he said, crossing to her, 'wait for the big reveal. Try one on.'

Looking slightly suspicious, she obeyed. Then winced.

'Hey, that hurt!'

'Sorry. I should have warned you. It was the device connecting to your nervous system.'

'The *what* doing *what?*'

'Come on over to the sofa and I'll explain.'

As soon as they were sitting side by side, he said, 'It's my research into the biochemical basis of memory, of identity. Look at that primitive thing over there.' He indicated the black unit with the winking red light on its top that he had used some weeks earlier for his previous demonstration. 'Well, everything it does, this little wristwatch can do. It stores your memories.'

She looked horrified. 'It stores my memories! What if I don't want them stored? What about when I have toothache or when I'm mad at you? I don't want those stored, for Chrissake!'

He smiled indulgently. 'No, it doesn't automatically store everything. You have to *will* it to store something. Let's try an experiment. Think of an important event you've experienced recently. Conjure up the sights, the sounds, the smells, the textures under your fingers. *Want* to remember them!'

'OK,' she said slowly. 'I'll try. But if this doesn't work, I want my dinner. Immediately!'

He stood up and moved away from her, moving as quietly as possible, but having to swerve at the last moment to avoid backing into the fountain.

She sat there for some minutes and then opened her eyes.

'I think I obeyed your instructions, O Great One. Now what?'

'We play them back.'

'How?'

He looked a little shame-faced. 'Through the original recorder, I'm afraid.'

'Oh, that's great. So we still have to lug that around. I'm impressed. No, really I am!'

'Alright, Girl Genius,' he said, 'that's my next project. I'll see if I can replace that unit with something more portable. But before I worry about that, let's see if the first stage has worked.'

He pulled the black cabinet to his chair and sat down. From a drawer in its base, he took out a device composed of metal wire, which he opened up into the hair-drier shape Adekola had seen before. He placed it firmly on his head and sat back, eyes closed and with an expression of intense concentration.

After about five minutes, he took it off with hands that she could see were slightly trembling.

'Good God,' he said in a strangely weak voice, 'You actually understand that stuff? All those equations? I've underestimated you!'

'You saw today's briefing session?' she said, with just a tinge of awe in her voice, 'all of it?'

'No, no, just snatches. You're not used to the method yet. But I saw the work you're expected to do. And I saw something else.'

'What?'

'Not what. Who. I saw *her*. That damned woman.'

\*\*\*

Baldwin leaned back in her chair and sipped at her drink. It was basically whisky but contained a few parts per thousand of a mild narcotic—just enough to relax one after a hard day at the office. Or trying to explain trans-dimensional analysis to people who could be reasonably expected already to know it.

Her office was quite dim as she had lowered the window blinds some minutes earlier, but through one there was a red glow as the hidden sun tried to make its presence felt, before it slipped further down between the colossal walls of one of Greater New York's steel and stone canyons.

She was tired. *So many balls to juggle at the same time*, she thought. *So many variables to keep track of. So many trends to extrapolate and keep secret.*

What were the others doing? Why was she expected to carry the burden alone?

But then she smiled. Deep down, that was the way she wanted it. She wanted to be able to turn to them and say, *What exactly did you do? Why do you think you deserve anything? It was I who did it. I created the plan. I brought it to fruition. You are just the tools I used.*

The tumbler was nearly empty. She tossed her head back and drained the last drop and then slammed the glass down on the desk, glaring at the inert viewscreen.

*Well, if you're going to call—call!* she thought.

121

As if in answer to her demand, the screen suddenly flashed into life, displaying the image of a strongly built, thick-set man. His chin bore the blue-black shading of someone who has a permanent struggle with vigorous facial hair.

The two stared at each other, like wrestlers studying their opponent, seeing who would speak first.

He spoke. 'How is it going?'

She reached for the bottle and poured another few fingers of the amber liquid into the tumbler.

'Not as well as I expected. They're a pretty mediocre bunch. There are a few I think I could delegate some of the planning to. Eduardo Estefan, Tamira Adekola, Philip...'

'I don't need a roll call,' the man snapped, 'just a progress report.'

Baldwin leaned forward and switched the image off. She then poured another finger of the spirit into her glass and waited. After a few minutes, the screen flashed back into life and the same man appeared, looking somewhat agitated.

'Don't you ever cut...'

She leaned forward and removed the image again.

This time it took a slightly shorter period before the man reappeared. They stared at each other in silence. Baldwin took another sip of her drink, placed the glass slowly on the desk and leaned back, arms behind her head, staring fixedly at the screen.

Finally, the man spoke again. 'I'm sorry, Elizabeth. I...'

She raised a slim white finger, tipped with a carmine nail that shimmered in the light from the screen.

'I don't recall giving you licence to be on familiar terms with me. Kindly address me as "Professor Baldwin".'

The man's expression, already stern, hardened into living granite. He seemed unable to speak for a moment but finally he said, in a voice which sounded like it was passing through gritted teeth, 'Very well, Professor. I was under the misapprehension that we were colleagues in this enterprise. It seems that I was mistaken. I will be more careful in my dealings with you. But please don't think that indicates a feeling on my part that I am in any way subordinate to you. I may not have your grasp of mathematics, but I would remind you that I am the CEO of Solarian Technologies. Nobody gave me any handouts or helped me through some Country Club network. I clawed my way up, and I stood on the bodies of my enemies to get where I am today.'

'Literally?' Baldwin enquired sweetly.

He returned her gaze unflinchingly. 'I don't care whether you think I'm bull-shitting or not, Professor. I warn you: I'm not some bookworm who spends all his time looking through a telescope before going home to his mother. I fought to get to this position, to claim my authority, so don't underestimate me. You may think I'm some kind of monkey in a suit, but beware: this monkey bites.'

Baldwin was silent for a moment. This dialogue had not gone quite the way she had expected. It was time to row back.

'I'll bear that in mind when I buy my next banana,' she said smoothly, and then quickly switched tack, 'let's start again. To recap: I have enough material to proceed with Project Independence. I have just enough foot-soldiers to get by, and a few brighter sparks I can use as lieutenants.

'I see no reason to think there is any need to adjust the timetable.'

He nodded. 'Good. I have quite a few people who are investing in this damned thing and they're not the kind of people who handle disappointment very well. In fact, they have a tendency to get rather upset and smash up the crockery.'

She reached for the bottle but gave a small moue of disappointment to find it was now empty. She pushed the glass away and looked back at the man.

'I believe we understand each other, Mr Wójcik. I will call *you* next time. Say in seven days', just before I go up to Plato.'

He nodded. 'I look forward to it.'

And without further comment, he killed the image at his end.

She picked up the empty glass and rotated it slowly between

her hands.

*A dangerous man. I'll need to be a little more careful with him.*

\*\*\*

'Mommy, can I come with you to the Moon?'

Adekola ruffled the child's hair.

'No, sorry Jahia. Maybe in a few years' time. Would you like that?'

To Adekola's surprise, Jahia ran over to Parry, with tears rolling down her face.

'Daddy, daddy, Mommy won't take me to the Moon with her!'

Parry picked up the child and placed her gently on his lap. 'Mommy's very busy, darling. She'll take you one day, I promise.'

'But I want to go now!'

Adekola came over to father and daughter and carefully turned the child around so that they were looking at each other.

'I can't take you, Jahia, because it's dangerous up there…'

She caught Parry's look of alarm a fraction too late. The little girl wasn't entirely sure of the meaning of "dangerous" but it sounded bad and the dribble of tears changed to a seemingly endless flood.

'Daddy!' Jahia cried, 'don't let Mommy go! Make her stay!'

Parry gave Adekola an exasperated look as she silently mouthed "Sorry". He put the child down and, gently holding her shoulders, said, 'No, Mommy didn't mean that, Jahia. It's alright up there, safe as anything. Safe as the safest place you can think of. Just like when you watch Timmy and Sally on the television. They're safe aren't they?'

The child nodded, wiping away tears.

'Well, Mommy is going to be even safer than Timmy and Sally. Aren't you, Mommy?'

Adekola noted the emphasis on the last sentence and hurried over to the other two and together the parents hugged the child until she stopped crying.

But even as she did so, a worm of doubt arose in her mind.

Safe?

Why did that word instantly sound so hollow?

Why did this warm, loving environment she was now in, suddenly seem like a childish fantasy?

Why was there the feeling that malign forces were hovering just outside this circle of love, ready to bring her comfortable and comforting world crashing down in black ruin?

# Five: Plato Base

Adekola looked out of the small round window at the blue-white glory of planet Earth. She could see temperate cyclones curling like motionless Catherine Wheels in the Gulf of Mexico and could trace a long line of rippling cloud that stretched the entire distance from the Bahamas to Europe. That segment of the planet filled most of her field of view, and at its rim there was a thin layer of blue haze—and then pitiless blackness.

*Earth's atmosphere,* she thought, *all of our little lives depend on that thin layer of air. How naïve we were to think that Earth was a permanent paradise for the human race. We were so sure of our importance, our place in the Universe, that we nearly destroyed our own habitat!*

Involuntarily, she gave a small shudder as the thought of humankind's near brush with extinction briefly crossed her mind. Then she forced her lips into a smile and turned from the scene below her and the dark thoughts that it had somehow invoked.

Philip Richards was sitting next to her, his large bulk attempting to spill out of the bucket seat.

'You seem nervous,' he said kindly, 'is this your first time in space?'

'No, my third,' she said, 'I guess I'm a bad traveller. I've been in LEO several times, but the Moon—it's another world.'

'That it is,' he replied, 'I've been to Plato before but I can't say I've gotten used to it yet. The low gravity: it always makes you feel like you're about to fall over. And being underground most of the time doesn't help much either.'

She gave him a slightly forced smile. 'You're not actually making me feel any better, Phil.'

He acted out a theatrical slap on the forehead. 'Sorry. I guess I must be a bit nervous, too. It makes me talk too much.'

Adekola looked around the cabin of the shuttle. There were six rows of very basic seats in the extremely spartan room that the passengers occupied. There were only two windows on either side; one of which she had had the luck to be next to. The room ended in a heavy-duty bulkhead behind which she knew the pilots were situated. There was no trolley service or in-flight movies: space travel wasn't that routine as yet. But there was a kind of packed lunch; unfortunately packed with food items that Adekola found more than usually inedible.

The shuttle was slowly rotating and as she glanced out of the window, the angular shape of the space station came into view. It still looked nothing like the great spinning doughnuts that Von Braun had visualised and had the look of having been randomly put together by someone who had been given only part of the blueprints. In places there were sturdy, rounded cylinders connected by fat tubes; in others there were cubes and rhomboids whose function Adekola was still unable to deduce, despite having seen them close up not long before. She had come up from Florida in a short-hop vessel, docked in one of the cylinders and been whisked down seemingly endless corridors with no time to take anything in. She had dim memories of rooms filled from floor to ceiling with banks of glowing equipment, strange metallic smells, and unfamiliar sounds that echoed and reverberated down winding, twisting tunnels.

After a quick meal and comfort stop she and her fellow travellers had been transferred to this Lunar Shuttle and now was on her way. The shuttle's thermal nuclear drive would make the Moon journey tolerably short; for which she was profoundly grateful. She had discovered, slightly to her surprise, that she did not enjoy travel in space.

The motion of the shuttle soon carried the space station from the window and, as the planet came back into view, she was instantly aware that it had shrunk considerably; already she could see most of its globe.

She felt a tiny shiver of alarm: she was really leaving Earth! In Low Earth Orbit the home planet was always there; its continents instantly recognisable; its blue seas comfortingly familiar. It seemed that one only had to reach out a hand to touch the warm soil of home.

But now that world, and everyone on it, was rapidly changing into a shrinking blue and white sphere, and it could not be denied that distance between them was growing by the second.

Richards could sense her unease and touched her gently on the shoulder.

'It's OK. When you get down you'll feel a lot better. Everyone goes through this.'

Adekola nodded dumbly, but when she looked back at the window, the planet had completely disappeared and there was only blackness. No stars were visible due to the brightness of the cabin.

Only blackness.

She sat back, determined to drive these fears from her mind. She nodded to Richards and gave him a slightly forced smile. She closed her eyes.

At least she wouldn't be seeing those bright flashes in the darkness of her closed vision as the early astronauts had; bright flashes which meant that a high-energy particle had just bored its way through the eyeball. The shuttle had its own miniature magnetosphere which deflected all but the most energetic cosmic rays or solar storms.

Just then, something white and brilliant appeared at the edge of the window, a small shining arc of light that made her blink after the blackness of Cislunar space. As she watched, the arc swelled into an entire segment of silver light as more and more of the lustrous object revealed itself. Hours later, she was looking at, or rather *down on*, the Lunar surface.

Like every other denizen of Earth, Adekola was familiar with the appearance of the satellite but this was different. This was a world! Although still thousands of kilometres from the surface, already the detail was astounding. She could see craters, craters inside craters, craters inside craters inside craters. She could see the smooth maria, dark and seemingly featureless against the white of the rugged highlands. There were sinuous rilles, snaking across the plains like frozen threadworms.

128

This was a world!

Then her destination appeared in the port: the great walled plain Plato, looking like a baleful Cyclopean eye staring back at her; lying just below the Mare Frigoris and to the west of the tremendous gash that was the Alpine Valley.

She knew from the pre-flight briefing that Plato was one hundred kilometres in diameter, and so she began to appreciate the scale of what she was seeing. It seemed impossible that she would soon be touching down on that huge expanse, near the northern crater wall.

Suddenly there was a rumbling noise and she felt the craft shudder slightly. A vibration began under her fingers, which were firmly clasping the sides of the seat. Plato and the Mare Frigoris disappeared from the window and the empty blackness returned.

She looked at Richards for reassurance, but he was already waiting for her gaze and smiled and nodded. 'Retros,' he said, 'we're turning over so we can come down on the rocket blast.'

She smiled back. Of course! How else would one be able to land safely on this new, airless world?

A few minutes passed, and then there was a much stronger shudder which rang through the shuttle, and she felt the craft dip down momentarily and then rise again.

They had landed.

'Welcome to the Moon,' Richards said, 'Now you are a certified Lunatic.'

She stared at him blankly for an instant before getting the joke and laughing, both at the humour and from an undeniable sense of relief. A red-lit sign flashed above her.

"REMAIN SEATED. DO NOT UNDO YOUR SEATBELT UNTIL YOU RECEIVE DISEMBARKATION PERMISSION."

A few more minutes passed and then a green-lit message appeared.

"YOU MAY NOW PROCEED TO DISEMBARKATION."

There was an immediate commotion as everybody tried to

get out of their seats at the same time. She pulled her small luggage case from the rack above her and waited until the crush had thinned somewhat. Richards waited with her.

'OK,' he said, 'here we go!'

They passed through a large flexible tube which had corrugations reminiscent of the bellows of a concertina and into another, much smaller, vehicle. After all the travellers were seated, an amplified voice said, 'Welcome to the Moon. We will be off shortly to Plato Base and it will take this Moon Crawler about twenty minutes. My advice to you all is to try to relax, and when you leave the vehicle move around slowly and carefully at first until you become accustomed to the lower gravity, which as you know is only a sixth of Earth's.

'So, off we go. I'll roll the shields down so you can enjoy the view.'

The circular hatch through which they had entered closed and there was a jerk as the Crawler pulled away from the shuttle. The lights snapped off and with a metallic whine, the roof broke into halves which retracted, revealing a transparent covering through which their surroundings and an ebony, starless sky burst in upon them.

The sky was devoid of stars but was not empty. About twenty degrees above the horizon hung a magnificent crescent of shining blue; streaked and speckled with bands and swirls of white—Earth. The area behind the crescent was not black but was dimly illuminated by what Adekola knew was moonlight. When the planet was in its full phase it would be a disc four times wider than the full moon. Adekola stared at it, trying, but failing, to imagine the billions of human beings carrying out their lives upon its surface; all the things that were happening there at that very moment: birth; death; lovers conjoining; some humans enjoying triumphs; some knowing defeat and despair. For a few giddy seconds, she felt the vast, indifferent immensity of the Universe. Then her mind recoiled, and she pushed those thoughts away.

She took her gaze from that majestic blue-white bow and

looked around at her immediate surroundings.

They were not far from the northern rim of the tremendous walled plain that was Plato, and on the strangely near horizon, less than three kilometres distant, she could see the austere rounded bulk of the crater wall rising up against the blackness; every detail on its blasted and fissured surface visible with pin-sharp clarity in the airless environment. Adekola thought briefly of how many thousands, millions and billions of years had passed since lava had flooded into the impact basin she was now traversing and had cooled to create the basaltic plain of Plato; of how aeon piled on aeon had crawled by since then, with nothing to disturb the emptiness apart from the strike of a meteorite.

And now humans were here; bringing their plans; their designs—and their needs and desires.

And as a sign of their presence, Adekola spied a metal dome ahead on the fissured plain, its burnished surface dazzlingly reflecting the rays of the fierce sun.

The Crawler approached it, its caterpillar tracks throwing up the bone-dry dust in grey parabolas that took a noticeably long time to fall back, and stopped a few metres away. Once again, the concertina tube extended and locked onto a port in the dome's side. There was a whirring noise as the tube wound its way into an air-tight connection and then the door in the Crawler opened again.

Richards looked back at her and nodded in the direction of the open door.

'Home sweet home! Well, at least for a few weeks.'

His job of providing reassurance apparently over, he stood up and headed for the door, leaving Adekola to her thoughts. And so it was that she was one of the last to leave the Crawler and head into the final stage of her journey.

The dome was only an elevator station and held nothing except the doors to those shafts. The base itself was many metres below ground level in a long-dead lava tube, shielded from the deadly torrents of primary cosmic rays and Solar protons which constantly blasted the Lunar surface with invisible death. With her fellow stragglers, she entered one of the elevators and, with a satisfyingly smooth motion, was whisked down to the hidden inhabited levels.

The elevator door opened and immediately they were met by a crowd of people smiling with welcome and beckoning them into the innards of the brightly lit complex.

She looked around: the base clearly had been constructed inside some kind of rocky tube as the undecorated grey walls had an obvious curve to them. It was a little unnerving to imagine blazing lava bubbling and burning its way through this tunnel, melting its way through solid rock with ineluctable power.

But that was millions of years ago, she reminded herself; now all was peaceful.

Nothing would happen.

Nothing could happen.

She was shaken out of her imaginings of cascades of destroying lava by a slim young woman coming up to her and her fellows, bearing a smile almost as bright as the fierce sun of the surface.

'Hi,' she said in a lively voice, which seemed to be carrying genuine pleasure in seeing them, 'Welcome to Plato Base. I'm Ximena. And you are…'

She rattled off all their names without a second's hesitation, nodding to each one of them as she did so.

Adekola studied the woman. She seemed to be in her twenties, with dark hair in a fetching bob. She was wearing a deep blue uniform, comprising loose trousers and a short jacket over a V-necked top. Just above the swell of the right breast was a circular badge showing two spheres linked by a double-headed vermillion arrow. Around its circumference were the words "Project Independence" in gold letters. Over her shoulder, she bore a plain leatherette satchel.

'Did you have an enjoyable trip?' she enquired of all of them, smiling as spoke, and nodding as she listened to the mundane replies. Adekola said nothing, which Ximena picked up on immediately.

'And you, Tamira—I can call you, Tamira, can't I? Sounds like you didn't have a nice trip.'

'It was fine,' Adekola replied, 'it's just me. I've discovered I'm not a good flier.'

'That makes two of us!' Ximena laughed, displaying perfectly spaced teeth, all whiter than the purest ivory. Her face relaxed from its smile, but still remained friendly and welcoming. 'And now to business. You are Group K7. Remember that, otherwise you might miss a few important announcements.' She laughed: 'Like when dinner is!'

The others laughed dutifully and Ximena smiled again. 'And now to show you to your quarters. Now, when you start walking, take it very slowly at first. Gravity here is only seventeen per cent of home, so it takes some getting used to. We don't want anyone falling over and banging their head on their first day! But don't worry, we have arranged transport for you. Please follow me.'

With that, she turned and headed off down the tunnel. As Adekola followed she became aware of the difference in gravity. This was the first time she had walked any distance in low gee and it felt like she was walking on springs, combined with a disconcerting feeling that she was going to fall over.

*I've finally managed to lose some weight!* she thought, wryly.

'Not far now!' Ximena called gaily over her shoulder.

Nor was it; the young woman turned into a side passage, and there was an open vehicle with rows of seats on both sides, sitting on a single rail.

'Voila!' she said, indicating the vehicle, 'Ladies and gentlemen—your carriage awaits!' No sooner were they seated, with Ximena at the back to watch over them like a ministering angel, then the vehicle gave a slight jerk and then silently glided forward through its own, much smaller tunnel.

'Where do you get your power from?' a man next to Adekola asked their guide.

'Mainly solar at the moment,' she said, 'our storage facilities can get us through the Lunar night just fine.'

Unlike her fellow traveller, Adekola had done her research

133

on Plato Base.

'But you have fusion reactors as well, don't you?' she said.

'Indeed we do! Four massive fusion reactors. But they're not on-line at the moment.'

'Then why do you need them?' the same man continued.

Ximena's voice dropped very slightly, as if she were about to reveal a great secret.

'Why, they're for Project Independence. We'll need oodles of power then!'

The man opened his mouth to ask another question, but then apparently thought better of it.

'Not long now!' Ximena trilled.

The vehicle emerged into an area as wide as the original part of the complex. On the far wall was a set of doors with numbers on them.

'Here you are,' Ximena said, as the vehicle soughed to a gentle stop, 'your beautiful homes for the duration.'

As they all climbed off the transport vehicle, she said briskly, 'Gather round. These are your house keys', and gave each of them a small rectangular object, made of a red plastic. 'Dinner is at 18:00, and the cafeteria is within easy walking distance of your rooms.' She paused and looked around at all of them. 'Any questions?'

Adekola had one. 'What happens for the rest of the day? When do we start work?'

Ximena beamed at her. 'My, aren't you the keen one! For today—nothing. You've had a long, tiring journey. About four hundred thousand kilometres, I believe! After dinner, just relax in your rooms and we'll all meet up in the morning. You'll find an agenda in there, so nothing to worry about.'

Adekola stood there, staring down at her key, then back at Ximena, not sure if there was anything else she should ask. But Ximena made the next move.

'Well, that's it! I hope you have a real good time here on the Moon, like everybody else. As the saying goes, we're just one big, happy family!'

With that she turned her back on them, her smile instantly vanishing, and was whisked away on the transport vehicle.

Adekola looked around at her fellows, none of whom she had had a good look at before and shrugged. 'Welcome to the Moon,' she said flatly.

The others nodded, and then they all headed to their rooms. The number of her door had appeared on the key as soon as she had taken it from Ximena and she was soon sitting in a comfortable chair in the room.

However, she was not comfortable; in fact she had suffered an immediate feeling of claustrophobia as soon as she entered, for the room had obviously been carved from the solid rock of the lava tube and had bare walls of the now-familiar, dispiriting grey basalt. Her dwelling comprised a living space with a small table with a bowl of fruit on it, and in a corner there was a refrigerator; there was a televiewer screen set into one of the walls; there was a small separate bedroom; a shower room, and nothing else. No windows. Just grey rock.

*I can't stay here!* she thought in gathering panic, *it's like a prison cell!*

Just then there was a pleasant musical tone and the televiewer screen flashed into life.

A human face appeared on it.

A face framed in tumbling blonde locks.

Elizabeth Baldwin.

'Hello, and welcome to the Moon,' the face in the viewer said, 'I am so glad you can join us here in what promises to be the start of one of humanity's greatest achievements; one of the greatest adventures of our species: Project Independence. I will meet you all personally tomorrow, so I will say no more about my plans at the moment. But you must all be a little confused by the rapid pace of what has happened to you recently. You are almost certainly a little disconcerted by your apartment and feel that it's a little confining.'

*You got that right, lady!* Adekola thought, trying to send that message at the electronic image.

'Don't worry,' the smiling face continued, in that honeyed voice which seemed able to allay all worries and send the listener into a relaxed state of blissful acceptance, like an aural soporific drug, 'your room can be tailored to your requirements. There is a manual just below this screen. I know that the lack of windows here will concern some of you, but as scientists you must remember that we are many metres below the Lunar surface, safe from the blasting radiation up there. But let me give you an example of how you can make your room more congenial.'

Instantly the grey walls became a scene of an ocean shore beneath a cool blue sky freckled with fast-moving clouds. Adekola thought it might be Cape Cod. Then the seascape was replaced by a tropical scene of a mighty waterfall, crashing down in white spume and spray from a red sandstone mesa into an emerald rainforest.

And so it went on.

'There are hundreds of visions to choose from,' the electronic Baldwin continued, 'the displays give off only minuscule amounts of heat so you can leave them on continually. You can choose from hundreds of scenes and program them to appear in any order you like. The choice is yours.'

Another lovely smile.

'And now I will leave you. There is food and wine in the refrigerator but don't forget dinner is at 18:00. I'll see you tomorrow. Bye for now.'

And Adekola was alone.

# Six: Project Independence

The alarm trilled gently and, unwillingly, Adekola opened slightly gummed-up eyes.

She could remember little of what had happened yesterday after arriving at Plato Base. She was able to recall sitting down in the noisy cafeteria, surrounded by people she didn't know and eating bland, extremely chewy food. Most of it she understood from her research was algae- or fungus-derived and had been textured into various shapes and then flavoured with a variety of spices; most of which had been concocted in the lab. She knew that somewhere in this sublunar complex there were great vats of slowly convecting nutrient broths, carrying green clouds of algae; all under the blaze of lights adjusted to the best spectrum for plant growth. Her research had also told her that the base had been established in Plato to allow easy access to the resource of the frozen water hidden under the north pole.

Elsewhere in the underground caverns there were dark regions where edible fungi were cultured.

And both fungi and algae would be combined, mixed, blended, twisted, baked, fried, into food for the researchers.

An ingenious system, designed to ensure maximum self-sufficiency for this little human outpost and sustain its precarious existence on a hostile, unforgiving world.

A remarkable achievement.

But the food was terrible.

And now she had to face it all over again at breakfast!

But as she emerged from the shower, her vigorous towelling was interrupted by the same musical tone she had heard from the televiewer the previous day. The screen flashed into life and, inevitably, Elizabeth Baldwin's smiling face appeared. Her smile wavered infinitesimally at the sight of Adekola hiding her nakedness under a large towel, and the latter realised with a start that this session was live.

'Oh, I've caught you at an inconvenient moment,' Baldwin

137

said, regaining her composure, 'I assumed that you'd be up and about by now. So sorry dear.'

Adekola wrapped the towel firmly about her to ensure her modesty was not threatened.

'Yes, good morning, Elizabeth. Sorry, I'm not really a very early riser.'

'Well, I'm afraid we're all larks in Plato Base; something you must get used to. Anyway, the reason I'm calling is that I've decided to advance the plenary session by half an hour. It'll be at 10:30 hours in the Conference Hall; there's a map at the back of the agenda so I'm sure you'll find it. Please be punctual.'

Adekola gave a nod, somehow feeling that she had been magically transported back to her school days. 'Yes, I'll be there, Elizabeth.'

Baldwin's image returned the nod, but her expression had altered in some indefinable way. 'Yes, I'm sure you will. And one other thing, dear.'

'Yes?'

'In Plato Base, I'm "Professor Baldwin". I'm sure you'll understand, Tamira, but it's important to me that everyone understands their place in the hierarchy. I make the decisions and I take the rap if anything goes wrong.' The indefinable expression was wiped away and the bottled sunshine of her normal smile returned. 'See you there!' she finished brightly.

The televiewer went dead, leaving Adekola with a swirl of mixed emotions.

Somehow the morning had not got off to a good start: hardly had she left the shower before she had been admonished by her boss while still towelling herself.

She glanced at the clock and realised guiltily that Baldwin had been right: she had to move!

On arrival in the cafeteria, she discovered that it was only half full as most of the personnel had already completed their breakfast and left. Hurriedly, she filled her tray with the usual unappetising mixture of algae- and fungi-based delights and sat down. She was pleasantly surprised to see Eduardo Estefan sitting opposite her. He raised a glass containing a dark green liquid.

'Good to see you, Tamira. You got the message from the Boss, I guess.'

She bit into an algal patty and had to speak with her mouth full in order to make up for lost time. 'Yes, *mmmphh*, I *mmmphh* did. I *mmmphh*...'

He held up a hand and grinned. 'It's OK. Enjoy your breakfast. But remember, this is the big day, so you mustn't be late. Today's the day we find out what we're supposed to be doing up here. Be given our orders.' There was a twinkle in his eye when he added, 'And with Baldwin, it'll definitely be orders we'll be given.'

She nodded but did not attempt to speak.

He drained his glass in a single movement and standing up, said: 'See you there. Let's hope she's not too hard on us.'

She gave him a silent wave and carried on glumly munching her breakfast.

She was nearing the end of the last tasteless item on her plate when she was suddenly hit by a wave of very raucous laughter. She turned to see the source and found herself looking at a group of men occupying a table some distance away. She stared at them for some time: they did not look like the normal run of scientists/technicians that made up the personnel in Plato. They were all burly, muscular men whose physiques seemed on the point of splitting their tight technician uniforms apart. Several were heavily tattooed with the kind that respond garishly to ultraviolet light, and others combined shaven heads with bushy beards. One caught her looking at them and, putting his glass down, returned her stare with one that gave her a sudden chill. Somehow intimidated, she quickly looked away.

She looked at the device on her wrist, which as well as functioning as the memory recorder, served as the simple timepiece it resembled.

Time to go!

*\*\*\**

139

The great Conference Hall reminded Adekola of the room on Earth where Baldwin had first revealed her grand plan; it was almost as large but differed from that room, of course, in not having any windows. It had no pleasing views of Earth's natural wonders either, just the drab, forbidding grey of Lunar rock.

But it did have a dais with a huge screen at the back, and on that dais, as one might have surmised, Baldwin stood, hands behind her back, waiting for her people to assemble. Those in the front rows might have been able to detect a faint expression of impatience on the usually serene countenance of their leader. She was wearing a uniform which bore a different colour to everyone else's: it was a shining yellow-bronze, and as she waited motionless for the stragglers, she looked like a splendid statue moulded from the finest gold.

Finally all were seated, Adekola being one of the very last to achieve that status. As she sat down she saw that the screen behind Baldwin was active and showed in simple glowing characters the name BALDWIN and from that illustrious name there three thin lines descended to join up with three other names in smaller characters.

And those names were: ADEKOLA ESTEFAN RICHARDS.

She remembered then that the agenda had said that she should go straight to her seat on the dais; where Estefan and Richards were already sitting.

With several *Excuse Me's* and *Pardon Me's* she made her way through the row of annoyed people and rather sheepishly found her way up to her allotted seat, managing to avoid Baldwin's glare as she did so.

'Now we're all here,' that lady said, throwing a glance at Adekola which the latter skilfully avoided, 'we will begin.'

Baldwin moved to the front of the dais and stood silently for a moment, studying her people, her tools. Then she spoke.

'Project Independence. You all know the words, but what do they mean? How will you help me bring my plans to a triumphant conclusion?' She turned to the three on the chairs.

'Let me welcome your three team leaders. They will introduce themselves and tell you their backgrounds and specialisms. First, Eduardo Estefan.' She withdrew from the front of the stage. 'Eduardo, the floor is yours.'

Experiencing a pang of alarm, Adekola watched Estefan walk to the front. She had not read in the agenda that they were required to make a speech—and public speaking held a particular horror for her. But not Estefan, apparently, for he immediately launched into a smooth recital of his qualifications and work history. Adekola listened dumbly to him, gradually feeling more and more inadequate as Estefan's list of achievements seemed to continue without end.

Finally he finished, glanced at Baldwin, who acknowledged him and indicated that he should take his seat. Richards was next, and if anything, he was even more at ease than Estefan, and incredibly managed to crack a few successful jokes, although Baldwin did not appear to notice.

Adekola watched him return to his seat and then found that her legs had unaccountably turned to rubber. She walked unusually carefully to the front of the stage and found herself looking timorously at what to her looked like an endless ocean of faces; although in truth, it was only a hundred.

For a few moments, she had no idea of what to say. The sea of faces stared up at her, expectantly. The silence seemed to press down on her like a heavy, invisible cloak.

Then she spoke, at first stumblingly, haltingly; but gradually her confidence began to build and towards the end of her account of her career she felt slightly light-headed with success.

She smiled down at them, gave a brief wave, and headed back to her chair. She passed Baldwin who gave her a quick glance and said, 'Not bad, Tamira, but it was a lot shorter than I expected.'

Completely deflated, she sat down and spent the next few minutes staring at her hands.

Baldwin was back at the front of the dais and speaking with clear authority, in that musical voice of hers which somehow forced the listener to accept every word.

...is necessary,' Adekola heard Baldwin say, as she brought her attention back to the present.

Adekola's mind raced. What was she talking about? Could it be...?

*What is necessary?* she thought.

'Negative matter; yes, you heard me aright. Some have argued that it is forbidden by the equations of relativity,' Baldwin continued, and then looked around at the throng below her, 'but let me tell you, I have studied those equations and I can tell you that Einstein was a long way from knowing everything. His relativistic interpretation of gravity had to give way before the quantum theory, to name but one instance of his shortcomings—if any more were needed.

'Exotic matter, specifically negative matter,' Baldwin said, 'that is the key. That will unlock the potential of the wormhole. And without wishing to insult your undoubted intelligence, let me make clear for the last time that I am not talking about antimatter, which is a much more everyday phenomenon. No, negative matter is matter which is opposite in its sign to gravitation. To it a *pull* is a *push*. To it a *push* is a *pull*. That's what you will help me to bring into existence. We here in Plato will gestate and give birth to the wonder of the age: negative matter. And when we have it, the road to humanity's new home in the Centauri system will be open.'

She paused and then thrust her arms at the grim grey roof.

'And we will gather in the harvest of stars!'

There was an astounded silence for a few brief moments, and then her audience broke into wild applause. She stood there, nodding, smiling, drinking the applause in like nectar.

Finally, the clapping faded away, and she said, 'Any questions?'

There were no indicator lights in Plato so when a woman decided to ask a question, she had to hold up her arm, like a humble student.

Baldwin acknowledged her.

142

'Professor,' the woman began, sounding distinctly timid, 'is it not possible that negative matter exists naturally and we could simply collect it, rather than have to laboriously create it?'

Baldwin looked annoyed. 'You obviously have not understood a word of what I said. Negative matter is negative to gravity. If there were any in the Solar system, it would have interacted with the normal matter and been repelled. It would have been driven away from the concentrations of positive mass and would now be beyond the boundary of the observable universe.' She snorted. 'If you want to go and look for it, be my guest. I have better things to do.'

After that, there were no more questions.

The plenary session broke up into the three teams in three separate conference rooms. There they found Baldwin's detailed instructions on their line of research. In her conference room, Adekola opened a sealed envelope with her name on it and found Baldwin's especial message, just for her.

It was couched in that lady's terse, parsimonious style. There was not an unnecessary word; not an unnecessary comma. It laid down Adekola's duties regarding the management of her team; her objectives; and, most importantly, the timetable for the delivery of said objectives.

It took her quite a while to absorb it, and she had to read it three times, finally wondering, with more than a little bitterness, that as the instructions were so detailed whether it would have been simpler if Baldwin had just run the whole project by herself.

And there was another message, clearly lurking between the carefully phrased lines.

And that message was:

DON'T FUCK UP—OR ELSE.

\*\*\*

*Come on, come on!* Adekola thought, staring at the blank televiewer screen. *Where the hell is he?*

This was the appointed time; she was sure of that. She had

143

correlated Lunar time with Eastern Standard Time and was certain that she had the right moment.

Then, to her immense relief, the screen flickered once and then there they were: Parry and Jahia, smiling out of the screen.

'Look, there's Mommy!' said Parry, pointing.

'Mommy!' the child cried, clapping her hands.

Adekola felt a rush of emotion; a sudden fierce desire to abandon this entire enterprise and get on the next shuttle.

Parry somehow picked that up. 'What's the matter?' he said.

She spread her hands, indicating her confusion.

'I…I don't know, Idris. I'm not sure I've made the right decision. It's Baldwin…she's…'. Adekola paused for a moment, then 'Idris, I want to come back! I miss you all so much! I…'

There was an unavoidable delay of just over two and a half seconds for a two-way conversation in Earth-Luna messaging, due to the finite speed of light, but the delay before Parry answered was considerably longer than that.

Then he said, 'You stop that right now! This is a wonderful opportunity for you; when you complete this project, your name will be recorded in the annals of science forever! You can't throw it all away!'

'I miss you all so terribly,' she murmured.

'We're not going anywhere. We'll be right here waiting for you until you come back. Of course, Baldwin's difficult. Like all driven leaders, she's a pain in the ass, but that's the way it is. You just have to suck it up. Now, stop this—you're upsetting Jahia and this is supposed to be a fun family time.'

With an effort, she brightened up and they spent some time in family chat.

Then Parry said, 'How's the memory recording going? You can't let these times be forgotten.'

She raised an eyebrow. 'Idris, in case you haven't noticed—I'm on the Moon.'

He tutted. 'And I thought you were a physicist. The signal can piggy-back on the standard communication wavelengths between you and Earth. So get to it, girl.'

144

She nodded. 'Sorry, I didn't realise that. I'll try it later. And Idris, I have a furlough in two weeks. Keep the bed warm...'

She watched him as her message crossed the black gulf between the two worlds.

When she saw his face light up, she knew he had received it.

'You bet!' he said, displaying the classic ear-to-ear grin.

After they had signed off, she activated the part of the wristwatch that enabled the download.

She leaned back and closed her eyes.

She saw the space station; she saw the shuttle and its journey through the unforgiving vacuum of cis-Lunar space; once again she looked down on the cold, dispassionate eye that was the walled plain of Plato; she saw Ximena welcome her to the Base; she looked up at the golden figure of Baldwin on the dais, shining in the spotlights in scintillating glory like a magnificent, all-knowing goddess.

*A goddess*, she thought, *and what do goddesses do to mortals who don't make the necessary sacrifices to them?*

# Seven: The Eavesdropper

'It's there!' Adekola said, staring at the monitoring display, 'it's there!'

She stood up ram-rod straight and raised her arms above her head. 'Only gone and bloody done it!'

Moreau called from the other side of the lab. 'Sorry Boss— it just decayed.'

'What!'

Adekola rushed to his side. 'Show me!'

Glumly, he tapped his finger at the scrolling display of numbers. 'There you are, Boss. Gone. Zilch. Diddly squat.'

Adekola stared at the numbers, willing them to show that her prize was still there.

They refused to obey.

'But it was there, wasn't it?' she said to Moreau, 'tell me I'm not going mad, please!'

Moreau looked down at her, and for an instant she thought she saw pity in his eyes.

'Yes, Boss. One whole picogram. Not enough to sustain a wormhole as long as my...' He hesitated, 'my little finger. And now it's gone.'

'You mean it was repelled by the regular matter?'

'Nope. It just vanished. It ain't in this universe. It ain't here. It ain't there. It ain't anywhere. And none of the sensors reacted fast enough to get a single data point. Not one.'

'Thank you for your colourful exposition, Henri,' she said, trying to keep the bitterness from infecting her speech. It wasn't Moreau's fault; she mustn't shoot the messenger. If it was anyone's fault, it was hers.

She re-ran the experiment in her mind. She had been so sure. She had had lovely visions of sauntering into Baldwin's office and slapping down the report in front of her boss's astounded eyes. Negative matter. Tamira Adekola's stupendous achievement.

And now all she could report was a picogram of negative matter existing in this universe for a picosecond. The other teams had already done that—two days' earlier.

She walked over to the massive transparent cylinder which ran the entire length of the room and disappeared into the walls at both ends.

Something, something, had come into being inside that cylinder, had been born from clashing force-fields of incredible space-twisting energies which had burned brighter than the sun for a few picoseconds; something strange, wonderful, not of this continuum.

What had happened to it?

She knew that her people were all looking at her, waiting for instructions. And she wasn't sure she had any. Her mouth dry, she eventually said, 'Let's run it again. Increase it by point triple-zero one electron-volts.'

They did, with the same result.

'OK, gang,' she said, knowing that they would detect the weariness in her voice, 'Let's call it a day.'

Back in her room, Adekola lay on her bed. On her wall, the waves of a great blue-green ocean rose and fell lazily below a sky of electric blue.

The televiewer flashed into life.

Adekola groaned inwardly. *Why won't she leave me alone?*

Inevitably, it was Baldwin.

'What progress?' she said, skipping any conversational preamble.

Adekola sat up.

'None so far, Professor.'

A tailored eyebrow rose.

'None? None? How much time do you need, Tamira? I've showered you with resources that any lab on Earth would be jealous of, and I keep hearing the same thing from you.

'None. And frankly, I'm getting a little tired of it.'

The image of Baldwin disappeared and was replaced by a matte rectangle of blackness as Baldwin cut the connection.

The ocean continued its mighty rise and fall on Adekola's wall.

But all she saw were the layers of grey rock that lay between her and the pitiless stars; stars that Baldwin hungered to reach and tame. Adekola considered her position: had she over-reached herself; been promoted beyond her actual ability? It was not that unusual, she pondered; in her career she had met many people who were living on past glories, who were unaware that the tide of scientific research had passed them by long ago. Was she one?

And then she sat up and swung her legs to the floor. No! She was not one of that forlorn crew!

She hurried back to the lab. It seemed strange to be in it alone when she was used to the constant noise of the technicians scurrying around the place; shouting orders, indulging in harmless badinage. It seemed as if some bereavement had taken place, leaving it deserted and dead.

She activated her console and re-ran the data from the experiments. She stood for a while and then sat down nearer the screen, almost pressing her nose against it.

She flicked the findings back and forth and then zeroed in on smaller and smaller time intervals. She re-ran the video of the experiment, decreasing the time periods to values so small that uncountable quadrillions of them would not amount to a second in the macroscopic world.

And there: a small purplish flash, occupying a period of time unimaginably small, smaller than the time taken for an electron to jump from one shell to another.

'Computer,' she said, a little startled by how loud her voice sounded in the empty room, 'I am looking at Experiment A2-iota. Examine the time period now on my console.'

'I am there, Tamira,' a pleasant contralto voice replied.

She moved the cursor, marked the start point, and then moved it to show the end point.

'There is an energy flux inside the marked time range,' she said, in rising excitement, 'describe the energy so marked.'

148

There was silence. Usually, the computer answered the question as soon as the human had uttered it. In computer terms, the period of this silence equated to geological eras in the realm of those slow-moving entities possessed only of wetware. Like Adekola.

Then the contralto voice: 'The energy flux does not equate to any known portion of the electromagnetic spectrum. Neither is it gravitational.'

'But I can see it!'

'What the human eye is seeing is an aftereffect. Something existed in our universe for 0.984 picoseconds which is not part of the standard model of forces. However, I have been able to retrospectively collect data which constrain the parameters of its entry and disappearance.'

Adekola felt her face burn with a rush of excited blood.

She jumped to her feet.

'Got you!' she shouted.

*** 

Baldwin looked up from her terminal as Adekola burst into her room.

'It is customary to knock and await permission before entering my office,' was her icy greeting.

'Yes, yes, I know, I'm sorry, Elizabeth... Professor Baldwin. But I have something to show you!'

Baldwin leaned back. 'It had better be good. I don't take kindly to unexpected disturbances.'

'Then let me show you these!' Adekola dumped a sheaf of printouts on her superior's desk.

Baldwin lifted the first sheet with a distinct air of resignation.

She studied it languidly. Then Adekola saw her suddenly stiffen and immediately reach for the next printout. And then the next.

Expectation crackled in the air like static electricity.

Baldwin had obviously forgotten that Adekola was there as

149

she studied paper after paper. Once she typed something into one of the several keyboards on her desk.

Then, remembering she was not alone, she looked back up at her uninvited guest.

'And you derived these results this evening?'

'Yes.'

'And you have told no-one but me?'

'No-one.'

'Can you see the implications of these results?' A delicately shaped fingernail tapped halfway down the third sheet. 'Especially this one?'

'I had noticed nothing particularly unusual about that reading.'

Baldwin smiled a half-smile. 'No, of course not. How could you be expected to do that with your background.'

Suddenly, Baldwin appeared eager to be rid of her.

'Yes, yes, you've done very well. Exceptionally well, my dear. I'm proud of you. Leave all this with me and I'll give it my full attention.'

'And the findings?'

'Will be my findings. You have shown the way, and for that I'm grateful. But I really don't think your team can take this much further.' She smiled again. It seemed to be a complete smile this time, but there was something wrong with it. 'Now, it's quite late. Why don't you run along and have a well-earned rest? It's nearly time for your furlough, isn't it?'

'Yes,' Adekola replied, becoming increasingly annoyed at what was clearly a thinly-disguised dismissal.

'Yes, back to that lovely man of yours. The Australian. Tell me, how did you manage to catch him?'

'I beg your pardon?'

'Let me put it as gently as possible. I mean, I'm beautiful. You're not.' Baldwin's smile became predatory. 'Get over it.'

Adekola turned on her heel and left Baldwin's room, without attempting to deliver her normal upbeat comment.

\*\*\*

Adekola sat at her usual table in the cafeteria, staring into space, as aware of the comings and goings around her as she was of the slow turning of the satellite beneath her feet. The noise of her fellows swept over her, unnoticed, inconsequential.

Could she carry on like this? Working for a woman like Baldwin?

She remembered the joy with which her team had learned of her breakthrough; of how the other teams, although piqued at being beaten to the post by her group, had warmly congratulated her.

But Baldwin. She had shown obvious excitement with the findings, but her praise had been perfunctory, formulaic. She had revealed her true feelings for Adekola: she was a tool, an instrument. No more. No better than the metal and ceramic instruments she had on her desk.

Adekola had shared her feelings with Parry and even downloaded the memory of the meeting, but it had not helped to ease her distress.

Her peripheral vision told her that someone had sat opposite her, but she did not look up. Then she heard a welcome friendly voice and realised that the sizable bulk that was now opposite belonged to Philip Richards.

'Well, well,' he said, 'you don't look like someone who's in line for a Nobel Prize. You look like a little girl who's just dropped her last lollipop.'

The ridiculous image forced her to smile, and she acknowledged him and said, 'Phil. It's good to see a friendly face.'

'Good to see you as well. One day I'll be able to tell my grandchildren I met a real-life genius.'

She waved a hand. 'Oh stop it, you flatterer! I had a lucky break, is all.'

'Yeah, it's funny that I've never had a break like that. Now tell me what's wrong.'

She hesitated. To reveal too much of her feelings might make her look mean-spirited, petty. But she looked at Richards, at his open expression, his smiling lips, and decided to risk it. She

151

needed to unload her feelings.

'It's that woman!' she finally exploded, 'That fucking woman!'

She smiled self-consciously, 'Pardon my French.'

Richards grinned. 'Sorry, I never took French. But I know what you're feeling.'

'You do?'

He leaned forward and for a moment it looked as if he was going to take Adekola's hands, but did not.

'You're feeling hard-done-by. You're feeling that you just been used; used for what you can give her and then thrown away.'

She gave a weak smile. 'That's exactly how I feel!'

'Tamira, Tamira, I'm afraid you've led a bit of a sheltered life. Academia is full of people like Baldwin, driven people who want to carve their initials across the Milky Way.

'She wants to go down in history, alongside Galileo, Newton, Maxwell, Einstein. We have to accept that we are her disciples, her acolytes—I'm not sure of the exact terms here, but you know what I mean. Ask yourself, honestly, are you really in the same league as our Lord and Mistress? I know I'm not.'

'No, I know I'm not. I'm probably not even in the league directly below her. But that's not all.'

'Oh?'

Tamira hesitated. To say more would reveal her insecurities regarding her womanhood compared to Baldwin. She decided to press on, carefully.

'She says things about me personally; about my appearance. About my partner. Things that really hurt.'

Richards pursed his lips. 'I don't think I can help you much there. I've always known that I'm nothing to look at; just a walking tub of lard. But I've learned to forget about that.'

Adekola did lean over and did take his hands. 'Oh, Phil, that's just ridiculous. I've seen worse than you.' *No, that wasn't the right thing to say!* 'I mean, you're a lovely man. You've got a great personality.'

152

Richards looked like he was sucking something sour. 'Yeah, that's what all the girls say.' He shook it off. 'Anyway, you've got nothing to worry about with Idris. The way you two talk is…'

She removed her hands. 'Idris? I've told no-one here about Idris. How do you know about us?'

He ran a hand over his forehead and looked away into the busy cafeteria. 'Damn, I've given myself away, haven't I?'

She stared at him stonily. 'Speak.'

'Look, Tamira, I'm not such a nice guy as you think I am.' He lowered his voice so she could only just catch his words. 'I eavesdrop.'

'What!'

'Now, don't get me wrong; I'm not into weird sex, or anything like that. It's a kind of… kind of insurance policy.'

'You're not making yourself any clearer.'

He straightened and spoke in a flat, unemotional voice. 'I have a talent for hacking into secure communication channels; a kind of side-effect of my research. I usually check on what the big guns are saying about me, so I can keep one jump ahead of them.'

'I am not your manager, so that doesn't explain your behaviour.'

'No, no, of course not. Look, you've got to believe me, I haven't been deliberately stalking you or anything. It's just that I picked up some odd traffic between Plato and Earth. It looked like a simple communication channel, but there was something heterodyned on it: something incredibly complex. I'd never seen it before. So I followed it for a couple of times, to see if I could understand what was going on. In the course of that, I'm afraid I got the gist of what you and Idris were saying to each other.' His head dropped down. 'I know you must hate me. I only did it twice, and then I came to my senses. And I've never done it again.'

A glacial silence had fallen. Eventually, she broke it.

'Oh, Phil, Phil! What have you done? The one person I thought I liked.'

He leaned across the table, a hint of desperation in his expression.

'You can still like me, Tamira. The first time was an accident. The second was wrong, I accept, but I haven't done it since.'

'As the second was yesterday, that's easy to say.'

He turned his head back and forth in his distress, 'I know, I know. But you have to believe me. I really, really wasn't going to do it again!'

Adekola stared at the man; the one man who had shown interest in her on this dead world and made her laugh with his silly jokes.

She decided that carrying on with no friend was too hard a price to pay for yet more anger, righteous or otherwise. She extended a hand.

'OK, Phil, I believe you. But never, never again, right?'

Relief visibly washed over him. 'Thank you, Tamira. I'm an idiot, I know. I've spent too many hours alone over printouts. Thank you.'

They sat and talked and gradually their old, relaxed behaviour reasserted itself, and toward the end of the conversation, he had her in fits of helpless laughter with an extremely convoluted funny story.

But just as they were about to part, he looked her in the eye and said, 'At the risk of reopening old wounds, there is something I learned from my eavesdropping.'

'Phil, I don't want to know,' she said, bristling again as she began to rise from her chair.

'No, no, this might help you in your dealings with the Great One.'

She sat back down. 'Go on.'

Once again, he dropped his voice and leaned nearer to his dinner companion. 'She's in communication with someone on Earth. And she's not using standard, TransTerrestrial channels. She's using a sophisticated encryption that I haven't been able to crack yet. It seems she's talking to someone that she doesn't want anyone else to know about!'

# Eight: The Sphere

The hypersonic part of her return was over, and for that Adekola was profoundly grateful. The orbital transfer vehicle had been shaken like a rat in a terrier's mouth as it arrowed down through the exosphere into the mesosphere. Although she was scientifically certain that the inferno outside caused by the craft's blindingly fast passage through steadily thickening layers of air could not penetrate into the passenger section, it was still nerve-wracking to know she was merely metres away from plasma at thousands of kelvins.

Or at least it had been for her; the other passengers had not appeared to be even slightly concerned and had either been asleep or reading.

Oh well, she was not a good flier: that had been made abundantly clear to her recently. But no matter—she would soon be seeing Parry and Jahia again! She felt her spirits lift at that thought and decided to enjoy the rest of the flight.

Through the window, she could see the green finger of the Florida peninsula poking into the dazzling blue of the Gulf of Mexico. There was a swirl of a tropical cyclone heading into the mainland, but it looked like the landfall would be in Alabama; too far west to bother her.

Tropical cyclones were still very common in the Gulf/Caribbean area as the subtropics were still cooling down from their close brush with killing heat. It would be decades before comparative calm returned.

She smiled as she thought how it would be a much better world for Jahia, than the one her mother had grown up in. Not for her the heatwaves which had pressed down on the cities like the breath of a cosmic dragon. She could still remember how she used to lie naked in her bedroom with the blinds drawn and feeling the sweat pour off her blistering skin as the air became the exhalation of a blast furnace; and how movement, speech and, eventually, even thought, became impossible.

She remembered how water had once again become a commodity to be fought over instead of an unnoticed adjunct to comfortable living. Of how the infrastructure and social bonds which had kept societies together had come perilously close to collapse.

And the violence.

There had been violence.

She thrust those thoughts back down into the substrata of her mind where they belonged, angry with herself for allowing them to invade her happiness.

There were some experiences she would not be recording for future generations of the Adekola/Parry lineage.

Florida lost its appearance as a peninsula and became simply a green carpet dotted with endless lakes of every possible size, dazzlingly brilliant in the noonday sun. The land rushed up to meet her, and soon she was seeing individual buildings, trees, bushes…

There was a slight bump and a rushing noise as of a great wind.

She was back.

The indicator panel above her warned her not to unfasten her seatbelt or attempt to move and so she continued to sit, looking out of the window at the busy spaceport.

Everywhere she looked there were great gantries, bearing various types of suborbital craft on their metal shoulders. Some more distant ones were in the process of being raised to the vertical in readiness for a launch into the bright blue skies above them.

But as she sat there, she became aware that something was wrong. It was as if someone had suddenly teleported a great block of stone into her innards. Just raising her arm seemed to require a noticeable effort, as if she was holding a dumbbell.

Then she relaxed. She was back all right; back to a gravitational pull a whole six times greater than what she had become used to at Plato. Even small motions now required a substantial effort.

156

As if to confirm that thought, the Captain's voice came on the intercom.

'Well, ladies and gentlemen, welcome back to Mother Earth. I hope you had a pleasant flight; sorry about that bit of turbulence back there; quite normal, I assure you.

'But please listen carefully: do not attempt to leave your seats or make any sudden motions. You are now back in a full one-gee environment and it will take you some time to adjust. If you attempt to stand up quickly, you will almost certainly have a blackout. Just sit tight and people will be coming on board to help you with the disembarkation procedures.'

Adekola sat back. She had done this kind of thing on other occasions; but she had never spent so long in a low-gee environment and was unsure of how long recuperation would take.

One thing was obvious to her: human beings could not live long on the Moon without irreversible physical changes.

After what seemed an interminable wait, she heard the exterior doors slide open and then a group of people came aboard, pushing collapsible wheelchairs. A smiling young woman helped her into one and then guided the chair down a ramp onto the bare concrete of the landing pad.

She was immediately struck by the quality of the air. This was the same air which she had been breathing before leaving for the Mare Frigoris, but how different it felt now! It was hot and heavy with moisture, but beyond that, there was the smell of living things and an active environment; aromas of vigorous, exuberant vegetation; of salt being blown in from the Gulf; of the lingering traces of propellant gases; of human smells; of machine smells. The air was so loaded with its cargo of the signs and smells of superabundant life that it seemed impossible that mere air could hold it all!

She realised then how still and dead was the air in Plato Base.

This was the atmosphere of a living world. The air of life itself!

She tried to turn her head to speak to the person pushing

her wheelchair but could not quite do it.

'Much happen while I've been away?' she finally said to the young woman who was doing the pushing.

'Usual nonsense in Washington,' was the laconic reply, 'A bad cyclone passed nearby last week. That's about it.'

Adekola fell silent; even casual conversation seemed tiring.

She was propelled into a building which was blissfully cool after the cloying, humid outside air. There were rows of beds, laid out in a similar fashion to those found in a blood donation facility.

'You'll lie here for an hour,' the woman said, 'then you can see visitors. Whatever you do, don't try to get up suddenly. If you need to unload before we lie you down, tell me now and I'll take you.'

'I'm OK,' Adekola said, 'You said an hour before visitors?'

'That's what I said,' was the brisk reply, and the woman was gone.

Adekola lay on the bed, thinking of the hour that stretched ahead before she could see Parry and Jahia. An eternity!

But not long after that thought, she fell dreamlessly asleep, to be woken by the gentle pressure of a hand on her shoulder.

'You can get up now,' a female voice said, 'we'll take you to the visitor room.'

There was another short wheelchair ride and then she was in a spacious room with many tall windows letting in the bright Floridian sunshine. Dotted throughout the room were softly upholstered chairs, placed symmetrically around circular tables.

And around one were Parry and Jahia!

The wheelchair came to a halt and her chauffeur helped her to her feet.

'I'll walk you to your family,' the woman said, and helped the unsteady Adekola walk to the chair.

With intertwined arms, they crossed to where her family sat waiting for her.

'God, I feel like an old woman!' Adekola gasped.

'It'll pass in a day or so,' the woman replied, 'You haven't been in Zero-gee and that makes a big difference. The drugs help as well; remember to take them at the same time of the day for a week.'

Adekola was no longer listening; she slid onto her chair and stretched her arms out.

Jahia was the first to join her, shouting 'Mommy! Mommy!'

After the inevitable kisses, Parry joined them, saying, 'Hello, Moon Maiden. Did you bring us any green cheese?'

It was not long before Parry was loading her luggage into the car; after searching for an item which the luggage robot had mislaid, of course.

'Why does that always happen!' he muttered, remembering not to utter any bad words in front of Jahia. The car, however, did not fail them and drove them swiftly and silently to the airport and, after a wait which was not too prolonged, into the aircraft.

Soon Florida fell away behind them, and the spectacular towers of Greater New York hove into view on the misty horizon.

Parry turned to Adekola to point them out.

She was asleep.

***

Several days had to pass before Adekola began to be certain that her real legs had not been replaced by lead prostheses.

It was wonderful to be back in the flat; just to be looking at the little central fountain or drinking in the rugged landscapes displayed in Parry's paintings was a soothing balm to her churning mind. The day when she could actually stand under her own efforts and stare at Parry's favourite painting was one which lived long in her memory.

*Under Arenig Fawr.*

She wondered if Parry would ever take her to the ancestral home of his family.

But it was wonderful just to sit back and not worry what

Baldwin's next demand was going to be; not to stand in front of her team and report that something had gone wrong again and that everyone would have to try harder.

Such peace. Why had she put herself through such trials in the first place?

Parry had not yet asked much about her first stay in Plato Base; he knew she just wanted to sit quietly and drink in the normality; to revel in the cosiness of it all.

She spent most of the time playing with Jahia and showed genuine distress when Elena had to take her away to the nursery.

'Can't she skip it for a while?' she asked Parry, 'After all I'll be going back soon.'

'She needs her friends as well as you,' Parry had replied, 'I've told her you won't always be up there. That one day, you'll be coming back for good.'

'Back for good.' Adekola nodded. 'That's what I really want.'

'That's not what I heard,' Parry said, finally broaching the subject of the Lunar research, 'I heard you made a major, major breakthrough.'

She laughed. 'I got lucky. Baldwin made me so angry that I just marched out of her room and went to the lab. And then I saw it. If she hadn't pissed me off, it would never have happened!'

Parry grinned. 'Yeah, I should be so lucky!'

\*\*\*

The days of the furlough passed all too quickly for Adekola. She began to become withdrawn and tended to speak only when spoken to. Only when playing with Jahia or talking to Elena about Jahia did she show much animation.

Parry knew very well what the reason was and tried to ignore it.

And then:

'Tamira,' he said, pulling her away from staring out over the cityscape, 'Look, I know why you're so morose but you've got to

160

look at the long view and what this will do for your career. We are talking about big events here; no, not big—colossal events, which will shape the entire course of future human history. You should be proud of what you're doing up there. You should be glad to get back. And grateful.' He paused, as if what he was about to say was difficult for him. 'Tamira, look, what you're doing will resonate down the centuries. My work—well, it'll just be a footnote; it'll be of some help in medical matters, but that's as far as it will go. So snap out of it!'

'*Snap out of it,*' she repeated, dully, 'That's easy for you to say. You don't have to work with that woman. There's something wrong with her; something deep inside. I believe she has some kind of plan, some agenda, which she isn't sharing.'

'What could that possibly be? TTS is a non-profit organisation. There's no way she could make money out of what's a purely scientific enterprise. The Centauri plan is to provide a safety net for the human race. After all, we've had one near brush with extinction; we know how easily everything could collapse. We need a second home. That's what Project Independence is about—there's no money involved.'

'Maybe it's not money. I agree I don't see how she could get that. But if not money, it's about *glory,* fame, renown, power. Maybe she wants to be the top bitch when the meat is fought over. She's evil.'

'That's a terrible thing to say. You should be ashamed of yourself.'

She turned to him, her face horribly twisted in anger. '*A terrible thing to say?* Oh, I know what your game is, Idris Parry! You're just like all the other men she's got grovelling at her feet!

'You want to fuck her, don't you!'

A silence fell.

Parry removed his hands from Adekola's shoulders and turned away. He crossed the room and sat down, saying nothing.

She stared at him, her mouth moving without words. Then she rushed to him and sat on her heels in front of him.

'I'm sorry, I'm sorry!'

161

He stared at the great window, looking over her head, not looking at her face. Tears glistened in the corners of her eyes.

'*I want to fuck her.* Well, you've said some things in the past, Tamira, but that's too much. You've gone too far this time. Fucking Elizabeth Baldwin is the last thing I want to do. If I were ever to do that, the world would be ending.'

Now the tears were falling.

'Idris, I know, I know! I shouldn't have said that, I know! I'm sorry! My head is all messed up! I'm sorry! I'm so sorry!'

Parry looked at his wristwatch. 'Best if you don't download these memories, Tamira. Jahia will be back soon. You can have a nice time playing with her.'

And with that he left the apartment, leaving Adekola sobbing on the couch.

*** 

It was quite some time before Adekola and Parry could look into each other's faces and smile again. Several wasted days passed before they dared to kiss again.

But eventually they did, and the taboo subject of Elizabeth Baldwin was not mentioned again for the remainder of the furlough. Even so, Adekola could not stop her thoughts from turning to the day when once again she would have to leave the living world of Earth for the dead and sterile Moon. And beyond that day, loomed a dark shadow; the shadow of a person whose name was not to be uttered.

But one day, not long before the end of her stay, Parry came home in an ebullient mood and wearing an unusually broad smile.

'Well,' Adekola said on seeing him, 'if you were a cat I'd think there was no more cream left in the house.'

'Something like that,' he said and stooped down to open his briefcase, 'I've got something to show you.'

He beckoned her to stand near the table and took out a small box from his briefcase. Adekola noticed he was wearing thin gloves, something she had not seen before.

He opened the box and took out a small white ball; a ball that had the nacreous sheen of mother-of-pearl. He placed it carefully on the table and then stood back, waiting for her reaction.

'A ball,' she said, 'a small white ball. What is this? Have you taken up baseball? Billiards? Or...'

She'd run out of games or sports involving the manipulation of small white spheres and so just looked at him, quizzically.

'Pick it up,' he said, 'then sit down immediately and close your eyes.'

She obeyed. He watched her intently and then grinned when her face was transformed by wonderment. She put the ball back on the table, almost dropping it, and then looked at Parry with eyes like saucers.

'Idris,' she gasped, 'I saw it all: the beach in Carolina; the meal; the flight to Plato! But I saw things that I don't consciously remember downloading.'

He sat down beside her. 'Yes, the software's been upgraded. The downloading works continuously in the background now, but only at a low level. If there's a really important event which you want to capture in Hi-Def, so to speak, you still have to consciously do the downloading.' He looked at her, like a child expecting praise, 'So what do you think, pretty cool, huh?'

She looked at the ball. 'It's incredible, to have all that in something so small! So this is your masterpiece, then?'

To her surprise, he looked slightly sheepish.

'Well, yes and no. I had the concepts, but it was McGillivray at the research institute that made it a practical reality. So we call it the "McGillivray-Parry Memory Storage System", or MPSS, for short.'

'I think I'll just call it "The Ball", for short!' she laughed, but then became serious. 'But Idris, what if I lose the damn thing and some stranger picks it up? I don't want just anybody reliving my memories. I mean,' and she smiled archly, 'I might want to remember making love with you!'

He grinned, happy, relaxed, all memory of the shadow that had come between them expunged.

'No, that can't happen. The sphere has sensors that read the DNA pattern of the person holding it and won't respond if there's no family link. And it only becomes fully active if it detects that the holder is an adult; or has gone through puberty, at least. And it's not just memories anymore—if the recipient brain is sufficiently organised, knowledge can be transferred as well. Our knowledge.'

'But the bit about the genetic link. That means eventually it won't respond at all, once the DNA link becomes really thin.'

He nodded. 'True. But with the best will in the world, I don't think your great-great-great grandchild will be that interested in the memory of you standing on a beach in South Carolina.'

She beamed. 'It's wonderful. And I can see now what a blessing it will be for people suffering neurological decline. It will allow them to store their treasured memories and not lose contact with who they really are.' She became serious. 'What you've done here is what really matters: improving the lives of people who are suffering. What I'm doing is just too remote from people's lives. There's no guarantee we can find a way of getting to the Centauri system or do anything worthwhile, even if we do. Either we'll find the planets can't be made habitable or we'll start squabbling and end up fighting each other, as usual.

'But you've done so much more. You've reached out and helped people.'

Once again, she fought back tears, but this time for a different reason. She leaned forward and their lips briefly met.

'I love you.'

'I love you too,' he said.

\*\*\*

Adekola, Parry and Jahia stood side by side, each holding the other's hand, looking at the ancient ruin. They saw a low wall of red stone with a series of low arches. Beyond the wall a

164

pleasant bay was visible, dotted with pleasure craft.

'Santa Rosa island,' Parry said, 'Very pleasant. But why are we here exactly?'

'This is where my family came from. We were so-called "Free Negroes" living in the Pensacola area. When Florida passed to the States they decided to end the status of those people, so my ancestors left Florida. But this is where we started.'

'So your people never were slaves?'

'Not in Florida,' was the ambiguous answer, 'but this is where we began. I wonder what I would see if they'd had your memory downloader in those days.'

'Perhaps best you don't have access to those memories.' Parry indicated the ruins, 'And this is…'

'Fort Pickens. Dates from the War between the States.'

Parry gave a small grimace. 'Slavery again. I'm afraid I don't like this place, Tamira. Too many reminders of how bad things were. How stupid people were. I'd like to think we're over all that now; all that fratricidal violence and hate.' He reached a hand down to ruffle Jahia's hair. 'You're a lucky little girl, Jahia. You're living in a better world now. We've learned from past mistakes. Those bad times can never return. The worst is behind us.'

From the little girl's expression, it was obvious she wasn't quite following her father's line of thought, but, having picked up on one phrase, she beamed and said, 'I'm a lucky little girl!'

Parry heard his partner sigh.

'I think things will be better from now on, but,' and she turned to Parry with a look of longing, 'but for me: Plato Base.'

He returned the wistful look and then turned back to Fort Pickens, and all three stood there for a while, gazing out over Pensacola Bay.

\*\*\*

The day had come. Their autonomous taxi had whisked them away from Pensacola and they were now heading straight for the spaceport.

165

Adekola sat with Jahia in the front, while Parry on the back seat gazed, somewhat forlornly, at the semi-tropical landscape.

Some time had passed since anyone had spoken. Adekola kept thinking of things to say, and then changing her mind at the last moment.

Then, suddenly, Jahia piped up.

'Mommy, I don't like my name!'

Adekola looked down at her daughter with some surprise.

'You don't? What's wrong with it?'

'There's nothing *wrong* with it,' the child replied, twisting her fingers together as if nervous about what she was saying, 'it's just there are nicer names.'

'There are?'

'Yes, Mommy, my friend in nursery, I like her name.'

'And what is this nice name?' Parry inquired.

Jahia twisted around to look at him. 'Kalli. I like Kalli.'

'Well, Jahia's a nice name too. You'll like it when you're older. It's a lovely sounding name. Just wait and see,' he said, giving a reassuring smile.

Jahia pouted, but after a few seconds she brightened and announced, 'Well, when I'm a mommy and I have a little girl I'll name her Kalli.'

Adekola relaxed. The last thing she wanted in her last few hours before boarding was a silly argument about names.

'That's a lovely idea, Jahia,' she said, 'You do just that!'

# Nine: Discovery

Baldwin leaned back in her chair, with her arms behind her head.

*Any moment now*, she thought.

As if in response to that thought, the televiewer flashed into life and the image of a man appeared. Baldwin studied the face, although she knew it well; it bore robust, coarsely carved features, including a square jaw marked with the blue-grey of vigorous stubble.

She was looking for signs of uncertainty, of weakness.

There were none.

It was the face of a man who would be better as a friend than an enemy.

Wójcik.

The man's expression changed into what could be interpreted as a smile, although it carried not the slightest hint of warmth, of camaraderie.

'Elizabeth,' he said.

Baldwin took her arms from behind her head and leaned towards the screen and started to say "Professor" but got no further than the first syllable.

'What progress?' Wójcik said, apparently taking some pleasure in cutting her off.

Baldwin stared at the screen for a few moments, wondering if she should make another attempt to insist on her title, but thought better of it. The lag between Plato and Earth gave conversations a disjointed feel.

Time was too precious for niceties. In any case, she had good news.

'I've made a breakthrough,' she announced, realising with slight surprise that she was smiling at Mr Wójcik, perhaps for the first time in their relationship, 'one of my people got a reading which I'm reasonably sure I can use to produce what we need.'

'How sure?'

She frowned. '*Reasonably* sure.' Even now, she could not

resist taunting him. 'Perhaps "reason" is not a term I could find in your vocabulary, Mr Wójcik, but that's all your getting.'

He began to speak, but she decided to return the slight he had given earlier and cut him off. 'I intend to move very quickly now, and I estimate that I can produce the required material in no more than a few months—let's say six weeks.'

He seemed satisfied at that, sat back, rubbing his chin.

Baldwin thought if she had been with him, she would have been able to hear his stubble rasping under his fingernails and shuddered very slightly.

'That is good news,' he said, 'or should I say, *reasonably* good news. As you know, my investors, both inside ST and outside, are pressing me hard. They, like all businessmen, want to see a healthy return on their investments and they don't like timetables that are always being extended. And they are, perhaps, even less patient than I.' His cold gaze drilled into her as he gave another smile-that-was-not-a-smile. 'If that is possible.'

She shrugged; exaggerating the movement for effect. 'Your endearing personality traits are of no interest to me, Wójcik. I've told you before and I will tell you again, there is no-one other than me who can pull this off; no-one in this entire fucking Solar system.'

'An interesting adjective,' he said, and the look he gave chilled her slightly. But he shook his head, and continued, 'No matter. We will leave it there for the time being. But be warned, Elizabeth, my people are watching you continually.'

Time for one last barb. 'Yes, I had heard that orang-utans were extinct, so I was pleased to see you were able to find some and put them in your employ.'

And with that, she cut the link.

She picked up the paperweight which lay on top of Adekola's findings. Lovingly, she stared again at the figures, which only she had been able completely to interpret.

*Poor dumb bitch!* she thought and returned to studying her paperweight. Under a crystal dome lay a corrugated piece of what appeared to be a pink stone.

Coral from what used to be the Great Barrier Reef.

*Australia,* she mused, *where* he *comes from.*

Then she took a bottle containing an amber liquid from one of the drawers in her desk and poured herself a slug. Her thoughts returned to her encounter with Wójcik.

*Got him!* She thought.

\*\*\*

The first person Adekola recognised on entering the cafeteria was Philip Richards, whose face lit up when he saw her.

'Tamira! Where have you been?' He came up beside her. 'Where have you been all my life?'

She was about to issue a put-down but decided at the last moment that Richards wasn't the kind of man to do that to, and just smiled and said, 'Phil, good to see you too.'

They sat down together.

'What's been happening since I've been down below?'

His expression changed, and he sat back, running a hand through his thick black hair.

'Hell on earth. Or is that hell on moon?'

'Explain.'

'What do you think? We haven't been turned into Pixy Land since you've been away. If you thought Baldwin was tough before, wait until you see her now. She makes Genghis Khan look like Santa Claus, and that's on a good day.'

Adekola groaned inwardly. *Why did the damn woman have to be so difficult!*

'What's it all about?' she finally said.

He looked at her. 'It's all down to you, dear Tamira. Since you gave her that data she's turned into a whirling dervish.'

Adekola didn't know the allusion, but she got the gist.

'She thinks she knows how to produce negative matter in bulk,' Richards continued.

'That's why we're here, Phil,' she said gently.

'Yes, but I didn't know we were supposed to produce

megatonnes of the stuff by yesterday. It's like someone's riding her, forcing her to make us do the impossible.'

'Oh well.' Adekola tried to be philosophical. 'She wouldn't be Baldwin if she didn't behave like that. But, Phil...' She leaned closer and for some reason found herself holding his hand, 'Just think of what'll happen when we do it! Just think! We'll go down in history! We'll have the stars in the palms of our hands!'

Richards looked unconvinced. 'Yes, but what will we do with them? Will we export violence and hatred? War?'

Adekola had a brief remembrance of Fort Pickens; a place that was just a minute symbol of all the terrible things that had happened to the human race in its short time on Earth.

But there were far grimmer relics of the suffering humans had visited on each other, if one cared to look.

Adekola did not. She changed the subject.

'The last time we spoke, you said you'd discovered something about Baldwin. Some odd communications.'

Philips suddenly looked nervous and, to her surprise, looked over his shoulder for a few moments.

'Yes, but I don't want to talk about that now. I'm giving that a rest.'

'Why?'

He looked around again. 'The last time I went into the communications link, I thought there was someone else there. Not saying or doing anything. Just watching me.'

'Oh.'

'And that,' he said, picking up his fork and trying to look nonchalant, 'is all I'm saying about it.'

Adekola looked at him intently. Was he actually worried about the consequences of what he had done, or was he just giving off an air of mystery for effect? She decided not to pursue the matter, and the conversation switched to inconsequential chat.

Richards talked of his home in upstate New York and of how he was looking forward to seeing his parents again. It looked like there was no-one else in his world, and Adekola nodded in a friendly fashion as he told tales of his early life and how pleased he had been to see snow return to his small town, after having only read about that mystic material in old books.

Finally, with his meal and his conversation finished, he bade Adekola a friendly *au revoir*. Adekola watched his rounded bulk disappear through one of the exits and felt a brief twinge of sadness; both for Richards and herself. He alone seemed to be not absorbed in his work; he wasn't thrusting to get the data that would bring recognition; fame; and most of all, the approval of Baldwin. *We need more people like Phil,* she thought, somewhat wistfully.

She looked down at her empty plate and decided that she had not eaten enough. *Damn it!* she thought, *I'll start that diet tomorrow!*

She walked to the food dispenser and was looking down at the monotonous items on offer when suddenly a hard body bumped into her side and pushed her sideways. She turned and saw that it was one of the large muscle-bound men she had noticed earlier who had pushed her aside and was now studying the same menu items that she had been, apparently oblivious of her existence.

'Excuse me,' she began, 'but don't you think you should...'

He turned, and she found herself looking up into cold grey eyes, eyes as unyielding as case hardened steel. The expression that went with the eyes was cold; cold as the gulfs between the stars. Something reached out and chilled her heart.

'If you know what's good for you, you black bitch,' were his words, in a deep rumbling voice, heavy with some accent she did not recognise, 'I would learn to keep your fucking mouth shut and not annoy me.'

She stood dumbfounded and shocked into silence. Never in her life had anyone ever spoken to her like that. Not even when she had encountered the hard men in the run-down suburbs of her childhood. And certainly not in the academic world in which she had spent most of her adult life. In that realm there was spite, jealousy, back-biting—but nothing like this.

171

She dropped her plate and left.

Later, in her room, she decided to do something about the incident. Ximena was supposed to be looking after the new arrivals—she would raise an official complaint with that young lady!

After the briefest of intervals, Ximena's perpetually smiling face appeared on the televiewer in response to Adekola's call.

'Tamsin!' she exclaimed as if finding a lost child, 'wonderful to see you again! How's it been?'

*Didn't take her long to forget my name!* Adekola thought bitterly, but ignored the error and went on to relate the story of her unpleasant encounter in the food hall.

Ximena appeared to listen intently, showing only the smallest possible smile that could still be described as a smile, and then when Adekola had finished, said, 'How awful! You must be terribly upset!'

'I am,' Adekola replied, 'but I didn't call you for sympathy. What are you going to do about it?'

Ximena looked puzzled. 'Do about it? Why, nothing. It could have been anybody, couldn't it?'

'I gave you a full description. His appearance is quite striking. There are only two other men that look anything like him.'

'Yes, yes, but Tamsin, we have to be grown-up about things like this.' Her wide smile returned. 'You mustn't be afraid of bad words; words can't hurt you, Tamsin.'

Adekola stared at the young woman, beginning to find the eternal sunshine of her smile rather irritating,

'It's not just "bad words", Ximena, his entire attitude was aggressive. Frankly, I found him distinctly intimidating. In any case, who was he? He didn't look like anyone involved in our research.'

Ximena hesitated and her smile shrank infinitesimally. Then she said, 'From the description, I believe he's one of the men who work on maintaining the fusion reactors. They'll be on-line soon, you know!' she added brightly.

'That's nice. Could I speak to his manager? His attitude to women, and,' she added, after a moment's thought, 'women like me in particular, was highly unsettling.'

Ximena's hands appeared on the screen as she raised them suddenly. 'Now come on, Tamsin! We're all adults here, for God's sake! These things happen; it's just give and take. If I can say so, it sounds like you're a teeny-weeny bit thin-skinned. And are you perhaps, unconsciously, of course, displaying prejudice against those who you think aren't quite up to your academic standards?'

Adekola found she couldn't speak for a few seconds, realising that somehow she had ended up as the bad guy.

'So you're not going to take this any further?'

There was no smile. 'No.'

'Then there's no more to discuss,' Adekola snapped, 'Thanks for your help.'

And just before she cut the connection, she said, 'Oh, and by the way, the name is "Tamira".'

She crashed onto the bed, her mind whirling.

Had she overreacted?

Then she had an idea. Her wristwatch device was permanently running in background mode.

She couldn't trust the memory she had in her mind: it was already beginning to fade.

Getting out her computer pad, she sent a message to Parry.

In it, she asked him to check whether there had been a recording on the sphere of the incident in the cafeteria and, assuming there was, what was his opinion.

After an hour, no message had appeared. She waited, holding the pad in front of her, willing a message to appear.

None appeared, and she fell asleep.

She awoke with a thick head; her mouth was dry, and she felt drained.

There was a message on the pad and her eyes grew wider as she read it.

SAW THE MEMORY. I'VE SEEN THAT MAN BEFORE
SOMEWHERE. CAN'T REMEMBER WHERE BUT I DO
KNOW THIS.
KEEP CLEAR.
HE IS DANGEROUS.

\*\*\*

Baldwin pushed her computer pad away and ran a tired hand over her forehead.

Her head ached and with good reason.

She picked up her empty glass and reached for the bottle.

Empty as well.

Oh well, she wouldn't need it for a while.

There was a pile of paper on the desk in front of her, covered in abstruse symbols.

Abstruse to some, perhaps, but not to her.

To Baldwin, they were as basic as the letters on the brightly coloured pages in a child's first Reader.

The message that those symbols encoded was not simple, however. The message, couched in the languages of mathematics and symbolic logic, was vast and profound.

It told of how a simple ape-like creature on one insignificant planet, circling an undistinguished star, could reach out into the galaxy and bend mighty, fundamental forces, which had reigned hitherto unchallenged in the darkness, to its will.

A great feeling of power, of *thumos*, surged through every cell in her body. She felt momentarily dizzy as she gloried in her prowess, her achievements, which would bring an entire galaxy to heel.

Abruptly she stood up, scattering to the floor the papers that carried the apotheosis of the epic struggles of her intellect. The empty bottle joined them. It bounced but under Lunar gravity did not break.

And then her face changed so it carried an expression which could not be fully described in simple language; perhaps the face

174

of a triumphant goddess whose power had been dazzlingly demonstrated.

She raised a fist to the ceiling, but she saw far beyond it, beyond the wispy nebulae, the crashing neutron stars, the farthest island universe.

'Got you!' she roared.

# Ten: Proof of Concept

The change in Baldwin's behaviour was so great that no-one failed to notice it. Suddenly the pitiless slave-driver was gone and in its place was a friendly, understanding and, yes, forgiving person. One who had even developed an interest in her staff's families, Earthside.

Adekola had lost count of how many times her superior had enquired after Jahia's health and educational progress. She began to wonder if Baldwin's previous aloof personality was not preferable.

Something had clearly happened to that lady; some tremendous weight had been lifted from her shoulders. The endless demands for more data had dried up completely, and her staff no longer feared her shadow falling over their workstations at the exact moment they had decided to rest for a second.

There was only one conclusion to be drawn, Adekola said to herself; she had completed her analyses of the means of generating a stable wormhole and was preparing to do just that.

And that was shown to be the exact truth, as Baldwin made clear during her next Heads of Department meeting.

'I am extremely pleased to announce that we can now proceed to the penultimate phase of our preparations,' she said, and then, remembering something, added, 'thanks to your hard work, of course.'

Adekola's eyebrows rose slightly on hearing that phrase, and for a second she jokingly entertained the idea that the real Baldwin had been replaced by a shape-shifting alien which had just given itself away by uttering a sentence which the original would never have said.

'And now,' Baldwin continued, 'I am certain that I can generate significant quantities of negative matter; sufficient, that is, to stabilise a wormhole so it can be put to practical use.'

There was a ripple of applause to which Adekola heartily contributed.

Whatever her personal feelings about her boss, the achievement was a tremendous one; one that would surely shape the entire future of humanity.

'I take it that this is where the fusion reactors come in,' Estefan said.

'Exactly. I have already given the order for Reactor One to be brought on-line. I will need only a few percent of its output for my proof of concept experiment.'

Another ripple of excitement.

'And that is...?' Estefan asked.

'In a few days' time I intend to generate about ten grams of negative matter.'

Yet more excitement.

'But that is the easy part,' Baldwin said, and her expression projected a calm assurance, a certainty, of personal power, 'the trick is to stabilise it. That I can now do. I will generate a field around the matter long enough for it to be embedded in our reality. The field will also anchor it to the substrate on which it manifests. The field will likely collapse after a short interval, but while it exists, I will harvest all the remaining data I need.'

Adekola noted sourly that the pronoun "we" had disappeared.

'The final experiment will, of course, take place on the Lunar surface.'

'Why is that?' Richards said, 'I would have thought we could better perform the measurements if it was done in controlled conditions in the lab.'

Baldwin's expression became one of tolerant forgiveness.

'Philip, when the field collapses the negative matter will immediately depart its surroundings at Lunar escape velocity. Do you really want a chunk of negative matter blasting a hole through the roof of Plato Base?'

'Oh,' said Richards, looking embarrassed, 'no, I suppose not.'

\*\*\*

Some days later, Richards came to see Adekola.

'Glad to see you, Phil,' she said, 'Please come in. What can I do for you?'

He looked distracted, as if he had been thinking about something else and he had just met Adekola by accident. Nevertheless, he accepted her invitation and sat down heavily on her one guest chair.

'Yes, yes,' he said, 'what can you do?'

She sat near him, waiting patiently.

'You seem agitated, Phil. Calm down and tell me what you want.'

For an answer, he passed a small box to Adekola.

'And this is?'

'My findings. I've been back in the communication network and these are my findings.'

'I thought you said you weren't going to do that anymore.'

'That was you and Idris. There was something in Baldwin's channel I didn't understand so I went back in.'

'And now you understand it?'

'Partly. I want you to keep this as a record in case I…'

'You're not making any sense. Why a box? Why didn't you send it electronically?'

He shook his head vigorously. 'No, not electronic. Nothing electronic. Too easy to track.'

She got up and stood over him. 'Stop this, Phil! You're behaving like a child in some silly school play. All this mystery and cloak-and-dagger nonsense. This isn't a Mafia operation—this is a research establishment!'

He looked up at her. 'Is it now? Is it?' He stood up and reached for her hands. He was uncomfortably close, and she withdrew. 'Is it? Baldwin's talking to someone about Project Independence, and there's something she hasn't been telling us. I downloaded part of a conversation and then it went into an advanced encryption mode which I haven't been able to crack. Perhaps you can do it.'

'Me? That's not my field at all; I'm a simple physicist, not a cryptographer.'

He began to walk up and down in the narrow confines of her room, forcing her to stand with her back to the grey rock wall.

'Someone's gotta do it. And quickly.' He stopped his restless pacing and looked at her.

'Idris! He'll be able to do it. All that coding of neurological impulses. He or someone in his team.'

She held him by his shoulders and looked him straight in the eyes.

'I have no intention of burdening Idris with any of this ridiculous conspiracy theory. Phil, Phil, I think you really have been working too hard. Something's gotten into you and you need a rest. It's all Baldwin's fault, I'm sure, but not in the way you seem to be implying. Just because she's obsessed with this vision of hers, she expects everybody else to be. Well, we're not. Unlike her we've got our own lives; our own families.' *Well, maybe that was the wrong thing to say to you, Phil,* she thought to herself, but continued, 'Surely your furlough must be due soon. Time to visit your parents again, you'd like that, wouldn't you?'

'Yes, yes,' he said, 'get down there. Maybe not come back, eh!'

She gently turned him in the direction of the door. 'Look Phil, I'll take care of your box and maybe I'll take it down with me on my next furlough. Idris likes that kind of thing and maybe he'll take a look at it for you.'

He brightened, and the hunted look faded slightly. 'Yes, yes, that would be good!'

For a moment it looked like he was about to try to kiss her, but fortunately he must have thought better of it and instead headed for the open door.

'So you will let Idris have a look at it?'

She nodded. 'Yes, if I remember, Phil. We're all very busy, but I'll do my best.'

She waited for a few minutes to be certain he'd gone and then sat on the bed with the box in her hands.

Should she even bother to open it?

She opened it.

There was a hard copy of a conversation between Baldwin and an unidentified man.

The conversation seemed very bad-tempered, but there was nothing to suggest any underhand activity going on, just two people who obviously didn't like each other sparring verbally. There were a few obscure references to "investors".

The only other thing in the box was a memory stick. By its weight, it was a very advanced one.

She stared at it, irresolute. Should she get involved in Richards' fantasy games?

What if Baldwin found out she had a record of one of her private conversations? It could well be the end of her career.

She passed the stick from one hand to the other, her thoughts whirling in a confused jumble.

Why the hell had she got involved with Richards in the first place? It looked like he was more than a bit unhinged.

Then she did something she could never quite explain.

She switched on her computer but disconnected it from the network so it was just an isolated, dumb machine. She connected the stick and looked at the rolling display of its contents. She stared long and hard as each line rolled into view from the bottom of the screen. Hard and long, she looked, determined not to let them defeat her.

The document was completely meaningless to her; it might just as well have been written in Etruscan.

Defeated, she switched the computer off and disconnected the stick. Then she just sat there, staring into space.

Tales of conspiracies, with no evidence to back them up. Indecipherable messages to unknown persons.

It didn't add up to much.

She put the stick back in its box, closed the simple lock and put it in her bedside cabinet.

That was that.

\*\*\*

They stood there on the grey regolith of the Lunar surface, staring at the strange apparatus.

There were two great terminals, each as big as the average human torso, and separated by a metre wide gap. The terminals were the ends of a single great arm that came out of a massive machine that had enormous power cables extending from its rear into the near distance. After ten metres they plunged into the desiccated dust to connect with the output from Fusion Reactor One. At any moment unimaginable power would come flooding through those cables and into Baldwin's enigmatic machine. Unimaginable power—and just a small part of the output of one of a bank of four mighty reactors.

Adekola looked around; this was her first look at the surface since her arrival on what felt like an incredibly long time ago, but was in fact only a few months.

The terrain was brightly lit except where great boulders threw inky, impenetrable shadows; shadows which would plunge astronauts into sub-zero temperatures should they enter one. And yet the sun-blasted soil a few centimetres away was near the boiling point of water.

She turned her gaze from the sterile soil to the sky. She had found that if she did not include a part of the dazzlingly bright landscape in her field of view, eventually the stars would emerge, but she was not looking for stars. Instead, she focused on a great dark blue-grey disc that was just distinguishable from the unbroken blackness on which it rested.

Earth.

But the darkness was not completely unbroken. On one edge of the disc, seemingly touching it, the sun blazed with terrible ferocity, undimmed by atmosphere. And it was slowly sinking into that edge, although Adekola knew it was actually a long way behind it.

A Solar eclipse was about to occur and she could not take her eyes off it, although she was supposed to be looking at the machine.

Fraction by fraction, the great, obscure disc swallowed up

the sun until it was entirely gone.

And the disc of the home planet was suddenly outlined in a fiery red as the hidden sun's rays were refracted through the atmosphere, and Adekola found herself standing on a red-lit plain looking up at a great circle of scarlet glory, as every Terrestrial sunrise and sunset was simultaneously emblazoned on the sky. There was only a little of the pearly corona visible, as the Earth was so big it hid most of the sun's outer layers. With a little twinge of homesickness, she imagined Parry looking up at the sky and seeing a reddish Moon, going through a Lunar eclipse. She even imagined his gaze sweeping over the northern wastes of the tenebrous Moon, perhaps catching a few photons reflected off her form as she stood there, bathed in the red light of the eclipse.

'Tamira!' a voice suddenly shrilled inside her helmet, 'we're here to take measurements—not admire the scenery!'

'Yes, sorry, Eliz—Professor Baldwin,' she quickly responded and bent over her equipment.

She took a quick look at her fellow scientists. They too were intently studying the readings on their machines but the red light gave the whole scene a weird, diabolic feeling as all that she could see of them were black silhouettes, looking not entirely human in their heavy vacuum suits, against an eldritch background of dull red; the dull red of dying coals.

*Abandon all hope, ye who enter here!* she thought to herself and gave an involuntary shiver. Then, pushing all extraneous thoughts to one side, she concentrated on her readings.

Or rather reading, as every panel showed the same figure: 0.00.

Time passed, each empty second being replaced by another empty second.

She thought for a moment she heard Baldwin mutter something, and then—there it was!

Between the terminals a strange indigo-violet glow appeared: or was it truly indigo-violet?

Somehow that colour hinted at shades that the human eye

was not supposed to be able to register; colours for which there were no names in the languages of humanity; colours that twisted and swirled to confuse the retina and the brain.

And then in the centre of the slowly churning sheet of diaphanous light there appeared an object; a small cube of a material of the same colour as the lambent sheet that enveloped it, but deeper, richer, more impossible for the eye fully to accept.

She heard Baldwin shriek, 'There it is! Negative matter! Make sure your machines are on automatic record, for God's sake!'

Adekola had checked before the object had appeared, but she rapidly checked again.

If her machine wasn't recording while this wonder was occurring! The thought was terrifying!

She heard Baldwin again: 'This is the breakthrough. I determined that negative matter is not fully stable in our three-dimensional reality; it requires an extra physical dimension. What you are seeing is a three-dimensional cross-section of a four-dimensional hypercube. It...'

She stopped. The enveloping sheet of that indefinable sheath of light had vanished; leaving the glowing cube sat on the grey Lunar dust.

For only a moment; then it shot upwards at an ever-increasing speed.

'It's gone,' Baldwin breathed, speaking in the tones of one who has just witnessed a miracle, 'repelled by the mass of the Moon; then by the Solar system; then by the gravitational field of the entire galaxy!'

Adekola looked up into the blackness, but the weird cube had long since disappeared into the interplanetary medium; soon it would feel the gravitational power of bodies mightier than the Moon; soon it would be repelled by the Sun and be flung into the great emptiness between the stars.

What would its ultimate fate be?

Why, to pass beyond the boundary of the Observable Universe; into the unknown.

Adekola felt a fire flood through her veins; felt exaltation; felt a tremendous pride in being part of this intellectual triumph; felt that along with the rest of the human race she could look up at the stars and shout, 'Beware! I am Humanity and I am coming for you! I will make you mine!'

In that instant of intellectual ecstasy she loved Baldwin; was prepared to fling herself at Baldwin's feet and worship her.

She became aware that the others had turned, forming a circle around their leader and were clapping her; silently in the Moon's vacuum, of course.

Eagerly she joined in while Baldwin stood at the centre of that circle, bathed in the admiration and adoration that swept over her.

Then Baldwin spoke. 'Friends and colleagues, I thank you so much. This is your triumph almost as much as it is mine. A new chapter has begun today in the history of the entire human race. Today, thanks in no small part to you, is the last day when we shall feel confined to this insignificant part of the Universe. Each day from now on we will be closer to the time when we will fulfil our destiny and gather in a harvest of stars!'

She took one last look at the empty sky and then said, 'Now we will go back and celebrate.'

The grouping of her admirers broke up and began their loping return to Plato Base.

Adekola also glanced at the sky. However, unlike Baldwin, she stared for a few moments at the home planet, still enclosed in its ruddy circlet. How would Parry react when he heard of her triumph? Would he…

A choking cry that broke in upon their communal communication channel shattered her reverie.

'Help! I can't breathe! I can't…'

She whirled around in time to see one of their number collapse onto the ground, sending up a slow-motion cascade of dust.

The name on the person's helmet was RICHARDS.

They all ran towards him; their motion inappropriately

comedic in the low gravity. Adekola was the first to reach him, and she could see a fine jet of vapour issuing from the junction of his helmet and neck. Tiny ice crystals had formed at the base of the jet where the water in his air had simultaneously evaporated and frozen. Adekola took a small set of pincers from her own tool pack and tried to pinch the edges of the tear together.

'Cover that gap!' Baldwin yelled, 'quickly!'

'Where's the repair kit?' Estefan yelled, 'Who's got it?'

Baldwin whirled to face one of the technicians. 'You're supposed to have it! Give it to me!'

He gave a small pouch to her, and she struggled to open it. 'It won't open!'

The others crowded around her and struggled to open the medical kitbag.

It seemed to take forever to Adekola, who had thrown the pincers away and had put her hand over the tear in Richards' suit.

Grimly, she had noticed that the pressure of the escaping air had stopped. She did not dare to look through the helmet faceplate at her friend.

Finally, after what seemed an age, they reached her and she slapped a sealant patch over the tear.

'Richards! Can you hear me?' Baldwin cried.

There was no answer.

When they got Richards back inside the base, the reason for his silence was clear.

He was dead.

# Eleven: Alarm

On entering the base, they divested themselves of their suits as fast as possible. Baldwin had radioed ahead and the medical team were ready. Richards was rushed to the sickbay as fast as they could push the trolley he lay on, silent and immobile.

For the next half an hour the medics strove valiantly to drag him back from death; to restart his heart; to see his chest rise and fall with inhalation and exhalation.

To no avail.

Richards was dead and would remain dead.

On hearing of the failure to save Richards, Adekola burst into seemingly endless tears.

She had not known him long, but he had been the nearest thing to a friend that she had had on this miserable ball of rock. She remembered his tales of his beloved parents and their simple lives in upstate New York; of how his father had railed against progress and refused to have a robot in the house; prophesying that all this meddling with nature would not end well.

She had listened to Richards' stories of his searches for love and how his brief relationships all had just faded away, always after promising starts.

And now he was gone, due to a simple, stupid accident.

How could it have happened? Modern suits were supposed to be foolproof; the materials used in their construction were supposed to be self-healing so that life-threatening rents could not develop.

And yet they had.

There would have to be an inquest, of course.

There had been remarkably few fatalities during the settlement of the Moon, despite the horrible environment. The dangers had been foreseen and planned for. All bases were underground, usually in old lava tubes. The surface was just too dangerous, due to the pitiless ionising radiation and the constant stream of meteors, some micro-, some not. The domed cities of science-fiction had proved to be impractical for those reasons.

Similarly, no long-term occupation of the Moon was contemplated. The wasting effects of low-gee were well understood and it was obvious that any prolonged stay would result in quadriplegia if the foolhardy colonist ever returned to Earth.

So any accident, especially a fatality, was an admission of failure; an admission that the satellite was not the safe place that all the brochures said it was.

The group shared their grief and then drifted apart, back to their rooms.

In the midst of her mourning for Richards, Adekola suddenly found herself feeling a small amount of sorrow for Baldwin.

What should have been the crowning moment of her career, indeed entire life, would now forever be remembered for the loss of life of a promising young scientist, not her moment of exultant glory. Not only that, but she would be investigated to see if there was any lack of safety measures on her part. Her entire position could be threatened.

*Poor bitch!* she thought and then put Baldwin from her mind.

Then she looked at her memory downloader, which masqueraded as a wristwatch, and thought about Phil Richards. She decided that he deserved more than a background recording and she conjured up his face in her memory and thought about his kindness and the help that he had given her. Then she remembered his funny stories, and her lips jerked automatically as she thought of the simple pleasure his ridiculous tales had brought her.

She focused her mind and sent those memories, and more, into the device.

*There,* she thought, *as long as the sphere endures Phil, you will not be forgotten.*

Then she slept.

\*\*\*

The next working day dawned, even though out on the dusty lava plain the ferocious sun had not sunk very far to the strangely close horizon. Had there been observers out on the grim floor of Plato they would have seen the thin bluish crescent of the planet Earth appear out of the darkness, as one of the many cycles of the Solar system began again.

It was a subdued team that Adekola met that morning as she entered her lab.

Only the most senior technicians had been with her during that terrible incident, so she was forced to relive it, to explain to those who had not been there what had been the manner of Richards' passing. Many had met him and all that had done so had liked him.

'Terrible,' one said, 'still the inquest will get to the bottom of it.'

'Yes,' another said, 'I've heard all outdoor excursions are on hold until they find out.'

Adekola nodded her agreement and said, 'OK. We wait for the findings. In the meantime, we have work to do!'

But as she gave the day's instructions, Adekola wondered if there was much that they could now do.

Baldwin had achieved what she had said she would achieve. The next stage of creating the wormhole would depend on what she decided to do—if she was still around to do any deciding, of course.

They did a few tests in that session; but basically all they did was confirm what had already been confirmed, and so Adekola decided to call it a day and finished early.

As she walked back to the monorail, she passed the room where the materials from that terrible day were being stored: the medikit that had refused to open, and most importantly, Richards' vacuum suit.

*We'll get the answers*, she thought, *and so no-one will ever suffer again the way that poor Phil did.*

She sat in her room and, for a few minutes, she was

188

motionless, cradling her head in her hands.

Then she suddenly looked up and thought: *This is ridiculous! Things aren't that bad!*

She decided that a cup of strong black coffee would help and began to rise from the chair.

And then she stopped; instantly alert.

There was something wrong with the room.

It was difficult to be certain, but somehow the room looked different.

There was a very slight indentation in the bed coverlet, as if someone heavy had sat there for a few moments. And as there was no room service in Plato Base, no-one should have been sitting there while she was out.

And the coffee cup.

Was it farther from the dish cleaner than it had been when she had finished with it that morning?

She began a circuit of the room, looking for things that were different when they should not have been.

There were no other differences.

Then she thought about Richards' box and hurriedly opened her bedside cabinet.

The box was still there, and the contents seemed as they were.

She quickly scanned the enigmatic lines of code. They looked identical, but as she had not decoded them earlier, she could not be certain that they were the same lines.

She sat back down.

What to think?

A vague depression in a coverlet and a coffee mug that might have moved a centimetre or two. It wasn't much to conclude that someone had been in the room.

In her nervous state, it was easy to start imagining ghosts in the shadows.

She put it from her mind. There was something much better to think about.

She had another family conversation with Parry and Jahia

189

that evening.

Immediately, Parry knew that something was wrong.

'What is it?' he said, 'is Our Lady of the Egomania riding your back again?'

After she had explained what had happened, he pulled a face and said, 'That's a tough break. I'll take a look at the memory later, but he sounds like he was a nice guy. But an accident with a vacuum suit—that's very unusual in this day and age.'

'Accidents happen,' Adekola replied, attempting a Stoic attitude which she did not really feel, 'Anyway, how are things down there?'

'Nothing much. Except Jahia's birthday is coming up—in case you'd forgotten that with all the activity up there. Will you be back for it?'

Adekola felt a twinge of guilt. In truth, the upcoming event had slipped her mind and she'd yet to ask for leave to attend her daughter's fifth birthday.

'Ahh, yes, probably,' she said, stuttering slightly, 'I wouldn't want to miss that, would I?'

Parry was stony-faced. 'No, you wouldn't, would you.'

***

The following day, Adekola asked for a meeting with Baldwin. She had become acutely aware that her original line of research had ended and was starting to feel distinctly under-employed.

When Adekola entered Baldwin's office she was a little disturbed by Baldwin's appearance. Up until that moment she had only ever seen two expressions on that woman's perfectly proportioned face: a smile, brighter than a nearby supernova, or a frown of disapproval at yet another display of ignorance by her staff.

Now Baldwin's features carried no emotion at all, which rendered her momentarily unrecognisable. As Adekola entered, she forced her face into an obviously synthetic smile and said,

190

'Tamira. Lovely to see you. How can I help?'

'May I sit down?' Adekola replied, realising that Baldwin was being a little slower than usual to consider her people's well-being.

'What? Oh, of course, please do sit down.'

Having completed the niceties, Baldwin leaned back and interlaced her fingers.

Adekola noticed that she had changed her nail polish. *Can't be too upset about Phil then,* she thought to herself, and then was instantly ashamed of being so judgemental.

'And the reason for this visit?' Baldwin enquired.

'Yes, well, Profess…'

'You can call me Elizabeth, in private,' Baldwin said, in the tone of a parent giving her child a special treat, 'No-one's listening.'

Realising that it was necessary to show gratitude, Adekola said, 'Thank you, Elizabeth, It's just that I was wondering what I am supposed to be doing now.'

Baldwin looked momentarily confused. 'Doing? Oh, I see, *doing!* After the proof of concept was so wonderfully demonstrated, you mean.'

'Yes.'

Her superior looked at her large computer screen for a minute and seemed to be thinking deeply.

'Doing. Yes, I must give you something to do.'

Adekola found she was becoming seriously irritated by Baldwin's detached attitude. 'Elizabeth, look here, I'm not a student on work experience. Like you, I'm a PhD, I…'

'Of course, my dear. I've read your thesis—on Reissner-Nordström-de Sitter black holes, wasn't it? A few errors, but they didn't compromise your main conclusions, I'm glad to say.'

Adekola was struck dumb. No-one had ever mentioned errors before. She had a sudden desire to get out of this woman's office at high speed. But…

'Yes, of course, it's time to put your talents to work on new challenges. Now we can create negative matter at will, it's time to move on to the main event. I've already discussed this with Estefan.'

*Oh, have you now!* thought Adekola bitterly, wondering why every interview with Baldwin left her seething about something or other.

'Yes, the wormhole. You'll need to read my paper on how we can manipulate the negative matter to stabilise them. I'll have it sent to your workstation. And your personal one as well, of course, so you can carry on reading it when you're off duty.' Baldwin's gaze fixed itself on Adekola. 'The paper has already been peer-reviewed and accepted by the necessary bodies, so there's no danger of plagiarism by letting you have it.'

Adekola decided to believe Baldwin's last comment was simply an inappropriate joke, and after she had thanked her, a silence fell.

Finally, Adekola said, 'Philip dying like that. Such a tragedy. Such a young man.'

Baldwin remained impassive. 'Yes, indeed. He had some signs of ability, which I could have nurtured. A great loss.'

'It's important to find out how it happened,' Adekola said, 'We'll have to wait for the official inquiry.'

Baldwin gave a nod of agreement as she turned away, dismissing Adekola from her thoughts.

'Indeed we will.'

***

Elizabeth Baldwin might have been accused of many things by those who knew her but one accusation that could never be levelled against her was that she was inefficient. And so it was that Adekola was not in the least surprised when she got back to her room to find the necessary documents already waiting for her on her personal computer.

With a little trepidation, she opened the first and started studying it. Her first reaction was panic: at first glance it looked as impenetrable as the encoded printout that Richards had given her.

*Get a grip, woman!* she thought to herself, *you can do this!*

She looked again; knowing from her prior dealings with Baldwin that the document would be elegantly structured but with absolutely no concessions to those who might be lacking in the necessary background. If Baldwin judged that the reader should know a concept, it would not be explained.

And so it proved. Line by dense line, Adekola struggled with the complex, tightly written paper. Several times she skipped a section, only to return to it after some time and gradually see it begin to make sense before her straining eyes. She was working at the very limit of her understanding, but after two hours she decided that she had understood the main thrust of Baldwin's work. Once again, she was overcome with a helpless respect for the woman, a respect that might be deeply begrudged—but respect it was. No true scientist could reach any other conclusion. If any human was going to tame the stars, that human would be Elizabeth Baldwin.

Then as she lay back on the bed, mentally drained, another thought struck her.

*Fuck!* she thought *I forgot to ask her for leave for Jahia's birthday!*

\*\*\*

Adekola stood in front of the screen, using her light pen to indicate the relevant section of the equations. She was doing her best to give a condensed version of Baldwin's main conclusions, but it was hard-going. Not every one of her technicians had the necessary background in higher mathematics. They were all competent in the physics of what they were doing, but Baldwin had ascended into such rarefied heights of abstraction that not all had the wings to follow her.

'How does Line Four follow from the two lines above?' a young woman said, her hitherto porcelain-smooth forehead now deeply corrugated.

It was a tricky one, Adekola had to admit.

'Well,' she started, and then stopped.

The terrible sound of the emergency klaxon had just blared out, crushing all ordinary sounds into nothingness.

They had all heard that noise before but only as part of emergency drills; and the ear-splitting blasts had always been preceded by gentle voices explaining that they were about to experience a training drill.

There had been no gentle voices.

Which meant—this was an actual emergency.

The lights in the lab flashed red.

Fire. The worst possible emergency. Fire in a building from which you cannot escape is the worst possible emergency.

Adekola tried to remember where the muster station was, but to her horrified surprise found that she could not!

But Moreau had seen her confusion and was instantly with her.

'Come on, Boss! Let's get out of here!'

She followed him blindly, and the only thought in her head was *Jahia's birthday!*

But as they ran towards the muster point, it became clear where the fire was.

She could see black smoke seeping around a closed door and in the centre of that door was a dull red spot, showing the force of the flame behind it.

*That's where they stored Richards' suit!*

Then abruptly there were people wearing protective gear, cutting the door down and sending huge blasts of seething white foam into the room beyond. Adekola stopped her headlong flight and stood watching as the emergency workers fought their way further into the room, through the hungry flames that licked around them like the tongues of fiery vipers, all the time spraying the dampening foam. The smoke grew thicker and blacker. The dreadful klaxon blared its bone-shuddering scream continuously.

And then a man came out of the smoke, waving an arm.

'It's OK!' he yelled. 'we've got it under control. But stay back! Go to your muster stations and wait for further

194

instructions!'

Adekola looked around, realising that Moreau had gone on without her. But the man's words had calmed her fear, and now she remembered how to get to the station.

When she finally found it, all her staff were already there.

'What happened to you, Boss?' Moreau asked, apparently annoyed that she had not taken his advice.

But before she could speak, the klaxon stopped and a blessed silence swept over them.

The red flickering in the light ended and there was a momentary flash of green.

Then a voice came over the Base public communication channel.

'The emergency is over. The fire has been extinguished. It is now safe to return to your place of work.'

'Did you see where the fire was, Boss?' Moreau asked as they began their return to the lab.

'Yes. It was in the storeroom where they were keeping Richards' suit and the medikit.'

She stopped as a sudden thought struck her.

But it was Moreau who said it.

'That means they won't be able to find out what was wrong with the poor guy's suit.'

She looked at him, but somehow through him.

'Yes, that's right. They won't be able to find anything. Anything at all.'

# Twelve: Memories

Adekola woke from her nightmare, her hands bent into claws, her eyes wide with staring madness.

She had been trapped in a terrible whirlpool of darkness, of clinging, sucking blackness that would not let her go, however much and long she begged and pleaded.

The darkness would hold her forever.

So vivid had the dream been that for a few seconds she could not believe it had not been reality. Gradually the now-familiar contours of her room swam into focus and she dared to believe that the ordeal was over.

She swung her feet onto the floor as relief washed over her and was soon drinking a mug of strong, black coffee. Gradually her belief in that she was back in the real world grew stronger and she began to chide herself for being so badly affected. It was not as if she believed that dreams could foretell future events—that was a pre-scientific delusion.

As she got dressed, she wondered what could have caused such horror to visit her in the synthetic night of Plato Base. The sudden death of Philip Richards had very badly shaken her—could that be the reason?

She dialled up her breakfast along with another mug of the strongest black coffee allowable; a beverage so strong that the dispenser asked her to confirm her choice. As she sipped it, her mind re-ran the recent events. Was there something that was disturbing her on the unconscious level? She tried to use her training in analytic thinking.

Datum 1: Philip Richards' death. An accident involving a vacuum suit in an age when accidents were not supposed to happen with vacuum suits.

Datum 2: The medikit, designed for use in emergencies, that had been difficult to open.

Datum 3: The destruction of both the vacuum suit and the medikit in a fire: the one emergency which was most feared and therefore the most prepared against.

Datum 4: The possibility, which now seemed to have moved up the probability scale, that someone had interfered with her room.

What did it mean? Could there be a malign force loose on the base that was behind these events? If so, what intent could be behind its actions?

Then Richards' words came back to her: his assertion that something secret was happening; that there were secrets in an institution predicated on openness and trust.

Suddenly a peculiar thought came to her, bulleting up from the deepest region of her mind; a command which she had never before received.

*Trust no-one.*

The coffee seemed more bitter than even its caffeine overload could account for as she drained the dregs. A worm of fear began to stir down in the foundations of her sanity.

What to do? What to do?

She thought deeply and rapidly. Was she in danger? How could she be? If Baldwin was somehow behind these events, she could see no threat in Adekola, surely? Brilliant though Baldwin undoubtedly was, she needed assistants in her great project and would not jeopardise its consummation by acts of actual violence. Adekola gave a wry smile: her staff were already sufficiently afraid of her.

Still, there was evidence that not all was well on Plato Base. She would take precautions.

The televiewer trilled to indicate an incoming communication, and she was snapped instantly out of her black mood.

It would be her partner asking when she would be joining her family for the great upcoming event, namely, Jahia's fifth birthday.

And so it was.

Parry and Jahia appeared on the screen and the child instantly began shouting,

197

'Mommy! Mommy!'

Parry just grinned. 'How's Mommy today?' Parry inquired, 'we're not interrupting another one of your Nobel-winning discoveries, are we?'

She smiled at them; all her fears and terrors of the night blown away in an instant, 'No, no, this is my rest day. We can talk for as long as we like!'

'Very good,' Parry continued, 'Look, Jahia's drawn you a picture!'

Jahia immediately held up a multicoloured drawing. It showed a dark-skinned stick figure standing in what must have been intended to be a Lunar crater. The stick figure had a circle drawn around the head and at the top of the picture was a black streak, in the middle of which was shown an object which must be the child's idea of the planet Saturn.

'It's lovely,' Adekola said, 'what is the circle around my head, darling?'

Jahia pulled a face. 'It's your space suit helmet, silly. There's no air on the Moon!'

They all laughed at Mommy's silliness.

After some more family talk, Parry's face became serious and he asked, 'So when are you coming back down?'

She was about to answer when a strange change came over her. She felt suddenly cold.

*Trust no-one.*

'Did you remember where you'd seen that man?' she asked, trying to keep her tone causal.

Parry looked indecisive. Then he said, 'He reminded me of a bloke who was accused of some nasty gangland murder a while back. But it can't be him. What would he be doing on the Moon? Must be my mistake: forget it.'

*Perhaps, perhaps not,* she thought but said nothing.

She decided on an experiment; a test.

'I'll be back soon. I wouldn't miss Jahia's seventh birthday for anything.'

As she uttered the lie, she held Parry's gaze steady in her

own and slowly tapped the side of her nose.

He stared at her, his mouth half-open. Then some kind of understanding dawned in his expression and after a moment or two he said, slowly, 'Of course not. You wouldn't want to miss her seventh birthday.'

After that, the conversation seemed to dry up and when it finally ended, Adekola found she was shivering slightly.

***

'So, Tamira, how's your analysis of the potential resonance instability going?' Baldwin enquired.

'It's not going at all, Professor,' Adekola replied, with an unusual note of levity in her response.

Baldwin's brow creased. 'I beg your pardon?' she said in a dangerous voice.

'It's not going because I've left the problem with Moreau. I'm on leave from tomorrow, remember?'

Baldwin's expression lightened. 'Of course, little Jahia's birthday celebrations. It's her seventh, isn't it?'

'Yes, it is,' Adekola said, smiling even though a rapier of ice had entered her heart.

Baldwin gave Adekola no further thought after they had parted.

She had many things to occupy her; many, many things.

Some were mathematical; problems to be wrestled with on the icy mountaintops of pure thought where she trod unperturbed and unafraid.

Some were to do with physical issues; of how to balance force with force; how to set force against force.

Some were… more "managerial".

She was sitting at her desk, not long after she had bid *bon voyage* to Adekola, when the door to her office was abruptly opened. She looked up to see a muscular, bearded man occupying most of the doorway.

'I prefer people to knock,' she said, without any noticeable

199

intonation, other than a pure statement of fact.

'And I prefer get paid on time,' the man said, striding up to the desk. 'I just solved little problem for you. Remember?

Baldwin looked up at him, as if studying a minor blip in the readings that she had seen many times before.

'There's a slight problem with the transfer arrangements. The authorities have closed one conduit; we are busy opening another. Your boss knows all about it.' She stood up and indicated the door. 'Now get out.'

He did not move.

She moved to within nearly arms-length of him. People tended to back down when she did that.

The man did not.

Instead, he looked her up and down; obviously approving of what he saw.

'There're other ways of paying. You good-looking woman.'

And with that he reached out and cupped her breasts, grinning widely as he did so.

Baldwin reacted with blinding speed. She whirled away from him, picked up her paperweight and smashed it hard against his left temple. He crashed against the doorjamb under the force of the blow and as he righted himself, he felt his temple and looked at the blood on his palm. Then he looked at Baldwin with murder in his eyes.

'I kill you, bitch! But first I cut out cunt and eat it!'

Baldwin was back behind her desk. Her breathing was normal and her eyes were full of contempt.

'I think not,' she said, as if rejecting an item on her lunch menu, and from a drawer drew out a revolver and then, almost unnoticeably, depressed a small button on the desk. She leaned back in her chair, apparently completely at ease. 'You will do nothing except suffer the consequences of what you did. I was very fond of that paperweight. It's irreplaceable now that the reef has gone.'

He moved slightly towards her.

She lined up the revolver on his heart.

'Stay exactly where you are. One more step and you're just a slab of meat.' She smiled. 'Which is not much different from your current state, you pathetic anthropoid.'

He turned for the door.

'Stop!' she commanded, 'I'm not through with you yet! Turn and face me!'

He obeyed, to see Baldwin leaning slightly towards him, a wicked smile on her face and with the revolver held rock-steady at the beginning of a trajectory which terminated in his left ventricle.

'What you didn't know is that every time someone opens my door, an automatic recording is made of everything that happens in this room. A short while ago I alerted your employer to your actions and he has been watching the recording.' She cocked her head. 'Am I right, Mr Wójcik?'

A deep voice, laden with menace, spoke from the air above their heads.

'Yes, I have been watching this sorry spectacle. I am very disappointed with you, Kuznetsov. So disappointed in fact, that I would like you to come and meet with me so we can talk this whole thing over. As civilised gentlemen, you understand.'

Kuznetsov had gone very pale, a change which had not gone unnoticed by Baldwin. Her smile was wolfish.

'A short time ago you threatened to remove a part of my anatomy of which I am inordinately fond. I suggest you start worrying about your own reproductive apparatus. Or, on second thoughts, perhaps you won't be using that equipment anymore. So sad. Such a waste.'

She waved at the open door with her revolver.

'Off you go. Mr Wójcik doesn't like being kept waiting. You don't want to make him even angrier than he already is, do you?'

Alone again, Baldwin leaned back in her chair, looking at the ceiling. Her heart rate and pulse were almost normal.

*Damn it to hell*, she was thinking, *how am I going to replace that paperweight?*

\*\*\*

Jahia's birthday party was coming to an end, Adekola thought, with a touch of relief. Bits of cake were scattered everywhere, some now ground deep into the carpet and would be the Devil's own job to get out. There were puddles of orange squash on the table, lapping around disposable plates still covered with scraps of party food.

A quarrel had broken out between two little girls over who had the best party dress and Parry was vainly attempting to get them to see reason and make peace. *Can't take this much longer!* Adekola thought. She realised now how quiet and calm Plato Base usually was. It was very unusual to hear raised voices or see any kind of argument, other than of the scientific variety. Baldwin's censures were always delivered in a quiet, calm voice, and her preferred weapons were irony and sarcasm.

Not so here. Adekola's ears were still ringing after the sonic onslaughts she had endured during the party games. The girls' shrieks had been the most annoying, as they were invariably of the penetrating, ultra-high pitched variety.

Now she could see that Parry was definitely winding the activities down and had finally got the two girls to kiss and make up.

'Now say goodbye to Jahia, there's good boys and girls,' he was saying, and Adekola winced as the entire throng yelled 'Goodbye Jahia!' at the tops of their voices.

One by one the parents arrived and eventually her family was alone again

Parry sighed and reactivated the fountain. The danger of one of the children falling into it, and somehow managing to drown, had been simply too great.

'That's over for another year!' he said with noticeable relief. He glanced at the mess. 'I suppose I'll have to trust the house robot to clear this up. Or at least not make it worse.' He glanced at Adekola. 'I must say you weren't a lot of help.'

She gave a weak smile. 'I know. I'm sorry. All the noise. I've got out of the habit of being around children.'

'Well, you'd better get back into the habit, as you're the

mother of one. It seems to me the quicker you get that damn project done and come back for good, the better.' He turned to look at Jahia. 'Darling, you're not supposed to eat cake off the floor. Why don't you go to your room for a little while so that Mommy and I can have a little rest.'

To both parents' surprise, Jahia did just that.

There was a silence for a while and then Parry said, 'Now perhaps you'll tell me what's wrong.'

Adekola looked at him, wondering if now she should release her fears and share her suspicions.

'Idris, there's something wrong up there. I'm a bit frightened.'

'Wrong?'

'I think my room is bugged.'

His eyebrows lifted. 'That sounds unusual for a research establishment. Go on.'

She told him more details of how Richards had died; of how things that should not have happened, had happened; of how the evidence of the suit and the medical kit had been destroyed; of the indentation in the bed and, crucially, how Baldwin had fallen into her little trap of the wrong birthday.

'So, it's quite certain that my room is bugged, and Baldwin is in on it.'

Parry's face was impassive and then he finally said: 'You shouldn't go back.'

She looked at him helplessly. 'Don't you think I've considered that! But the money's so good and we do need it.'

'We can get by on mine.'

'I don't want to *get by!* I want us to have the life we deserve after all the work we've done. Why should every mindless media star have more money than they know what to do with while we're struggling? It's not greed—it's just what we should have as a reward for all those years of poverty while we studied!

'And it's not just money. This project is vast, tremendous! It will reshape the world. And I want my name to be up there with Baldwin's.'

'You want to be famous,' Parry said, sourly.

'All right—fame. It's nothing to be ashamed of. Every scientist wants to be remembered for their contributions to the race's body of knowledge. You do too, with your memory gizmo.'

'My memory *gizmo*,' he repeated, 'glad to see you've mastered the technicalities. But if Baldwin's in on it, why do you still want to work for her? Is she not the mastermind?'

'No, I don't think she can be. She wants to carve her name across the stars; she wants to out-Einstein Einstein. It's science all the way with her.'

'So who is behind all these machinations which you think you've discovered? Baldwin must know about them at the very least.'

Adekola produced a somewhat helpless expression. 'I don't know for sure! It must be some form of industrial espionage. Maybe Baldwin's just been caught up in it; got out of her depth.'

Silence fell again.

Then Parry looked up and said: 'Richards. He gave you an encrypted document and thought that I'd be able to read it. Have you brought it with you?'

She looked down at her lap. 'No.'

Parry threw up his hands. 'You're a fine espionage agent, aren't you!'

She was angry now. 'If I'm right about them being in my room, then it's almost certain that they've changed the document for a dummy, rather than just taking it. That way they wouldn't alert me to what's going on. It was only my little trap that made it clear that there is a bug—so I can't be that stupid!'

Silence again.

Jahia put her head around the door.

'Stop shouting. It's my birthday.'

After they had calmed Jahia and she had gone back to her room, they spent some time staring at each other, immobile.

Then Parry suddenly started and his gaze at Adekola became intense.

'You said you looked carefully at every page of the Richards' document.'

'Yes. But I know what you're going to say—No, I didn't memorise it and download it. How could I? It was gibberish to me.'

Parry's gaze bored into her. 'There is a way.'

'What? How?'

'You didn't memorise it, I understand that. But as long as you looked intently at every page your subconscious will still have a record of what you saw.'

'But I can't recall it!'

'Of course. That is the definition of the subconscious. But with my techniques, I can retrieve them.'

Alarm sprang into her face. 'What! Will it hurt?'

He smiled gently. 'It's not surgery. Just deep brain stimulation by electrical means. It'll mean a splitting headache afterwards, but that's all.'

She leaned towards him and took his hands in hers.

'Then let's do it!'

\*\*\*

Adekola's right hand made small movements on the paper. She was sitting in a white antiseptic room in Parry's research facility. On her head was something like an old-fashioned hair dryer; a very heavy, old-fashioned hair dryer. It rested on two horizontal arms on either side of her neck so she did not bear the weight.

She drew a few more symbols.

'Alpha. Zero. Alpha again,' she intoned in an uninflected, robotic voice. 'That completes the document.'

'Good,' said Parry, who was standing slightly behind her so he could see what she was writing, 'Now, I'm going to slowly reduce the power. You will gradually become aware of the room again and you will know that you are perfectly safe. I'm reducing—now.'

Adekola's eyes shut as the stimulation slowly faded. After about five minutes, while Parry anxiously stood over her, her eyelids fluttered and then she opened them wide. The stimulation helmet rose gently from her head and folded itself away.

She looked around, to confirm that she was still in the room that the experiment had started in and then Parry moved in front of her.

'Welcome back,' he said, looking more than a little relieved.

'Idris!' she said, with eyes now wide open, 'It was incredible! I could see every character, just as if I was actually holding a paper document!'

'Well, maybe not every character,' he said gently, 'I think you missed a few here and there. But my people should have enough to work on.

'But I doubt if we will have cracked it before you have to go back.'

She held out her hands to him. 'That doesn't matter. Now I know that you're there, looking out for me, I'm not worried. Between us, we'll cut Baldwin down to size.'

## Thirteen: A Hungry Blackness

Adekola woke up screaming.

Parry was instantly awake and switched on the light.

He found his partner covered in sweat and with bulging, staring eyes that focused on nothing; seeing nothing.

He shook her gently to try to snap her out of whatever it was that had gripped her.

'Tamira!' he said, 'it's OK! It's me! What's wrong?'

She turned those unseeing eyes on him, and for a second or so he looked into a terrifying emptiness. Then her eyes seemed to focus, and she fell onto his shoulder.

'Oh, Idris, it was horrible! I was sucked into darkness, into blackness. I'd lost Jahia, I'd lost you—I'd lost everything! Just the blackness—it wouldn't let me go! I pleaded with it but it didn't care. I was just nothing to it!'

He stroked her hair and made calming noises as best he could.

'It's OK, Tamira. There's no blackness. You're with me and Jahia is just next door. It was just a silly dream.'

She looked around as if searching for proof of his words. She saw the bedroom and relaxed slightly. But as he held her he could feel that she was trembling.

'It's alright,' he said, 'Everything's all right.'

She sat up in the bed and put her hands either side of her head, rocking back and forth slightly, like a frightened child.

'It's the second time I've had that dream, Idris. You don't know what it's like. It's so real!'

He forced her to look directly at him.

'Dreams are dreams. They can't hurt you.' He shook her. 'Do you hear me! Dreams can't hurt you!'

'Then why do I keep having that dream?'

'Having a dream twice does not constitute "keep having it." You are under tremendous pressure up there. No wonder you're having bad dreams. If I'd gone through all you have, I'd probably have snapped by now. Look, one day, all this will be behind you. You'll have your name in lights, and you'll never have to see Elizabeth Baldwin again, ever. The only people you'll have to see will be Jahia and me. Just Jahia and me.'

Her eyes glistened moistly in the soft light of the bedroom as she looked up at him. 'Promise?'

'I promise.'

They both lay back with eyes closed, but behind Adekola's eyelids, dark fears danced, mockingly.

It felt that morning would never come; Parry had a fitful sleep, sometimes asleep in a shallow slumber that had no restorative quality; Adekola rarely even dozing.

But morning did come, and it found Adekola sitting listlessly in an armchair, gazing out over the city, but not seeing it.

Finally, Parry asked, 'You're determined to go back?'

She nodded slowly, as even that small action required effort. 'I have to. I want a small piece of Baldwin's triumph. As long as I keep my nose clean, it'll be alright.'

The day wore on; neither of them could think of much to say.

A reasonably efficient automaton called Eddie delivered their lunch; parts of the meal were even pleasant.

It felt as though both of them were living with a tremendous intangible clock that filled their apartment and was counting down the days, hours and minutes before Adekola had to board the shuttle to the space station and thence to Plato.

And then Parry said, 'I think I might know what might be behind all these shenanigans on the Moon.'

Adekola made a face. '*Shenanigans.* Not a very appropriate word, Idris.'

'Let's not quibble over words. McGillivray put me onto this bloke who might throw some light on things.'

Adekola gave a small wince at the word "bloke" but tried to look interested. 'Go on.'

'He works for a large legal firm and knows quite a bit about interplanetary law. He might be able to work out what's going on up there.'

She shrugged. 'OK. Let's hear him. As long as I don't actually have to do anything, like put a bug in Baldwin's brassiere.'

They both smiled at that image, and for a moment, it felt as if their personal dark cloud had lifted somewhat.

Parry indicated the televiewer. 'His name's Charles Marston. He'll be calling in a few minutes.'

When Marston appeared on the screen, he was obviously a man of advanced years, but he had those indefinable signs that revealed that he was, in fact, much older than he looked. That, in turn, meant that he was wealthy enough to afford age-slowing drugs and was, therefore, a member of the international elite. His iron-grey hair showed no sign of recession and his face was not much more lined than Parry's. But there was something about the eyes: in a way that Adekola could not put into words, they were eyes that had seen many things over many years.

'Good afternoon,' he said, in a dry, clipped voice, 'I understand that you believe that I might be able to advise you on some matter.'

Parry explained his and Adekola's concerns over Project Independence.

'But neither Tamira nor I can think of any way that illegal activities could be going on up there. How could any organisation be making money from such a venture?'

Marston was silent for a short while, then, 'I know of Elizabeth Baldwin. She is a brilliant scientist who has made many breakthroughs in physics and astronautics. She doesn't strike me as a criminal mastermind. But it is possible that she has got herself mixed up with dangerous company. Maybe they have some kind of hold over her.'

'But where would the money be coming from?' Parry said.

'It's a common misconception that the exploration of space is a purely non-profit enterprise,' Marston said, with each word clearly pronounced and distinct from its fellows, 'there is a little-known section in the Treaty which allows for profits to be generated. If a commercial organisation can prove that they are the first to reach an astronomical body and have done so with no help from the public purse, then they are granted ownership of said body and have sole rights to any revenue which can be derived from that ownership. I believe that that section was inserted after lobbying from various multinational companies. At the time it was held that interstellar activities, in particular, would be beyond the reach of private finance and so it was taken to be basically a vacuous clause.'

Parry glanced sharply at Adekola. 'Could that be what's going on?'

She shook her head. 'I don't see how. We know a lot about the Centauri system. It doesn't have anything that we don't already have in the Solar system. It's just ice, rock and iron, like we have here. There's no money to be made. In fact, it will absorb vast amounts of finance through the terraforming procedure. We'll be sending resources there, not bringing them back.'

'Then why go there at all?' said Marston, somewhat sharply.

'It's purely a plan to give our species a second home,' Adekola replied, 'after the traumas we've been through, we now know how fragile our biosphere is. It's a way of seeing we survive the Great Filter.' She could see that Marston did not understand that phrase. 'What I mean is, you don't put all humanity's eggs in one basket.'

'I see,' said Marston, 'no doubt a noble enterprise.' His gaze shifted to Parry. 'Is there anything else I can help you with?'

'No, thank you Mr Marston.'

'Then you will excuse me. I have a great many demands upon my time.'

And he was gone.

Adekola and Parry sat in silence for a while and then Parry said, 'Looks like we're no further forward.'

'No,' Adekola replied, 'we're not.'

\*\*\*

210

Adekola looked around her room. It was exactly as she had left it, except the plates and mugs had been washed and put away, probably by one of the few domestic robots that Plato Base could afford.

She looked around with little enthusiasm; that "First Day At University" feeling that she had had when she first arrived was long gone. More and more the entire complex was feeling like some kind of penitentiary, with Baldwin as the Chief Jailer.

She placed her small suitcase by the bed, which she then proceeded to stretch out on, wondering what that lady had planned for her tomorrow, her first full workday. Whatever it was, it would not be a slow and gentle reintroduction to her duties.

Nor was it.

Baldwin held a meeting at an ungodly hour the very next morning, leaving Adekola feeling that her head had touched the pillow only minutes earlier.

'Time to move on to the real reason we are here,' Baldwin announced, scanning the meagre ranks of her most senior staff, 'the creation of negative matter on demand was merely a necessary, not a sufficient, condition for our true goal, which is of course a stable wormhole capable of spanning the distance from here to Alpha Centauri.' She looked around. 'I know that you are as impatient as I am to bring about that great triumph, and together we will do it. The mathematics are very advanced but we have the task of translating the equations into hard reality. While you've been away, Tamira,' she added, giving her subordinate a hard stare, 'we have been constructing the projectors which will take the energy from the fusion reactors and produce the first wormhole. We will proceed in short steps, of course. The first wormhole will only be a few hundreds of thousands of kilometres long. Approximately four hundred and three thousand kilometres, in fact.'

'Does that reach anything, other than Earth?' Adekola asked and received a stony stare in return.

'It will reach the L4 or L5 Lagrange points, Tamira,' Baldwin said, 'I assumed you would deduce that. Anyway, we need to think about managing the tests. Four people are the minimum that I need to be sure of success. I must have people who know their way around devices that will be pouring out complex data. It is most unhelpful that Richards is not available.'

'Yes,' Adekola said, attempting to fix Baldwin's gaze upon her, 'I dare say Phil would find it unhelpful, if he was around to offer an opinion.'

The irony was lost upon Baldwin who merely nodded abstractedly.

Having failed to embarrass her boss, Adekola added, 'Moreau would probably be up to it. He's pretty sharp.'

'Yes, I know something of his work,' Baldwin said, 'I'll put him on the team.'

'That will mean an increase in his salary,' Adekola pointed out.

'Oh, will it?' Baldwin said, 'Oh well, that can't be helped.' She looked around. 'It's great to see your enthusiasm, my friends and colleagues. It will not be wasted, I promise you. Tomorrow we start!'

*Tomorrow the stars!* thought Adekola, *I've heard something like that before*—but she said nothing.

*** 

The training session began early the next day.

The control room for the Project Independence was a great vaulted room, reminding the insignificant human beings which it contained, of the chancel of a tremendous Gothic cathedral. Sturdy girders criss-crossed each other in the roof in a design reminiscent of delicate fan-vaulting, but a fan-vaulting reborn as mighty metal struts. The struts swept down the walls, and became more like the massive ribs of a tremendous, beached leviathan. A sloping bank of glowing instrumentation comprised one whole side of that great chancel, with softly glowing screens sending gentle multicoloured radiance far across the room, and with rows of lambent lights shining like the dance of elemental spirits viewed from afar. It was magnificent, beautiful, the spirit of science made manifest in metal, ceramic and semiconductors. Beautiful, but a beauty which disguised a musculature of incredible power, like the supple form of a tiger.

Baldwin stood in front of the vast bank of instruments, looking more than ever like the High Priestess of some esoteric religion; a High Priestess who alone wielded the power to summon potent elementals from the void.

Adekola, despite herself, despite her determination to be unmoved, felt humbled by the woman and the awful power she clearly held; felt insignificant in this magnificent temple to Baldwin and the forces which, like faithful dogs, came and went at her command.

Somehow to bend the knee, to bow down before her, did not seem ridiculous.

Moreau looked distinctly worried, and Adekola found it necessary to encourage him.

'It'll be alright, Henri,' she said in a conspiratorial whisper, 'Baldwin's not as bad as some people say.'

He did not look particularly relieved. 'If she's half as bad as they say, it'll be quite enough', he said, giving a good impression of a rabbit who had just found a stoat blocking the route to its burrow.

The object of his fears was now sitting facing her staff. Her eyes seemed to blaze in the coloured dimness.

'You have all read the papers, of course, and fully absorbed their implications,' she said. Out of the corner of her eye, Adekola saw a wince from Moreau at that statement.

'Let me recap,' Baldwin continued, 'We will generate about four kilograms of negative matter. That will be enough to reach the L5 point. The N-matter—as I propose to term that incredible material from now on—will be incorporated into the wormhole matrix and prevent it from collapse. The output of Fusion Reactor One at five per cent will be sufficient to generate a stable wormhole of the desired length. I intend to keep it in operation for about ten minutes, which will be enough to confirm that it has indeed reached L5. Who can tell me what will happen when the terminus of the hole reaches L5?—Yes, Estefan?'

Estefan put his hand down.

*God, it's just like being in school!* Adekola thought.

'Any mass just beyond the terminus will be pulled in and traverse the hole to be ejected at the near end. Our end.'

'Precisely,' Baldwin said, looking almost pleased, 'So we have to be very careful where we point our wormhole. If we pointed it at, say the Pacific Ocean, several kilotonnes of salt water would be deposited on top of us—and obviously, we don't want that!'

There was polite laughter, although Moreau didn't realise it was required and remained conspicuously silent.

'Therefore it is important that we can shut down the wormhole instantly should unforeseen events take place. Any one of us will have the authority to do that and to make sure that there is no confusion, should an emergency arise, the method of shutdown is childishly simple.' She crossed to the bank of instruments and pointed to a large red switch a short distance up the slope of instruments.

'Switching that to the left will immediately terminate wormhole production. Switching it to the right will initiate the production. Obviously, it is now in the central or neutral position.'

Moreau put up his hand. 'Am I right in saying that the principal part of the wormhole will be in the higher dimensional manifold, with just the terminals confined to three-dimensional space?'

'That is correct,' Baldwin said, 'but that was already made clear in your briefing paper.'

Adekola thought that it was about time she reminded Baldwin that she was also present.

'The main part of the wormhole is in the higher dimensional manifold,' she said, trying to sound calm and omniscient, 'but three dimensional space is a proper subset of the manifold. What if there was an object lying between the source and the target of the wormhole; would not that perturb the wormhole throat and warp it towards itself?'

'It would,' Baldwin replied smoothly, 'but space is vast. The density of matter is very low; it would take a tremendous mass to distort the throat. We can safely discount that possibility.'

She looked at her staff one by one and then walked slowly towards them. It was as if she was glowing with an internal radiance in the soft light of the control room. Instinctively, her people backed away slightly as she approached.

She stopped.

'Now take out your work programs and we will go through them together. We will generate the wormhole in seven days' time.' One by one she looked at them and under that gaze they all wilted slightly as if their innermost secrets were being revealed. 'Seven days' time. We generate the wormhole.'

# Fourteen: Wormhole

The days passed in a whirlwind of work. They tested the software over and over, running it through powerful AI-driven checking systems and managed to find and eliminate a few minor errors. Great machines now stood sentinel on the Lunar surface; four great parabolic dishes, interspersed with four scaled-up versions of Baldwin's devices for generating N-Matter. The huge dishes all were pointing upwards, and at present the axes of the dishes converged on a point two hundred metres above the barren landscape.

Fusion Reactor One was brought on line and gradually fed with its fuel, some of which was helium-3 from the soil of the Moon itself. The super and supernally powerful metallic hydrogen magnets were gingerly brought into life and the field strength measured against Baldwin's calculations.

The tension grew palpable as the great day approached, a sparking electricity in the air as if a tremendous thunderstorm was closing in on them. Adekola did not know whether to be exhilarated or terrified as the days drained away. As the hours swept past, faster and faster it seemed, she found it more and more difficult to sleep; but she knew she must sleep, for any loss of concentration might be catastrophic.

A great video screen was now in operation and showed the assemblage of mighty machines out there in the vacuum of the Moon's surface, all pointing upwards as if in expectation of a wonder in the sky.

And that was exactly what everyone was expecting.

The entire base was on edge; all other work seemed trivial and inconsequential. There was only one purpose for the whole personnel and that purpose came from Baldwin; streaming from her like a physical force.

Then it was The Day.

The three senior scientists and Moreau, who, to Adekola's relief and respect, had not buckled under the pressure, took their

216

seats in front of their assigned instruments. Around them, like worker bees, a crowd of technicians stood poised to obey any orders which might be barked their way in addition to their standard responsibilities.

Adekola looked at her palms and could see sweat glistening in their creases. She wondered if this was not in fact the supreme act of hubris on the point of Homo sapiens. They were about to unleash forces which no creature built of transient organic matter could be trusted with; forces so powerful that they belonged in the heart of a star or in the first terrible milliseconds of the Big Bang. Prometheus had stolen fire from the heavens and his punishment had been terrible.

For an instant she thought she was going to rise from her chair and simply walk out of the room; get the shuttle to Earth and spend the rest of her days with Parry and Jahia. Perhaps she would take up crochet or garden design. She could put her mind to anything as long as it did not carry world-wrecking potencies in its slightest aspect.

Then those thoughts blew away as a klaxon blared.

Too late. Now she must stay and do whatever it was required that her leader required of her.

'Sixty seconds,' she heard Baldwin call. Their leader was occupying the central position in front of the myriad of instruments. Before her was the large red switch that would bring their preparations to a climax.

The seconds came and died in lightning succession.

The klaxon blared again.

On the nearest screen to each of the main protagonists a naked zero abruptly replaced tumbling numbers which had been shooting upwards in a seemingly endless sequence.

Baldwin's face was like that of a devotee entering the threshold of Paradise; her face was numinous, transcendental.

Beyond the northern rampart of the walled plain that was Plato, Fusion Reactor One woke from its slumber. A barrage of laser blasts heated a mixture of helium-3 and deuterium, each blast taking the temperature higher and higher, reaching

217

temperatures beyond the comprehension of biological beings: first thousands of kelvins, then hundreds of thousands of kelvins, then millions of kelvins. In the reaction chamber, a small sun came into being; the constituent ions of its plasma held in the adamantine grip of magnetic fields as strong as those of a pulsar. Greater and greater rose the temperature and the pressure until ions began to fuse into helium-4 and protons.

And power flowed from Fusion Reactor One; first a trickle, then a stream, then a raging torrent of mighty energy.

The four leaders stared at the displays before them in wonder, watching the numbers climb higher and higher, but also watching for instabilities which would doom the project and perhaps doom Plato Base itself.

Baldwin flung the red switch to the right.

And then on the screen, the four smaller machines glowed with an indigo-violet light that somehow was not indigo-violet, and the great parabolic dishes also began to radiate, but theirs was the dull red of a cooling ingot pulled from the furnace.

What would happen? Adekola thought. Would anything happen? Would they go back to their rooms with the world's greatest anti-climax hanging over them?

The field of view shifted. Now it was looking to where the parabolic dishes were pointed.

And there at the exact centre of their field of view, a small shining sphere came into being; a sphere whose inner regions were starless blackness but whose circumference glowed with a silvery radiance.

A wormhole.

A great roar went up from everyone in the Control Room. They could even faintly hear muffled celebrations coming from the other side of the door.

Estefan leapt from his chair and went to congratulate Baldwin but she just smiled and waved him back.

'Keep your eyes on the instruments until I say otherwise,' she said, but her tone was forgiving, not chiding. 'As you see, the mouth is spherical from all vantage points, just as theory

218

predicts.'

Adekola had not taken her eyes from the wormhole and was watching how the light flickered around its entrance as the spatial distortion twisted the light of the stars into gleaming bands. On her screen below the image, she saw the message 12.4 KILOGRAMS IN THROAT.

Then she heard Baldwin say, 'That's enough!' and the indigo-violet light vanished; the parabolic dishes dulled to grey and the shining wonder of the wormhole instantly snapped out of existence, leaving a circular after-image on Adekola's retina.

Then the clapping began as a circle formed around Baldwin but she smiled gently and pointed to the viewing screen.

'Watch,' was all she said.

Adekola had not taken her eyes from the screen and saw thin curtains of grey dust slowly settling on the wonderful machines and the terrain around them, drifting slowly and gently in the weak gravity. 'What is that?' she asked, finally turning to look at Baldwin.

'Dust from the Kordylewski clouds,' she said, 'the L4 and L5 points trap dust as they're gravitationally stable.'

Adekola pulled a face. Of course, she should have known that.

But this was no time for self-doubt: she had played her part in a truly incredible achievement. This day would be remembered for as long as there was a human race and her name—Tamira Adekola—would be remembered for that time as well. Whatever tremendous accomplishments humanity would make in its assuredly glorious future, they would never forget this date. She, Estefan, Moreau and, of course, Baldwin had given the human race the key to the stars. For an instant, she felt slightly dizzy with the immense import of the last few hours. She looked around at the vast vaulted room with its flickering multicoloured lights, and momentarily, she felt as if the whole thing was some kind of play and she had blundered onto the set. Soon the Director would notice her and drive back into the wings.

But no, this was reality! Her reality! Her glorious reality!

She slid off her chair and joined the others who had formed a little grouping in the centre of the great room. All were laughing and smiling. Adekola noticed that Baldwin's smile was somehow completely different from her usual beam of sunshine and realised that, for perhaps the first time in their relationship, she was witnessing a genuine, unaffected smile from that lady.

Then Baldwin said something unexpected.

'To the bar!' she beamed, 'the drinks are on me!'

And so it was a somewhat squiffy Adekola who stumbled into her room some hours later, crashed onto the bed and then leapt up again as she realised she had forgotten her video session with her family.

When she finally managed to open the link, she stumbled over her words and was rewarded with a disapproving look from Parry. Even Jahia seemed annoyed.

'You've been drinking,' was all he said in way of greeting.

'I have!' Adekola replied, unabashed. 'And I don't care!' And proceeded to give the reason why she didn't care.

Parry's face softened as she told her tale and when she had finally finished her rather slurred account, he smiled and said, 'Well done! You deserve to let your hair down.'

'I wish you were with me, Idris,' she continued, and with a wicked tone added, 'We could really, you know… celebrate in the old-fashioned sort of way!'

'That we could,' said Parry, with a glance down at Jahia, 'but we'll have to wait.'

They talked for some time longer and Adekola learned all about Jahia's new friend in nursery and how they would stay together for ever and ever.

But just before Earth's rotation was about to take Parry and Jahia out of range, a thought rose to the top of her rather befuddled mind.

There was something she should ask. What was it?

Then she had it, but remembered she had to ask it in a convoluted way.

'That puzzle I left with you,' she said, fighting back hiccups, 'any luck?'

His face was impassive. 'No. No luck at all.'

\*\*\*

It was an unwelcome call from Baldwin that shattered Adekola's much-needed sleep the next morning. Baldwin's face appeared on the televiewer and she raised an eyebrow when she saw Adekola's face peering over the duvet.

'Oh, still in bed, Tamira? I thought you'd be up and about by now.' Baldwin did not seem to be suffering at all despite her Brobdingnagian consumption of alcohol the previous night.

'I'll be up now,' Adekola managed to mumble.

'That would be nice, Tamira. If you could hurry along to my room, I'd be grateful.'

*What does she want now?* Adekola groaned inwardly, but Baldwin's next words were like a bucket of cold water thrown over her.

'There are some men who want to speak to you.'

Adekola dressed in the shortest time possible and was soon in Baldwin's room.

Two middle-aged men were sitting in front of Baldwin's desk and turned to look at the door as she hurriedly opened it.

'Ah, here she is at last,' said Baldwin, her standard smile switched back on again, 'Gentlemen, this is the Dr Tamira Adekola I told you about. Tamira, these are Mr Thorne and Mr Kapoor from the Serious Incident Investigation Office.'

Both men nodded in greeting but their gaze was forensic, cold; the gaze of the medical student about to begin a dissection.

'I told them you were with Philip Richards just before he died,' Baldwin said sweetly, 'And you might be able to help them with their enquiries.'

'What?...yes, yes, I was,' Adekola said, looking from one man to the other and then back again.

'Mr Richards' death was very unusual,' Kapoor said, in a dry, whispery voice, 'it's most unusual for vacuum suits to fail in our

221

time. They are designed for every eventuality.

'Our investigation is of course severely hampered by the destruction of the suit and the medical equipment in the recent fire. We have studied the remains but they were so carbonised to be valueless.'

Adekola nodded dumbly, not knowing if she was supposed to comment.

'The autopsy on Mr Richards did show something unusual,' Thorne continued, 'there was an abrasion, almost a lesion, on Mr Richards' throat, as if a sharp instrument had come into contact with it.'

Adekola's own throat was now very dry. 'And how can I help you?' she managed to say.

'You were the first to reach Mr Richards and were in close contact with him before the others arrived.'

'Yes.'

'Did you notice anything unusual about Mr Richards' condition when you were alone with him?'

'Other than him dying, you mean?' Adekola said and then bit her lip. *Wrong thing to say!*

'Quite,' Thorne said, and his lips were so closely pressed together the word was almost a hiss. 'I believe you were seen pressing something onto Mr Richards' neck.'

'Yes, an adhesive strip to stop the air escaping! He was dying of anoxia!'

'I believe you had a pair of pincers which you were using before the sealant patch became available. We accept that there was a tear in his suit before you reached him, but is it possible that you used the pincers to enlarge that tear and in so doing made the nick in Mr Richards' neck and thus hastened his death?'

Suddenly it seemed that Adekola was alone on a great dark plain and a cold wind was blasting down from the north. In the distance, ravenous wolves were howling.

She fought her way back to sanity.

'I tried to save Phil! He was my friend!' she yelled.

Thorne and Kapoor were unmoved by the outburst.

'Do you still have the pincers?'

'I think I left them on the Lunar surface in the confusion. I don't have them anymore, that's all I know.'

Thorne glanced at Baldwin. 'I think we'll leave it there for the time being.' He turned his gaze back to Adekola. 'There's something about this incident that makes little sense, Dr Adekola. I take it you have no plans to return to Earth just yet.'

'No,' Adekola said dully, 'we're in the middle of a significant project.'

'So I understand. If we need you again, we will be in touch. We'll be around for a few more weeks.' He turned to Baldwin. 'Thank you, Dr Baldwin.'

She lifted her hands. 'Hey, any time.'

Adekola had to stand up to give them room to get out and then slumped back in her chair, staring at Baldwin.

'I don't think you have anything to worry about,' Baldwin said smoothly, 'I can't believe you had anything to do with poor Richards' sad death.'

Adekola jumped to her feet. 'You're damned right! Damned right! I was trying to save him!'

Baldwin looked at her coldly. 'Do calm down, Tamira. No-one's accusing you of anything, least of all me.'

After Adekola had left, Baldwin opened one of the drawers in her desk and took out a bottle containing an amber liquid. She poured herself a quarter of a tumbler's worth of the liquid and then leaned back, slowly sipping it.

And as she did so, the ghost of a smile played over her full red lips.

# Fifteen: The Probe

'I need your help,' Adekola said.

'Sure,' Moreau replied, 'what do you want?'

'I need you to come onto the Lunar surface with me. I want to look for something.'

Adekola related the story of how she had tried to save Richards.

'And for some reason, they seem interested in the pincers I used to try to hold the sides of the tear together.'

Moreau shrugged. 'I take it we won't have to go very far?'

'Two hundred metres. We shouldn't be out there long.'

Moreau nodded. Although vacuum suits gave protection against radiation, they did not confer invulnerability. And now there was the apparent possibility that they might fail.

'OK. You'll make the arrangements?'

Adekola agreed. Because of the hostility of the Lunar environment any excursions outside the base had to be officially logged with names, destination and expected time of return. One did not take chances with vacuum and hard radiation.

One hour later the two stood outside the building that housed the elevators to the sublunar base.

They both looked at the sky; with a sky like the Moon's, it was impossible not to. Earth was shrinking down from gibbous, and experienced eyes could have detected the continental outlines through the swirl of clouds in the sunlit section. The shadows cast by Plato's grim ramparts were in retreat as the two cosmic bodies continued their perpetual dance. But Adekola was not interested in examining the home planet, and the two set out across the grey plain; their loping movements sending up small parabolas of dust. Adekola realised that the monotonous lava plain had so few points of reference that getting lost on it was a worrying possibility, but on the Moon footprints last for millennia, so it was not too difficult to retrace the steps taken on that dreadful day.

224

She remembered throwing the pincers away when the sealant patch had been thrust into her hands but could not recall in what direction or how hard she had thrown it. Under Lunar gravity it could have travelled a long way. It might even have buried itself in the soft dust.

They trudged on, over the dead and deadly floor of Plato. Adekola glanced backwards; the elevator building already looked far away even in the pin-sharp clarity of airlessness.

But eventually, they came to a patch of badly disturbed regolith where clearly some turmoil had occurred. Many footprints led to the disturbed patch and almost as many led away. This was the spot where Richards had died.

'It'll be somewhere around here!' Adekola called, and Moreau stopped and immediately began to look around on the ground.

'It's here somewhere!' she muttered to herself and bent over, a more difficult operation than it might have seemed, because of the stiffness of the joints in the suit.

'Nothing here, Boss,' came Moreau's voice over the suits' communication link.

Adekola cursed silently, bent further over, lost her balance and toppled slowly onto the lifeless ground.

But then as she raised her head she saw it; half-covered in grey dust but still bright in the glare of the merciless sun.

'Got you!' she breathed. Moreau was with her now and helped her to her feet, triumphantly holding the pincers.

'There!' she said, holding it out so that Moreau could see it, 'not a drop of blood anywhere on it! Just as I knew there wouldn't be!'

'I never doubted you, Boss,' Moreau said, looking down at the small object in Adekola's gauntleted hand.

'Straight back...' Adekola started to say but stopped. 'Did you feel that?'

*That* was a shuddering, trembling sensation that started at their boots and rapidly ascended their limbs until both of them were trembling violently.

'Some kind of moonquake!' Moreau said, 'let's get down before we're thrown down!'

They both stretched prone on the Lunar soil while the quake surged to a bone-rattling intensity. The pincers flew from Adekola's hand and disappeared into a cloud of swirling dust. They lay there with their faceplates pressed down into the shivering soil. Adekola could see nothing but blackness; feel nothing but her body being shaken as if by a giant's hand.

*What a stupid way to die!* Adekola thought, out here in this Godforsaken place, looking for something that she knew was unimportant. If only she had stayed in the base!

Then it was over. Adekola rose slowly and warily to her feet, dust cascading from her. For a moment she thought Moreau had been swallowed by some fissure that the quake had opened up, but then a mound in the regolith stirred and a space-suited figure rose out of it.

'Well, that was fun,' Moreau's voice said in her helmet.

'Wasn't it,' Adekola said, 'Looks like I'm not having much luck these days. First I'm accused of murder then I'm hit by a once-in-a-thousand year moonquake.'

'Could have been a nearby meteorite strike,' Moreau replied, 'they're common enough.'

'Whatever. Well, the pincers have gone again. Back to square one.'

'Not exactly, Boss. You have a witness now. I saw them and they were as clean as your conscience.' He looked around. 'We should get back, Boss. We can't take any more time looking for that thing. If it was a quake, it may have loosened things a bit and we don't want to be out here if a big one comes.'

'You're right,' Adekola said, with some reluctance. She would have preferred physical proof but Moreau was right: there could be aftershocks, even if what had just happened had not been the precursor of something worse.

They turned around, seeing with no little relief that the elevator building was still there and apparently undamaged. They had not gone far when Moreau said, 'That's funny.'

226

'What is?'

'Over there. Something shining very brightly. It wasn't there when we came out.'

Adekola followed his pointing finger. There, about as far from the building as they were but ninety degrees to their current path, was a brilliant point of light. She checked the sun's position; it was almost certainly reflected sunlight, which meant that there was a very reflective surface where one had not been before.

'I'm going to take a look,' she said.

'Boss...' Moreau said in a voice which carried the message *Don't be so stupid!*

'Henri,' she said reprovingly, 'I'm a scientist. The unknown is my job.'

Moreau tried to shrug but the action was hard to perform in the heavy suit.

'Let's go,' was all he said.

They changed direction and walked towards the light. It soon became evident that the quake had cracked some kind of mound on the lava plain. Adekola had briefly noticed it on the way out but had dismissed it as simply another swelling in the rock produced by long-extinct volcanic forces when the Moon was young. But as they approached...

'It's artificial!' Moreau gasped, walking up to it; his long legs having carried him faster than Adekola.

As she joined him she could see it was a metal dome, on which broken slabs of rock had been attached to give it the appearance of a natural mound. But the quake had torn a great gash in one side and through that gap blazing light was streaming as something caught the sun's rays.

Moreau raised a leg to climb over the sharks' teeth of torn metal into the shattered dome.

'Careful, Henri!' she called, 'watch your suit on the jagged edges! I don't want another fatality out here!'

Somehow she knew he was grinning as he turned slightly to look at her, and then he was inside. She knew she had no option but to follow.

The light was being reflected not off some crude mass of unworked metal but a machine; a machine with lenses for seeing, and reticulated arms for grasping, now folded up against its polished sides. It was slightly taller than Moreau and everywhere they looked they could see their reflections looking up at them from the machine's shining depths.

'It reminds me of something,' Moreau muttered quietly to himself, but loud in Adekola's helmet.

Then suddenly a terrible fear struck her; blasting its way up from her deepest subconscious. She tapped him on the shoulder and, as he turned, put a gloved finger to her faceplate in a sign to be silent. Then she made a motion with her right hand to indicate that something should be switched off.

He stood statute-still for some minutes, staring bemusedly at her. She repeated the movement. Finally, he understood and turned his communication channel off.

They approached each other and touched helmets.

'Can you hear me?' she said as loudly as she could.

Moreau's muffled voice came to her, transmitted by sound vibrations directly through their helmets. 'Just about. What the hell's the matter? Why are we acting like we're some kind of spies?'

'You said, it reminded you of something. I had the same thought and I know what it reminded me of. I know what it is.'

'And?'

'It reminded me of the probes they used in the twenty-first century to explore the Solar planets. That's what it is—a probe!'

'Of course! That's what I thought! But why?—we don't need that kind of probe anymore. We know all we need to know about the planets.'

'Indeed we do.' She looked back at the machine and then touched helmets again. 'Stay here. I'm going to look at the back of it.'

Leaving Moreau standing just inside the dome she moved carefully around the machine. And stopped. There was something on the back of the device but in the fathomless Lunar shadow she could not make it out.

She took a flashlight from her tool pack and sent a circle of light onto the machine.

She saw the letters "ST" in a bold, stylised font above what appeared to be a heraldic device of some sort. She bent closer. It was an eagle grasping a sun disc in its talons.

And she had seen that eagle and sun somewhere else. As a much smaller image.

Where?

She completed her circumnavigation of the machine and joined helmets with Moreau again.

'Boss, would you care to tell me what is going on?'

'I wish I could, Henri. But I can tell you this: there's something going on in this base that we're not being told about. Have you been told about this machine—this probe? No. Why was it hidden?'

'You mean someone's manipulating Baldwin? But that's crazy—she lives, breathes and shits science. That's all she cares about!'

'Is it? I don't know what's going on but I tell you this— something *is* going on; something that someone is keeping secret!' She paused. 'We've been off the net too long. We'll switch back on when I raise my arm. But don't talk about this to anyone. Phil told me not to trust anyone and I'm going to take his advice. I suggest you do too. We'll walk back now and we'll say nothing about this machine—we'll just say how bad it was we couldn't find the pincers. Got it?'

'Well, I don't know, Boss. It sounds too crazy.'

She grabbed his nearest arm.

'Trust me. There's something bad happening in this base. And it could be something very bad!'

They walked back to the elevator station, saying to each other what bad luck it was that their search had been in vain.

*\*\*\**

'And so,' Baldwin said, addressing her senior staff and Moreau, 'we are approaching that wonderful day when we reach out and touch the Centauri system, almost with our own hands.' Her smile became broader. 'I exaggerate, of course. Forgive me a touch of poetic language but if any one were to write about our endeavours here, it would surely be an epic poem. A new "Iliad", perhaps. But certainly not "Paradise Lost"—no, it would be "Paradise Gained".'

Her staff gazed back at her, a little puzzled, a little unsure of where this speech was going.

They were not in the Control Room but in another immense space, inside another tremendous structure. There was nothing in it apart from Baldwin and her staff and the functional chairs on which they were sitting. At the end opposite to where they had entered, was a great roll-up door, obviously designed so that it could be wound upwards to reveal what lay beyond.

Baldwin looked tolerantly at her people, perhaps feeling an almost maternal concern at their bemusement. She pressed on.

'We know a lot about the Centauri system, of course. We have, after all, been studying it for decades ever since the new generation of telescopes became available, replacing worn-out relics like the James Webb. We have identified one planet which we believe we can terraform and in so doing provide us with a much needed second home, so we can escape the Doom of Stars.'

Moreau and Adekola looked at each other when that mysterious phrase was uttered, a movement which did not go unnoticed by Baldwin.

'Ah, I see, I am not taking you with me in my glorious vision. I told you I was in a poetic mood. What do I mean by those enigmatic words?' She rose from her chair, which as usual was facing them, and began to walk back and forth in front of them, but not looking at them. Adekola noticed once again the flowing feline grace which Baldwin managed to infuse into the simple act of locomotion.

'Ever since the twentieth century,' she continued, 'those of us capable of thought have noticed something inexplicable about this universe of ours: its silence; its emptiness. If life evolves on all planets capable of hosting it—and such worlds must be common in a galaxy as vast as ours—why is there absolutely no sign of them? Why is there a Great Silence?'

Estefan put up his hand but Baldwin ignored him: this was her exposition.

'Some scientists, and I count myself amongst them, believe this is because life, or at least metazoan life, is not common and that the universe is fundamentally hostile to the production of life. You may remember the little parable I gave a while ago about the lucky uranium atom. But I may be wrong.' She looked at them impishly. 'Yes, I know you find that hard to believe, but stranger things have happened!' Then her face became serious. 'There is a more unpleasant, a more unsettling possibility. It may well be that metazoan, and ultimately intelligent, life-forms are common in the galaxy. But something weeds them out, kills them off before they become mature enough to escape their little worlds. It is possible that they destroy themselves through terrible wars, or, as nearly happened to us, environmental degradation. But it is possible that it is the universe itself which brings the axe down, time and time again. And that axe could take many guises: it could be a superflare from that world's sun; it could be an endless volcanic episode, such as occurred at the end of the Permian; it could be the close passage of another star; it could be a nearby supernova; it could be a blizzard of comets. The list can be extended, of course. Some people refer to the murderous nature of our cosmos as "The Great Filter" but I prefer to refer to it as "The Doom of Stars", a phrase which I believe I have coined. I call it that because it seems to me that if there is an ending to our civilisation, it will come from outside ourselves.' She stared hard at them. 'So how do we escape the Doom of Stars?'

Dazzled by her vision, they found themselves unable to respond.

She lifted her arms, adopting a Messianic posture.

231

'We find a second home! We double our chances of escaping the Doom! And that is the real purpose of Project Independence—to make it more likely that we will not merely survive, but thrive and transform the Doom of Stars into a Harvest of Stars!'

She dropped her arms and stared at them, awaiting their reaction. Then there came the sound of clapping, echoing in the tremendous space. Adekola looked past Moreau and was not surprised to see Estefan clapping, and felt obliged to join him. Soon all three of her audience were clapping.

She acknowledged their praise and then lifted a hand to terminate it.

'I said earlier that we had learned much about our new home. Of course, its transformation into a habitable world will require vast amounts of energy and resources; a task that would be totally beyond us if we were to attempt to travel there by conventional means. That is why the project depends utterly on the creation of stable wormholes. But before we can travel safely there ourselves, we need more data. And that means sending probes to collect the data. Remember how totally astronomers misunderstood the planet Mars when all they had were telescopes? It was not until physical probes visited that world that its true nature was revealed. And so I will now reveal the probe I am going to send to Alpha Centauri. I will use one of the base's mass drivers to catapult it into low Lunar orbit and then manoeuvre it into the throat.'

Moreau gave Adekola a soft dig in the ribs, leaned in and whispered, 'See, I told you there was nothing sinister about that probe we saw!'

Adekola nodded, feeling a little relief that one mystery at least had been explained. She was tired to her heart's core of these endless problems, whose solutions were always just out of reach, just around the corner of a corridor in a long and fiendish labyrinth.

There was a rumbling noise and they turned to see the massive door rolling up and something shining beginning to move into the room, being propelled by a group of technicians.

Moreau grinned at Adekola and then turned back to watch the probe coming nearer.

His smile faltered a little.

The probe was basically a cube. It had a feathery communication antenna, stretching out twice its width. There were many cameras and sensors sprouting from most of its surface, giving it the appearance of a metal hedgehog.

On the side approaching them were small red letters which spelled out: "INTERNATIONAL COUNCIL FOR THE PEACEFUL EXPLORATION OF EXTRASOLAR SPACE."

'Godammit!' Adekola hissed to Moreau, 'that's not the probe we saw!

\*\*\*

Adekola lay on the bed. Totally drained and defeated.

She could not make sense of all the things that had happened: Richards' strange warning and then his death; the two probes, one of which came from an organisation she recognised, the other a total mystery. A conversation between two people who didn't like each other, followed by an encoded text. And officials who seemed to think she was guilty of murder, despite zero evidence.

Things like those were not supposed to be happening in staid research organisations, where arguments were usually about which figures should follow a decimal point. Science was all about openness and sharing: there were supposed to be nothing hidden, no dark secrets.

Yet there were secrets in Plato Base. Secrets that must be important enough to require her room to be bugged.

There was only one ray of light and that was her weekly conversation with her family.

Eagerly she activated the televiewer and waited for the screen to show Idris and Jahia.

When they appeared, after what seemed an interminable

wait, Parry looked particularly serious.

'What's the matter?' she said, suddenly alarmed.

'Nothing, absolutely nothing,' he said, although his tone indicated otherwise.

She looked at him quizzically. 'So what's been happening?'

'Not a lot. Jahia's fallen out with her best friend at nursery. We've upgraded the memory recording software.' He paused, and his eyes flicked momentarily to the left, as if he were unsure of what to say next. 'Uhh, I was thinking of taking Jahia to the park on Sunday. She wasn't sure if that's where we were going but that's our true destination.' There seemed to be an unusual emphasis on that final phrase. She stared at him blankly.

'That's the—*true destination?*' she repeated.

'Yes. The true destination.'

The conversation ground to a halt. They stared at each other like total strangers whose communication channels had crossed. Then Parry reached behind himself and produced a generously-sized sheet of paper.

Adekola looked at it. It showed a distinctly badly-drawn quadruped which might generously be interpreted as a dog, looking at what appeared to be a very large asterisk. This was getting weird.

'Jahia drew this for you,' Parry said. Then off-camera Jahia could be heard saying, 'I didn't draw that, Daddy!'

She appeared on screen, looking agitated. 'I didn't draw it, Mommy!'

Parry looked worried. 'Well, maybe not, darling. Maybe Daddy drew it, I can't remember.'

Jahia turned from the camera to her father. 'And on Sunday, we're visiting my new friend, remember Daddy?'

'Oh, yes, sorry Jahia.' He looked back at Adekola. 'Sorry, that's our true destination.'

'So that is your true destination?' she said, getting the distinct impression that she was trapped in an avant-garde comedy sketch.

'Yes.' His eyes flicked down to the sheet he was holding up

to the camera. 'That's our true destination.'

She gave up and tried to divert the conversation into more normal topics but it seemed Parry's heart wasn't in it.

After the conversation had ended and the televiewer screen had reverted to a blank grey rectangle, she lay back on her bed, resting her head on her crossed arms and staring at the ceiling.

A weird phrase kept bouncing off the walls of her mind.

*True destination?*

What in the Nine Hells was that about?

# Sixteen: The Rings of Neptune

'Proof of concept is complete,' Baldwin said, 'Now we must spread our wings.'

Her senior staff, who day by day found themselves confined more and more to the role of acolytes, waited on her next words with growing anticipation.

*We're like pets waiting for a treat!* thought Adekola, *Come on, let's have it!*

'I have determined that we will do one more test run within the Solar system,' Baldwin continued after she had determined that her theatrical pause had persisted for long enough. 'So I— we—will generate a wormhole which will reach into the outer regions of the system.'

'How far will that be?' Estefan asked, the tremor in his voice indicating barely-suppressed excitement.

'30.1 Astronomical Units.'

Adekola did some rapid mental data retrieval. 'That—that's the orbit of Neptune.'

'It is the distance of Neptune itself,' Baldwin said, her face as usual suffused with a mixture of the sunshine of relaxed assurance and the steel of irresistible determination. 'We will capture a ring particle and transfer it to the Moon. Then we will ready for the big jump across the interstellar wastes to our true destination.'

Adekola's head jerked upward, breaking her study of her stubby fingers. That phrase again! Was it a coincidence?

The others were unaware of her sudden alertness, although for a fleeting moment she thought she had caught an odd look from Baldwin.

'Yes, our true destination,' the latter continued, 'A distant star system which will hold tremendous riches for humanity.'

'When do we start?' Estefan said, his tone and body language suggesting that he was prepared to go to Neptune in person and bring back a chunk of celestial matter for his

Mistress.

'We know the procedures well enough now,' Baldwin said, 'Four days will be enough. And we will up the output from Fusion Reactor One to ten percent. That will give us enough power to drill through Neptune and come out the other side!'

They all laughed, except Adekola, who could only manage a smile.

\*\*\*

And so, the days to the countdown flew by ever faster. And Baldwin was right; the actions which they had agonised over on the first trial now seemed to come naturally to them as if they had been doing them all their lives.

'Sixty seconds.'

Adekola saw the Reactor once again rouse from its dreamless sleep and begin to climb the ladder of steadily increasing temperatures until they reached numbers which seemed incredible, impossible; temperatures which most stars could only dream of; temperatures to cause the fabric of space-time to tremble.

One motion from Baldwin, one movement of her slim arm, and the energy now held captive in Fusion Reactor One would be set free and sent flashing into the mightiest machines that humanity had yet devised. And together they would create a wonder, a marvel, something long deemed impossible. And it would reach out across emptiness to the realm of the great Ice Giants and bring back some of the matter attendant on the outermost Giant.

For an instant Adekola's head seemed to swim with the enormity of it all.

And that would be accomplished with ten percent of the power of one reactor. What would the combined power of all four be like!

The human mind could not comprehend it; would recoil from trying to comprehend it.

Adekola could look at the numbers but they carried no image, no vision of that power.

They were just numbers.

'Get ready.'

Baldwin's imperious voice snapped the cobwebs of her imaginings and brought her back to the vast Control Room. She looked around. She and the three others were in the places of honour nearest to the central part of the enormous bank of controls and instruments.

The more distant positions were held by the "lower orders", as Baldwin had once been heard to refer to them; technicians who stood and served but were still essential to the success of the project.

Baldwin snapped the red switch to the right.

Again the indigo-violet light which was not quite indigo-violet came into being; once again the centres of the great dishes glowed dying-ember red—though perhaps a little brighter this time.

The screens showed something else come into being, high above the Lunar surface.

A shining sphere whose central region was a chilling, dead, ebony nothingness but whose circumference shone with the distorted images of remote galaxies, twisted into a ring of pearly radiance.

And Adekola could see that it was somewhat bigger than the first wormhole, swollen with the extra gigajoules that Fusion Reactor One was pouring into it.

'Readings!' came Baldwin's commanding voice again.

There was an excited murmur as everyone transmitted their data to Baldwin, like workers swarming around their queen bee.

And then Adekola's screen flashed a message in front of her questing eyes.

450.98 KILOGRAMS OF MATTER IN THROAT.

Baldwin's eyes were fixed on her own screen and then as she saw what she had been waiting for, she flung the red switch to the left. The shining sphere snapped out of existence as if a celestial soap bubble had just popped.

On another screen, Adekola saw an irregularly shaped object enter from above and crash silently onto the Lunar surface in a great eruption of grey dust.

'That's it people,' she heard Baldwin say, in a joyous voice, 'let's go out and see what we've captured.'

It was a brief journey in the crawler and soon the four senior staff were standing on the pitted surface staring at a fresh crater in the Moon's battered face. And in the centre of that crater was a gnarled block of reddish-grey material that was visibly shrinking as great jets of vapour shot out from ever-changing points on its surface.

'A particle from the Égalité ring arc, if my calculations are correct,' Baldwin's voice came over the suit intercom, 'The Moon is too hot for the volatiles in its composition, so soon it'll just be a nub of silicate rock.'

'Are we doing anything with it, now we've captured it?' came Moreau's question.

'No. Why should we? It's just a worthless hunk of rock. We're after much more exciting prizes.'

And with that, they returned to the base.

***

After that tremendous high, there came the inevitable reaction. There was no party after the successful conclusion to the second test. Baldwin gave them a few brisk "thank-you's" and then they were dismissed. Moreau suggested to Adekola that they went for a celebratory drink but her heart wasn't in it. After declining politely, she found herself back in her room, staring at the blank televiewer screen.

If only Parry was with her—or that she was with Parry!

Something was wrong with this project; she knew that. So instead of feeling joy and wonder at what they had achieved together, there was this virus of doubt, eating away at the foundations of her mind.

Had she known what was being played out in Baldwin's room at that very moment, her doubts would have crystallised into a thing of terror.

'I was in contact with Mr Wójcik only recently,' that particular woman was saying, 'there is no need to send one of his goons round to threaten me. Especially one whose mugshot is on every news channel on Planet Earth.'

The large man on the other side of her desk gave a brief, unconvincing smile. Whatever that expression was, warmth was definitely an emotion it did not carry.

'I fear you have underestimated me, Professor. Whatever I am, I am not a "goon." I know how you humiliated one of my colleagues some time ago, but I warn you not to attempt anything like that with me. I am in a somewhat higher echelon than that unfortunate gentleman; God rest his soul. And I know all about your penchant for recording conversations.'

'Lawks a-Mercy,' Baldwin said, in a theatrical falsetto, 'looks like you've got me. What's a poor girl to do?'

'This is no time for childish play-acting, professor. Mr Wójcik does not appreciate people wasting his valuable time.'

Baldwin matched his cold stare. 'So, what more can I tell you? That I have already been there and got the stuff? Science doesn't work like that.'

'Mr Wójcik is unhappy with the rate of progress.'

'Is he!' Baldwin exploded, 'Is he, now! I have just brought about two of the greatest breakthroughs in all history, and it's not enough! Not enough, you tell me! If you can't understand what I have accomplished here, you really must be a goon!'

The large man bore the outburst patiently and without any reaction, and then, as if Baldwin had not spoken, said: 'He wants to move straight to the target.'

'And he didn't have the balls to tell me that himself?'

The man took a leather pouch out of his jacket and undid it, revealing a gleaming knife with a serrated edge.

'Mr Wójcik is in possession of all his bodily equipment. However, if you should be so foolish as to be uncooperative, the same may not be true of you in the future.'

Baldwin snorted. 'Very impressive. But let me tell you something. If I should disappear after an unfortunate accident like Richards, then my tremendous programme is also finished. No riches. No untold wealth. No power. Get rid of me and who will take my place? Adekola? Estefan? I can outthink that pair in my sleep. And what hold do you have over me? I've no family. No dear little children for you to abduct and torment. No aged mother in a nursing home that you can terrorise. You deal with me and me alone. Got that, Mr Higher Echelon?'

Silence fell.

The man continued to glare at Baldwin with a dangerous mixture of fire and ice in his eyes.

Finally, he spoke. 'You know, I could use this thing on you, just for the fun of it. And it would be fun.'

She leant back in her chair, and slowly placed her hands on the back of her head, knowing that it accentuated the swell of her breasts.

'No doubt there's something else you'd like to use on me, but forget it. When all this is over maybe I'll let you sniff my panties one day. You'd like that, I'm sure.'

He made an involuntary move towards her but stopped himself with obvious difficulty, his face like magma.

She laughed and held up her hand, palm towards him. 'OK, I think I've made myself clear but I've got good news for you. You won't be the bearer of sad tidings to Mr Wójcik. As a special favour to him—not because of any threats from you, of course—I will advance the project. I'll skip the next test and go straight there. But not because of him. Or you. But because I want to.'

The man's expression was still one of anger but it slowly became suffused with evident relief. He nodded. 'Thank you, Professor.'

She smiled sweetly. 'Think nothing of it.' Her gaze flicked towards the door. 'You may go now.'

And so it was, at the next Heads of Department meeting

241

Baldwin seemed to be fizzing with excitement as her staff trooped in, all wishing that she was less of a morning person.

When they had all sat down, Baldwin rose from her seat and stood in front of them, her eyes seemingly shining with an inner radiance.

'I have great news for you,' she said, 'I have decided to skip the next few tests and go straight to our final destination.'

Estefan broke into a round of applause and Moreau followed slightly less enthusiastically until he noticed that Adekola wasn't applauding at all, and stopped.

'Bravo!' Estefan cried, 'wonderful! Typical of you, Professor!'

Bur Baldwin was looking at Adekola, not Estefan.

'You look a little concerned, Tamira,' she said, 'scientific breakthroughs don't excite you perhaps?'

Adekola looked up at her.

*Dammit, why am I always seated when she's lording it over me!*

'It seems a little hasty,' was all she said.

'Hasty?' said Baldwin, her normally alabaster forehead corrugating slightly, 'why is that, dear?'

'To go from the orbit of Neptune to Alpha Centauri is a gigantic step.'

'If you think about it, the ratio between the L5 point and Neptune is very similar to the ratio of the distance between Neptune and Alpha.'

'It's not the ratios that are important,' Adekola protested, 'it's the absolute distances. Neptune is about thirty astronomical units away, while Alpha is nearer two hundred and seventy-eight thousand AU away!'

Baldwin turned away and sat back down.

'Well, Tamira, I never thought I'd find out that one of my people is antiscience.'

Adekola gasped. 'Antiscience! Me!'

'Why yes. What other reason could there be for deliberately choosing not to explore, to choose not to lift the veil on the mysteries of the cosmos? To stay home and never head out into

242

the great ocean of discovery.'

'That—that's not it! That's not it at all!'

Baldwin looked at Estefan and Moreau. 'Could you excuse us, gentlemen, Tamira and I have a few things to discuss? I'm sure you must have lots of things you could be doing.'

Moreau looked at Adekola but she did not meet his eyes. He got up slowly and joined Estefan who was already heading for the door.

When they were alone, Baldwin said, 'So Tamira, what's it all about?'

*This is it!* Adekola thought.

'Professor...'

'Elizabeth.'

'Elizabeth,' Adekola began diffidently, feeling all her resolution beginning to fray, 'there are things happening on this base that I don't understand.'

'Such as?'

'Moreau and I were out on the Lunar surface and we found a probe, a probe that had been hidden. And when you revealed your probe, it wasn't that one.'

Baldwin nodded. 'I see. That is very sinister; I'm surprised you didn't go to the authorities immediately.' She smiled again, and it was the tolerant smile of the expert correcting a simple, but understandable, error on the part of the student. 'So because you didn't know about that probe it means that somebody, almost certainly me, is up to nefarious acts.'

'I'm sorry?'

'Tamira, you don't know about that probe but I do. There are other teams up here and they have their own scientific agendas.'

'But why was it hidden?'

'It wasn't. I knew of it. You didn't. That doesn't mean it was—ahem—"hidden." If I may point out the obvious, you are not sufficiently senior to know of all the Base-wide activities. I am, and I do.'

'But why was it being stored on the surface?'

243

'My, you are the curious one, aren't you? But why are you asking me?—I've just told you that it's nothing to do with me. I imagine it's to be used in a high radiation, airless environment. So please find something else to grill me over.'

Adekola felt her confidence disappearing like water on the Lunar surface. She went quiet.

'Anything else, my dear?' Baldwin inquired.

This was no time to hold back, Adekola told herself. Time to give Baldwin both barrels.

'Why is my room bugged?'

Did Baldwin blink then? Adekola wasn't sure.

'Bugged? What makes you think that?'

'I told Idris about Jahia's seventh birthday in our televiewer conversation. When I asked for leave, you quoted "seventh birthday" back at me. But it was Jahia's fifth birthday.'

Baldwin rocked back on her chair, clapping her hands in amusement. 'So that proves a conspiracy. Tamira, you really are priceless. I know nothing about children, even your sweet child. I just guessed Jahia's birthday to show I was interested in your family affairs. I'm afraid you'll have to do better than that.'

'What about Phil?'

'What about him?'

'His death was strange, suspicious. Vacuum suits don't fail these days.'

'My dear, you have nothing to fear. Thorne has been in contact with me. He has decided that there is insufficient evidence to proceed against you. You're in the clear.'

'I'm in the clear because I'm innocent!' Adekola snapped. 'Innocent! I cared for Phil! It seems I was the only one here who did!'

Baldwin stared at Adekola, coolly, dispassionately. 'My dear, I hope you're not *protesting too much*, as they say. I always thought you weren't in any way involved, despite how it looked.'

The discussion seemed to have finished. Adekola stared at her interlocked fingers, desperately trying to think of some other accusation. Then Baldwin spoke again.

'Tamira, is there perhaps another reason for your mental state?'

Adekola looked up. 'Like what, Professor?'

Baldwin leaned forward and spoke quietly, confidentially, girl to girl, 'Is it possible that you are in fact jealous of me?'

Adekola stiffened. 'What!'

'Now calm down, it's only natural. I'm used to it.' Baldwin smiled in a self-deprecatory manner, 'I know your career hasn't exactly sparkled, and your qualifications are about average. But you're not alone in that. It's the way things are.'

Adekola stared dumbly at her.

Baldwin waved a hand, dismissively. 'And about Idris. You've nothing to fear there. I agree he's cute and you're lucky to have him. But I would never take him off you. I...'

Adekola leapt off the chair, took one step towards Baldwin, stopped, turned.

And walked out of the room.

# Seventeen: The Message

The noise of hungry diners beat around Adekola and Moreau like far-off surf as they stared at each other over the remains of their half-eaten meal.

'And that's what she said,' Adekola said and held her arms wide in an expression of baffled defeat. 'I've asked around but no-one's said anything about another team planning to launch a probe.'

'I haven't heard of one either,' Moreau said, 'but Baldwin's right. This is a big place. We don't know everybody and we can't ask everybody.'

Silence fell for a moment and Adekola distractedly stirred the remnants of her fungal protein strips. 'They must already be loading it onto the mass driver in preparation for launch. If I could get a good look at it!'

'You'd find it difficult, Boss—but I might be able to.'

'How's that?'

Moreau looked slightly embarrassed. 'Well, the girl in charge of the mass driver. Carina. She and I—uhh—well, we had a bit of a thing going. A while back.'

'Do you think she'd let you into the launch area?'

'She might. But it's awkward. She said she never wanted to see me again. In order to get anywhere, I'd have to say that I wanted to start up again. And I don't. I'd be stringing her along, and that wouldn't be right.'

There was silence again. Adekola looked directly into Moreau's eyes.

'You're a good man, Henri,' she finally said, 'one of the best I've met. Normally I would never respect a man who deceived a woman but I feel that there's something monumental going on here. And you and I seem to be the only ones who know that. The launch could happen at any time and I know they load the driver a considerable time before they actually fire it. I suspect Baldwin's planning to switch the probes and launch the one we saw on the surface.'

'And the one we saw?'

'We never got a good look at that. We never touched it. We saw it from quite a distance and then it was snatched away. We don't even know if it was a real probe. It could have been a mock-up, stitched together from aluminium foil.'

Once again there was silence. Then: 'OK, Boss. You think there's some kind of plot going on and that's good enough for me. I just hope Carina forgives me.'

Adekola gave him a soft smile. 'Perhaps one day I'll speak to her when this is all over and ask for forgiveness on your behalf. To understand all is to forgive all, someone said.'

Moreau grinned. 'Well, I don't think it was Carina!'

\*\*\*

Carina Bianchi looked up from her monitoring screen as she became aware of someone standing beside her. Her eyes widened when she saw who it was and then became tight slits as she hissed, 'Well, look what the cat dragged in! What are you doing here!'

Moreau had adopted a hang-dog look and he slowly raised his gaze from Bianchi's shoes to her face.

'Hello, Carina. It's been a while.'

'That it has. I repeat: what do you want?'

'I wanted to say I'm sorry. Really sorry for the way I treated you.'

Her face softened. 'You are? You've never said that before.'

'I've had time to think. I see now what a fool I was to let you go.'

Bianchi's lips trembled on the edge of a smile. 'Go on.'

And Moreau did, and after half an hour the two were observed to be laughing together by Bianchi's bemused colleagues. They were even more bemused when they saw Bianchi touch Moreau's cheek with obvious affection.

Eventually Moreau dared to make his move.

'I understand you're getting ready for a launch?' he said, trying to make the question sound as casual as possible.

'Yes,' she smiled, 'that dreadful Baldwin woman. We're doing one of her projects. Do you know her? God, she's awful. I think she hates women!'

'No, I can't say I know her. Say, I wonder if I could ask you a favour.'

'Well, that depends,' Bianchi said with an arch expression lightening her face, 'I might ask you for a favour or two in return.'

'It's my little cousin. He's very into mass drivers. Has models and pictures of them all. He's asked me if I could get him a picture of the Plato one, as it's one of the biggest.'

'You've never mentioned a cousin before. What's his name?'

'Pierre,' Moreau replied, thinking very rapidly on his feet, 'A lovely little boy. I'd really hate to disappoint him.'

She pursued her lips. 'Well, strictly speaking, it's against regs.'

'I did promise him, Carina. Maybe I shouldn't have, but I did.'

She stood there, obviously thinking it over. Then: 'OK. But just a quick look. Then out!'

'That's fine. Just long enough to take a picture. You've got Baldwin's payload ready?'

'Yes.' She was suddenly suspicious. 'Why do you ask`?'

'Well, they look better when they're ready to fire, that's all.'

And so it was, ten minutes later they were standing in the gargantuan hall that held the lower end of the great rails that comprised the mass driver. When activated, the superconducting magnets would hurl a magnetised capsule into Lunar orbit without the need for propellants. It consisted of two massive rails, each the width of an average sequoia tree. At present the loading area was pressurised but when firing, the massive doors would open, exposing the rails to the Lunar vacuum.

Moreau approached the cupola that held the payload. It had a lid but it was not fully closed and as he approached, he could see the top of the probe protruding slightly.

'You know how this baby works, of course,' Bianchi said, obviously proud of her machine, 'superconductors induce eddy currents in the cupola's aluminium coil and the driver's immensely strong magnetic field blasts it into space—Hey, where are you going!'

Moreau had jumped onto one of the rails and for a moment swayed precariously on its curved surface. Then he was next to the open cupola and holding his camera over the partially revealed probe. Then, relief washing over him, he jumped back down.

'You shouldn't have done that!' she scolded, 'if you'd scratched the rail...'

'But I didn't,' he grinned, 'All done! Thanks a lot!'

She escorted him briskly back into the control area and, placing a hand on his shoulder, smiled as she looked up at him.

'So...' she purred, 'when are we getting together?'

He turned away.

'I'll be in touch.'

With a blank face and compressed lips, she stared at him as he walked out of the control room.

Twenty minutes later, Moreau and Adekola were outside his quarters. Adekola had insisted that they stay out of the room in case surveillance had now extended to Moreau.

They were huddled together over Moreau's camera, looking down at an image.

'It's not the best pic I've taken, Boss,' he said, 'but it's clear enough.'

'It is,' Adekola said, slowly and carefully, as if something had happened that she would have preferred not to happen, 'it's clear enough all right. That is not the probe Baldwin showed us. It's the probe we saw on the Lunar surface.'

They lifted their heads and their stares locked together.

'Now what do we do?'

\*\*\*

249

Adekola lay on her bed, drifting out and in of wakefulness. A crisis was approaching: one she did not want. All she had wanted was to play her part in the scientific discoveries of the century—nothing more. She did not want the coming struggle; did not want any struggle.

Parry and Jahia. She saw their faces; she heard their voices. That was what she wanted. If seeing them in peace and quietude would mean giving up her scientific career—so be it. It would be a small price to pay.

She settled into a more profound slumber. But it was not a calm one.

Once she saw that hungry blackness; watching her; waiting for her. She could feel it hunting for her; seeking to devour her. But she pushed it away; did not let it dominate her sleep.

Other images drifted past her mind's vision in that unquiet sleep.

She saw Baldwin; golden-haired, calm, ethereal Baldwin. A goddess at large in the fragile, pathetic world of humans. Baldwin: the source of her current misery. She pushed the image away.

Then she saw the picture that Parry had held up during one of their televiewer meetings.

A picture of a dog and an abstract image. Perhaps an overgrown asterisk. Perhaps a child's representation of an explosion.

Meaningless.

But the picture kept returning.

Was it badly drawn after all? What if it held a meaning?

Was the dog shown in a crude representation, or was it a reasonable picture of a very young dog—a puppy?

And the giant asterisk—had she misrepresented it also?

Could it be…

She woke up with her eyes wide open, the message thundering in her brain.

She knew that Parry and his associates had cracked at least part of the code that Richards had recorded. And he had been trying to tell her the central message in the only way that he could without alerting the watchers.

And she had been too dim-witted to understand it!

But now she did.

She also knew where she had seen the logo of the eagle and sun before.

She knew what the initials on the unknown probe stood for.

And now there could be no more procrastination; no more excuses; no more delays.

She knew what was at the very least, the central part of Baldwin's hidden plan.

And it was time to confront her.

# Eighteen: Thumos

'So what do you want to talk about?' Baldwin asked, leaning back, totally at ease in her big chair.

Adekola felt an electric force coursing through her, a power that she had never felt before when confronted by Baldwin. It was a calm certainty that this time she would not be reduced to the position of an over-awed student, the status of a humble, penitent acolyte. This would be a conversation between equals.

'I want you to tell the truth,' she replied quietly and firmly, 'The truth about what you're up to here in Plato base.'

'Why, nothing you don't already know, Tamira dear.'

'Professor Baldwin,' Adekola said, 'I don't want you calling me "Tamira" and I especially don't want you calling me "dear." From now on, until we part, address me as "Dr Adekola".'

'Very well, Dr Adekola. Why do you think something is—' Baldwin made quotation marks in the air with her hands, '*Going On.*'

'Stop fencing, Professor. Your subterfuges are over. Let me enumerate what I have learned. I have determined that the probe you showed us some time ago was a dummy. The probe you are really going to place into your wormhole is the one that Henri and I discovered hidden on the Lunar surface.'

'This is fascinating—go on.'

'I also know what the imagery on that probe refers to. The eagle and sun image is the one I saw on that ornate and rather vulgar ring worn by the unpleasant man I encountered in your office some time ago, and just happens to be the logo of a certain company.'

'Which is?'

'The letters on the probe were "ST" which rather obviously stand for "Solarian Technologies". You are working for them.'

A strange silence fell in Baldwin's office. For a moment, Adekola thought that time had stopped and that she and Baldwin were forever marooned between two instants of eternity.

Baldwin seemed absolutely motionless; even her eyelids did not blink. Then she moved, and the sudden resumption of motion gave Adekola a little start.

'Very good,' Baldwin said, in a curiously flat voice, 'but not quite good enough. It is better to say that Solarian Technologies is working for me.'

Adekola shrugged. 'Whatever. I'm sure I will work out the full relationship before our talk is over. But I haven't finished my revelations.'

'Please continue.'

'I know what your true destination is.'

Baldwin leaned forward, reducing the space between their two faces to an alarming degree. 'Oh. You have, have you. And what is the *True Destination?*'

Adekola also leaned forward so that the two women's faces were now almost touching. 'The planetary system of a star other than Alpha Centauri.'

'And that star is...?'

'Sirius.'

Baldwin leaned away from the other woman, looked up at the ceiling for a few seconds and then began clapping as she returned her gaze to Adekola.

'Brava, doctor, brava. And how did you determine that?'

'My partner has somehow managed to decode a message between you and an unknown other, which I now strongly believe to have been the CEO of Solarian Technologies. Idris was very careful not to give himself or me away to prying eyes. He held up an image. An image which I now realise to have been a rebus for "Dog Star." And "Dog Star" is an old name for Sirius. To make its meaning even more clear the dog was a puppy and some know Sirius B as "The Pup." '

Baldwin nodded. 'Yes, I saw that picture. Very clever, I thought. I wondered how long it would take you to solve it. Rather longer than I expected, I regret to say.'

Adekola would have flushed with anger if she had been capable of changing her skin tone but she was angry all the same.

'Your days of insulting me are over, Professor. But before I go to the authorities, I want the whole picture. Why have you betrayed the International Council and, in so doing, betrayed the entire future of the human race?'

Baldwin placed the fingers of both hands together, tip to tip.

'There are many reasons. I will shortly explain why I have in fact ensured the survival of humanity, rather than doomed it, as you are implying. But first a few concepts.

'Are you familiar with the notion of *thumos*?'

'No.'

'I thought not. "Thumos" is an idea deriving from Classical Greece. It encapsulates the idea of greatness, of standing out from the herd, and, more importantly, getting the respect and admiration from that herd, a respect that one has earned, one has deserved. It embodies the concepts of striving, of struggle, of contempt for the everyday, the quotidian. The individual who embodies thumos is in many ways equivalent to Nietzsche's *Übermensch*; the being who creates his own values, his own morality.' She smiled. 'Or in my case, *her* own morality.'

'And you are the embodiment of thumos? Thumos made flesh.'

'I am. But that does not mean I am contemptuous of humanity. I am contemptuous of human individuals, like you, but not the race as a whole. I want to help it. And in order to help it, I must lead it. But I'm afraid, doctor, that you still haven't asked the central question. And of course, not being able to ask the central question is a sure indication of your status as a second-rater. Or perhaps third-rater.'

'Be tolerant with me. I'm just a beginner. What is the central question?'

'Why go to Sirius rather than Alpha?'

Adekola tried to keep her face emotionless. Amazingly, that question had not occurred to her.

Baldwin swivelled her chair so that she was looking away from Adekola. She began:

'It all started when I was doing my second degree and I had

time available to me on the *al Eayn* telescope. I was doing some research on quantum entanglement, and some subconscious command made me examine the Sirian system. I discovered a huge belt of planetoids, rich in the Lanthanide elements, especially praseodymium, dysprosium and erbium. In concentrations higher than anything in the Solar system where they're vanishingly rare. Megatonnes of them!'

'So?'

'There you are, doctor! You don't keep up. Recent research has shown that the lanthanides can be used to stabilise quantum computers and make them robust, reliable everyday objects.' She leaned forward close to Adekola, a dangerous light in her eyes. 'Think, doctor, a quantum computer in every home! And as a side effect, it would revolutionise robotics. Instead of the clumsy jokes we have now, we could have an army of efficient, effective humanoid companions to aid us as we go out to the stars. Why with an army of intelligent, truly autonomous robots by our sides we'll have this entire galaxy by the tail! Settling the Centauri system will be a sideshow!'

Adekola felt herself beginning to quail under this woman's messianic certainties. She fought to keep herself as an equal partner in this debate.

'So you will be the great leader of an adoring humanity. But is there anything in it for you, other than abstract glory, that is?'

'At last, doctor! You are finally beginning to show some practical intelligence. Yes, of course there is. And that "thing" is riches—incredible, incalculable riches!'

'How so?'

'When I launch the probe into the Sirian system, that system will become the property of Solarian Technologies. Are you aware that if a private company reaches an astronomical body first then that body becomes its property?'

'I am aware. But it has to do it without public funding.'

Baldwin nodded. 'Brava again, doctor. But you seem to be unaware that I spun off TransTerrestrial Solutions some time ago as a private company. And I am its legally registered CEO. So the Sirian system will be a joint venture between Solarian Technologies and *my* company. None of this would be possible without my wormholes, so there is no danger of Mr Wójcik deciding to buy me out violently. I have nothing to fear from a man who struggles with the Ten Times Table—even if he is CEO of Solarian Technologies.'

'So what did he contribute?'

'The capital to persuade the International Council to allow me to form an independent company. His organisation had the necessary contacts to raise the sums involved and he has helped me to set up various funds which will increase both my wealth and my control over world finance. And, of course, he will have a monopoly on the new computers and new robots.'

'So you just bribed the Council?'

'Basically. I did have to sleep with some of them.' She laughed. 'I say "sleep". One old guy was so nervous that in the end he couldn't get it up. I was then able to blackmail him with the threat of making that public. That was an amusing diversion.'

Adekola pulled a face. 'Please. Too much information. So what happens to you when all this goes public, as it will have to?'

Baldwin shrugged. 'Why should anything happen to me? Have I actually done anything illegal? Am I the first entrepreneur who has bent the law a little? It's a grey area. And in any case, I'll shortly be able to hire the best lawyers on Earth. Nothing will happen to me. Money is the single greatest determinant of power known to humanity. And as time goes by, more and more people will realise the wonderful thing I've done for them. Year by year I will become more influential, more respected, more loved. I'll have the best anti-ageing drugs money can buy, and I'll be able to fund research into better ones. I intend to be around for a very long time. You might call it "thumos".'

'But one small point, Professor. Sirius is about twice as far away as Alpha Centauri. Can you extend your wormhole that far?'

'A good point, doctor, but one I have, of course, already considered. It will take the combined output of all four fusion reactors—but they will be enough. You can quote me on that.'

'But there are still unknowns. We have intensively mapped the space between the Solar system and Alpha in considerable detail. We know that there are no obstacles, such as free-floating planets, on the line of sight between here and Alpha. Can you be that sure over at over twice the distance?'

'Once again, a good point, doctor, and one I cannot be quite so dismissive over. I have not exhaustively mapped the intervening space. But the diameter of the wormhole throat is infinitesimal compared to the vastness of space. It is very unlikely that it would meet anything in such a gigantic volume of space. No, Wójcik will get his rare earth metals and I will get my money.' She laughed. 'I must be careful, I'll have so much I'll have to ensure it doesn't collapse under its own mass into a black hole!'

Adekola did not laugh. She stared at the beautiful woman on the other side of the desk and wondered if once again, she had been outwitted. Then she remembered something.

'Phil Richards. Did you have anything to do with his death?'

Baldwin's face became absolutely still, absolutely emotionless. 'I had nothing to do with poor Phil's death. It was a tragic accident.'

'A very improbable one.'

'There you go again, doctor. Under the frequentist interpretation of probability, any non-zero probability must eventually be actualised. I had nothing to do with his death, you have my word on it. I was aware, of course, that he was spying on me but I intended to have the same conversation with him that I am now having with you. And then he was taken from us.'

Adekola relaxed slightly. At least she wasn't dealing with a murderer.

'So you admit you were bugging Phil. And are bugging me.'

'Yes. I am a control freak, I admit it. I demand absolute loyalty from my staff and I need to know that they are fully on-board with me. I went too far. I'm sorry.'

'You're not an easy woman to work for, that's for sure. Bugging your own people is more than a little extreme. But I'm certain it says more about what kind of person you are, than it ever said about me and Phil.'

'So where do we go from here?' Baldwin said.

'It's very simple. You go public with what you've done. I'll need confirmation from the International Council that you set up TransTerrestrial Solutions legitimately. If you didn't, then it's a short to medium length prison sentence for you.'

'No.' Baldwin's face became like steel, without the slightest hint of softness, of gentleness. 'That I cannot accept. The launch to Sirius must go ahead. You know what the Council is like. It's a talking shop for old men. It'll be years before they reach a decision, one way or the other. My career will be over, even after I'm exonerated. Look, Tamira, I know it would insult you if I offered you a slice of the profits, so I won't, but your career would be over as well. If people think I'm the Big Bad Wolf, won't that rub off on you, as my trusted second-in-command?'

'I thought I was a second or third rater.'

Baldwin made a dismissive gesture. 'I was angry at being questioned. I don't take criticism very well. But I know that without you, I'd still be searching for a way to generate negative matter. You gave me the clue I needed. But don't you see, even if you're not interested in the money, that this is your big chance for scientific immortality? You and I together—two ballsy women who opened up the stars to humanity and finally put our civilisation on strong—no—on indestructible foundations!'

Baldwin put out her hand to Adekola. 'Tamira, I can't do this without you. I need you!'

Adekola was silent, while thought after thought chased each other through her turbulent mind. Then she looked up from her hands and stared at Baldwin.

'If Moreau and I help you this one last time, then you'll go to the Council?'

Baldwin nodded. 'Of course. You have my word on that.'

'And after that, you and I will part. We will part forever.'

'Yes.'

The two women shook hands and as Baldwin pulled away, she said, 'Yes. You and I will part forever.'

# Nineteen: Behemoth

'It all seems too easy,' Parry eventually said.

'In what way?'

'Bugging you, just to check if you're loyal. Who would go to all that trouble?'

'Baldwin would,' Adekola said, firmly, 'That's the kind of ultra-micro-manager she is. I've never given her any work without her checking it twice before accepting it.'

Parry looked unconvinced. 'OK, we'll let it go. The important thing is—your damn project is finally coming to an end and you'll be coming home for good. No more Elizabeth Baldwin—ever. You must promise me that you'll have no more to do with that woman, no matter what she promises you.'

Adekola laughed. 'Don't worry about that. She'll have a lot on her plate when this rigmarole ends. She thinks she's going to be the richest woman in the Solar system, but it may not be that simple. She's the best there is in physics but the world of finance and company law must be new to her. She might be an old woman by the time it's sorted out.'

'Couldn't happen to a nicer person,' Parry grunted. 'But you must promise not to go off-world again. Jahia's growing up and you're missing half of it!'

Adekola winced at those words. 'Don't say that, Idris. You know I've only done it to boost our income. And bringing this project to an end will put my name in lights. All sorts of doors will open!'

'As long as Baldwin takes the heat for changing the destination of the wormhole. It's not exactly the Project Independence we all signed up to.'

Adekola felt a residual twinge of loyalty. 'Yes, but she's explained it will make the success of Project Independence much more likely. With improved robot helpers and robust quantum computers, settling the Centauri system will be a walk in the park.'

'OK,' Parry said, 'I hope this is one of the very last times we talk about Elizabeth Baldwin rather than us. Anyway, here's someone who wants to speak to you.'

Jahia came into the screen and Adekola gasped slightly on seeing how much she had changed.

'Hello Mommy,' the child said, 'when are you coming home?'

Waves of guilt swept over Adekola. *God, she's growing up so fast!*

'Soon, darling, very soon,' she managed to say, 'And Mommy's never going to go away again!'

'Yes,' Parry said, looking from Jahia to Adekola, 'Mommy's never going away again. No matter what doors open for her.'

Adekola nodded vigorously at the images on the screen.

'Yes, that's right. No matter what doors are opened.'

\*\*\*

'The probe is in low Lunar orbit,' Estefan said. 'We have established contact and all readings are nominal.'

'Very good,' Baldwin said, her eyes fixed on the softly glowing displays and their fluctuating numbers. 'Reactors ready?'

'They are,' Estefan said, 'the final test firings were completely on the button.'

Normally Baldwin would have criticised the use of figurative language but she was now too tense to make such minor corrections. Adekola could see the strain she was under by the fact that she had developed a slight tremor in the hands. If she had been sitting on the other side, she would have been able to see a pulse jumping in Baldwin's neck.

What she did see, however, were two large men sitting in the shadows in a far corner. They were reminiscent of the burly males she had seen in the dining area during her first breakfast in Plato Base.

*Why are they here?* she thought.

There was suddenly no more time to worry about the

inconsequential. The klaxon blared.

'First sixty second period,' Baldwin said in a strained voice that Adekola hardly recognised. 'Reactor One.'

Once again Reactor One sprang into life. Once again, a captive sun formed in its heart.

The klaxon.

'Second sixty second period. Reactor Two.'

Reactor Two soon held a blazing sphere of fusing matter.

The klaxon.

'Third sixty second period. Reactor Three.'

Reactor Three's core flashed into incandescent fury.

The klaxon.

'Fourth sixty second period. Reactor Four.'

Now all four mighty reactors were on-line but, like greyhounds straining at the leash, they had not yet released their titanic energies but still held them blazing in coruscant impatience in their dreadful interiors. Temperatures beyond comprehension, power unimaginable. Like the awful pressure of megatonnes of water seeking a weakness in a crumbling dam, those terrible forces hungrily sought release; release to break free to rend and annihilate entire worlds.

Baldwin flung the red switch to the right.

And out on the plain the eldritch indigo-violet light came into being.

But this time it was not a minor patch of luminescence.

The entire walled plain of Plato became stained in that unnatural colour. Indeed, it would have spread beyond Plato had not the crater's scarred ramparts blocked its path and flung it back on itself.

Observers on Earth saw a strange indigo-violet eye staring back at them from the Lunar wastes and were afraid.

And now the cascades of energy swept out from the four reactors, merging into an unstoppable flood of power; power which brooked no resistance to its imperious flow.

The massive parabolic dishes sprang obediently into life at Baldwin's command but this time their centres did not display a dull-red glow like the comforting colour of a banked fire.

No, each dish in its entirety abruptly blazed into savagely blinding white brilliance.

And above the Lunar surface a great and terrible black sphere came into being, surrounded by a shimmering ring made from twisted and warped images of unimaginably distant objects from the ends of the visible universe.

Adekola goggled at the size of it as it burst onto everyone's screens. A choking gasp of terror rose from all those present, with the single exception of Baldwin.

It was too huge, too overpowering, too ineffably mighty to be the work of weak and foolish humans. It lowered above the surface like a rogue planet, as if it were bearing down on them to crush them into nothingness.

The behemoth filled the whole of Adekola's screen, forcing her to zoom out twice to be able to see its circumference. She had an overwhelming urge to run, to hide and cower from this horrific entity. To plead and beg with it to leave them in peace.

Then Baldwin's voice came again and she felt a great sense of relief.

Baldwin was not frightened. It was she that controlled this monster. It would obey her commands like a faithful hound.

'Manoeuvring probe into the mouth,' she said, making small, delicate movements with the controls.

At the adjusted scale of Adekola's screen, the probe was too small to be detectable but after a few minutes, Baldwin said, 'Probe safely in the throat.'

She turned away from the controls and looked at her people. All her tension, her worry, her fear perhaps, had been washed away.

The old Baldwin was back; serene, untroubled, fully the mistress of all eventualities; radiant; beautiful. A goddess.

'We're on our way,' she said, in a quiet, unmoved, untroubled voice as if she were starting a simple car journey to the local shopping centre.

The applause was wild. Everyone, except the two men in the

263

shadows, rushed forward to congratulate her. She nodded with simple gratitude, displaying that special smile that had melted so many hearts before with its lovely radiance.

'Thank you. This is your triumph as well as mine. History will never forget us. Now back to your stations, please.'

Adekola had also risen but having been slower than the rest it took her less time to return to her devices.

There was a message on one of the screens.

She glanced at it, a happy smile playing over her features.

The smile froze, and she leaned forward, her brow furrowed.

What was this?

The message read: 30 OCTILLION KILOGRAMS OF MATTER IN THROAT.

She stared at it, unable to process its import.

She refreshed the screen, expecting the crazy display to reappear with something believable.

The message said: 30 OCTILLION KILOGRAMS OF MATTER IN THROAT.

She stood motionless, momentarily deprived of the ability to move. The blood roared in her head. The message could not be right—thirty octillion kilograms, why—why, that was fifteen times the mass of Jupiter!

One more try.

The message read: 30 OCTILLION KILOGRAMS OF MATTER IN THROAT.

Something had entered the wormhole at its far end; something monstrous was rising up out of the depths!

Now convinced of existential danger, she spun on her heel and screamed, 'Professor. Something's wrong! Come here, quick!'

Alarmed by her tone, Baldwin was with her in an instant. She too stared at the screen for some time, also unable to immediately absorb its terrifying message. Then:

'Something's entered the wormhole at the Sirian end.'

Adekola stared at her. 'Yes, obviously! But that mass—it's

264

gigantic! Bigger than Jupiter —and it's coming our way!'

'That much mass,' Baldwin muttered, 'perhaps a brown dwarf.'

'It can't be a brown dwarf,' Adekola shouted, 'a brown dwarf is far too big to enter the mouth. It must be something much smaller!'

Her mind whirled. That much mass. Small size.

Both women reached the conclusion at the same time.

'A collapsar,' Baldwin said, running her hand over her forehead, 'a neutron star, or...'

'A black hole,' Adekola finished for her. 'A fucking black hole. What have you done!'

Baldwin turned away and started running for her controls. 'It's OK! I can fix it!'

Adekola ran after her.

'You can't fix it. Every millisecond it's getting closer. This is the bloody doom of stars you were gabbling about! And you've caused it. Kill the wormhole!'

'No, no,' Baldwin muttered, as her fingers danced over the controls, 'negative matter. That will deflect it, you stupid bitch. We must reach the Sirian system!'

Adekola grabbed her shoulders and spun Baldwin around so that she was facing her.

'There isn't time! You've got to kill the wormhole. If that thing gets any closer its momentum will bring it down on top of us. Kill the wormhole!'

It was then Adekola felt strong hands on her shoulders and she in turn was spun around. And found herself staring up at Estefan.

'Leave the professor alone!' he shouted, 'she knows what she's doing!'

'Negative matter,' Baldwin muttered, as if talking to herself, 'must have negative matter.'

Estefan suddenly found himself torn away from Adekola as Moreau interposed himself between them.

'Get off Tamira,' he said, 'or I'll lay you out!'

The whole room descended into chaos as technicians abandoned their posts and began running for the door, screaming. It seemed as if the hitherto calm Control Room had been transmuted into the antechamber of Hell. The two men in the shadows stood up and began to move towards the struggling group.

Estefan was holding onto Adekola with one hand. Baldwin was bent over the instrument panel, still muttering. Moreau was trying to pull Estefan away from Adekola.

Then the two men were on them. A single blow sent Moreau flying, taking Estefan with him. The other man bore down on Adekola but in so doing collided with Baldwin, knocking her away from the panel.

Adekola seized her chance. She grasped the red switch and smashed it hard to the left.

The fusion reactors ceased their outpourings of power.

The indigo-violet light vanished.

The parabolic dishes changed from white-hot, to yellow, to orange, to dull, dying red.

The wormhole disappeared.

And a heavy blow sent Adekola into unconsciousness.

# Twenty: A Confession

When Adekola awoke, she found herself back in her room. She realised by the fact that her room was still intact and she was still alive that the black hole had not impacted onto Plato Base.

She swung her feet off the bed and very slowly stood up. She put her hand to the back of the head where a deep, throbbing ache resided. So it could not be that long after the terror in the Control Room, maybe she had relaxed too soon.

But as the hours dragged by and doom did not arrive she concluded that her action had indeed saved the Moon from being obliterated.

Then she noticed that her memory watch was missing.

*Does she know about that as well!* she wondered bitterly. *No matter. The memories of what happened are safely encoded. Idris and Jahia will know the truth.*

There was nothing to do; the televiewer was dead. The door was locked. No-one called. Each dead, meaningless hour was followed by another.

She fell asleep.

When she awoke there was a tray on the table bearing a pitcher of water, a tumbler, and a plate with some simple food items.

She drank some water and ate some of the food. Then sat back on the bed and watched the door.

She fell asleep.

When she awoke again the tray had gone.

And so it went on. Eventually the light dimmed and she realised that this particular day was drawing to a close. She lay there in the darkness, certain that she would not sleep, but eventually she did.

When she awoke the light was on, and there was a tray of food and water on the table.

Two more empty days dragged themselves to a monotonous conclusion. Adekola began to feel some of the horror of solitary confinement.

Then about half-way through the third day, the door suddenly opened, startling her out of her now semi-permanent dozing state. One of the large, muscular men stood in the doorway, filling most of it.

'Boss wants to see you,' he said tonelessly, 'come with me.'

To Adekola's surprise, she was taken back to the Control Room whose huge space was now empty apart from one figure.

Elizabeth Baldwin.

She waved to a chair in front of her and gave Adekola her old, dazzling smile.

'Tamira!' she said, 'lovely to see you again! Please take a seat.'

Adekola obeyed and the large man departed leaving the two women alone in the vast room.

'How are you now, dear?' Baldwin inquired, tilting her head slightly to show her concern.

'I told you not to call me "dear",' Adekola said through tightly compressed lips. Her heart was hammering.

'Now, now dear,' Baldwin replied, 'let's have none of that unnecessary nastiness.'

'What happened to the collapsar?' Adekola said, ignoring Baldwin's theatrical sweetness.

'Oh, that little thing. As I said, negative matter was the answer. Without me the thing would have gone through the inner Solar system on a wrecking-ball hyperbola. There wouldn't be much left.'

'Without you, there wouldn't have been a collapsar on a wrecking-ball hyperbola in the first place.'

Baldwin appeared not to have heard that comment and continued: 'A pulse of N-matter deflected it so that its perihelion was just inside the orbit of Jupiter. It's on its way out of the system as we speak. Never to be seen again. Its passage will shake things up in our region for a while so we're abandoning the Lunar bases, *pro tempore.*'

'You feel no responsibility for what you did.'

Baldwin shook her head. 'That's a big fat "No" from me,

268

Tamira. It was a one in quintillion chance that something happened to be on the line of sight from here to Sirius. That's all. Just bad luck.'

'Which would not have happened if you'd done a proper survey instead of rushing to get those pretty hands on all that money.'

Baldwin looked down at her hands. 'Oh, you like them, do you? I've got some new polish. Look.' And she held out her hands for Adekola to inspect.

Adekola rose from the chair and took two steps.

'Don't.' Baldwin lifted the revolver which had been resting in her lap the whole time. 'Sit back down. You don't think I'd be alone with you without any protection, do you? You look like a wrestler so maybe you could behave like one if pushed.'

Adekola sat back down, breathing heavily. She could see now that there was another small device in that lap.

'Where's Henri?'

Baldwin shrugged. 'To be honest, I'm not sure. But wherever he is, I can guarantee that he's beyond all earthly worries.'

'You had him killed.'

Baldwin stared back unmoved, emotionlessly. 'Next question.'

'You had Richards killed.'

Baldwin sighed. 'That I did, poor lad. And he never did get a girlfriend.'

'Why did you murder him?'

'Come on; you can't possibly be that stupid. He was about to find out that most of the Council didn't know that I'd hived off TTS. I'd only bribed or seduced the key players. If he'd told them, the whole timetable would have gone to Hell and Mr Wójcik would have been very, very angry with me. I knew that I was vulnerable to a half-decent legal team locking me up, but I knew if I could present everyone with a lucrative *fait accompli* then my oodles of money would start talking for me and I'd be safe.'

'Isn't your gangster friend very, very angry with you now? I don't see any superhighway from here to Sirius.'

'That is a distinct possibility. But to head him off, I have to do two things: One, Assure him that what has happened is only temporary, and Two, find someone to blame for this debacle who isn't me. Mr Wójcik is very primitive about these things. If I can't find someone else to blame he's likely to make me eat my own intestines before killing me.

'And that's where you come in.'

Fear pricked over Adekola's flesh like a swarm of biting ants. But all she said was: 'Oh? And why should I take responsibility? It was me who saved all of us. For all your wonderful intelligence, you were in a blind panic. If I hadn't killed the wormhole, the collapsar would have crashed down on all of us and eaten the whole bloody Moon! For starters!'

'That's your interpretation of events,' Baldwin said, shaking her head in pitying disbelief, 'but you *will* take all the blame and I *will* rebuild my relationship with Mr Wójcik.'

'There were witnesses. Those men who slugged me. They must be in Wójcik's employ. They know what you did.'

Baldwin laughed. 'For God's sake, Tamira! Grow up! Those yahoos had no idea what was going on. All they saw was you attacking me. They're inbred cousins to an Australopithecus with learning difficulties. As long as I throw them a banana now and again, they're happy!

'No. You will take the blame, Tamira.'

'Make me.'

'Of course. I didn't expect you to volunteer.' She pointed off to one corner of the room. 'Do you see that screen?'

Adekola nodded.

'OK. No doubt you have heard of "Deep Fakes"? it's a very old technology. First used in anger in the twenty-first century, I believe. But it is much, much better now. Mr Wójcik supplied the technology but I wrote the screenplay. Watch.'

Baldwin lifted the small object from her lap and her delicate fingers moved over its surface. The large screen in the shadows flashed into life.

Adekola gasped. It was her apartment and there were Parry and Jahia playing in the centre of the room, near the fountain.

'How do you know so much about my place?'

'Isn't Jahia adorable?' Baldwin said, ignoring the question, 'And Idris! How on earth did you bag him! He's so far out of your league, it beats the shit out of me!'

Open-mouthed, Adekola watched the little domestic scene, her heart aching. She wanted to reach out and touch them, to hug them, to kiss them. To nuzzle Jahia's hair, to feel Parry's arms around her!

'Keep watching,' came Baldwin's voice, crashing into her fantasy, 'this is the best bit.'

The door to the apartment suddenly burst open and two large men, looking very much like those that had been in the Control Room, rushed at Parry and Jahia. They were carrying long serrated knives.

For a few seconds Adekola watched the scene of absolute horror that was played out in front of her. Then she could take no more. She closed her eyes and put her hands over her ears.

'Stop it! Stop it! Stop it!' she screamed.

'It's amazing,' Baldwin remarked, 'one wouldn't think there was so much blood in such a small child.'

Adekola could tell that the screen had gone dark and removed her hands from her eyes.

'I know precisely where you live,' Baldwin said in a cold, calm voice, 'one word from me to Wójcik and what you saw will happen. And you will be to blame.'

Adekola stared long and hard at the beautiful woman opposite her.

'How can monsters like you exist in the real world?' she said, injecting each word with venomous hatred, 'how can things like you be real? Monster.'

Baldwin gave a thin smile. 'Have you learned nothing from me, Tamira? The laws of physics care nothing for Tamira Adekola: why should I? This universe is sublimely indifferent as to whether we wriggling things live or die. Despite what naïve

271

fools have prattled, this universe is not meant for life. It hates life. It kills living things with blasts of radiation, with supernovae, a million different ways to die. Why should I be any different? The universe is my teacher.'

She leaned back lazily, keeping the revolver trained on Adekola's heart.

'Now, back to business. Here's the deal. You make a taped confession, admitting that it was who you brought the black hole down on us and nearly destroyed the world. Make sure you say, "doom of stars". I like that phrase—it's so poetic!'

'Why not Deep Fake me confessing?'

'There are ways that experts can distinguish such fakes from the real thing. You will do the real thing.'

Adekola was no longer looking at Baldwin. Dully, emptily, she stared down at her hands; her fleshy hands with the stubby fingers.

'And what do I get?'

'The life of your family. Isn't that enough?'

Adekola finally looked up.

'I'll do it.'

*** 

'You're on camera,' said Baldwin, 'but please don't smile, dear. This is meant to be serious.'

Adekola stared at the lens; the lens that would soon be recording the lies she would be making; lies to save her family.

One thought kept echoing and re-echoing in her mind: *She doesn't know about the sphere! Idris and Jahia will know the truth!*

Baldwin had told her what to say and, being Baldwin, had made her go through it again and again, until every word came easily. To the last, she was the demanding perfectionist.

'Now!'

She looked at the recording apparatus. A red light had appeared. She took a shuddering breath.

'Hello,' she said. *Does one start a confession with a greeting?* she

272

thought wildly.

'My name is Tamira Adekola, and I have something very important to tell you.' She glanced into the shadows beyond the machine. Baldwin was there. The shadow was so deep that she could not tell if Baldwin was holding a weapon. Best to assume she was.

She did not look in that direction again.

'All the problems you are having, all the climatic changes; the disruption to your normal lives; the disturbances in the skies— I am responsible for all of them. I caused that dreadful object to enter our home space; it was I who brought this menace into your lives from outside; this Doom of Stars.

'For some time I have been working to undermine my superior Professor Elizabeth Baldwin. I repaid her help and kindness with treachery and malice. I subverted her plan to peacefully explore another star system and give our people a new home. I was jealous of her and wanted my name to go down in history. Unable to match her achievements, I decided to claim them for my own. For my own aggrandisement, I changed the destination of the wonderful mechanism that she had created through her determination and self-sacrifice.

'At the last moment, I seized control of the experiment and sent the probe off to another star system, one Professor Baldwin had said was too distant for us safely to attempt.

'And I paid the price. I accidentally captured that black hole and caused it to enter our system, with the results that you are familiar with.

'I paid the price. And now you are paying the price for my jealousy and my stupidity. Only Professor Baldwin's heroic efforts at the last moment saved us from an even greater disaster.

'I do not expect you to forgive me. I, and I alone, am responsible for this Doom of Stars.'

The red light winked out.

From the shadows there came the sound of cynical clapping. And then Baldwin:

'Brava, Tamira. Perfect. It is obvious to me that you made a

273

big mistake in opting for a career in science. The theatre has lost a great performer in you. All that applause you have missed out on; all those bouquets that could have been thrust into your hands; all the messages of love from your adoring public. What a silly woman you've been.'

Adekola said nothing. She knew that nothing she could say would have the slightest effect on Baldwin's plans for her.

One thing she was determined on: she would not beg.

'What now?' she finally said, her mouth so dry she could barely shape the words.

Baldwin ignored the question.

She came out of the shadows and she was indeed holding a revolver. Once again Adekola found herself looking up at her. Adekola saw those perfect lips part as she spoke.

'You know that object you captured is truly remarkable. It's heading back out into interstellar space but it's straightforward to track: it's so small it's shining very brightly in Hawking radiation. It will soon evaporate; soon in cosmic terms of course.'

Adekola was silent. What did anything matter now?

Baldwin placed her hand under Adekola's chin and roughly jerked it upwards.

'Look at me when I'm talking to you, dear. This is interesting. All you have to do is pretend you can understand it.

'Remember that little Ph.D. thesis that you did so long ago? Well, this hole is the one you wrote about—a Reissner-Nordström-de Sitter object. Now, isn't that a lovely coincidence? A kind of wheel coming full circle, isn't it?'

Adekola did not reply.

Baldwin snorted. 'Oh well, be like that! I'm trying to show an interest in your work and all you can do is just sit there like the dumb bitch you are.'

'You've never shown any interest in my work! All you care about is being so, so brilliant and pretty and making fools out of men! You have this burning desire to prove you're cleverest woman there's ever been, that you're better than everybody in the universe. You like to think that everyone else is just some

274

kind of pathetic monkey, taught to do a few tricks. That's because you are a psychopath!'

'Sticks and stones, dear,' murmured Baldwin, 'Sticks and stones.'

Adekola's voice was faster, louder as her rage took hold of her, sending her into trembling, shaking, frenzy.

'How can you do this to me,' she yelled, 'how can you do this to another woman?'

Baldwin shrugged. 'Oh, you're a woman, are you? Now you tell me!'

Adekola fixed the other with a burning stare of undiluted hatred.

'Are you quite so clever, Elizabeth? I think you've underestimated the effects that the black hole will have on the inner system. I think all that mass will distort the orbits of the Moon and the inner planets, making them more elliptical. God knows what that will do to the climate.

'And the asteroid belt. Will that be unaffected? The hole came very close to it. Imagine if a few of them are deflected into Earth-crossing trajectories!'

Baldwin did not answer but her face was cold and still. There was no smile on those lips. She did not speak.

'One more thing. Its perihelion was just inside the orbit of Jupiter. Where was Jupiter when that happened?'

Baldwin turned away. 'Oh, this is so tiresome! Can't you think of anything more interesting to talk about?'

'Like what?'

'Oh, affairs of the heart, shall we say!' Baldwin trilled, in a sick parody of a girlish giggle, 'the Moon is being abandoned. I'll be back on Earth soon. I think I'll take a visit to meet Jahia and that lovely Australian you've kept squirrelled away. I like him. He likes me. Perhaps we'll just see where our hearts will take us!'

Then Adekola did rise from the chair.

Baldwin raised the pistol. 'I think not.' She looked beyond her captive. 'Now!'

Suddenly Adekola found strong arms were winding a thin

cord around her. She struggled but the man was massively too strong for her. And the cord was unbreakable.

Baldwin nodded to the unseen man. 'Very good. Go now; I'll call you when I want you.'

Adekola carried on struggling for a while, but finally realising it was hopeless, slumped into impotent immobility.

'Idris will kill you.'

'No. He will learn to love me. Now, I've never cared for that messy business of actually giving birth, all that blood and slime, far too biological. But I will probably be able to care for Jahia. Who knows—she may grow up to be a great scientist. Like her new mother.'

Adekola screamed.

'Now, now, where's your scientific detachment?' Baldwin said. 'Don't worry. You won't be seeing it.'

'What are you going to do to me?'

'Why kill you, of course. Good God, you really are stupid. Did you honestly think I would have you hanging around, like some kind of pet? Ready to blab your version of events to anyone who would listen. Do you think I would trust you to keep silent all the time while I was fucking Idris? Now come on, be realistic.'

Adekola screamed again. Then, lowering her head, she stared long and hard at Baldwin.

'I can't kill you; I know that. But Idris will. Idris will.'

Baldwin smiled again. 'Yes, dear. We shall see.'

# Twenty One: Doom of Stars

Adekola returned slowly to consciousness. The strange taste in her mouth and the raging headache told her that she had been drugged.

She looked around, seeing unfamiliar surroundings. She was not in any room that she recalled from Plato Base. And yet—there was something about these surroundings that stirred a memory.

Then she had it. She was in a type of short-range shuttle. Almost immediately on that thought, she could feel a light vibration in the deck. If it was a shuttle, it was under power. She was going somewhere.

She looked around, her misty vision slowly clearing. It was definitely a shuttle. She had been lying on the floor but not far away were rows of the functional bucket seats which this type of craft carried. Near her was a porthole, to which she hurried.

Looking out, she could see the brightly lit Lunar northern region; the Mare Frigoris was directly below her, and she could see the Alpine Valley and the dark walled plain of Plato itself.

She was on a low Lunar trajectory.

But why was she in space? Why hadn't Baldwin just shot her where she sat? Why send her into space?

Was she alone? A wonderful thought made her shake. Perhaps she had been rescued!

'Hello!' she yelled, 'anybody here?'

Her voice echoed around her, rebounding in a decreasing crescendo from the far corners of the vessel.

She was alone.

She slumped into one of the seats, despair once again flooding over her.

As she sat there she noticed that not far away there was a televiewer and below it a handwritten note had been attached,

She walked over to it and read the note.

It said: PRESS THE RED BUTTON.

277

What scheme of Baldwin's was this? she wondered, now under no illusions that she was not still in captivity. She pressed the button.

Almost immediately, Baldwin's smiling face appeared.

'Tamira!' Baldwin said, her face seeming to display genuine pleasure, 'I hope you're feeling better after your little nap. Don't try to reply to me; this is a recording. I'm already on my way to Greater New York.

'Now you're no doubt wondering why you're on a shuttle and why I haven't killed you as I said I was going to. Well, I am going to kill you but in a special, truly wonderful way. You see I've been very busy and I've found a way of generating a wormhole without all those silly people running around, thinking they're doing something important. A software solution. The wormhole will only be in existence for a very short time so you needn't worry about the collapsar being pulled back into the inner system. It will shudder for a few seconds but then continue on its merry way, back into the outer darkness. But the amusing thing is, you'll be inside it.'

Involuntarily Adekola's mouth fell open in horrified astonishment.

'My dear,' the recorded Baldwin continued, 'now you've recovered from the shock, I will explain. You see, the story is that you were so disgusted with yourself, so full of self-loathing, that you have decided to commit suicide by flying into the black hole. You knocked me out and stole a shuttle, having first switched on the automatic wormhole generation mechanism which I showed you a few months ago. Of course, I hadn't devised it back then but no one will ever know that. I doubt if anyone will be visiting Plato Base for a very, very long time.'

'Monster,' Adekola whispered into the emptiness of the shuttle, 'monster.'

'Now, here's something that a top-notch scientist like you might find interesting: the shuttle is carrying a large amount of N-matter to make absolutely sure that the wormhole doesn't start pulling the hole back into the system. A belt and braces solution, if you will. There is actually a small possibility that it will save you from spaghettification when you cross the event horizon. I can't be sure; the equations are fiendishly difficult, and I haven't had time to solve them. And to be quite frank, I can't really be bothered.'

The smile on the face of the recorded Baldwin became radiant. 'But think of it! What an honour! What a triumph! The first human being to cross into a black hole! Your name will live forever.' The smile vanished. 'Of course, generations to come will curse you and say that such a fate was what you deserved and that they will hope you were torn into little, teeny-weeny bits when you entered the hole. So you will be doubly famous. Or is that infamous? I'm not quite sure.'

Adekola began to weep. With her head bowed, she watched her tears form little shining drops on the metal floor.

'Now look,' Baldwin continued, 'I really must be going now. I'm not quite sure when you recovered consciousness but the wormhole should have formed by now and you should be just about to enter it.'

The image blew a kiss.

'Bon voyage.'

The televiewer went black.

Adekola looked around desperately. She didn't doubt that Baldwin had spoken the truth and she was about to suffer a fate unparalleled in all of human history.

Was there a way off this shuttle? Even a vacuum suit that she could get into and then eject herself? Anything other than what Baldwin had planned for her!

Panting in her desperation, she looked behind her. This was the smallest type of shuttle and she could see that there were no suits at that end. She turned and ran forward towards the nose.

The doors opened and she found herself in the pilots' cockpit.

And there it was.

The mouth of the wormhole.

An evil black sphere, ringed with the blurred, twisted images of distant stars and galaxies.

It was growing bigger and bigger as she watched.

There was to be no last minute escape.

And then she was inside the throat.

Ahead of her she saw shining rings of light; glowing rings that she knew were photons captured by the spatial lensing of warped space. To either side the soft light was stretched into the crazy patterns like those of an old fashioned fairground mirror; ahead were ring after ring of light, interposed with fathomless darkness, shrinking down to a vanishing point.

A great calmness came over her. There was nothing more to do. There could be no more struggle, no more striving.

Ahead the light echoes ended and beyond them there was nothing but the deepest, darkest, starless night.

She knew that blackness.

She had seen it in her dreams and known it was waiting for her; waiting for her to enter the dread cave of no return.

She held out her arms as if embracing the darkness.

And Adekola felt the event horizon take her.

# Twenty Two: The Visitor

Parry watched the meteorite as it flashed above Greater New York. Its head was a brilliant yellow-white and behind it stretched a swirling tail of angry black smoke. It was gone in an instant, heading out towards the Great Lakes. Some minutes after it had disappeared, he felt the building sway slightly and then came the noise of the impact like the distant roaring of a gigantic lion.

*That was close!* he thought *And they're getting bigger!*

'What was that thing, Daddy?' Jahia said, and she hugged his leg in her fear. 'I didn't like it.'

He smoothed her hair. 'It's alright, Jahia. Daddy's here. Those things can't hurt you.'

*If only that were true!* he thought. *But it's not. If one of those things should come down on the city...*

Should he leave? he wondered, head out of the city?

But where? Nowhere was safe. One point on the planet was as vulnerable as any other. Since the black hole had disturbed the swarm of near-Earth asteroids many had collided and the shards and splinters were being spread over the orbits of the inner planets. And eventually one that had not been shattered, and was still possessed of megatonne menace, would come thundering down, annihilating whatever was beneath it.

There was nowhere to go; nowhere to hide. All anyone could do was weather the storm and hope that they would still be alive after it ended.

'Go and play for a while, Jahia' he said, 'then Daddy will come and read to you.'

It was no good putting a children's programme on the viewer; emergency reports were now interrupting the normal schedules on an increasingly frequent basis. Although his daughter could not understand all the words, she could certainly pick up the tone of worry and, yes, outright fear that was now infecting the airways.

After his daughter had gone to her room, he paced back and forth near the window, occasionally glancing out to see if any other peril was streaking across the sky. Outside there were ominous reminders of the encircling dangers which from nowhere had burst into everyone's lives and brought fear into their every waking moment. Two days earlier a blazing fireball had come down into the city and exploded a few hundred metres above the great towers. The resulting shockwave had smashed hundreds of windows and flying meteoric shrapnel had bitten great gouges into the stonework.

*If only those fools hadn't decided to save money by not developing proper asteroid defences!* he thought bitterly, *always the short-term. Always penny pinching!*

What to do?

He looked across at the memory sphere which held a record of the terrible things his partner had witnessed. The power of her emotions during the crisis had flashed between the worlds and deeply engraved themselves within its depths. He had seen them in the sphere. Like Adekola, he had recoiled when the final wormhole had burst onto her screen. Like Adekola, he had pushed Baldwin out of the way and smashed the control switch to the left, killing the awful thing that had sprung into terrifying existence above the Moon.

And afterwards, there had been no more thoughts transferred to the sphere; no more messages from Adekola's conscious and subconscious.

Only a terrible silence.

He had tried contacting Plato Base, but it was soon clear that the entire complex was being evacuated, abandoned. Those people he did manage to contact and who knew of Adekola, did not know where she was. A few assured him it was because the entire place was in turmoil and everyone was trying to get on the shuttles and back to Earth. It was very difficult to locate any particular person, they told him, but everyone would get off the base eventually. He would have to be patient.

He had tried booking a shuttle to the Moon but every seat

was already accounted for. They would not waste resources getting someone to the Moon when the overriding priority was to get people back from the Moon.

He contacted the Council, but the officials there, more used to wrestling with abstract problems in cosmology than with unfolding tragedies, were worse than useless.

He looked at the sphere willing it to reveal more of what had happened on that dead satellite but it did not answer. Reluctantly, he put it away in its box.

Whatever the future had in store for him, the sphere must not be harmed. It alone held the truth! Some day that truth would be revealed!

Where was Tamira!

And where was Baldwin! She would have the answers!

He clenched and unclenched his fists while his mind whirled. He smashed his fists against the window in his despair, and then just stood there with his head resting against it, and quietly sobbed.

Then he stood up straight. Jahia must not hear him. She was already frightened and he would not make it worse.

He spent some time reading with her and when she had drifted into a nap, he smoothed her hair, kissed her and left her there, curled up on her bed. A thumb had found its way into her mouth.

He sat down again and checked the time. Where was Eddie with their lunch?

Just then the doorbell chimed. His brow furrowed. Strange, he wasn't expecting anyone and Eddie didn't need permission to come in.

He activated the door viewer and was rewarded with the face of a woman, a face that was framed in an aureole of shining, cascading hair. Elizabeth Baldwin!

She would know!

She came in and sat on the sofa opposite him. He marvelled at how serene and untroubled she looked.

And beautiful. She was as beautiful as he remembered;

perhaps even more so. She had the calm assurance of someone whose lofty ambitions had been triumphantly achieved.

'Idris,' she said in that honey-dipped voice, 'it's so lovely to see you.'

'Never mind that!' he said, 'where's Tamira! Have you seen her!'

'Yes, of course, I've seen her,' she said, looking at him from under impossibly long lashes, 'but as to where she is—I'm afraid I'm not quite sure.'

'You were her superior. She was your responsibility. Don't tell me you just ran off and left her!'

'No, no," Baldwin said, in a strangely wistful voice, 'I would never just leave her. I owe her more than simple desertion.' But then she brightened up. 'But I do have a message from her!'

'You do! Let me see it!'

Baldwin pulled a computer pad from her bag, made some adjustments to it and then passed it to Parry.

'Here you are, Idris.'

Parry stared at the screen. It was blank at first and then Adekola appeared on it.

She was sitting on a chair in a dimly lit room. She looked exhausted and, yes, frightened. Then she spoke.

'Hello. My name is Tamira Adekola and I have something very important to tell you.'

Parry watched in growing horror as Adekola told of her treachery and how she, and she alone, had brought this dreadful crisis upon the world; she and she alone.

He angrily thrust the pad back at Baldwin.

'No! that can't be right! She didn't do any of that! I saw the fight in the Control Room. If anyone's to blame it's you. You changed the destination of the wormhole! I saw it!'

Baldwin's lips twisted into a self-satisfied grin.

'Ah, you did, did you. I thought so. Something about a sphere, isn't it?'

Parry looked at her with growing suspicion.

'What do you know about it?'

Baldwin leaned back on the sofa, stretching her long, shining legs out towards Parry and kicking off her shoes.

'Never mind about that. The questions is, what are you going to do about the dear girl's confession?'

'What do you mean, do? Other than deny it vigorously?'

Baldwin wound a golden lock around a finger. 'What would you say if I told you that in two hours' time your partner's confession will be broadcast on all the major networks of the world. All over the world. Every atoll in the Pacific will see it. Every research station in Antarctica will see it.'

Parry's hands became balled fists. 'Why are you telling me this!'

Baldwin's face became alive with excitement. Her eyes seemed to sparkle. Her legs, hitherto pressed tightly together, moved apart slightly.

'Idris, I want to make love with you.'

'What!' he leapt to his feet, towering over her. 'You're mad! Get out!'

She also stood. Her eyes looked up into his, but not by much, for she was only a little shorter than he, even without heels.

'What if I told you that if we made love, I have the power to prevent that video from going public? Tamira's reputation would be safe. And I would tell you where she is.'

'What? What do you mean, prevent the video going out? How could you do that?'

She moved closer, placing her palms on his chest. He could smell her perfume, her fragrance, her womanliness.

'Never mind that, Idris, I am Elizabeth Baldwin. I can do many, many things. I can create exotic matter. I can conjure wormholes from the vacuum and make them reach out to touch another star. Trust me. I can make sure no one else ever sees that video. Just make love with me and I will make it so.'

Parry stood staring at her, trapped in a whirlpool of insane indecision.

'You promise that?' he finally said. He was astounded at how dry his mouth felt.

She moved her palms in slow circles on his chest. She moved even closer so that he began to feel a gentle pressure from her breasts.

Then Parry heard Jahia say, 'Daddy, who is the nice lady?'

Baldwin cocked her head in Jahia's direction, without looking at her.

'Best to get the child back in her room.'

Parry pushed Jahia, none too gently, back into her room, saying, 'Daddy will talk to you soon.'

He turned away from the child's room.

Baldwin had already taken off her top and was standing there, her magnificent breasts only half-hidden by her bra.

She smiled at him lovingly as her hands worked behind her back for a few moments. Then her bosom fell free as she threw the garment to the floor.

'Do you like these, darling?' she said, and slightly cupped her breasts so they rose proudly against her chest.

Parry stood there. He felt as if he was in some crazy dream, some ridiculous fantasy.

He could feel his heart going into overdrive as this glorious goddess approached him.

A slim hand pressed itself against his crotch, and the two of them felt his response.

She placed her lips against the nearest ear and whispered, 'I know you want me. And you can have me. Let's not waste any more time!'

Now long past caring, he divested himself of his clothes. He could hear Jahia saying something from the other side of her bedroom door but ignored it. His world was Elizabeth Baldwin. She stood in front of him, holding the last of her stockings between her legs. Slowly she pulled it up, revealing a fuzz of aureate down where those silken legs met.

She threw it to the floor and held her arms out to him.

'Come,' was all she said.

He crossed to her and their lips melded together. She tasted of honey and fine wine.

Her roseate nipples were hard points rubbing back and forth against his chest as her sumptuous breasts mashed against him. She held his penis between slim fingers, gripping it, then pulling away, teasing it, forcing him, almost against his will, into steely hardness.

She leaned back onto the sofa, pulling him down on top of her. He saw the face of a golden angel; he felt a yielding body moving beneath him; he felt the pressure of her hands on his back, pulling him down, pulling him in.

She looked up at him, their faces almost touching. 'Fuck me, Idris,' she whispered gently, 'fuck me hard!'

They became one as he surged into her. She cried out: 'Oh, Idris, my love! Yes!'

He did not know how long he took. He was only conscious of a warm wetness enveloping him and the desire to thrust and thrust into this soft whimpering thing that squirmed and bucked beneath him.

Then there was sweet release, and in his moment of ecstasy he slid from her moist embrace into a heap on the floor. For an unknown time he did not know where he was, who he was.

When his eyes focused again he saw that Baldwin was putting on the last items of her clothing. Sitting in his armchair she slid her feet into elegant shoes.

She looked over at him as he started to dress.

'Well, that was a disappointment,' she said coldly.

'What?'

'You heard.' She stood up and picked up her bag. 'You didn't stimulate me properly and you came far too soon. As I said, a disappointment.'

He completed pulling his trousers on.

'God, you're a cold one,' he said, 'I'm sorry I let you down. Maybe I didn't find you that exciting.'

'Don't make me laugh,' she said, 'you were well away. Anyway, some people say that sometimes the imagining is better than the reality. Looks like they're right.'

'Never mind about my shortcomings!' he snapped, 'what about that video?'

'Oh, that.' She looked at her watch. 'It'll be going out in an hour's time.'

'What!'

'I just wanted to see what you were like, that's all. And to fulfil a promise I had made with your partner. Now, don't feel too sad, rainy face. You weren't really that bad; the circumstances must have been a little difficult for you.'

'You promised!'

She looked at him, shaking her head. 'What is this! Are you some kind of child! I lied. Get over it.'

She felt for something in her bag. 'And now before I go, there is something I want.' She pulled out a revolver and pointed it at him. 'Give me that sphere, Romeo.'

'What! Why!'

She laughed. 'God, stupidity really is rampant in this family. I sat in on every one of your conversations with your One True Love. I knew all about those wristwatch things. I didn't understand how it was done, I'll give you that, but I knew that somehow memories were being recorded.' She waved the pistol back and forth. 'Now give me the sphere so I can destroy it.'

'You said you'd tell me about Tamira!'

Baldwin grunted. 'Oh, yes. Her. She's far, far away. The poor girl. So much stress, she's quite gone to pieces.'

'What do you mean, you crazy fucking creature!'

Baldwin looked at him pityingly. 'The black hole. I put her in it. That information will be made public as well; a tragic suicide. But what a way to go!'

Jahia's door opened, and the girl came out.

'Is the nice lady going now, Daddy? And what were all those funny noises?'

'Jahia, get back in your room!' Parry thundered, 'Now!'

Jahia reluctantly obeyed as Baldwin watched her with an amused smile playing on lips now smudged by smeared lipstick.

Then the door opened and Eddie, the robot butler, came in,

directly behind Baldwin.

'Your lunch, sir,' it said.

Baldwin, startled, took her eyes off Parry.

He saw his chance and dived for her. She twisted so he shot past her and crashed into Eddie, sending the robot crashing into the meal trolley.

As it lay there, Eddie said, repeatedly, 'Here is your lunch sir. Here is…'

Baldwin backed away from the pair and took a position against the window.

'Not bad, Idris. You do have balls, it seems.'

Another wave of the pistol.

'Where were we? Ah yes. The sphere. Now. Give it to me and you live. Refuse and I kill you and take it anyway. It'll take me a bit longer the second way so, give it to me. Now.'

Parry stood up and moved back into the centre of the room.

The fountain was still sending its pleasing parabolas into the air..

The clouds were still drifting over Arenig Fawr.

Everything was normal.

Normal that is apart from Baldwin and her pistol.

He turned towards the box that held the sphere.

And then there was a terrible noise and something blindingly brilliant flashed past the window, trailing a roiling mass of ebony smoke.

The meteorite hit a building not far away and the shockwave followed almost instantly.

The window burst in, sending Baldwin sprawling, the pistol flying from her hands.

In an instant, he was upon her, throwing her onto her back. Baldwin fought back like a tiger, her perfectly manicured nails tearing great gouges in his face.

He rammed his knees onto her arms and sank fingers of steel into her neck and in a paroxysm of hatred began to choke her.

Then for some reason he paused and stared down at her.

A goddess looked up at him, a face of unendurable beauty framed in that lovely corona of spun-gold hair.

She managed to whisper some words as his hands tightened again.

'Don't do this, Idris. I love you.'

And so Idris Parry killed Elizabeth Baldwin, there on the floor of his apartment as the smoke from the fallen space rock drifted in through the shattered window.

## Twenty Three: The Recording

Parry stared down at the corpse of Elizabeth Baldwin. Even in death, she was beautiful; her hair, in which every glorious summer there had ever been had found their embodiment, was spread out on either side of her head in a lovely fan.

Only the staring eyes and the blue-black marks on her neck spoiled the image.

Parry could have wept for the terrible doom which had come upon her; a woman who had possessed transcendent ability, who could have been one of humanity's greatest saviours. Her whirlwind life, her triumphant, matchless intellect—all for nothing.

But then more pressing issues crashed into his mind. Whatever Baldwin's crimes, he had murdered her. Perhaps she had deserved death but it was he who had given it to her in his mad rage.

Then an even more pertinent fact hit him. He had murdered her, which meant that he was no longer an ordinary citizen. He was a murderer. And murderers are punished.

He heard his daughter's door open.

'No, stay there!' he shouted, 'everything's all right! I'll be with you in a moment!'

To his immense relief, the child obeyed.

*She must not see Baldwin!* he thought. He looked around the small apartment.

What could he do?

He could not think long term; he only knew Jahia must not see a corpse. Finally, he dragged the sofa away from the wall; the sofa on which he had Baldwin had had sex—he could not term it love-making. This sofa: such a short time ago. And now everything had changed.

He pulled the body behind the sofa and pushed the furniture back as far as it would go. Then he sat in his armchair, thinking rapidly. He became aware that Eddie was still lying on its back, still repeating 'Here is your lunch, sir. Here is your lunch, sir,' in an infinite loop.

That was one madness-inducing stimulus he could do without. He crossed to the automaton, found the relevant switch and silenced the thing.

As he did so, Jahia's door opened. The child's sorely-tested patience had evidently run out. She looked at her father and then recoiled slightly.

'Daddy, you're bleeding!' she said, pointing at his face. He felt his face and the fingers came away bloodied.

'It's nothing, darling,' he said, in a voice which sounded incredibly phoney to him, 'I'm alright.'

He crossed to the shower room and looked at his reflection. Great parallel red lines were ripped down his cheeks. He applied ointment to the wounds that sharp fingernails had inflicted only minutes earlier and then returned to his daughter.

'Look, Daddy's fine,' he said, 'just a few scratches!'

Jahia looked unconvinced but did not press the matter. Instead she looked around and said, 'Where's the nice lady gone? And what were those terrible noises, they frightened me.'

'Oh, she had to go,' Parry said, wondering if the truth was written on his features, 'She's very, very busy.'

'She's very beautiful,' Jahia said thoughtfully, 'I'd like to be beautiful.'

He hugged her. 'You are, Jahia, you are. And when you grow up you'll be even more beautiful than that lady.'

That seemed to satisfy the child and she smiled at the thought of the beauty to come. But having solved the missing lady problem, more immediate concerns came to the fore. She noticed the inert form of Eddie and the overturned meal trolley.

'What happened to poor Eddie? And where's my lunch?'

'Eddie's OK,' Parry said, 'Look, I'll make him talk again.'

He reactivated the robot, commanded it to erase the module it was running and to skip forward to delivering the meal. The robot righted the trolley and proceeded to place the food on the table. However, it did not notice that many of the food items had mashed together after the trolley had tipped over, and Parry found he was eating his Ffish with jelly and custard. Jahia seemed to like it.

But Parry found that he had no appetite. His thought kept returning to the body that lay only a few metres away from him and his daughter. As soon as Jahia had eaten her fill, he told Eddie to take the rest away, and soon he was alone with his daughter.

And a corpse.

His thoughts returned to what he could do, what he must do. It was then he saw Baldwin's pistol lying near the sofa. Jahia had not seen it. He crossed rapidly to it and hid it in his jacket. What should he do with it? Dispose of it, that would be the wise thing to do.

Or would it?

There was no telling how far society would decline under the terrible changes it was undergoing; perhaps a weapon would come in useful.

He would keep it for the time being.

Then he decided that there was something else he must do. He was grimly certain that Baldwin had not been bluffing when she said that Adekola's false confession would soon be transmitted across the world. He had lost track of time: it was probably being broadcast even as he sat there, head in hands.

He had to do something to preserve the truth for future generations; to let posterity know that his beloved partner was innocent. He felt a strong suspicion that the world's situation, bad though it now was, would get worse. Much worse. Something told him that humanity had only just begun its slide into an abyss of horror and despair.

He turned to his daughter. 'Well, that was a funny meal, wasn't it?'

She nodded.

'I liked it. Can we have it again?'

'Maybe. Now, Daddy's got a bit of work to do. Can I ask you to look at a book for a few minutes?'

After the child had returned to her room he took the sphere from its box, thinking that Baldwin had been so very close to it, all the time she had been an uninvited guest. He activated his memory watch, switching it to the video recording channel from its background memory mode.

He sat facing it, although he knew that his location was irrelevant.

'Hello,' he said, 'you can see me but I cannot see you. All I know is that you are a descendant of mine. I don't know if you are my daughter or a child of my daughter. All I know is that a line of inheritance, of blood, links us. We cannot communicate, I'm afraid. You may ask questions but I cannot hear them, and so I cannot reply to them.

'You may wonder why the sphere that you are holding is showing these things to you. You must be wondering that, so I will assume that you have already asked the question. And it is a good question.'

Just then there was a roaring sound from outside and he glanced at the window to see a bright dot racing across the sky, pulling a train of cloudy blackness behind it.

Far enough away.

He continued giving his talk to the unknown person in the future; a person he would never know but someone who would be carrying strands of DNA linking him or her to him and his partner. Baldwin would be frustrated in one part of her plan at least; future generations would know who it was who had brought the Doom of Stars upon them. They would know that his beloved Tamira had been innocent; a woman who had harmed no-one; who had lived for love and for the happiness of her family. Surely there must come a day when someone would arise and force the truth upon what was left of humanity.

He thought again of what Baldwin had done and hurriedly ended the recording.

Then he wept.

After a few minutes, he became aware that Jahia was standing next to him and had placed her hand on his face.

294

'Why are you sad, Daddy?' she said in a frightened voice, 'is it something about Mommy?'

He looked at her, her face blurred into a strange collage by the tears.

'Yes, Jahia. You must be brave. I have something to tell you.'

\*\*\*

Sometime after Jahia had fallen asleep after her crying had worn her out, Parry knew what he had to do.

He must leave Greater New York; leave North America. Society had not degenerated so far as to be indifferent to murder. It would, but not yet. Jahia must not lose her other parent.

He must move quickly; the two of them could not share an abode with a corpse for very long.

Then he knew what he would do.

His family home was still there in the wild lands below Arenig Fawr.

He spent the rest of the day setting up the arrangements to transfer his assets to that European island.

He sent his letter of resignation to the laboratory.

He packed the minimum of clothing that they would need.

He booked the flight.

He decided not to take Baldwin's pistol; he could not risk trying to get it on the plane.

'Jahia,' he said, 'would you like to go on a lovely holiday?'

'Yes, Daddy, but I don't want to be away too long. I've got a new best friend now.'

Parry smiled sadly. 'Yes, I understand Jahia. I'll see what I can do. You might like it so much you won't want to come back.'

Jahia's face indicated that she thought that unlikely.

Parry said no more. Now was not the time for too much honesty.

'When do we go?'

'Soon Jahia, very soon.'

Nor was it.

He received the message that the robotaxi was waiting not long after he completed the last of the actions that he needed to do to wind up his affairs in Greater New York.

He stood at the doorway, looking back at his apartment thinking of all the times he had had there with Adekola, all the love they had shared, all the plans that they had made, the life together that they had looked forward to.

All destroyed by the woman who now lay dead behind the sofa.

How long would it take before they found her?

He shrugged. He wondered how actively the law enforcements agents would be looking for him. Society was beginning to fray at the edges but it still had a long way to fall. Following his trail would be easy now that everybody left a digital trail behind them.

He knew that there was a window of time in which he could be apprehended and sentenced. Eventually, they wouldn't be looking for anybody. But that time had not yet come.

He knew it was meaningless, but as he started to close the door, he said quietly and calmly, 'Goodbye, Baldwin. Rot in Hell forever.'

## Twenty Four: Under Arenig Fawr

The flight was not without incident. The atmosphere was very turbulent and the plane was thrown around so badly that several passengers were injured. Jahia was very frightened and Parry spent much of the flight doing his best to comfort her. And once, when they were about half-way across the great ocean, he saw a blazing bolide come down from a great rent in the dark clouds and smash into the ocean. The wave from the impact must have been a kilometre high but they were too far away to see what path of destruction it took.

Fortunately at supersonic speeds the crossing was only a few hours and it was not long before they were disembarking in a rainswept London.

Parry looked up at the sky, seeing with concern how wild and turbulent it looked. Great billows of black cloud were speeding overhead, periodically being illuminated from within by savage blasts of lightning. Rain was spattering across the tarmac as he had seen many times before but it was unusual to see rain so hot that it almost immediately started evaporating in twisting columns of steam.

The man at the customs desk looked up from Parry's records on his screen and gave a friendly grin.

'Bloody awful weather. Couldn't you have brought some better weather with you?'

'No, sorry,' Parry said, 'but I'm going to Wales. I hear the weather's much better there.'

The man threw back his head and laughed.

'Man, are you in for a shock!'

Parry tried to return the grin but he found his sense of humour had deserted him. He wondered briefly if it would ever return.

\*\*\*

Parry looked around at the rugged hills. They were not high enough to be mountains but even so they were impressive, seeming to carry the weight of the lowering grey clouds on their stony shoulders.

*The Land of Eagles*, he thought to himself, wondering if those magnificent birds would survive the coming cataclysms. What would survive? What could survive?

It had taken quite a while to regain possession of the old family home, which had been turned into a hotel earlier in the century, and then abandoned due to obscure financial irregularities; long since forgotten. It had not taken long for the wild, upland weather to rip the shingles from the roof, blow in the windows and infest the wooden beams with destroying fungi.

Parry had had the money to restore it, but he was conscious that now he no longer had an income he would have to be more careful with his remaining money. But gradually the old building became a fit place to live in. He loved the exposed beams and the ancient walls which he knew to be white under their covering of ivy because the stones were held firmly together with lime plaster. But especially he loved the huge inglenook fireplace, which on the many cold evenings under Arenig Fawr held a blazing log fire. Many times he would sit before it, watching the logs flicker and fall in upon themselves as they burned themselves out, and his mind would roam in the corridors of the past, reliving his triumphs and failures.

But two women in particular haunted those recollections.

One with long, flowing blonde tresses; the other with short, curly black hair.

One he had loved.

One he had killed.

And Jahia—she was very restless in this remote, windswept area. She had difficulties in making friends with the local children, who tended to mock her accent and lack of understanding of the natural world. But as she matured, he was able to explain more and more of the reasons why they had to leave everything behind; although he had not yet had the courage

298

to tell her that her father was a murderer. For the last four years, he had lived in constant fear that the police would suddenly turn up at the house and charge him with that offence. It would not have taken a forensic genius to conclude that the owner of the apartment in which Baldwin's body had lain was in some way responsible.

*How would he react?* he wondered.

But they never came and as the rainy days drifted past he stopped wondering why.

It was not until many months had withered away that he discovered why they had never come.

In the meantime, while he waited for that fateful knock on the door, he studied the scientific reports about the slowly unfolding disaster that was now afflicting the Earth.

And now as he stood there in the gusting wind, looking up at Arenig Fawr, he believed he now had a fundamental understanding of exactly what form the coming catastrophe would take. All the reports agreed; the orbits of the Moon, Mars and Earth were becoming more elliptical, more elongated. That could only mean that the climate would become more extreme, more dangerous.

Again, he looked up at the rugged hills. The heather should be blooming now but it was not. And was it his imagination or was the temperature distinctly higher than it should be at this time of the year at this altitude? He shook his head. There would come a day when he would not need to ponder; to wonder.

He would know. He would know that an irreversible change had come upon the fragile human world. Just how fragile that world was would be revealed before much longer.

He decided that he had enough of standing there looking at the barren hillside and turned back to the cottage.

The house was empty when he got in; Jahia was no doubt out roaming the hills trying to occupy herself. He had tried to continue her education via the digital network with some success but he knew she resented being torn away from the world she had known, removed from her friends, from Elena. But how

299

could he explain why he had done it? How could he explain that he had fled that world because he had killed a fellow human being?

He had put the box containing the sphere in the tall cupboard by the bay window and told her that she must not try to access it yet. She was still too young to learn that her father was a murderer and in any case it was unlikely that it would respond to someone so young.

He knew the record of his violence was engraved on the sphere, and after arriving in Wales, he had thrown away the memory-watch, thus ending more memory encodings. He did not expect anything to happen to match the tumultuous events already inscribed on it. And what coda could he add to the recording of Baldwin's death?

It marked the end of what he wanted to record, or feel needed to be recorded.

What more could he now expect from life?

The black hole was now clear of the main part of the Solar system, heading back to the lightless gulfs from which it had been snatched. He had learned that the light echo of Adekola's crossing of the event horizon could still be discerned in the most powerful telescopes, but would soon be too far for even them to perceive. It was yet another cruel joke that due to time ceasing to have any meaning in that region of warped space his partner's death would be preserved for millennia to come, until that terrible object finally evaporated.

He heard the door fling open, crashing against the wall with some violence.

'Jahia?' he called, 'is that you?'

'Sure, dad,' came the sardonic reply, 'Who're you expecting—some movie star asking for your autograph?'

She came into the room and flung her coat onto an armchair and slumped on top of it.

'Why is it so freaking hot around here?' she complained, 'I go up on the hills to get fresh air and it's like a goddamn sauna!'

He looked at her, feeling a mixture of guilt and admiration;

admiration of his daughter who was about to become a long-limbed teenager, and guilt for taking her away from the world she had loved.

'I'm afraid the world is changing, darling,' he said mildly.

'Yeah. Because of what Mom did. Thanks a freaking lot, Mom!'

'I've told you that's not true, darling. I've told you that one day you'll be able to find out what really happened.'

She glared at him. 'So you keep saying. Christ, if those retards in that crummy village ever find out I'm her daughter—God help us all!' She stood up. 'I'm going to my room.'

As she opened the door of her room, she looked over her shoulder and said, 'And stop calling me "Darling." It's weird!'

Parry smiled with a smile which was slightly wistful. His daughter was growing up fast.

But into what world?

He went to his daughter's room and knocked on the door and asked for permission to enter.

He found Jahia stretched out on the bed, looking at her computer pad.

'Can we talk, dar—Jahia?' he said diffidently.

'Sure. What do you want to talk about?'

'I know, you're not happy here.' He resisted an urge to reach out and touch her. She wouldn't like it. 'But before long the big cities won't be safe. Everybody will be trying to get out and into the countryside. There may well be food riots, and who knows how bad things will get.'

'So why couldn't we have stayed in the States? Gone to Montana or somewhere like that?'

Once again, he hesitated. He could not bring himself to tell her the real reason so their mutual unhappiness would continue. There was no way out.

'Is it so bad here?' he continued, 'I know there are no bright lights but there are—there are boys here.'

She continued looking at her computer pad and not her father.

301

'Yeah, right. If you want to be with some guy who works the drains in a hydroponics plant.'

'Look, Jahia, put that pad down for a moment.'

She obeyed, slowly and reluctantly.

'I can't tell you why but there is a reason we're here. It's all recorded and one day you'll read it all.'

Her brown eyes stared into his grey.

'What, on that sphere thing? I'm not touching it.'

He groaned inwardly. She had expressed many times the determination not to look into the sphere. Would all his work be in vain? All those memories wasted?'

'OK,' he said, 'I'll tell you the real reason. I...'

Once again, their eyes locked but as he tried to form the words his mouth went dry and he knew he could not do it.

'I know why we're here,' she said, after accepting that he wasn't going to speak, 'It's because Mom wrecked the world. She brought that thing into our space and it fu—messed up the whole world. That's why we're hiding away here! To avoid getting lynched!'

'No, no, it wasn't your mother. It was another woman!'

She went back to her computer pad.

'Then get her on the phone, dad. I'd like to hear her side of the story.'

He looked at his daughter, realised he had no more to say and went back to his armchair.

He sat by the great fireplace. Still no need for a fire.

What could he do now? He knew, better than everyone else in this neighbourhood, what was coming. The cities must be avoided. There was a hydroponics plant here that could provide food if everything started going to Hell. And if that failed there were oldsters around who knew something about growing things in dirt. They might even know how to butcher an animal...

The idea appalled him and he thrust it from his mind.

He would go down into the village tomorrow and see if there were any social activities that Jahia might be interested in. There was a middle-aged widow, Mair, who ran the library—she

302

might know.

Another wry smile.

Of course, he had more than a suspicion that she was interested in him and would like to be on more familiar terms. But that was not going to happen. Despite being still a reasonably young man, he had recently realised that he no longer had any interest in women. He must not lead her on. Lead her…

His head bowed and then he was asleep; asleep in front of the empty fireplace.

*** 

True to his word Parry walked down to the cramped little town. He was finding it more difficult these days, especially when walking back up. There were strange aches and pinching feelings in his sides, which had only recently appeared, and he noticed he was getting increasingly out of breath, even with simple tasks.

*Old age doesn't come alone!* he thought, giving a thin smile.

The village was not large and it didn't take long to find the library. He liked it because it had a wide selection of actual print-on-paper books, which had come back into fashion recently.

So he was very surprised to see the door of the building wide open and a noisy group of people standing in the doorway, tossing books into the street.

He could see Mair in the midst of the throng, trying ineffectually to stop them.

He rushed up to the group and shouted, 'Stop this! Why are you doing this?'

The man nearest to him turned and his lip curled when he saw Parry.

'Keep out of this, Yank! We're cleaning this place up!'

'And how are you doing that?' Parry said, picking up one of the books at his feet.

It was "Practical Astronomy for Beginners."

'We're clearing out all the science nonsense if it's any of your business.'

Another book flew from the doorway, delivering a glancing blow to his head.

He picked it up.

"Intermediate Organic Chemistry."

Parry had had enough. 'Stop this , you fools! Science is what has produced all the good things which you take for granted!'

A stocky man shouldered his way through the crowd and looked down on Parry.

'Oh, has it now? And what about that bloody thing that black bitch brought down on us? Wasn't that science? And now all the seasons are changing and they say it's all down to her and her science! We've had enough of it!'

The others cheered at that, raising their fists.

'You're all fools!' Parry yelled, 'you'll need science to survive what is coming! Without it you're just—just…' A very old expression came to him then. 'Lambs to the slaughter!'

Somebody behind the big man shouted, 'Get back to fucking America and take that kid of yours with you! We don't want either of you in our town!'

The big man had turned away and Parry grabbed his shoulder to turn him back.

He wasn't sure what happened next but he felt a crushing blow in his face and the world went black.

He came around to find Mair mopping his face with a moist cloth and looking at him with obvious concern. He saw that they were in the library and that the floor was carpeted with books, many of them torn.

He felt his jaw. 'That hurt,' he muttered.

'I'm not surprised,' Mair said, in the lilting local accent that he loved, 'he really hit you.'

'No sh—yes, he did.' Parry rose unsteadily to his feet. 'God, they've made a mess of this place.'

'Yes, it's been building up for weeks. But now the news has got so bad it just tipped them over the edge, I suppose.'

Parry looked around at the destruction. 'They've ruined your library, that's for sure. So much for knowledge.' He suddenly realised that he hadn't checked on Mair. 'Did they hurt you, Mair?'

She smiled. 'No, things aren't that bad—yet.' She touched his shoulder and left her hand there. 'Idris, are things going to get much worse?'

He was slightly taken aback. It had been years since a woman had used his first name. He hadn't even been sure she knew it.

He took a deep breath. 'Yes, Mair, they are. The world's orbit is changing. And the Moon's. I'm afraid things will get a lot worse.'

She looked down at the torn books at her feet.

'I thought I'd reached rock bottom when Harri died. But now I'm afraid for myself. And you must be afraid too, Idris, for your daughter.'

'I am.'

She lifted her other hand to touch him, so that she was resting her hands on both his shoulders. 'That dreadful woman! She's ruined all our lives!'

Parry was too weary to protest. After all, it was true, but not in the way Mair thought.

'Yes, she did,' was all he said, leaving the "she" unspecified.

He gently removed her hands and started looking through the books. There were quite a few astronomy books with the colourful images that Jahia had liked when she was younger.

'I take it you won't be putting these back on the shelves?'

'No. What's the point? They'll only throw them down again. And they might be angrier next time.'

'Could I have them? Jahia might like them.'

Her eyes seemed to sparkle. 'Certainly! I'll drive up with some tonight. Just put the ones you want to one side.'

'Thanks,' he said, hoping that her smile wasn't displaying too much anticipation.

\*\*\*

He heard the car crunch to a stop on the gravel outside the front door.

*She's here,* he thought and rushed out to help her.

The evening was warm and close and it felt as if sweat was misting his forehead as he helped her with the boxes of books.

They piled the books on the big table and he heard her say, 'Wow! These print books are so heavy!'

He turned to her and his heart sank. She was wearing bright red lipstick and her auburn hair had been styled.

'Thanks, Mair,' he said, thinking *What should I do now?* 'Can I get you anything?'

'A drink would be nice,' she said, 'if you have some that is!'

'Yes, yes,' he said, 'I think there's whisky somewhere.'

He brought the bottle and two glasses.

'How do you take it?'

'Oh, neat will do fine. We're only young once!'

He poured the smallest amount he could decently get away with into the two glasses. Mair indicated the sofa.

'Is OK to sit down?'

'Oh. Sure,' and he started to move towards his armchair.

'Don't be silly!' she giggled, 'we're friends aren't we?' and tugged him gently towards the sofa.

They sat together, some distance apart, sipping the whisky. He stared directly ahead.

Then Mair turned to him and said, 'Do you know what, Idris?'

'No what?'

'You're one gorgeous man. I'd like to think we could be friends.'

'We are.'

'I mean, close friends.' She moved closer. He could smell a cheap perfume. 'It's been lonely for me, Idris. Nothing ever happens around here. You're the only man with a brain for a hundred kilometres. I like that.' Her eyelashes dipped. 'And I hope you like me.'

She leaned in towards him, and her lips parted slightly.

He put out a hand to stop the inward motion.

'Thank you, Mair. The books will be very useful. I'm sure Jahia will like them.'

He never saw Mair again.

***

The years passed.

The planet Earth continued its slow rotation around the galactic centre in an ever-widening helix. It remained supremely unconcerned by the turmoil and suffering on its surface.

Jahia had a few short relationships with local boys but nothing came of them.

Then there came the time when she had to nurse Parry through the final months of his cancer, after the last of the drugs had gone.

After he died, she took the astronomy books with the best pictures, some clothes, the box containing the sphere and left for the camps around London.

She never did look into the sphere.

And she never again stood in those uplands where her father had died, under Arenig Fawr.

# BOOK THREE: Spes Nostra

# One

Kalli stepped out of the ruined hut, narrowing her eyes as the gusting wind hit her. It was warmer than she was used to.

She looked up into the dim, cloud-swept sky, listening and looking for the helicopter.

And suddenly, there it was—a black dot moving against the grey billows. It rapidly grew bigger and, for a few moments, she wondered if she should signal to it before she realised it was homing in on her communicator's signal. Soon the dot was large enough to clearly identify as a helicopter. The downdraft from the rotors beat down on her and she almost stepped back into the hut before she stopped herself; she wanted to see all of this.

The craft touched down and the rotors stopped their whirling. The engine died, and after a few moments the door opened and a slim figure stepped out.

Jason! Why did her heart flutter when she saw him?

He strode up to her, his eyes seemingly shining as he took her in.

'Kalli!' he said, 'you haven't...'

He stopped and looked her over quizzically.

'Well, I was going to say that you hadn't changed a bit. But you have. There's a different look about you. You look older.'

'Well, thank you, kind sir. You've got a white hair in your beard, did you know that?'

He laughed. 'Attagirl! No, don't get me wrong, I didn't mean that in a bad way. I mean, you look more mature, more womanly. I don't know why; I can't explain it. You just do.'

She studied him. Whatever he thought of her, he was exactly the same. The same easy manner, the same way his lips were always the verge of a smile or grin. The same air of a boy who may or may not have done some mischief in the very recent past.

'I've been through a lot,' was all she could say at first. But then as she got used to his presence, she told him the story of the trawler and the destruction of her Village.

'That's a tough deal,' he said, 'but it's always dangerous living near the coast. The tides are too dangerous. Estuaries tend to get those big tidal waves. I would have thought they'd have known that.'

'They liked to eat,' she replied coldly, not liking the implied slur on her people.

He slapped his hand on this forehead. 'Hah! I'd forgotten who I was dealing with! I'll have to learn my place all over again!' He looked at her again. 'You have changed, you know. The way you speak is different. It sounds like you're now older than me, more experienced than me. What have you been up to?'

She looked at him in silence. Was this the time to tell him of the sphere and all the tumultuous events it had shown her? To tell him that through its power she had seen the clouds pass over Arenig Fawr; been alongside her grandmother in Plato Base and seen that first flash that revealed negative matter; that she had struggled to save Philip Richards on the desiccated dust of the Moon; that she had battled Elizabeth Baldwin as a black hole bore down on the Solar system? That in a few seconds she had experienced a lifetime of epic struggle?

Instead, she said: 'I'm hungry. I can't remember when I last ate. Do you have anything?'

Realising that she was not ready to talk, he grinned and said, 'Sure. We'll eat in the chopper. And then, to coin a phrase, I'll take you away from all this.' He lifted the arm that the wolf had bitten. 'You didn't ask, but it's OK now. As they used to say in the movies—just a flesh wound.'

Kalli didn't understand at least half of that statement, but she didn't ask for clarification—much of what he said was a mystery to her.

She looked past him to the remains of her Village at the bottom of the slope and indicated it with a movement of her head, 'Is there anything you can do for them?'

He followed the movement and then looked back at her. 'Not a damned thing. There's no shortage of people in need in this world, Kalli.'

She nodded reluctantly and then took one last look at the Village, knowing that she was about to leave it forever.

After they had eaten she said, 'Well, Jason, where do we go from here? Am I still an R.I.F. girl? The kind you collect?'

He brushed some crumbs from his beard. 'Yes, I think you are. I'm even more sure than when I last saw you. There's a calm certainty about you that you didn't have before. Yes, you are indeed an R.I.F. girl.'

'And what happens to R.I.F. girls? What is their reward?'

'Their reward?' He looked suddenly serious and turned from her so that he could look out at the grey estuary and not at her. 'Perhaps the chance of life.'

She mused over that for a few moments, and then, 'An enigmatic statement, Jason. That's not like you.'

He looked at her sharply. '*Enigmatic?* You really have been up to something.' And then seeing she would not make a reply, he said, 'Well, the R.I.F project is coming to an end. Time is running out. We'll go back to London to a nice little hostel and from there we'll take you to mainland Westrania, where they'll give you a battery of tests to make sure you're up to it.'

'Mainland Westrania.' She wasn't entirely sure of the meaning of that phrase. The sphere had not mentioned it. 'Would that be the United States?'

'Yes, that's the old term for part of it. Westrania is most of the North American continent and the offshore European islands. Like this one. The western hemisphere part is the most significant region so we call it the "Mainland".'

'OK.' World geography had not been important in the Village; survival from day to day had been. The political upheavals that had created Westrania must have occurred after the recordings to the sphere had ceased.

'And things are a lot better in Mainland Westrania? Than here, I mean.'

'Yes and no. There are more amenities, a higher standard of life. But there's a creeping rot there as well. Lots of very, very weird cults are springing up. Everyone's heard a rumour, or five,

311

about the End Of Days. Some of which contradict each other. Some of them say we are living in the "Days of the Beast"—whatever that means.'

She frowned.

'Will I have time to visit Greater New York? That's where my grandparents lived.'

'Well you could. But you'd be a little disappointed. Ever since the asteroid fell on it, it's been nothing but a very big hole. Still, it's starting to turn into a nice lake. The birds like it.'

Her face showed disappointed acceptance. Then:

'Well, if I can't go to New York, let's go to London,' she said. 'I am anxious to find out if I'm up to R.I.F standard.'

He grinned. 'Attagirl.'

***

They descended into the same square in which she had first seen Jason—when had that been? Was it ten thousand years ago? It felt like it, as she looked around.

The buildings were as she remembered, with the exception that now the snow on their tops was thinner and patchy. Even as she looked at one structure, there was a sudden faint rumble as a shelf of snow slid off the roof, crashing into the street in curtains of white.

'Summer's coming,' she murmured.

'Yes,' he said, 'let's hope it's not as bad as the last one.'

The helicopter was attended to by a group of Jason's colleagues who flew it away, presumably to its night-time hangar, and they crossed to the nearby hostel.

Jason was welcomed by a crowd of young men and women as they entered the building. Kalli was annoyed to see that some of the women were very familiar with her pilot, apparently thinking it was acceptable to drape themselves over him. One of them was somehow aware of the weight of Kalli's stare and turned to see who was responsible.

'Oh, we have a new girl,' she said, giving a distinctly

312

unconvincing smile. 'Who's this young thing, Jason? The one dressed in rags, I mean.'

Before Jason could reply, Kalli said, 'The name is Kalli. And I prefer not to be discussed in the third person.'

'Oh,' the girl said, 'aren't you the high and mighty one. You don't look old enough to be away from your mother.'

Kalli diminished the distance between them. 'I've seen things you couldn't even begin to imagine. So even if you're top of the R.I.F. class, please treat me with respect.'

The girl looked confused, opened her mouth, then shut it and walked away. The other girls followed, giving Kalli hard stares as they passed her.

When they were alone, Jason said quietly, 'There was no need of that, Kalli. They're not bad girls, just a little full of themselves. They're very proud of their status. They mean no harm.'

She ran a hand over her forehead. 'I know. I'm sorry. My head is splitting. I've been through a lot. Things I can't explain.'

He moved to her. 'You mustn't keep things to yourself, Kalli. You must share them. I'd like to think we're a team.'

She looked up at him, a warm smile spreading across her face. 'I will tell you all about it soon, Jason. But I'm still trying to come to terms with it.'

He shook his head. 'I don't understand. What is it that you've done? I know the trawler thing must have been very traumatic...'

There were several chairs in the foyer of the hostel, and she slumped into one. He stood over her, confused, not knowing what to do.

'What is it, Kalli?'

'Jason, when we had our first flight and you took me over the old London, you said that a great disaster had happened to the world. I now know how that disaster came about, but I think you know more than you have told me. You said about the chance of giving me "Life." That suggests that you think my life is in danger. Things are bad, I know, but tell me something: are they going to get worse?'

His face became still and expressionless. Seconds of silence passed and then he said: 'Yes. A lot worse.'

'I thought so. Little things you've said. This "R.I.F. Project"—it is for some kind of breeding stock, isn't it?'

'Yes. You are sharper than I remember. That's what people like me are doing. Collecting a breeding stock.'

'Which implies a need to restock the population.'

He suddenly threw up his hands. 'Look, this is not the time or place to talk about this! We've just arrived, we're both frazzled, and you've upset my friends two seconds after arriving. I think we need a good meal and then a good sleep and then start from the beginning tomorrow morning.'

She gave a self-deprecatory grimace. 'You're right. I've been a cow. But you've got no idea what's on my mind.'

'So you keep saying. But I'm not exactly doing a stand-up comedy show myself here. You've got to give it to me straight. Not tonight, I accept that, but soon.' Suddenly he bent down and put her face between his hands. His face was dizzyingly close. 'Look, you're a great kid. We'll do something different tomorrow before the real work begins. What would you like to do?'

She rose to her feet. They were very close. She wanted to touch him but did not.

'I want to go into London.'

'There's not much sight-seeing these days, kid.'

'I know. I want to meet my father again.'

# Two

The day dawned grey and overcast; a sure sign of approaching Summer.

Kalli sat in the dining area, being studiously ignored by the girls she had upset the day before. A few boys approached her, but she was not interested.

Finally, Jason joined her and she stole glances at him as she forked in mouthfuls of scrambled egg. It tasted much better than the food she had been used to in the Village: it was clear these people were used to a high standard of living.

'Sleep OK?' Jason inquired as he paused a forkful of yellow gloop on its path to his mouth.

Kalli nodded, although she had in truth, found the bed far too soft.

'And you like those new clothes I've gotten you?'

'They're lovely,' she smiled. And they were; soft, supple, pleasant to touch.

And clean. Very clean.

'So your father's living in London?' he continued, 'it's a huge place. What makes you think you'll be able to find him again?'

'I'm not sure I can,' she said, 'I'll go back to that bar I first saw him in. I've got a feeling he's a regular there.'

Jason pulled a face. 'I'll come with you. We can't have a young girl wandering around those streets. It's far too dangerous.'

Kalli gave him what she hoped was a disapproving stare, although she was secretly pleased by the suggestion.

'If you must,' she shrugged, 'although perhaps you've forgotten it was me who fought off the wolves.'

He smiled. 'Attagirl. But wolves in London walk on two feet, and some of them carry guns. And they might have plans for you other than eating you.'

She finished the last of the scrambled egg. It had been delicious! She wanted more but could see that those around her had had only one portion. Still, the chicory coffee was truly excellent, and she could sip that while looking at Jason. She decided it was time to find out more about what he knew about the world they shared.

'The world has gone to Hell,' she said, 'when we last saw each other you said you knew how it had happened. Could you tell me again?'

He reacted with a wry expression. 'Not the best early morning topic of conservation.'

'I want to learn, Jason. You don't want a girl who knows nothing, do you?'

She studied him to see if he would react to the implication that they were in a relationship but he did not. Instead, he finished his scrambled egg and leaned back, adopting a didactic expression.

'There was a scientist; a woman scientist. Her name was Bedwin. She was one of the greatest scientists the world has ever seen. She had developed a method which would allow people to reach the stars in a human lifetime.'

'And why was that important? The world was a paradise in those days.'

'It wasn't for conquest or anything stupid like that. She was a great benefactor of the human race. She had discovered a resource which would allow the proper development of computers and robots, to everyone's benefit.'

Kalli knew very well what computers and robots were, she had seen them in the sphere, but she wanted to find out how far Jason's knowledge went.

'Robots? Computers? There were none in the Village.'

He smiled thinly. 'No, of course not. There aren't robots anymore. But there are still computers. You'll see them in Pensacola. But they're still primitive things, not like what Bedwin had hoped to give us.'

'So how did we get in this mess?'

All trace of Jason's humour, his playfulness had disappeared. 'Bedwin had an assistant. Another woman. And this woman was

316

jealous of Bedwin and wanted the glory for herself. '

'What was this woman's name?'

'Not sure. Addick, or something like that. People don't like talking about her, you see. She tried to seize control of her superior's great project but didn't know what she was doing. She messed up badly and brought a black hole into the system.'

Kalli knew what a black hole was; she had seen that mind-shredding horror in the sphere. But she nodded to show that she was simply following Jason's exposition.

'And that "messed up" the orbits of the planets.'

'Yes.' He looked at her sharply. 'You seem to know what I'm saying before I say it. How did you find the time to learn about planetary orbits while you were out hunting seals?'

'I had books on astronomy,' she replied. *And that is entirely true,* she thought.

'So what happened to this evil woman?' she continued, 'This "Addick", or whatever her name was.'

'I'm not sure. Some people say she was so ashamed of what she had done that she killed herself by flying into the black hole.' He put up his hands. 'I don't know. It was all a long time ago. Anyway, Bedwin saved us all by finding a way to stop the black hole coming too close to the Earth. That's why you and me are here, Kalli. She saved us all.'

Kalli said nothing. Her mind was reliving those tremendous moments in the Control Room when utter annihilation had been only seconds away and how her grandmother had flung herself onto the control switch which was the only thing that had stood between humanity and eternity. To her amazement, she suddenly realised that her eyes were moist.

Jason saw her distress and reached for her hands.

'Don't be upset, Kalli. We can't undo what that woman did. But we can still make a go of our lives. There is hope.'

Suddenly she was angry. She jumped to her feet.

'Hope? To be a wonderful R.I.F. girl? A breeding cow! That's hope?'

She walked past the girls and looked scornfully down on

them.

'So looking forward to churning out babies for your masters, are you? That's all you want?' She spun on her heel. 'You're pathetic!'

On entering her room, she flung herself on the bed and sobbed.

\*\*\*

When Kalli awoke, she feared that she had alienated Jason, and when they met again later that day, she tried to apologise but he just smiled.

'Forget it, kid. You're not yourself. Losing all your friends in that tidal wave; it must have been Godawful. Let's move on.'

She nodded gratefully, all the time thinking, *I mustn't take it out on him. He's the closest thing to a friend I have in this world! Whatever happens on this dying planet, Jason must not suffer!*

She even found it in herself to apologise to the other girls; although it didn't look as if the apology had been accepted.

The grey day wore on; not getting any less grey; any less oppressive. The air was cloying and clammy as the steadily rising heat melted more and more of the old snow and ice. Looking out of one of the hostel's windows, she could see curls of vapour rising from the street.

Slowly the grey ceiling of the world became a darker and darker shade of gloom until it could not be denied that evening had fallen.

Jason came looking for her.

'Still want to go out into Old London Town?' he enquired, showing that lopsided smile she had come to love.

'Yes, I know there's not much chance of finding him, but I've got to try.'

'OK. But we can't hang around here much longer allowing you to feed your face. Pensacola awaits.'

A brief flutter of hope sprang into life in Kalli.

'What's it like, Jason? Is it a great city like I saw...' She stopped herself from saying *in the sphere* and concluded, 'in my books?'

'Well, it depends on your point of view,' was all he said, and she left it at that.

Jason had a map of the immediate area and so there was no danger of them getting lost in the ramshackle warren of its streets and it was not long before they found the bar in which she had first felt the approach of womanhood.

It looked amazingly unchanged and Kalli had to remind herself that although she had seen much and understood much since she was last here, very little actual time had passed.

The bald, thickly set man was still behind the bar, with two young women behind him.

She studied the man to be sure it was the same one who had been unimpressed with Jansen, but spent no time on trying to recollect the girls.

They were just girls.

Jason was obviously unfamiliar with this kind of establishment and was standing in the middle of the noisy and noisome throng, looking around with some bemusement. Kalli left him there and addressed the barman.

'I'm looking for a man; a black man with white hair. I won...'

The barman gave her a very fleeting glance and said, 'You're too young to be in here. Get out.'

Kalli was momentarily too shocked to say anything but after a moment said, 'I'm only asking if you...'

Once again she was cut off. This time he looked down at her, pointed to the door and snapped: 'You heard. Fuck off!'

But now Jason was with her. 'There's no need to be so aggressive, sir. Kalli was only asking for if you knew of this man, who happens to be her father.'

The barman was not mollified by Jason's explanation. In fact, he seemed even angrier.

'So, there's two of you. You don't look much older than the girl. Now, I've got regulars to serve, so get out before I throw

319

you out! Now!' Once again, he indicated the door.

Jason interposed himself between Kalli and the bar.

'Just answer the question and we'll be on our way.'

The barman looked up at the ceiling and then back at Kalli and Jason. Kalli was suddenly aware that a sinister silence had replaced the cacophony of the regulars.

The barman said 'Right' and flung up the flap that allowed egress from the bar area. In a second he was bearing down on Kalli and Jason, rolling up a sleeve as he came on.

He swung a ham sized fist at Jason.

And almost instantly found himself face down on the bar with an arm pulled tightly behind him. The girls behind the bar gave out high-pitched gasps and backed away. The silence from the crowd of drinkers ceased to be sinister and became merely alarmed.

'Now,' Jason said, grunting with the effort of keeping the bigger man pinned face down in a small puddle of stale beer, 'let's have no more unpleasantness; unlike you I'm trained in unarmed combat and I can break your arm whenever I want to. Kalli, ask this nice, helpful man your question.'

Kalli obeyed but strained to hear the barman's answer as his face was half in the beer. She nodded to Jason who slowly released him, stepping back as he did so. He held his erstwhile captive in a warning stare. 'Behave,' he said.

The barman turned to Kalli. 'OK, I know the guy. He comes in most evenings but this is his night off. He should be in tomorrow. He'll be in about midday and again in the evening.'

'Thanks,' Kalli said, and then looked at Jason, 'OK, we can go now.'

The crowd parted to let them through, and, just as they were leaving, Jason turned and, addressing the barman but loud enough for everyone to hear, said, 'Thanks for the help. We'll be in again tomorrow.' He grinned. 'We might even buy a drink!'

The air outside was penetratingly cold, and instinctively she drew closer to Jason, who, to her intense pleasure, put an arm around her.

'That was quite a display,' she said, smiling as she looked up at him.

He shrugged. 'Self-defence is just part of our training. When you go around the world like I do, there's no telling who you'll bump into.'

She turned her attention to the sky, and the reason for the cold was instantly obvious.

The clouds had disappeared and the deep black sky was resplendent with stars. Half hidden by the crowding roofs an enormous yellow crescent moon could be seen, looking like a tremendous celestial longbow. And higher above the horizon than she remembered it, shone that brilliant star, with the four dimmer stars in attendance.

She pointed it out. 'What is that? It's so bright!'

He threw it an unconcerned glance. 'One of the planets, I think. I don't know which one.'

'And the four little stars near it?'

He looked again. 'Four? I can only see three. Probably moons or just a line of sight effect; I don't know.'

She looked again. The sphere had not mentioned a brilliant planet with three or four moons, but she was sure that her books had. But when talking about the possible planet, it had been made clear that the moons were only telescopic sights.

So the mystery was unresolved.

She was about to ask Jason a more personal question when another mystery was upon her.

From the north west a brilliant star suddenly rose above the roofs; even more brilliant than the mystery planet, and unlike that object it was moving rapidly. It passed almost directly above them and then faded as it dipped towards the other horizon.

'What was that?' Kalli breathed.

It was quite dark now but Kalli was sure Jason was grinning.

'That, Kalli,' he said, 'is the Orbital Platform. Pass the tests, and that's where you're going!'

# Three

Kalli spent some time absorbing that statement, but shortly after they returned to the hostel, she stopped him from going any further into the building and said, 'Orbital Platform. So there is still some type of space travel. Just low Earth orbit?'

He pursed his lips. 'Well, I'm going to give you one mark out of two. There's a bit more going on than just LEO.'

'So why haven't you told me this before?'

'I could ask you the same question. It's obvious you're holding something back. You're not the same girl I was with when we flew over London.'

'One thing at a time,' she said, 'this puts a different slant on things. You have an Orbital Platform and you're collecting breeding stock. The two must be connected.'

'OK, I'll give you two out of two.' With a jerk of his head, he indicated two seats around a low table. 'Let's sit down.'

Kalli watched him making himself comfortable and, after he had hung his jacket on the back of the seat, she said, 'More than LEO. So we're going somewhere. How far?'

He took some time replying, spending those seconds looking deep into her eyes, watching for what reaction his next word would have.

'Venus.'

'Venus!' She looked somewhat alarmed, 'but that's impossible! It's Hell-off-Earth! Clouds of acid, crushing pressure, hotter than the inside of an oven. Completely impossible. There's no way we could be going to Venus!'

'You really are an unusual seal hunter, aren't you,' he said, looking at her with hooded eyes, 'but don't tell me we can't go there—tell the boys in charge. I'm just a grunt; I go where I'm told. Today this forgotten arm pit of Westrania; tomorrow Venus.'

She did not reply; instead she sent her questing thoughts down into the deep substrata of knowledge that the sphere had implanted into her subconscious.

Venus?

Yes, there was something about Venus engraved there. The Council had started investigations into... But Jason was speaking again.

'As you like big words these days, here's one for you—terraforming.'

She looked up sharply. 'Terraforming Venus? That would be very difficult.'

Once again her thoughts probed the sunless depths of her mind. Once again there was a reference to terraforming—but in the Centauri system, not Venus.

She gave up.

'So just a grunt are you?' she said, returning her gaze to Jason.

He laughed. 'Hey, it doesn't make me a bad person! And don't quote me on that terraforming thing, it's just a guess. I was trying to impress you.'

She looked back at him and felt a smile curve her lips.

'You already impress me, Jason. You don't need to try.'

He looked embarrassed. 'Well, that's good then. I think we'll leave it there for tonight, we've had enough excitement for one evening.'

She began to protest. 'No, I'm...'

He raised a finger. 'We'll leave it at that, Kalli. I'm bushed even if you're not. I haven't had to arm wrestle someone for a long time and I'm out of condition. We'll try finding your father again tomorrow. We'll try the midday shift. So goodnight and sleep well.'

And with that he pushed his chair back, collected his coat and with a wave was on his way.

Kalli watched him go with hungry eyes. This was ridiculous; he was treating her just as if she was his ward, his charge. How could things ever change?

Seeing no way forward, she rose wearily and went to her room.

As she lay on her bed, staring at the ceiling, she wondered how she could explain to Jason that she was no longer the naive and ignorant ingénue that he had known previously. How could she explain that she knew far more about the history that had led to this ruination of Earth and humanity; that she had seen a wormhole stretching beyond the farthest planet; seen a ravenous black hole descending on the Solar system?

And more than that, she knew who it was that had brought horror and despair into a peaceful world; that the dimly glimpsed figure whom he believed had been humanity's saviour had in fact been the one who had brought everyone and everything close to oblivion.

Would he not think she was mad?

Where was the proof?

She had thrown the sphere away after it had taught her all it held, but even if she had not, it would not have spoken to him.

How would an inert ball have proven anything?

It would not.

And as she lay there, trying to find her away out of the endless labyrinth, sleep finally took her.

*** 

The next day was as grey and moist as the previous day had been.

After a breakfast spent alone while young people laughed and chattered all around her, Jason finally appeared, explaining that he had had an early breakfast.

*Is he avoiding me?* she thought, looking at him as he talked to a table of smiling young women. She saw how they laughingly reached out and touched him, running their fingers up and down an arm. She saw how he smiled and laughed back at them.

When he joined her after what seemed like an age of high spirited flirting, he took one look at her face and said, 'Good God, what's eating you?'

'Nothing,' she said through tightly compressed lips, 'I'm

fine, just fine. Shall we go?'

He shrugged. 'OK. As long as you're up to it. You don't look well.'

'I'm fine,' she repeated, 'Just fine.'

They walked back to the bar in near-total silence. He tried to strike up a conversation but she simply muttered monosyllabic replies and he soon gave up.

She wanted to stop, to turn him to her and pound impotent fists upon his chest and scream *Look at me! Look at me! Why can't you read what's in my eyes?*

But she did not, and soon they were at the bar.

The place was just as packed as the previous evening. The barman looked up as they came in and immediately began polishing some glasses, throwing them the occasional wary glance.

Kalli looked casually around the noisy room, feeling completely disinterested.

'He's not here. Let's go.'

Jason tapped her on the shoulder and pointed.

'So who's that?'

Kalli followed the gesture and saw a black man with curly white hair in a corner. And saw that he was looking back at her. He had a somewhat shocked expression and was utterly motionless.

'We haven't come this way just to look at him,' Jason said, 'let's go over.'

Kalli found her apathy had evaporated with the actual discovery of Charles and hurried over to him.

He rose to meet her. 'Kalli! You've come back for me!' he said and put his arms around her. He tried to kiss her, but she pulled back. Taking the hint, he released her and sat back down.

'Come, come, join me here!' he said eagerly, 'what are you drinking?'

'Nothing,' she said, 'I'm just here to talk with you, Charles.'

' "Dad",' he said eagerly, 'my daughter calls me "Dad".'

Her face was expressionless as she looked at him. 'That's

why I'm here. To find out who you are.'

His smile vanished. 'What is this—some kind of test? Do I have to provide a DNA sample? A semen sample?' He suddenly noticed Jason, who was standing near the table. 'And who's this? The Paternity Police?'

'I'm Jason,' the latter said, and looking at Kalli, he added, 'don't be too hard on Kalli. She's been through a lot recently.'

Charles' expression softened slightly. 'I understand.' He turned to Kalli. 'I'm so glad to see you! I thought I'd never see you again!'

'Well, I'm here now,' Kalli replied, still somewhat coldly, 'I'd like to ask you a few questions, if that's OK.'

Charles was beaming again. 'Anything my daughter wants!'

'When we last met, you told me you were my father. Tell me about my mother. Start with her name.'

'I see. This really is a test. OK, her name was Jahia.'

Kalli softened slightly. 'Do you know her parents' names?'

'I do. Her father was a man called Idris. Idris Perry.'

Kalli decided that the slight mistake with the name was understandable after so long, and the period of chaos which had blighted the time between Charles and her grandfather.

'And Jahia's mother?'

Charles looked hesitant, and he looked from Kalli to Jason and back again.

'I don't really want to talk about her.'

'Why not?'

'You know why!' Charles said, and his voice was suddenly loud and thick with bitterness. 'She's the one who did this to us! Look around you at how low we've become! How wounded we are! How sick and dying! She did that—the she-devil!'

Kalli fought to keep calm. So much wrong had been done to her grandmother. Baldwin's immense shadow still lay over the years, staining them with its injustice and cruelty.

Finally she felt calm enough to speak.

'And how do you know this?'

'Jahia told me. She was much closer to events than you are,

Kalli. She knew how her mother had betrayed the scientist she worked for.'

Kalli decided to change track. 'Tell me, Charles…'

' "Dad" '

'Tell me, Charles, did your partner ever show you a small sphere, a ball shall we say?'

Charles was puzzled. 'What's that got to do with anything?'

'Did she? And if she did, what did she say about it?'

He leaned away from Kalli and an invisible wall of coldness seemed to have developed between them.

'I saw it once. A small shiny ball. I asked her what it was and she said her father had given it to her. He'd said that if she held it for a while it would tell her lots of things; it would answer many questions.'

'But she never did look—hold it?'

'I never saw her with it again. She said that if her father had wanted her to know things, he should have told her outright instead of hiding behind some stupid ball. Those were exact words, I think.'

Kalli was silent. She thought she knew why her grandfather had relied on the sphere to speak to Jahia. He had been ashamed of his act of violence, of murder. He could not bring himself to tell his daughter but at the same time had wanted the truth to be told. He had not foreseen that his daughter would refuse ever to use it.

And so the truth had not been revealed.

And Baldwin's shadow still lay upon the fleeting years.

'And you deserted her.'

A hunted look came into his eyes. 'It's easy for you to judge me! You weren't there! She had no more love for me! I was just a walking ghost; she looked through me as if I wasn't there. I knew she'd had a bad time looking after her father, and it had taken all the joy from her life. So I knew I wouldn't be missed.'

'Your daughter might have missed you,' Kalli said. Her gaze was bitter and unforgiving. 'You never gave her—me—a chance.' She no longer doubted that the man opposite was her father.

She looked up at Jason who was still standing patiently by her side.

'OK. We're done here. Let's go.'

But on standing she found Charles' hand tightly gripping her arm.

'No,' he said, his voice tight and strained, 'you're not walking out on me. I can see the two of you are nicely dressed and well-fed. You people don't know what it's like here.' He looked around furtively. 'You don't know what I have to do to afford my liquor. I won't let you just leave me, nose down in the dirt. I'm coming with you. I want what you've got!'

Kalli stared back. 'You think I've had it easy, do you? You know nothing about me since you left. You don't know what I've been through. My mother was wounded, suffering, but you took the easy way out. And left her to bring me up. Without you she couldn't do it for long so she took me to the Village where they at least fed and clothed me. You lost your hold on me the day she went looking for you and you weren't there. We're going. Try to stop me and Jason will break your arm.'

Charles released her, and she straightened herself, turning her back to him.

To Jason she said 'That's that. I'm finished with London.'

As they walked out, she could hear Charles calling after her, 'Kalli come back! You can't leave your father! Come back!' And then, more faintly as they were crossing the threshold, she heard him say, 'You're as bad as your grandmother!'

When they were some distance from the bar she suddenly could not walk on. She slumped against Jason and he had to hold her tightly to stop her falling onto the slushy ground. Salt tears stung her eyes as she looked up at Jason.

'How could I do it, Jason? I've left him, left my father to fester in this Godforsaken place! My father—what have I done!'

He held her tightly and she was only aware of his support, his strength. Nothing else. He crushed her against him.

'I'll see if anything can be done,' he whispered down at her,

328

'perhaps we can get him a job at the hostel. Something simple, undemanding.'

She looked up at him, smiling fitfully as he wiped away the tears. 'Yes, yes,' she said, 'please do that. Please.'

She stood straight and he released her.

She looked up at the grey sky and it seemed as if the clouds were moulded from the terrible shadow of Baldwin.

*My grandfather killed you,* she thought, *but still you haunt us. If there's a way to undo the lie that you have entangled us in, I will find it and I will drag you down from the throne you have usurped! Whatever it takes, I will do it!*

She turned her mind from recent events and Charles' pleading desperation.

She never thought of him again.

Then she looked at Jason and forced her lips into a longer smile.

'Let's go,' she said, 'I want to see that Orbital Platform.'

# Four

They hadn't gone far into the hostel when Jason grabbed her arm and brought her to a halt. She looked at him with some alarm.

'I want a word with you,' he said, 'we'll find a nice quiet corner, and then you'll tell me what's been going on.'

After sitting down, Kalli found herself subject to an icy stare from Jason.

'Right,' he said, 'no more flim-flam. What have you been up to since I last saw you? Why are you so different? How do you now know things you didn't even know existed before? What's this sphere thing you grilled poor Charles over?'

Kalli knew that it was time for the truth.

'Make yourself comfortable,' she said, 'it's a long story.'

He leaned back, his gaze softening very slightly.

'My grandfather was a brilliant scientist. He developed a way of encoding memories.'

Jason's right eyebrow raised itself slightly at the word "encoding." But he said nothing.

'He put a record of his days onto a memory device, a ball, a small sphere. And his partner's experiences, as well. My grandmother.

'The sphere told me about their lives in a way that was more than just telling. It felt like I *became* them at vital moments in their lives. And it also imprinted knowledge in my brain, my subconscious. Knowledge that I don't know I possess until I need it.'

'That sounds a very handy little gadget. Much better than poring over all those boring textbooks late at night. Can I take a look at this ball, this magical sphere?'

'No, I threw it away.'

'That was an odd thing to do. I would have thought you could have made a fortune hiring it out to college students. And think of all the things it could have taught me.'

'It wouldn't have reacted to you—spoken to you.'

He looked simultaneously sceptical and annoyed. 'It wouldn't talk to me? What, it doesn't like guys with green eyes and neatly trimmed beards?'

'No, no, don't be silly!' Kalli had a feeling that her exposition was not going too well. 'It only responds to people with a certain DNA sequence.'

'I've never heard of any technology which can do that. Or "encode" memories, for that matter.'

'The technology died with my grandfather. Idris Parry.'

Jason leaned forward and took her hands in his. She let him.

'OK, Kalli. I believe you. Something about you has changed and there hasn't been enough time for you to have taken a college degree in between seal hunts. Even without this magic crystal ball with a built-in genie which pops out when you rub it, I believe you.'

She smiled with pleasure at his faith in her but the smile soon vanished as she thought of what was the next thing she would tell him. But his next words made it impossible for her to dissemble anymore.

'So your one maternal grandparent was a genius. I suppose the other one was too.'

Kalli bridled at his tone, and flatly replied. 'She was and her name was Tamira Adekola.'

Kalli saw his causal posture suddenly stiffen; saw his friendly gaze become coldly alert; hostile.

'Adekola? You don't mean "Addick", by any chance?'

'Adekola was her name. You may know her by the corrupted name of "Addick".'

Jason stood up abruptly, looking around the room as if searching for an escape route. Then he looked down at Kalli.

'You mean to tell me that your grandmother was the one who fucked the whole fucking world up! That she destroyed everything beautiful and civilised and safe and...' He ran out of adjectives. 'She was the one! Your grandmother!'

'Sit down, Jason,' she said, fighting to stay calm in the face of this storm of emotion, 'I haven't finished.'

331

He looked around the room again, obviously deciding whether he should go or stay. But he stayed and sat down again but leaned back to minimise the possibility of contact with Kalli.

'Speak,' was all he said.

'You have to trust me,' she said, feeling desperation cloud her thoughts, 'I'm not making this up. The sphere...'

'Ah, the magic sphere!' he interrupted, and looked away from her. 'Made by cute little elves in Fairyland!'

'Damnit Jason!' she suddenly blazed. The others in the room cut off their own conversations and stared at her. 'I'm not making this up! Why would I come up with a story that would make you hate me! It's got to be the truth, you stupid man!'

He looked steadily back at her, silent. Then, slowly, he said, 'That's right. Why would you come up with a cockamamie tale that would make the whole mothering world hate you? Why would you do that?'

'Yes, yes,' she snapped, 'I didn't have to tell you about her. I could have kept it to myself. But now I'm going to tell you all of it, and you'll damn well sit there and listen to it! And at the end if you don't believe me, you can fuck off back to Pen-whateveritis is and take all your pretty girlfriends with you!'

He grinned at that and said, 'Ouch! And I was so looking forward to taking those pretty girlfriends with me! Now I'll have to listen to you instead!'

She glowered at that, but he smiled again and said, 'Tell me everything you know. Everything.'

And so she did.

She told him of Parry's experiments with memory recall and why he had wanted to do that.

She told him of Plato Base and Project Independence; the plan which would have made humanity almost immune from random extinction events.

But most of all, she talked of Elizabeth Baldwin; surely one of the greatest intellects that the world had ever seen and how she had prostituted her genius through a lust for power and riches.

'So how did your grandmother get the blame?'

Kalli paused. 'There was a video confession which was broadcast over the entire Solar system. I don't know how she was forced to make it as her memory recordings stop before then. But she must have been coerced. I've seen how she seized control from Baldwin at the critical moment and prevented the black hole from impacting the Moon and then Earth itself. The confession is false. I know it is.'

'And the suicide? The flying into the black hole?'

Kalli's face was grim. 'Once again, I don't know how Baldwin did it. But she did. She forced my grandmother to take the hit and then murdered her so that the truth would never come out. But for all her cleverness, she didn't know everything. My grandfather stopped her getting her pretty little hands on the sphere. I know the truth.' But then Kalli's determined expression morphed into one of helplessness and her tone became tearful. 'But I can't convince anyone!'

He was holding her hands again. 'Stop beating yourself up. You've convinced me. I believe you.' He gave her hands a slight squeeze. 'And if there's a way of finally beating Baldwin, we'll find it. Together.'

She beamed. 'Yes, Jason, we'll do it. The world will finally know the truth.' And then her expression became serious again. 'Now I've been straight with you. But there's something you're holding back.'

'Oh, what's that?'

'Our civilisation has taken a tremendous hit. There was a terrible loss of life and in lots of places we've been flung back to a hunter-gatherer lifestyle. But we've survived. We still have machines and computers. The seasons are much worse now and there are terrible tides that make the coasts dangerous. But we're still here! There's no reason why we can't adjust to this new situation and gradually rebuild back to where we were before Baldwin came along. It might take a thousand years, but so what? But all this talk of breeding stock; this crazy idea of colonising Venus. That sounds like we're racing against time. It sounds like there's something even worse coming.

'What is it?'

He looked at her long and hard while she waited for him to speak; to reveal the coming peril.

Then he spoke.

'There is something coming. And it will be worse. But as I told you, I'm just a grunt. I don't know exactly what it is. But there's one thing I do know.'

She leaned forward, anxious to hear the revelation.

'What's coming is the end of the world.'

# Five

Despite the grave significance of Jason's statement, Kalli soon realised that he was telling the truth about how much he knew. He had simply picked up snippets and rumours back at his headquarters, but no-one had made any definitive statements. He understood the project involving Venus to be a direct response to the coming climax, but exactly how it was to ward off that disaster he had no more idea than Kalli. She was a little shocked to discover that he hadn't even been aware of the horrendous nature of that other planet.

But another, lesser, climax was upon them. It was time to move back to the North American heartland of Westrania. She met two other young men and one young woman who had been Jason's co-workers in the collection programme. The young woman and one of the men had been working on the European continent as far as the fluctuating border with Eastrania. It was not known if the Eastranians were also running a collection programme but it seemed likely.

In a quiet moment, when she had Jason to herself, she asked him, 'How do you people go about collecting R.I.F. girls? I mean they don't go about with labels on them.'

'No, they don't. The "F" part is the easiest, of course. We just go by age to save time. There's no actual fertility test. The "R" and the "I" are the most difficult. Basically, it's down to the judgement of the collectors like me. Of necessity, we have to immerse ourselves in the local cultures and get to know people, which is very time-consuming. We have to be judges of character, but you soon get to know what signs to look for. We have to stick to the major population centres to have the best chance of a good...' he paused, ' "harvest". That means we miss out on people who would have been suitable but who live out in the sticks. I would never have—uhh—collected you if you hadn't fallen over in front of me.'

'Lucky old me,' she commented drily, 'And how do you get

335

them to sign up?'

'We show them videos of the life they could be having in Westrania proper. Even the poorest parts are better than this backwater. Of course, we mention the little detail of an off-world life, as well. And it's not just girls.'

'Oh?' Kalli was intrigued.

'No, we collect boys as well; in a rough 1 to 5 ratio. We assume the boys are ready to do their duty, if you know what I mean. Males are disposable but we'll need some.'

'I think I've learned enough, thank you,' Kalli said, wrinkling her nose slightly, 'I'm sorry I asked.'

Jason grinned but, wisely, said no more.

Then came the day that all the young people had to leave the hostel. There was much hugging, handshaking and cheek kissing but in the end all were shepherded onto two rickety coaches. To Kalli's disappointment, she found that Jason was going ahead to the airfield in the helicopter.

Then she found herself forced to sit next to the young woman she had clashed with on the first night.

'Oh, hello,' the latter said, as she sat down, 'fancy meeting you here.'

'It's a small world,' Kalli observed. Then it occurred to her that it was stupid to continue a feud which had no real cause. She turned, extended her hand, and said, 'Hello again. My name's Kalli.'

The other looked somewhat surprised but then said, 'I'm Sara. Pleased to meet you.'

'We got off to a bad start,' Kalli said, 'but I hope we can all get along now. After all, all of us have been "harvested". I never thought I'd end up being compared to a potato.'

Sara obviously was possessed of a literal frame of mind, for she seemed slightly confused by Kalli's last comment. But she decided to pass over it, in the spirit of newly acquired friendship.

'Yes, exciting, isn't it? Did you see all those lovely pictures of where we're going? All those swimming pools and those wonderful restaurants! We can get our hair done whenever we want!'

Kalli concluded that Sara's priorities were somewhat dissimilar to her own but soldiered on with the manufacture of light conversation. 'But what about this Venus plan? Aren't you a bit nervous about the idea of moving to another planet?'

Sara shrugged. 'Not really, it's a new start, isn't it? This part of Westrania is dead on its feet, and I've heard stories that the whole world is going to Hell in a handcart. I really don't think that things are going to get any better; let's face it, the whole bloody world has turned into a shitfest. No, I'll want kids one day and I want them to have the best possible start.'

Kalli was intrigued by this strangely optimistic slant that the other girl had on abandoning Earth and continued, 'I've heard it's rather hot there. On Venus, I mean.'

Sara looked puzzled. 'Is it? Still, the Summers can get pretty hot here, can't they?'

*Hmmm*, Kalli thought, *did Jason overlook the "I" part when he recruited you?*

'How long have you known Jason?' Sara asked, getting into the swing of chatting.

'Not long,' Kalli said, 'he picked me up when I fell over.'

For a moment Sara looked bemused again, but true to form decided not to inquire further.

'He's quite a dish, isn't he?'

'Quite,' Kalli said, wondering why her voice suddenly sounded so hollow.

She was surprised when Sara took her arm and pulled her a little bit closer.

'I tried it on with him once,' she whispered conspiratorially.

'Is that right?' Kalli croaked. *Now that sentence definitely sounded hollow.*

'Yes,' Sara said, with a slight giggle, 'but he wasn't having any. He's got a girlfriend back in Florida. Perhaps we'll meet her.'

Kalli looked directly ahead to where the driver was visible beyond the ranks of young people.

'Yes, that would be nice.'

Sara tried to continue chatting with her newfound friend but was puzzled to find that she had abruptly retreated into silence and could not be made vocal again.

*** 

Kalli found she lost all interest in conversation after Sara's bombshell and spent most of the rest of the journey gazing moodily out at the miserable landscape as it sped past.

The disappearance of the snow was now well advanced, and large patches of bare earth were apparent in all directions. She recalled the President's words when he had announced that they were past the midpoint of Winter. When had he said that?—it seemed like an eon ago. So much had happened. Jansen, Ethan, the Village—all gone.

Later she had found her father and then deserted him, as he had deserted her. No, she had done more than that—she had driven him away.

And it had seemed for a brief moment that she had found companionship, but that had been revealed as yet another false hope.

And now what lay ahead? A trip across an ocean with the promise—or was it threat?—of a much greater journey at the end of it. Suddenly, it all seemed pointless.

Why struggle? Failure was virtually guaranteed. Baldwin's dead hand lay over everything; crushing out all hope.

And then, abruptly, they had arrived. She raised dull eyes to realise that they had just passed through a gate in a huge wire fence and they were at the airfield.

Sara tried engaging her in conversation again, telling her that this place had once been a bustling airport back in the days when people crisscrossed the globe for pleasure in those incredible days when resources were plentiful and life was easy.

Now most of those buildings—the shopping malls, the restaurants, the bars—were gone, with just low, military-style buildings as their replacements. She could see that three helicopters were present; one of which was presumably Jason's.

And on the runway were two large aircraft with strange bulbous noses.

Kalli and her fellow travellers disembarked and were directed to one of the squat buildings. Once in, they were seated in rows before a low stage on which sat three people: Jason and two of the other "Harvesters"

The young woman Harvester rose to speak as the last of the travellers took their seats.

'Welcome, one and all,' she said in a melodious, accentless voice, 'we are just about to embark on an incredible journey. The most important journey you will ever take. Let us not mince words: you young people are the hope of all of humanity. It is no secret that this world of ours, this Earth, is badly wounded. I don't need to remind you of how we got into this dire position; of how one woman brought the Doom of Stars down upon us.'

*Yes,* Kalli thought, *but which woman!*

'Some people think we are wounded beyond hope of recovery,' the speaker continued, 'I am not one of them; I think the best days of our planet are yet to come. But I recognise the need for an insurance policy; a safety blanket. You people are that insurance policy. You are immensely privileged. You have been lifted from the squalor and despair which has hitherto characterised your lives. We have taken you from that and given you hope. In turn, you will give hope back to the rest of the people; those not fortunate to experience your adventures.

'You will be the heroes of a new Mayflower; resolute settlers of a new land. The rest of the world will envy you as you carve your names on the monuments of history.'

*What the hell does that mean!* thought Kalli, as she looked around at her fellow travellers. They were all looking rapturously at the woman on the stage; it seemed as if their eyes were shining with an exultant pride. She looked back at the stage. The young woman was seated and Jason was getting to his feet. He came to the front of the stage. His gaze swept over his audience; swept over Kalli, but he did not see her. He turned slightly to look at

339

the young woman and then back to the audience.

'Well, I'm sure we all agree that Jane has given us a wonderful vision of the future, a future which you will create. You are a golden generation; a generation that will redeem us all and recover all that was lost; all that was stolen from us by that woman.'

*I told him who that woman was!* Kalli thought bitterly, *Was he listening!*

Jason changed from being messianic to business-like.

'And now to practicalities. We will shortly embark on our plane journey and fly to Sanford airport in Florida. After a short rest period, we will then go on to Pensacola.' He grinned. 'Pensacola is a great city. And it also happens to be my home!' He punched the air above his head. 'Yay!'

The audience broke into amused applause. All bar one, that is.

One of the audience put up a hand. 'I thought Jacksonville was Westrania's winter capital?'

'It is. But the launching site for the transfer craft is at Pensacola. Those politicos don't want their afternoon naps disturbed by rocket blasts!'

The whole audience laughed rapturously at that. All bar one.

There were a few more practicalities to explain and discuss, and then the meeting broke up. Kalli hung around to see if she could talk to Jason but along with the other two Harvesters he disappeared through a curtain at the back of the stage and did not reappear.

And so it was, an hour later Kalli sat with the others in the transfer lounge watching the aircraft being loaded.

The reason for their bulbous noses was now obvious. The front of the planes broke open like horizontal jaws and the helicopters and four-wheel drive vehicles were winched or driven into the cavernous interiors.

*They really are bringing their expedition to a close*, Kalli thought, knowing, as perhaps the others did not, that helicopters would never again be flying over ruined London. The Harvest was complete.

Shortly after Kalli found herself sitting in the window seat of a three-seat row in the middle of the plane. She listened with scant attention to the safety announcements and then felt the craft give a great shudder as its engines sprang to life. Almost immediately, the view out of the window began to change as the aeroplane manoeuvred into its take-off position.

The engine noise developed into a mighty roar, and abruptly she was looking down on the dead, snow-pocked landscape. In the distance, she could see the grey blotch that comprised the remnants of moribund London. A dying city in a dying landscape.

Kalli looked past her faint reflection in the window at the receding landscape. More and more of the stricken land was becoming visible. Soon she could see the grey tongue of the estuary on whose shores she had spent her childhood. She could just about make out the drifting ice floes on its surface as tiny white specks.

Soon all detail was lost and the land became a featureless mixture of brown, grey and white.

She knew with a grim certainty that she would never set foot on that land again. Never again would she see the fallen towers of the original London; the squalid hovels of the new London; the torn remnants of her Village where nearly all those she had known had been taken from her in that pitiless surge of water under a swollen Moon.

Ahead of her was a terrifying Unknown. The promise—or was it threat?—of leaving the world into which she had been born.

But she thought of her grandmother, Tamira Adekola, who had also left the home planet for the unknown.

And the thought comforted her.

*I am following you, grandmother,* she said to herself, *and there is unfinished business for me to complete!*

# Six

The journey took seven wearisome hours above a tumultuous grey sea over which monstrous waves had dominion. Several times it seemed as if a colossal hand had reached down, grabbed the aircraft and shaken it like a toy. There were a few screams from different parts of the passenger compartment, but Kalli did not contribute.

Kalli knew that Jason was on the same plane as she and once went looking for him, but was told to sit back down by the woman who had spoken at the meeting.

Eventually, the journey neared its end. From her window Kalli saw a green, mist-wrapped land come into view, dotted with a myriad lakes of all sizes.

With a thrill of excitement, Kalli realised that this at long last was the fabled land of Florida; a country where it never grew cold; where luscious fruits hung down at just the right height for picking, and where birds bejewelled in an infinite palette of gorgeous colours darted among the trees. It surely was the nearest thing to Heaven on Earth! And she was here with…

And then she remembered. And a little of the excitement died.

There was a sudden bump below her, and she knew that they had landed.

Eagerly she looked out, expecting to see the multicoloured birds flitting around like beautiful butterflies.

And was rewarded with a view of grey tarmac and low, military-looking buildings; remarkably similar to those she had seen at the start of the journey.

Her brow furrowed. Oh well, this was just the entry point to Florida. Once they had crossed its boundary things would be different.

They trouped off the aircraft and began the walk to the terminal building.

Kalli was surprised and disappointed to see that the sky here was the same furrowed grey expanse as hung above the offshore island she had recently quitted. It was as if a freshly ploughed field of ashen soil was somehow suspended above her. And the air—yes, it was warmer than she was used to, but it was sticky, cloying, and seemed to be laden with the reek of rotting vegetation. There were no gorgeous colours in any direction she looked.

The group passed close to a perimeter fence, and Kalli was startled to see a small crowd pressing up against it, waving banners and shouting something. As they walked closer, she could read some of the larger letterings.

One banner read:

WOE TO THE SERVANTS OF THE WHORE OF BABYLON

And another:

YE ARE CURSED BY THE VOICE OF THE SEVEN THUNDERS

She turned to the nearest R.I.F. girls for an explanation but they just shrugged.

'Some kind of weirdos,' one said and turned away.

Once inside the terminal, they had their temperatures taken and were asked to give a blood sample; neither of which had been expected. Then after their meagre luggage had been collected, they moved on to a large concourse where the four Harvesters were waiting.

Kalli stared at Jason, hoping once again to catch his eye but once again failing.

It was Jason who spoke.

'Welcome to Sanford and the mainland of the Western Democratic Republic,' he said, and then his face split into a wide grin, 'and my home state!'

He punched the air again, but this time everyone was too jaded to respond. Taking his cue from their lack of response, he continued, 'Well, obviously you're all tired. We'll be putting you up in sleeping quarters for the rest of the day and then we're off in the morning.'

343

'What didn't we fly directly to Pensacola?' one of the males asked, in a tone which suggested he was displeased by the arrangements.

'Well, there is an airport there but only high-security planes go in directly.' Jason essayed another smile, but this time he didn't quite make it. 'I'm afraid you're simply not important enough!'

A few groans indicated that he had misjudged the mood of his audience. He continued, after another failed grin, 'Well, you're all exhausted. It's not the best of flights these days.'

'You can say that again!' someone shouted.

Another said, 'What did that crowd want? The ones outside the fence. They didn't seem too pleased to see us.'

One of the other male Harvesters spoke up. 'Just harmless eccentrics. Every state has them. You must have them in...' He faltered and turned to the woman, who whispered in his ear. He turned back. 'In Britain.' He turned back to his companion, mouthing something; but Kalli was sufficiently accomplished at lip reading to get the addendum: *Whatever that is.*

They were queuing to get their keys when Kalli realised that Jason had come up to her.

'How are you doing?' he said, 'sorry about that dreadful flight, but these days that was one of the good ones.'

She stared at him coldly. 'I'm very well; thank you.'

He looked slightly startled at the frosty response and said, 'Kalli, are you sure you're alright?'

'I'm perfectly fine, thank you,' was her reply and then she turned her back on him and moved away as the queue shifted.

He was left staring at her back in puzzlement as the queue slowly took her away.

\*\*\*

When Kalli arrived at her sleeping quarters, she found she was sharing them with another girl, who was already stretched out on one of the bunk beds. Her new companion lifted her head and said, 'Hello, I'm Deirdre.'

Having exchanged introductions, Kalli also stretched out.

'Looking forward to your new life?' she asked.

'I'm looking forward to getting out of Westrania,' the other replied, with surprising firmness.

'Why? We've only just got here. To the real part of Westrania, I mean.'

Deirdre was on the bed below Kalli and she got off hers so that their heads were almost on a level.

'Haven't you heard? This place is a real mess; gangs and cultists are taking it over.'

'I hadn't. I'm afraid I've been living out in the countryside. It looks like I haven't kept up.'

Finding Deirdre's face a little too close for comfort, Kalli sat up and, hugging her knees, waited for the next revelation.

'You don't want to listen to what the President says,' Deirdre continued, speaking in a husky whisper, as if afraid others were listening, 'according to him we've never had it so good; that things are better now than they were before that Addek bitch fucked everything up.

'But I've got folks over here, and they let me know what's going on by a frequency most radios can't pick up. And things are bad. And getting worse.'

*So much for restaurants and getting your hair done whenever you want!* Kalli thought, *what else has Jason lied about?*

'Then why come?' she asked, after a pause spent thinking about Jason.

Deirdre spread her arms. 'What choice have we got? Are things any better back where we came from? Everything's rotting, falling apart, turning to shit. And my folks have told me something else.'

She paused, waiting for Kalli to say *And what's that?*

'And what's that?'

Deirdre's whisper became almost inaudible. 'The world is coming to an end.'

Kalli did not respond immediately. This was not the first

345

time she had heard those doom-laden words. It was becoming a commonplace. So she just said, 'I see. That does sound pretty bad.'

'Pretty bad! You're a cool one! Anyway, that's why I signed up for this Venus gamble. It's the only thing worth fighting for. That's why I felt goddam lucky when they said I was R.I.F.'

'I don't think life on Venus will be…' Kalli searched for a phrase that would not be a cliché, but in the end simply said, 'a walk in the park, a bowl of cherries.'

'So what? It gives us hope. I didn't come here to get my hair done—I came here to live!'

'And your folks over here. They want to live; to go to Venus?'

Deirdre slowly shook her head to demonstrate her pity.

'You really are a country girl, aren't you? Haven't you read about Noah's Ark? This isn't going to be a joy ride that every idiot gets on for free. These guys will give us our ticket to get on the Ark. But those mugs out there are not going to make it!'

\*\*\*

The next morning, after a breakfast which was much better than any of the ones she had had previously, they waited outside for their transport to Pensacola to arrive.

Deirdre's words from the day before echoed and re-echoed in Kalli's mind.

Why hadn't she been able to reach the same conclusion? Looking back, surely it was obvious.

Item: Some kind of catastrophe, some kind of cataclysm was waiting for humanity in the not too distant future.

Item: The only way to escape this cataclysm, this catastrophe, was to leave Earth and migrate to Venus.

Question: Could the entire population of Earth do that?

Answer: No.

There was another conclusion to be drawn from these syllogisms and that was that the turmoil, the disasters, which had been visited on suffering humanity did not constitute the fabled Doom of Stars.

Which in turn, meant that it had not yet happened.

It still lay in the future.

And that would be—the Near Future.

She became aware that most of her company had already left: there was only a group of about nine or ten left.

An all-terrain vehicle drew up, seven got in and were soon heading for the gate, beyond which lay the outside world.

That left Kalli and another girl. A girl she was pleased to see was Sara.

'Who are we waiting for?' Kalli asked after another ten minutes had passed.

Sara looked around, and then said, with a big smile lighting up her face, 'Here he is!'

Kalli turned around.

It was Jason.

'Hello ladies,' he said, as he joined them.

'Hi, Jason!' Sara beamed.

'Hello,' Kalli said, flatly.

Once again, he looked at her with concerned eyes.

'Are you OK, Kalli?'

'I am fine. Absolutely fine.'

'Is anything wrong?'

'No, everything is fine,' she said, trying to develop the most unconcerned expression that had ever graced her features, 'Perfectly fine.'

Jason looked extremely baffled by that response but evidently decided that he had other things to worry about.

'Where's our transport got to?' he muttered, drawing out a slim object of metal and plastic from his breast pocket. He was in the process of activating it, presumably to contact the driver, when a battered vehicle came through the hastily opened gate and came directly towards them. It shuddered to a halt in front of his group, sending up a splatter of dried mud.

A middle-aged man wound the window down and called 'All

347

aboard!'

Jason stared at him for a moment or two.

'You're not one of the usual drivers,' he commented.

'Well, I'm all you've got,' the other replied, 'do you want to go to Pensacola or not?'

'We do.' Jason turned to the two young women. 'OK, my girls, sling your cases in the back.'

They obeyed, but as Kalli passed Jason, she looked him in the eye and said in a clear, careful voice, 'Jason. I would be very grateful if you would not describe me as one of "Your girls".'

With that, she climbed in the back, leaving Jason to stare at her disappearing rear in perturbed puzzlement.

# Seven

The vehicle was half an hour into its bone-shaking journey when Sara finally asked, 'How long will it take to get to Pensacola?'

Jason was sitting next to the driver and did not take his eyes from the blurred landscape, which was flashing past them. He seemed to be looking for something.

'Between six and seven hours. The roads aren't what they used to be.'

'Six to seven hours!' Sara exploded. 'That's as long as it took to cross the Atlantic!'

Kalli said nothing; like Jason she was staring at the scenery but, unlike him, her eyes did not appear to be focused on anything in particular.

Jason shrugged, 'Things are not what they used to be.' Suddenly, from the depths of his mind, an ancient scrap of poetry came to him: '*Things fall apart: the centre cannot hold.*'

Sara did not seem to be familiar with the quote and snorted, 'Thanks a lot!'

Kalli said nothing.

More kilometres sped beneath the vehicle's wheels. The driver was unusually taciturn for a worker from the Launch Site, Jason thought, where was the usual banter of what ridiculous things the high-ups had asked for now? And as he was mentally wrestling with that issue, he was spending more of his time scanning the surrounding landscape, his eyes narrowing, his face becoming tenser.

Finally, he turned to the driver and said, 'This isn't the right way to the Launch Site.'

The driver's gaze remained locked on the road ahead. 'There's been trouble on the main route. That's why we're going the long way.'

'I haven't heard anything on my comm.'

The driver shrugged. 'That's not my problem, fella.'

Jason frowned and reached into his breast pocket for the

349

small communication device. As he did so, the vehicle made a screeching left turn into a much narrower, even less well-maintained, road and the jerking and bumping of the sudden change of direction caused the device to fall from his grasp. The all-terrain vehicle barrelled along an ever-narrowing road until it came into the environs of a large building and then came to such an abrupt stop that Jason bounced off the windscreen. He was still holding his head when the driver jumped out, came round to his side and, opening the passenger door, shouted, 'That's it! Everybody out!'

Kalli and Sara looked at each other in rising alarm as the man walked along the side of the vehicle, banging it as he went, and shouting 'Out!' Their alarm increased to screaming pitch when they saw that his other hand now held a revolver. They scrambled out and helped Jason out of the cab. He was still holding his head and seemed disoriented.

Kalli looked around and saw that two men had been standing near the house and were now coming towards them. One of them was carrying a long weapon of some kind. As they came closer, Kalli could see that the one carrying the weapon was a strong-looking individual, probably in his thirties. The other was much younger, a tow-haired youth, who looked no older than eighteen and was possibly younger.

The man with the weapon, which appeared to be some kind of semi-automatic firearm, nodded to the driver and said in a deep voice, 'Well done, Joe. The Pastor will be pleased.' He then turned to the three ex-travellers. 'Follow me, please.'

He moved behind them while the youth pointed to an open door in the side of one of the wings of the building; a structure which at first glance looked as if it took the form of three wings in the shape of a straight-edged "U".

Jason was still not speaking and was stumbling slightly as he walked. They passed an object which was the size of an articulated truck, but as a huge camouflage tarpaulin covered it, it was impossible to identify. Kalli took one look behind her as they were about to cross the threshold. The man with the

350

automatic weapon was close behind them, but she could see their erstwhile transport being driven away. The man waved the gun slightly to show that he wanted them inside.

They obeyed.

They walked down a long corridor and emerged into a room brightly lit by strip-lights and whose walls were covered in wooden panels which had some kind of inscriptions on them. Kalli was too frightened to make any attempt to read them. At one end of the room was a table next to an object which she could not identify, but to students of ancient customs would been recognisable as a crudely carved lectern. Behind the table was a man who rose when they entered and came around the table to greet them, wearing an expansive smile.

'Greetings my flock, greetings. Welcome to my Church.'

Kalli studied the man. He was of medium height with a round face which bore equally round, rimless spectacles. He was well advanced in the progression of baldness, as was evident from the broad pink areas visible between plastered down strips of hair.

Jason had recovered somewhat and said angrily, 'What the hell do you mean by abducting us!'

The man raised an admonishing finger.

'We will have none of that in the Lord's house. I am a tolerant man but impious language I will not accept.' He indicated some chairs in front of the table and said, 'Please sit down. You have had a bit of a shock, so please sit down.' He noted their reluctance and once again said, 'Please.'

They all sat. Kalli was in between Jason and Sara and she noticed Sara sobbing quietly.

'Tell us who you are,' Jason said, with barely suppressed anger seething in his voice.

'Gladly,' the man said, 'You may call me the Pastor. I am the Pastor, for we will have none of that episcopalian nonsense here. I do not believe in bishops.' His voice rose slightly. 'Bishops are the wolves dressed as sheep that prey on the innocent flock, and I will not tolerate it!' He smiled softly and when he spoke again,

351

his voice was also soft. 'Now I am the Pastor and you are now part of my communion, my flock, praise be to He Who Reigneth On High!'

Jason looked at him stonily. 'We do not want to be part of your flock. We were on our way to the Launch Site and you appear to have kidnapped us!'

The Pastor spread his arms. 'Let not your heart be troubled, my son. You shall indeed go to the Launch Site. When I have fitted you out for your mission, that is.'

Kalli finally found she could speak, although she discovered her mouth was horribly dry.

'What mission?'

The Pastor looked at her, and his eyes were not kind. 'Whore, you are not familiar yet with the ways of the Church. A female may not speak until a man has given her permission to speak, but as you are new to our flock, I will forgive you. This time.'

Ignoring Kalli and her question, he turned back to Jason.

'Now my son, you have the look of intelligence about you, one who thirsts after the cool, clear water of righteousness.'

'I do,' Jason said, now obviously trying to keep his tone flat and unmenacing.

The Pastor looked pleased. 'I knew it! I have found my disciple who will carry out the Lord's work!'

'And what is the Lord's work?'

The Pastor raised a finger. 'Now my son, do not display the sin of pride. All shall be revealed to you in time. In fact,' he said, moving to the lectern, 'that is why I have brought you and your female sinners here into my chapel. Please show forgiveness in your heart if I tell you things that you are already aware of. Please forgive, as I am only a humble vessel of the Lord.'

He mounted the lectern, and looked down on his sparse congregation. The man with the automatic weapon and the youth stood in the background, in front of the door. The Pastor looked at the ceiling, raising both arms.

'Oh, hear me! I speak unto these people as Jonah spoke unto

the people of Nineveh and they repented! Let no mote of sin remain in their hearts!' He looked down at the three captives and his face became suffused with a great emotion. The strip-lights sent flashes of actinic brilliance from the lenses of his spectacles as he moved his head in a growing frenzy.

'These are the Last Days!' he said in a voice that had gained enormously in volume and timbre, 'the Last Days that have long been prophesied!' His voice had become like thunder, as if it were electronically amplified, but no equipment was visible. *'Then I watched as he broke the sixth seal And there was a violent earthquake; the sun turned black as a funeral pall and the moon all red as blood; the stars in the sky fell down to earth, like figs shaken down by a gale; the sky vanished, as a scroll is rolled up, and every mountain and island was moved from its place.'* He looked down at the seated three, who, against their will, had been transfixed by his oratory. 'And that is the literal truth. All that St John the Divine prophesied has come to pass! We have seen the mountains torn down, islands thrust into the depths of the sea, and great cities, like whorish Babylon herself, have been annihilated by His wrath! Who shall stand against Him? Yes, it is written of the great men of the Earth: *During that time these men will seek death, but they will not find it; they will long to die, but death will elude them!'*

Sara broke into loud sobbing, her head in her hands. There was a great roaring in Kalli's head as of an approaching whirlwind. Seeking reassurance, she glanced at Jason only to see the muscles and tendons working in his jaws as he strove to control himself.

'This the Age of the Beast!' the Pastor cried, 'he has been given dominion over the peoples of the earth to speak his blasphemies. But we, The Lord's warriors, must don the armour of the Lord and defend the Faithful as the Great Day approaches.'

He pointed at Jason. 'And He has moved in me and, through me, He has chosen you, my son, to carry the great sword of Divine Vengeance upon the blasphemers who seek to do the Beast's will and hide from the Lord's righteous anger by trying

353

to leave this world in bodily form.'

He came down from the lectern and stood in front of Jason, so close their knees were almost touching.

'You will be my faithful disciple as together we destroy the Launch Site!'

Sobbing, Sara rose from the chair and made as if to run out of the room.

The Pastor whirled.

'Stay where you are, whore! I will not permit you to leave this place until I have given your man permission to release you! Be warned, child, if you attempt to leave this holy place against my express will, the Lord shall smite you!'

Sara looked at Jason in desperation, her mouth working, but no sound emerging. Then she started running to the open door.

The Pastor roared, 'Strike down the unbeliever!'

There was the bark of the automatic weapon; a short scream, and Kalli knew that Sara was no more.

Then it was Kalli who was screaming.

The Pastor stood over Jason and struck him a stinging blow across his face.

'Boy! Control your whores in this Holy Place, or you too will be judged unworthy!'

Jason half rose, but then slumped back down.

'Excellent,' the Pastor said gently, 'you are forgiven, boy. Now it is time you rested before your great task tomorrow. I have prepared sleeping quarters for you and your whore. But be warned, do not attempt carnal knowledge of her under my roof.'

The flaxen-haired youth approached them and led them, uncomplainingly, out of the room. Kalli was glad to see that Sara's body had already been removed, but there was still a large and very fresh red stain on the floor.

The youth led them in silence across the central courtyard, although Kalli noticed he was throwing surreptitious glances at her. They passed some bulky objects lying on the ground, that at first glance looked like large wooden crosses.

He opened a door, and with a sweep of the arm showed

them that this was where they would sleep. After they had entered, he locked the door.

There were two separate beds, a small table, a washbowl, a pitcher of water and a chamber pot. Nothing else.

Kalli flung herself on the nearest bed, sobbing bitterly. Jason stood silently watching her. He did nothing. There was nothing he could do.

Eventually, Kalli rolled on her back and stared at him with eyes overflowing with tears.

'This is all your fault!' she snarled, 'why didn't you leave me back there! Why bring me to this hellhole! You know he's going to kill us both, don't you!'

'That has occurred to me,' Jason said quietly. 'But don't blame me for the Pastor. I knew things were getting bad here, but I didn't know they'd gotten so crazy.'

She jumped up. 'Have you still got the communicator?'

He shook his head. 'No, I dropped it in the van. I assume the Pastor's got it now.'

She ran up to him and beat her fists against him. 'So what are you going to do now! How are you going to tell your girlfriend that this is your last night on Earth! Tell me that, you bastard!'

He pulled her fists away from his chest and shook his head. 'What girlfriend? I haven't got a girlfriend.'

She looked up at him, her chest heaving. 'What! But Sara, she told me you've got a girlfriend over here!'

He gave a wry smile. 'We're not supposed to get involved with the girls we collect. So I always say I'm in a relationship, so I don't have to hurt their feelings. I say that to all of them.'

Kalli collapsed back on the bed and covered her face with her hands.

When she finally revealed her face to him, her face was completely different.

'I've been such a fool,' she whispered, 'why didn't I just ask you? I've ruined everything; I've wrecked our last night of life.'

Jason stared at her. 'So much for trust. But actually I don't remember saying that I'd committed myself to you, Kalli.'

She shook her head, and for a moment it looked as if she was going to burst into manic laughter. 'No, you didn't! It was all me! It was all in my head! I've been living in a stupid fantasy!'

Jason looked at her. His eyes were sad, and moisture glinted in them.

'Let's lie down, Kalli. And hold each other. We don't know what's going to happen. Let's have some tenderness in this crazy madhouse we're trapped in.'

They lay down together; side by side. The light was dim.

Kalli whispered, 'Jason, we're going to die. If he doesn't kill us tomorrow, he'll kill us the day after. I can't die like this; not knowing love. Make love with me, Jason, please!'

He stared at nothing for a while, then he rolled on top of her.

They kissed. She gripped him tightly, holding his face, smothering it with kisses. She felt his growing masculine demand.

'Yes, Jason,' she breathed, her eyes shining as she looked into his, 'Yes!'

He rolled his head from side to side, groaning in his indecision.

'I, I – I can't, I can't, Kalli! How old are you?'

'It doesn't matter, Jason. I'm here with you. You're here with me. We're all that matters. I want you to do it, Jason, I want you to do it!'

But he rolled off her and stood up. 'I can't, Kalli. Not here. Not knowing he's not far away with that sick mind; an evil mind that justifies killing with some twisted words!'

He crossed back to the bed she was lying on, and sat beside her, gently touching her hair.

'I will love you, Kalli, because I want to. But not here. Not with him nearby, probably listening in right now and panting as he paws himself.' He leaned nearer to her and kissed her forehead. And when he was very close he whispered, 'We will laugh and love together when we are somewhere else, far away, sometime in the future. But first things first; before I can do that, I have to kill the Pastor.'

# Eight

They did not remember how long they sat or lay in the room before unconsciousness finally claimed them. They did not remember how many times they awoke from shallow sleep, wondering for a few seconds where they were before they recalled the horrific reality of their situation.

But then, after much dozing and waking, the door of their prison opened and the two men, the younger and the older, came in.

The younger man placed a tray on the table. On the tray were two lukewarm bowls of oatmeal, a fresh pitcher of water and two plastic tumblers. Once again, the young man, or youth, Kalli could not be sure of his age, seemed to give her lingering glances. She stared blankly at him until he looked away. All that time, the older man kept a rifle trained on them.

They ate their meagre breakfast without enthusiasm. Kalli pushed hers away when she had only eaten just over half.

'It tastes like a dog's vomit,' was all she said, glancing at Jason.

'You should finish it,' he said, 'you might need the energy.'

'Really? How much energy do I need to take a bullet in the brain?'

He did not answer but, saying, 'Excuse me,' took the chamber pot into the corner to use it.

Time passed. Half an hour? Two hours?

They could not tell. But then the door was unlocked again, and the two men escorted them back into the main block.

The Pastor was waiting for them.

'Good morning,' he said, rising to greet them, 'Please be seated.'

They sat together on one side of the table. The Pastor glanced at Kalli and then Jason.

'Tell the whore to sit in the corner,' he said, 'she has been wicked.'

358

'I will not,' Jason said, 'she is not a whore—she is my friend.'

Kalli stood up. 'It's alright, Jason. I'll go. I don't want to cause you any trouble.' She moved from the table and sat in a corner of the big room.

The Pastor leaned slightly towards Jason. 'You did well, my son. I watched the whore try to seduce you, but you repulsed her like a true Son of Light.' But his expression changed from neutral indifference to stern disapproval. 'But then I heard you say bad things about me, bad things which the Tempter must have put into your mouth.'

In her corner, Kalli could hear his words and a cold shiver ran through her. So the Pastor had bugged the room, as Jason had guessed. But had he overheard everything that Jason had said? Had the Pastor heard Jason's whispered comments about planning his demise? Rigid with fear, she awaited the outcome.

'What bad words were they, Pastor?' Jason replied, his voice seemingly firm—to Kalli's ears. But what of the Pastor?

'You know, my son. You implied that I was watching the whore and using her lewd display as an excuse to yield to the temptations of the flesh.'

'I may have said that. I was exhausted and worried.'

'No, my son. That is not enough. You must wholeheartedly repent. For without repentance, there can be no forgiveness. Our Lord said we must forgive someone seventy times seven if they repent. So do you repent?'

Jason looked at the Pastor. There was only Kalli, the Pastor and himself in the room. Perhaps if seized the Pastor and threatened to…

Then he noticed, just under the folded arms of his interlocutor, the metallic glint of the muzzle of a pistol. The Pastor, it was now clear, was not foolish enough to deliver himself weaponless into the hands of others.

'I truly repent,' he finally said.

The Pastor seemed to relax. 'Praise be to the Lord! I had feared that I would have to kill you and look for another instrument of vengeance. And time is so short! The Beast roams at will, seducing the foolish, amazing them by bringing down fire from Heaven and other blasphemies!'

Jason felt his tension relax slightly, knowing that he was safe from immediate death. But if he had not noticed the pistol...

He tried a different approach.

'Pastor, may I ask why you are so certain that these are the Last Days as prophesied by the Divine Saint?'

'That is obvious, my son. The great tumults that have struck the world; the fires, the earthquakes, the tempests. All these are prophesied.'

'But all these are explained by science, Pastor. The orbital shifts caused by our near encounter with the black hole.'

'No!' Jason recoiled slightly as the Pastor brought the flat of his hand down onto the table with a loud report. 'No! Science falsely so called! The Tempter devised this wickedly named science to lead us astray. His invention of science is why we are being punished. And he has almost succeeded in seducing the Children of Light. He has sown many thistles in the garden of true belief and they have sprung up with poisonous thorns to rend and maim the weak-minded of our brothers. First, he fashioned bones of fish and reptiles from stone and placed them in the earth so that the people would believe that they were the remains of creatures that had held dominion over the world thousands and thousands of years ago! Oh, my son, such cleverness! Truly, he is a fallen angel. Then he tricked them into believing that their great grandfathers had been monkeys! Oh, so many people were led away from the straight and narrow path. I weep for them, my son. I weep.'

Jason looked at the Pastor silently for a few minutes, noticing the wide, staring eyes, the flecks of spittle at the corner of the mouth. Then he tried once more.

'But Pastor, why do you hate those who are trying to leave the Earth in rocket ships? Why are you determined to destroy the Launch Site?'

The Pastor leaned back and, to Jason's surprise, removed the pistol from his lap and placed it on the table. Jason's gaze flashed from the pistol to the Pastor and then back to the pistol. Was it within reach? Could he…?

'You disappoint me again, my son,' the other said, 'I see your covetous eyes on my weapon. But you will not take it. You will not take it because you begin to feel the growth of His Grace within you, and you know that I am the instrument of that Grace, which I pour into you; my vessel.' And before Jason could say or do anything else, he moved the pistol, so it was completely out of reach. 'Now to answer your question about our fallen brothers at the Launch Site. They are corrupted almost beyond redemption, my son. They know that they are truly damned and face the Second Death in the Lake of Fire. So what do they do? Do they humbly abase themselves, cover themselves in sackcloth and ashes like the sinners in Nineveh? Even now it is not too late, the fools!

'But no. They compound their sins beyond all hope of salvation. They commit the sin against the Holy Spirit, for which there is no forgiveness. In their crazed madness, they seek to escape His Wrath by moving to another world. As if the Lord was lord of only one small ball of rock! So it is my holy duty to frustrate their wickedness by bringing all their works down in the cleansing fire, just as the great Tower was overthrown!'

The Pastor seemed to have used up all his energy with that last outburst for he lapsed into silence and, putting the pistol back on his lap, leaned back and closed his eyes.

Silence filled the room for several minutes. Jason glanced at Kalli, who looked back at him helplessly.

Then the Pastor stirred.

'Well, I think I have given enough exegesis to lift the scales from your eyes, Jason.'

Jason lifted his head suddenly at the unexpected use of his name.

The Pastor smiled gently. 'Oh yes, I know all about you, Jason. I have chosen you especially.'

'And why would that be?'

'I know that in order to get into the complex at the Launch

Site a code must be supplied. You have sufficient rank to use those codes. I also know that the codes are generated randomly at the end of a period which is normally also chosen randomly.' He smiled, 'Except one of my agents on the site—and yes, I have many—altered the timing of that generator. So starting tomorrow, the code will not change until they realise that there is a problem and find the alteration my servant made. We should have a few days to employ the code without fear of being caught using an old one.'

'What's this got to do with me?' Jason said, his whole body now iron-rigid again.

'I admire your modesty, Jason. It is a commendable virtue. But in your case, the modesty is false.' He looked away from Jason for a moment and called, 'Greg! Bring it in!'

Kalli looked at the opening door, and the tow-headed teenager came in. As he passed, he once again stole a glance at her. Kalli felt a stab of fear. The youth obviously found her arousing. Did the Pastor's moral convictions require him to keep his minions under firm control?

The youth approached the table, and respectfully placed a small object in front of the Pastor. He then withdrew, not before casting another surreptitious look at Kalli.

Jason looked at the object.

It was his communicator.

The Pastor picked it up. 'You dropped this when you arrived, but as you can see, we retrieved it. Now this piece of the Devil's handicraft responds to your retinal patterns. It will transmit the code as we approach the complex and let us in.'

'And if I refuse?'

The Pastor shook his head pityingly. 'I have already said the code will not change immediately. After we remove one of your eyes, it will still be fresh enough to permit the communicator to transmit that code. And do not think that will be the end of you. You may have noticed some large crosses as you were taken to your sleeping quarters.

'We will crucify you and your whore. Now, when our Lord

was on the cross, His Father was merciful and took him away quickly. But often it takes days to die upon the cross. You will endure days of hell and then wake up in Hell. But that is not what I want for you.

'Come willingly with me and help me destroy the Launch Site. Then there will be a moment's flash of light and you will be taken from this place of darkness and wake up in Heaven.' He jerked his head in Kalli's direction. 'If you will not be merciful to yourself, be merciful to your whore. You will be crucified facing each other. Do you really want to spend your last days seeing nothing but her agony?'

Jason seemed to have been transformed into stone. He was utterly motionless but the tendons and veins in his flesh could be seen standing out like whipcords. Even from her distance, Kalli could see the tremendous strain he was under.

Finally, he moved slightly.

'What do I have to do?'

The Pastor nodded and smiled. 'Well done, my son. You have chosen wisely. I have a tanker truck at my disposal, but it will not be holding rocket fuel. I could not obtain enough of that. It will, however, be holding several tonnes of an impact-sensitive explosive; enough to destroy most of the firing gantries at the Launch Site. I hope I do not kill too many of the personnel there, because vengeance is the Lord's.'

Jason held out a hand. 'Alright, I'll do it.'

# Nine

'When are we doing it?' Jason asked in a flat, dispirited tone.

'Right now,' the Pastor said, 'the Devil finds work for idle hands to do!'

Jason was very close to him and stood taller and stronger than the older man. Perhaps he was thinking, even at this late stage, of seizing the Pastor, but Greg and the other guard were standing nearby, both armed. So Jason did not move. Instead, he said, 'Won't they be suspicious if an unscheduled tanker suddenly turns up?'

The Pastor shook his head. 'Not with the correct code. My sources tell me they are so short of fuel so they will see us as manna from Heaven. And with you by my side, who they know and love, they will be so happy to see you that, like the heathen Trojans, they will fling wide the gates.' He smiled. 'That's why I am anxious to have all of your body as my companion rather than just a piece of it.'

He turned to the older of the two guards. 'I'm afraid you won't be with us on the path to glory, Eddie.'

Eddie nodded reluctantly. 'I was afraid you would say that. But there will be another day.'

'Indeed there will. I must leave you behind to rebuild and recruit. I very much doubt the blow we strike today will be the final cut. The Beast is not so easily overthrown—but let not our hearts be troubled. A great day is about to born!' He then looked at Greg. 'But you, my son, you will ascend in the fiery chariot that we will create and be seated at the Right Hand!'

Like Eddie, Greg showed displeasure, although for precisely the opposite reason.

'Eddie says he wants to go,' he mumbled, looking at his feet, 'he's older than me. Why can't he go 'stead of me?'

'Greg, my son,' the Pastor said, his voice having developed a dangerous timbre, 'are you not willing to do the Lord's work? Are you disobeying His commands?'

364

'The Lord hasn't spoke direct to me,' Greg said, but catching the Pastor's glare as he looked away from his feet, suddenly added, 'No sure, I'll go. Praise be the Lord!'

'Praise be!' said the Pastor. Smiling contentedly, he turned back to Jason. 'You too, my son, will be seated on the Right Hand.' Then he seemed to remember something and subjected Kalli to a hard stare. 'But the whore. It is not for me to judge her. But we cannot leave her here to spread her lascivious poisons— she will accompany us.'

It was then a terrible realisation crashed into Kalli's consciousness. 'What happens to us when we get inside the Launch Site?'

The Pastor looked at Jason. 'Still, she speaks without permission. But I do not have time to chastise her now.' He looked again at Kalli. 'Why you, me, your master and Greg—we shall all be snatched up to Paradise in a fiery chariot.'

'You mean we'll all be killed when the tanker explodes!' she said, glancing desperately from the Pastor to Jason. Jason's face was impassive: he had no reassurance to give.

'Now we must go,' the Pastor continued, 'time is short for us to meet Eternity!'

Jason and Kalli were pushed out of the building and made to stand near the great tarpaulin-covered object. Greg and Eddie pulled back the sheet, revealing an old-looking fuel tanker.

*Looks like they've gone back to diesel,* Kalli thought, *everything is falling apart, crumbling away into the primitive. How long before they're using flint axes?*

The Pastor stood admiring the tanker, rubbing his palms together in his joy. 'Magnificent! Truly the Lord moves in mysterious ways. Even a piece of worn-out metal such as this can become one of his weapons against the Deceiver!' He turned to Jason. 'You, my son, will have the honour of driving. I will be at your side with my revolver in case your courage fails you at the last moment and you decide to defy the Lord.'

'I've never driven one of these before,' Jason said, 'it's too old. I don't know what to do.'

365

The Pastor put on a look of disappointment. 'Come, Jason, gird up your loins. That comment is not worthy of you. I know your career, how you have been travelling the world in flying machines, collecting whores for your immoral purposes. You will drive. Let's have no more nonsense.' He then turned his attention to Greg and Kalli. 'Greg, take the female into the back of the vehicle and bind her securely. You have brought the rope?'

'Yes, Pastor.'

'Then be quick about it! You will stay with her to guard her. Perhaps you can think of some words of scripture which may comfort her as her end approaches.'

The tanker was basically a huge metal tube, and Greg took Kalli to its back and, picking up a small folding ladder which had also been under the tarpaulin, pointed his revolver firstly at her and then at the vehicle.

'Climb up and open the door,' he said, and then after a slight pause, added, 'whore.'

She glared at him but obeyed. The door opened to reveal the interior—a great cylinder, lined on either side with boxes, chained together.

*The explosive*, she thought.

Greg climbed in after her and was holding an object other than his pistol. He put it on the curved floor, touched a control, and sallow yellow light came from it. As the cylinder had no windows, it was soon the only light illuminating Greg as he turned to close the circular door. He seemed to be having some trouble closing it, as he had to make three attempts to get the door to shut. Even when he appeared to be satisfied, she could still see a narrow arc of daylight on one side. She looked around, trying to find some way out of this nightmare, but there was only her, Greg, the boxes of explosive and the lamp in front of her. She turned around. A rectangular hole had been cut in the end of the cylinder which abutted onto the cab, but that had been covered over with a sheet of what looked like plywood. No light came from around it.

'It ain't no good you lookin' around none,' Greg said, 'you

366

ain't going nowhere. Except Hell.' And with that he came towards her, holding a thin rope. 'Now I gotta hogtie you, whore.'

He bound her wrists together, grunting oddly in the process. Kalli noticed that he seemed to be brushing against her burgeoning breasts more than was necessary. Then he tied her ankles together. She tested the knots as soon as he looked away. They were not expertly done, but she would not be able to undo them by herself. His nearness to her body appeared not to have muddled Greg's concentration enough so he could no longer tie knots. She then realised she could hear voices behind her. Twisting around, she realised that they were coming from behind the sheet of plywood. It could not be particularly thick.

'It is time to go,' she heard the Pastor say, 'time to meet our wondrous Maker!'

Instantly there was the full-throated roar of the engine coming to life. The vehicle might be old in appearance but there did not appear to be anything mechanically wrong with it. They would be on their way to the Launch Site any time now. As if to confirm her thought, the tanker gave a sudden jerk and then she could tell it had started moving.

She turned back to Greg. He was staring at her, his face lit from below by the yellow light, turning it into a mask seemingly carved from brimstone. His eyes were sulfurous ovals in a face that the upward cast of the light had turned into that of a lecherous gargoyle.

Maybe she was in Hell already.

Suddenly she felt the urge to speak, to try to find out why all this was happening.

'You know we're all going to die, don't you?' she said, forcing herself to look directly at him.

He nodded. 'Sure 'nough. We're bound for glory. Praise be!'

'Who told you that? The Pastor? Why do you believe him?'

'The world's endin'. Any fool can see that. Hurricanes and earthquakes. Waves as big as mountains. Sometimes the Moon is so small you can hardly see it; other times it looks like it's gonna

367

fall right on top of you. The Summer is so hot that nothing can live down here. Winter's so cold up North, birds fall out of the sky. The Pastor done explain it all. That's as plain as the nose on your face.' He looked at her chest. 'Or your titties.'

'Why do you believe the Pastor?' she said, ignoring the salacious comment.

'He's a man of God. That's all anyone needs to know.'

That was that. There was no way through his wall of belief. It was best just to accept the inevitable.

But then something rose from the depths of her mind.

'Hey Greg,' she said, 'I think I gotta pee!'

He shrugged. 'So pee. Don't worry me none if you soak your pants.'

She looked at him askance.

'Could you help me take off my pants, so I don't wet them?'

He suddenly looked very alert and threw a glance at the plywood partition.

'I don't know about that,' he finally said.

Just then the tanker hit something in the road and the vehicle drunkenly lurched to one side.

*God!* she thought, *Impact sensitive! The whole thing might go up at any moment!*

The tanker righted itself and carried on its deadly journey.

She looked back at Greg, once again finding him staring intently at her.

'You like me, don't you, Greg?'

No answer.

'Tell me, Greg. Have you ever been with a woman?'

No answer.

'Have you seen a woman's body?'

He licked his lips, tried to speak and failed, tried again and said, 'No, I ain't.'

'You don't want to leave this world without touching a woman, do you? You know what it says in the Good Book—in Heaven they are neither given nor taken in marriage but are like the angels.'

368

'Yeah, the Pastor says that often time.'

She was running out of opportunities, she knew that. For all she knew, they might already be at the gates of the Launch Site.

'Have you ever seen between a woman's legs? Have you ever seen her,'—she used a forbidden word, knowing it would inflame him.

His face was flushed, his eyes seemingly bulging.

'No,' he finally managed to say.

'Then this is your chance. Your last chance before Eternity. Undo me and I'll show you.'

'Why've I gotta untie you?'

She gave him her broadest possible smile. This was it, no time to hold back. What happened in the next few seconds would determine whether she lived or died.

'Well, if I can use my hands you can watch me play with myself. You'd like that, wouldn't you Greg?'

For answer, he rushed forward and feverishly, with shaking hands, began to untie her.

She glanced behind him.

Yes, in his frenzy he had not brought the pistol.

He undid her hands and then her legs, all the time staring at her crotch.

And then his own crotch received a vicious kick from Kalli, a kick which had every gram of her strength behind it. He doubled up, involuntarily bending towards her. She smashed a desperate fist onto his chin, momentarily straightening him.

She knew she must keep the advantage. Greg was only a youth, but he would still prevail in any prolonged fight. He was balling his fists and roaring as Kalli crashed directly into him, sending him spinning backwards onto the door.

Under his impact it flew open, and she had a momentary glimpse of the road, blurred by the tanker's speed, just before he fell out of the tanker onto it. Her momentum almost flung her out of the tanker to join him, and for a few terrifying seconds she hung over the road, desperately clutching the door frame. It took a great effort to right herself and fall back into the belly of

369

the vehicle.

Then she could hear the Pastor shouting behind the plywood partition. She ran to it and ripped it away, tearing her nails in the process.

An arm holding a pistol came through the gap. The gun fired, blinding her with acrid smoke. The bullet ricocheted off the roof and out of the open door.

She grabbed the arm which was holding the pistol and slammed it against the side of the gap. The hand did not drop the pistol but neither did she release the arm; instead she forced it against the side of the gap with all her strength.

Through that narrow gap, she saw Jason take both hands off the wheel and deliver a pile-driving uppercut to the Pastor's chin.

'Kalli!' he yelled, 'get out if you can! Now!'

The tanker swayed alarmingly and began jerkily to turn. The speed dropped.

She ran for the open door and leapt out, heedless of what lay beyond. She landed on soft ground and, rolling over, saw the tanker swerve onto a bridge crossing a wide body of water. She saw a figure jump from the cab. From this distance, it looked like Jason. He landed in the water, close to the nearshore. She saw the splash and ran towards it.

The tanker continued its crazy crossing of the bridge, swerving from side to side, bouncing off the railings with the terrible cacophony of rupturing metal.

She saw a body in the water. Was it moving? She ran down the river bank. She was almost there.

The tanker hit the supports on the far side of the bridge. Instantly, it was replaced by a great, rapidly expanding ball of red and yellow flame, interwoven with deep black smoke, that hurtled towards her like a rapacious predator.

The shockwave hit her just as she was diving into the water to escape the lethal heat and hurtling daggers of shattered stone. From below the surface, she saw flames pass overhead and felt talons of fire bite into her. Chunks of masonry were falling all around.

And then unconsciousness took her.

# Ten

Kalli opened her eyes to see Jason's concerned face a few centimetres away. As he saw her eyelids flutter open, the concerned look faded somewhat.

'You made it!' he said, a great smile lighting up his face.

'Only just,' she groaned, 'I feel like I've been hit with a sledgehammer and then had my lungs set on fire.'

'You breathed in burning air just like I did, but you had a bit of luck—the collapse of the bridge caused a huge wave, and it must have pushed you back onto the shore,' he said.

'Just as well, as I can't swim,' she said. She tried to get up but then fell back with a groan. 'No can do.'

'Just take it easy, you've swallowed quite a lot of Perdido Bay water—something I normally wouldn't recommend. And you didn't seem to be breathing when I found you, so I tried artificial respiration—not easy with one arm.'

'One arm?' she gasped, and this time succeeded in sitting up. She saw his left arm was hanging limply by his side. 'What happened?'

'Hit by a flying chunk of masonry. Don't worry; it's a clean break, simple transverse fracture. I'll get over it.'

Having sat up, Kalli looked around. The bridge was completely gone, except for a few stumps of masonry on both shores, looking like the remnants of decayed teeth. Two of the larger pieces of shattered masonry were protruding from the violently agitated water, and slowly dissipating streamers of black smoke hung over the scene of devastation, as if reluctant to leave. Around them, the grass had been burnt brown, grey and black by the fiery breath that had swept across the water from the terrific detonation of the Pastor's cargo.

'That was one hell of a bang,' she finally said.

'No shit. If it hadn't been for the cushioning of the water, we'd be up there playing harp with the Pastor—or been chased by little red devils with pitchforks. I'm not sure which.'

'You're sure he's gone?' she said, scanning the water to be sure he was not at that moment emerging from the flood with vengeance on his mind.

'Certain. He was out cold after my haymaker. He didn't get out of the cab.'

There was no more to say about the Pastor. She thrust him from her memories.

'So now what do we do?' she finally asked.

'We wait. That explosion would have shook them up in China. Someone will come to have a look.' He glanced at the turbulent water again. 'We sure as hell aren't crossing that water without wings.'

Wings arrived quite shortly afterwards in the form of a helicopter. Jason waved at it with one good arm, Kalli with her two good ones. It settled close to them, blowing singed shreds of grass into their faces. A woman in uniform stepped down from the cabin and walked towards them, shielding her eyes from the flying fragments. As she neared them, she recognised Jason and her eyes lit up.

'Jason!' she said, 'I heard you were back in town. Couldn't you have found a quieter way of telling folks you're back!' She came up to him, still beaming. Then she saw his arm and went into a solicitous mode. 'Your poor arm, what have you done to it, you poor little darling!'

At that provocation, Kalli made a *hmmmpphhh!* noise and said quietly, 'Hello. I'm here too.'

The woman turned. 'Oh hello, I didn't see you there.'

'Obviously,' was Kalli's dry response. 'Well, now you lovebirds have reintroduced yourselves, is there any chance of getting us out of this war zone?'

'Of course,' the woman said, turning back to Jason, 'but what happened here? We heard the noise in the complex like an atom bomb going off. We thought the asteroids had started bombarding us again.'

'It's a long story,' Jason replied, 'but can I tell it in the chopper? We're more than likely going to go down with shock when all this sinks in. And I do have a broken arm.'

The woman blushed slightly. 'Sorry. It's just that I'm in a bit of shock myself seeing you again!'

Kalli gave her a killing glare, but the woman survived.

As the chopper began its descent, Jason pointed out two tall machine-gun towers either side of the entrance gate.

'They're new,' he said to Kalli, 'things are going south quicker than I expected.'

'Not quicker than I expected,' she said, 'I saw how all this got started. You haven't.'

He looked questioningly at her. 'That Baldwin woman?' he said over the clamour of the rotors.

Her lips became a thin line. 'Yes, the Baldwin woman.'

*How will I lift your shadow?* she thought to herself.

The helicopter landed and as Kalli was helped out she looked around.

So this was the fabled Pensacola she had heard so much about! And Jason's home!

There were low buildings in all directions inside the high wire fences. But they looked much the same as all the other official buildings she had seen on other continents.

What caught the eye were the tall spidery gantries, reaching up from blast-scarred and fire-blackened concrete into the turbulent grey sky. Four mighty launch gantries, and in three of them were stubby-winged shuttlecraft, ready to go through those dismal clouds into the clean blackness of space.

Jason saw where she was looking. 'Yes, that's why we're here, Kalli. If all goes well, you'll be in one of those babies before long.'

She smiled. A thrill shot through her: the thrill of the idea that her long, perilous quest was nearing its climax but also a thrill of concern as to what the next stage might bring.

They entered one of the low, functional buildings and Kalli was relieved when Jason's female friend handed the two of them over to the care of a white-coated man.

However, she blew Jason a kiss as she departed; an action

which did not go unobserved by Kalli. She let it go. Hopefully, that lady was deficient in R.I.F. qualities and Kalli wouldn't be seeing her again on Venus.

The white-coated man turned out to be a medic and after a quick examination said, 'A clean break, Jason. You'll be fine after we've strapped it up. But Carole radioed to me while you were on your way and told me what you've been through. You'll have to have counselling, of course, after such a trauma. I...'

Jason shook his head. 'No, doc. We haven't got time for that. I know I'm O.K. and Kalli,'—he took a quick look at her—'she's made of tungsten steel. Just fix me up so the damn thing doesn't fall off, check our lungs and we'll be on our way. There's the big meeting of all the evacuees coming up, and we have to be there.'

The doctor nodded. 'Of course. The Big Reveal. How could I have forgotten that?'

As they went into the surgery, she gave him a playful pinch and as he turned to look at her, she smiled and said, 'Tungsten steel. Don't forget to tell all your *ex*-girlfriends that.'

He grinned.

\*\*\*

But the doctor was not to be brushed aside quite so easily. Jason's arm was strapped to his chest almost immediately, but he and Kalli were forced to spend some time in isolation while their obs were studied. Eventually, after quite a few injections and medications, they were allowed to leave.

Jason then spent some time being thoroughly debriefed. He told his stern inquisitors about the Pastor's lair and gave them descriptions of Eddie, and also of Greg in case that individual had survived. He was shocked to find they had not considered the possibility that they had been infiltrated by cultists, but they listened impassively and thanked him for his information.

'But it's like dealing with the Hydra,' one said to him, 'we take down one of these gangs of fanatics and one day later there

375

are two more. There're no easy answers.'

Later in her room, Jason sat talking to Kalli. She was lying on the bed, he was sitting stiffly in an armchair, his left arm strapped to his chest.

'I don't entirely blame the Pastor,' he said quietly.

Her head jerked upwards. 'You what!'

'Well, the Pastor was a bad example. He was just a maniac who disguised his sadism in a wrapper of fake religion. But some of these groups, they're just looking for answers. If you look at it from their viewpoint, after all the false prophets who have come and gone over the centuries, the world finally *is* ending. They want to find some meaning in what is happening, some justification for their suffering.'

'I'm not sure there is any,' Kalli said slowly, 'I am the only person on Earth who knows exactly what happened, thanks to the sphere. I was there in the Control Room when the black hole appeared on the screens. Even at that moment, when the survival of everyone was in danger, Baldwin couldn't give up her dreams of power and wealth. My grandmother saved the entire human race and got blamed and murdered for it.'

Jason sighed. '*She saved the entire human race*—but did she? Maybe she only delayed the execution.'

Kalli put her head back on the pillow.

She did not reply.

After many minutes of silence, she finally spoke.

'So here we are at the end of the rainbow. We're ready to leave this planet and start a new life on another. Or are we?' She sat up. 'Sometimes I wonder if there's something you're not telling me. There're things about this so-called project that don't add up, don't make sense.'

'For instance?'

'For instance: If the entire planet Earth is doomed, why would a planet a hop, skip and a jump away be safe?'

He shrugged. 'I can't answer that. I'm not a scientist.'

'And if we were trying to convert a planet so it was suitable for human life, who in their right mind would choose Venus? It makes Hell look like a beauty parlour.'

Once again he shrugged. 'I don't know. I haven't had the benefit of being turned into a freaking genius by that mysterious sphere of yours. The one I never saw.'

She swung her feet onto the floor and stood up. 'If I thought you were holding back on me, Jason…'

He also stood and looked down on her. With his good arm, he gently stroked the side of her face.

'It's about time you started trusting me, Kalli. I have never lied to you. Maybe at the beginning, I didn't tell you everything I knew. Then you were just a lost teenager that I thought I'd never see again.

'You've raised good points. Points that I was too dumb to think of myself. You're not the same girl I helped to her feet in London. In some ways you are a combination of your grandparents, reborn.

'But you don't have to wait much longer. There's the big meeting in a few days' time when all those leaving this world will be told exactly what is expected of them. Then we will know everything.'

She looked back up at him. There was no excitement in her face, no joy, no contentment.

'Then we will know everything,' she repeated.

*** 

The great hall was as full as it could be. Kalli looked around. Most of the expectant audience were teenage females, obviously the chosen R.I.F. types. There was also a sprinkling of males, all of whom appeared to be young adults. At the far end of the great room was a stage with some empty chairs on it.

Looking at the scene through her grandmother's eyes, she was reminded of that stage where Elizabeth Baldwin had first revealed the outline of her great plan to an enthralled and enraptured audience. Would this plan also end in chaos and despair?

There was not long to wait. Three people, two seemingly middle-aged and one considerably older, came on to the stage.

There was some desultory applause, but the oldest man indicated that it was not necessary.

'Thank you,' he said, 'but you may not feel like clapping us when I have finished.'

He glanced behind him. 'My colleagues and I are the representatives on this planet of the team of scientists, computer technicians and engineers who have been building the last hope of humanity to escape the terrible disaster which is so nearly upon us. A long time ago, an outstanding scientist named the possibility of human extinction as the "Doom of Stars." A very melodramatic phrase, but one which has passed into common parlance. Well, that doom is now upon us and there is no escaping it.' He paused and looked around at his young audience, who stared up at him in rapt but somewhat apprehensive silence.

'You have been collected—"harvested" I believe is the somewhat offensive term you young people use—from all parts of the world. You were chosen—which is the word I find more apposite—for your mental and physical qualities. You will need those qualities for what lies ahead.

'When you were chosen, you were informed that your task, or rather your destiny, was to leave Earth and travel to Venus in order to create a new safe home for our species.'

He paused. 'That was not untrue. But it was only part of the story. I will now tell you what the complete plan is. After I have finished, I will, of course, take questions, although I believe I will have told you all you need to know in my talk. After I have finished, some of you may wish to withdraw from the Project. That is your right, and there will be no pressure put on you to change your minds, even if every single one of you decides the full project is not something you wish to be associated with. Should that happen, it would be the final note in the symphony that has been humanity. But so be it.

'Now I will elaborate on my opening words and describe the Project in its entirety.'

378

When he had finished, some of the audience did get up and walk out of the room.

But not that many, and Jason and Kalli were not among them.

There was, as the speaker expected, a flurry of questions, although the answers did not add materially to his description.

But one question was not asked in that first burst of questioning, and it was Kalli who asked it.

'When do we leave?' she said.

He looked in her general direction but did not fix his gaze upon her. Maybe he had vision problems—he was not a young man.

'In three weeks,' was the reply, 'I'm afraid time is not on our side.'

The crowd of people broke up, each back to his or her lodging.

Later that day, Kalli stood in her room staring out of her window, looking past the launch gantries at the evening sky.

Unusually, the sky was completely clear, and its great dome was becoming a fathomless shade of blue-violet.

A few stars had already appeared, and the emperor among them was a truly brilliant object, shining like a splendid jewel, and accompanied by four much fainter attendants.

# Eleven

'The big reveal,' Kalli said to Jason, 'I said there was something screwy about the original idea.'

'True. I swear to you, I didn't know. It was all above my pay grade.'

'It doesn't matter now. All that matters is deciding whether we're going. It also makes sense to learn that we are not the first people who have been sent.'

'Yes, at least three other groups. I wonder where they are now.'

She touched his good arm. 'Do you really want to go, Jason?'

He looked at her. 'Yes, of course. But I may not be able to come with you.'

Ice invaded her heart. 'What?—why wouldn't you go?'

His smile was wistful. 'I'm a male, Kalli. Males are ten-a-penny. Disposable tools. They may already have enough of us drones.'

She mulled that over.

'We'll see,' she finally said.

\*\*\*

Then came the day when officials took Kalli to another wing of the building, a wing that was white, antiseptic and clinical. There she met two sober, white-coated individuals who introduced themselves as doctors Eduardo dos Santos and Helena Grauber.

Dos Santos was the lead clinician, a florid, smooth-faced man with slick, jet black hair and an unconvincing smile.

'Good morning, Kalli,' he said, 'please be seated. This is the final part of your assessment before we let you leave for Venus.'

'You're too kind,' Kalli murmured, 'why do I need these tests?'

Grauber smiled at Kalli, but her smile was no more

380

convincing than that of dos Santos.

'A good question. You and all the other R.I.F. females were recruited by our peripatetic field personnel. But of course, their choice was based on subjective, qualitative criteria. Here, we will use proper medical procedures to ensure that you are fit to make the journeys.' Another attempt at a smile. 'Let me reassure you; we reject very few of the females who have been recruited.'

'I think I have already demonstrated the "R" and the "I" part of that acronym,' Kalli said, with an air of ungracious resignation, 'so do I now have to pass an "F" test?'

The two doctors briefly exchanged glances. Then dos Santos said, 'Well, not exactly. It's a general body check-up. Plus an estimate of your intelligence.'

'Oh,' Kalli said, 'so I have to solve puzzles as well, do I?'

'No, no,' the male doctor said, 'nothing as crude as that. We use an electroencephalogram and using various sophisticated algorithms we can arrive at a good estimate of your mental capacity.'

Kalli looked from the one to the other and then rose from her chair.

'Let's get on with it.'

Several hours later, after an MRI scan, a CT scan, ultrasound, X-ray, and finally the electroencephalogram, Kalli was back in the interview room. She looked, without any observable emotion, at the two medics.

'Well, how did I do?'

Both dos Santos and Grauber looked strangely uncertain, unsure of themselves.

After a few seconds of pregnant silence, Kalli said, in a somewhat louder voice, 'Well, did you find anything you shouldn't have?'

Dos Santos shook his head, 'No, not really. At least nothing to worry about.'

Grauber took up the explanation. 'You have suffered some lung damage from breathing in superheated air, but we can fix that. Your heart, kidneys, liver, vascular system, ovaries are all fine…'

Kalli raised an eyebrow. '*But*…let's have the "But".'

'It's the electroencephalogram readout,' dos Santos said, looking almost apologetic, 'we're not sure how to interpret it. There may have been a fault with the machine. However, we have another, so I'm afraid we'll have to ask you to retake it.'

Once again, Kalli rose from her chair.

Once again, she said, 'Let's get on with it.'

Another hour passed, and the three were back in the interview room.

'I hope there are no more tests,' Kalli said dryly, 'did you find a brain in there?'

Dos Santos nodded and then, speaking strangely slowly, said, 'Yes. Indeed we did, Kalli.'

'There's another *But* hanging in there, doctor,' Kalli said, 'you'll have to stop doing that. What is the reading that is concerning you?'

Once again, the doctors exchanged glances, then dos Santos said, 'There's nothing actually concerning us, but it is the truth to say that we are extremely intrigued. Your brain scan is unlike any we've ever seen before. You have a higher density of neurons that is normal, and the speed of transmission between those neurons is considerably higher than the mean, median or mode. To be frank, neither of us have ever seen anything like it. Can you help us to understand you, Kalli?'

'My grandfather was a great neuroscientist when the world was full of great scientists. He devised a method of recording and transmitting memories and knowledge from one brain to another. It works best when the individual is a young adult, but when the brain still retains its plasticity. I am that young adult.'

Grauber smiled, and this time the smile was more believable, 'Well, you don't talk like someone without a formal education, Kalli. Who was this neuroscientist?—We may have heard of him.'

'Idris Parry.'

Was it Kalli's imagination or had a slight chill entered the room?

'Idris Parry,' dos Santos said, seemingly weighing his words very carefully, 'Yes…wasn't he the partner of…?'

Kalli raised a hand. 'I know what you're going to say. I think it's best you don't.'

Both doctors were taken aback by the tone of command in Kalli's voice, and dos Santos stopped speaking. Both medics then stared at the prodigy before them for several silent seconds.

'So,' Kalli said, 'I assume I am fit to make those journeys you mentioned.'

Grauber nodded eagerly. 'Most definitely. You will be a great asset. Don't you agree, Eduardo?'

Dos Santos appeared to have lost the power of speech and then, visibly shaking himself, said, 'Yes, most definitely.'

'Thank you,' said Kalli, 'one more thing before I go. I understand that the number of males on these "journeys" is strictly limited. May I enquire whether a male called Jason has been selected?'

Both doctors were still staring at her when dos Santos suddenly realised he had been asked a question.

'Yes, I'll find out for you. Jason. What is the last name?'

Kalli was dumbfounded. In all their time together, she had never asked if he possessed a last name.

'I don't know,' she finally admitted, thinking that she had lost a smidgeon of her air of omniscience which had so impressed the doctors.

'I'll search for the name "Jason",' dos Santos said, and turned to his computer terminal.

After a few minutes, he turned the screen to Kalli, revealing the image of a young man with a closely cropped auburn beard and spectacular green eyes.

'Yes,' said Kalli in a soft voice, smiling in the process, 'that's him.'

She lost the smile a second later when dos Santos said, 'No, I'm afraid he hasn't been selected.'

Kalli stood up and approached the doctors. They were still

sitting, but even so she was not much above them.

'I believe you said that I would be an essential member of this project.'

'Yes, a very great asset, Kalli.'

'But I must tell you I'm not going.'

'What? But you must! I don't understand!'

Kalli pointed to Jason's image on the screen.

'If he isn't going, I'm not. If I am going, so is he. That is my statement of what is going to happen.'

Dos Santos turned to Grauber, looking as if he was going to say something; then, after apparently changing his mind, he turned back to Kalli and said, 'Yes, of course. I shall make the recommendation.'

*\*\**

Kalli was so anxious to tell Jason her news that she burst into his room without warning. He was sitting in an armchair, carefully stirring a mug of chicory coffee.

'Whoa there, tiger!' he said, looking up, 'where's the fire?'

'I've got some good news at last!' she beamed and proceeded to tell him.

He gave her a happy, relaxed smile when she had finished.

'That's great news, Kalli. Attagirl!'

She looked up at him, eyes shining with happiness, her arms around his neck.

'And, Jason, this means we can start planning! We can finally become a proper couple!'

She stopped smiling when she saw him shaking his head.

'Jason, what's wrong? Why are you looking at me like that?'

He disengaged her arms and pointed to the other armchair.

'Sit down, Kalli. We have a few things to sort out.'

With a drawn face she obeyed and sat waiting for him to speak.

'Kalli, it's too soon to talk about being a "proper couple". We have to wait a bit longer.'

'What!' she said, almost angrily, 'what is this? Are you giving me the brush-off!'

'No,' he said, 'I'm not. But it's not right just yet. You are almost a woman; you're so damned close. But you're not quite there yet. That's why we have to wait.'

'I knew it!' she shouted, 'you *are* giving me the brush-off! You want to go back to those girls with the big smiles and the big tits! The whole world is shit, and now the rest of my life will be shit!'

He crossed to her.

'Now stop that! I spoke the truth. Those other girls—they were just pretty shapes to play with for a while, that's all. You and I are destined to be together, I've known that for some time—and we will be. We just have to wait a while longer. At present, it's not right. But it will be. I will wait for you, Kalli. And then it will be *so* right!'

She looked up at him. Her eyes were moist.

'You mean that?'

'Every word. We'll face the Doom of Stars together and lick it.'

She stood up and threw her arms around his neck. This time he did not remove them.

'Jason, oh Jason, you're a good man! Sometimes I wonder what the hell I did to deserve you!'

He grinned down at her.

'Funny, I've been thinking exactly the same thing myself about you!'

And they kissed.

But then they parted.

# Twelve

The bone-shaking thunder of the rocket motors died, and silence washed over Kalli in a sweet, refreshing wave.

Through the porthole window, she could see the planet Earth as a marvellous white and blue segment, topped with a thin blue haze, and knew the haze to be the precious, life-sustaining atmosphere.

*I am leaving all I ever knew,* she thought. *Never, ever to see it again. And in cosmic terms, it will soon be just another failed world: destroyed by uncaring forces.*

Thoughts, memories, longings, passed through her mind as she watched the doomed planet turn below. She thought of Tomlinson, of Jansen, of Kiara, of Ethan, of Sara.

She knew three were gone, but what of all the others she had known, in those dead days which now seemed as remote as the Jurassic?

What of her father?

She would never know. That world was dead, in every sense of that dread word.

She turned to Jason and asked, 'And how long will it take to get to Venus?'

'We'll be travelling in powered flight, not ballistic. So, given Venus' position in its orbit—about a month.'

About a month.

Kalli visualised the relative position of the two planets, calculated the separation between them, allowed for their relative speeds and somehow instantly knew what their average velocity would be. More and more things were becoming clear to her…

'Thanks,' she said and turned back to the planet below.

More of that world was now visible, and she could see the swirls of cloud marking tropical cyclones in the Gulf of Mexico. Lifting her eyes to the north, she could see the bright glint of the snowfields that still reached halfway down the Canadian part of Westrania.

They would be in full retreat now as the terrible Summer approached; soon only the actual icecap would be left; perhaps not even that. Each Summer had been slightly hotter than the previous one.

None of the works of the human race was visible at this altitude, but as she looked down on the receding world, she thought of the people; all the millions of people—trapped, imprisoned with no possible escape, looking for a way out, but finding none, looking for answers as to why they were suffering—and finding none. The horrific, sadistic injustice that had been inflicted upon those people was beyond comprehension.

Suddenly, she was sobbing, and Jason reached out for her.

'I know what you're thinking, feeling,' he said gently, 'I feel it too. But it's not our fault. We didn't cause this wrong, this hurt. We are as innocent as they are.'

'But we're escaping,' she said, wiping the tears from her cheeks, 'Me, because I am a bloody R.I.F. girl, you because I chose you. But there's nothing I did to gain that status; I didn't struggle to get it. I was just lucky. Out of the millions as deserving of life and happiness as I—I am the one who gets the prize.

'Or, I think I am,' she added, 'We don't know what lies ahead.'

'No-one does,' Jason said, and they relapsed into silence.

Eventually, the Orbital Platform swam into view against the blackness; a central cylinder with four long spokes protruding at the cardinal points. And at the end of each spoke was a large vehicle with streamlined wings. Kalli observed that the wings were oddly far forward on the fuselage which puzzled her for some time until the answer rose from her subconscious.

*The front part detaches*, she realised, *it's designed for atmospheric flight!*

But that, in turn, was odd. Why would anyone wish to penetrate the atmosphere of Venus?

The transfer shuttle docked smoothly with the Orbital Platform, and some hours later the contingent transferred to the interplanetary spacecraft which hung patiently at the end of one of the spokes.

The interplanetary craft was much bigger than the shuttle, and as Kalli looked around, she thought it felt a little like being in the belly of a massive, metal whale.

'The front part of the ship separates for atmospheric flight,' Jason said, pointing to the far end of the vehicle.

Kalli smiled gently. There was no point in telling him she had worked that out quite a while ago, just by studying its design.

The ship was big enough to hold a cafeteria, and so Jason and Kalli gravitated towards that; (which is not perhaps the best term as the Orbital Platform and its attached vehicles were all in free-fall).

They spent some time talking with the other evacuees, talking about their hopes for the forthcoming struggles. They all knew that there would be many of those ahead.

It was evident that most of the passengers were young women, but Kalli looked on them with equanimity; she was secure in the knowledge of her bond with Jason.

He had, perhaps unwisely, mentioned that it would be his job to fertilise many of those females.

She had simply smiled a beatific smile and said calmly, 'Of course. How could it be otherwise? I'm sure they will get used to artificial insemination in time.'

He had just grinned and, wisely, never mentioned that possibility again.

The Captain's voice suddenly burst in upon them, driving away all smiles and laughter. They listened intently.

'Hello, everyone. Welcome aboard the Cytherean. We will leave Earth orbit in approximately thirty minutes. It will take us just under four weeks to get to Venus. I am assured that the weather is as bad there as it always is, so don't get too excited. You all have your assigned sleeping quarters, and you will find more information there when you decide to settle down for the journey. There is a viewing platform amidships, for those of you who want to say goodbye to Earth.

388

'Our acceleration will be very gentle so you will be able to walk around and you'll find that the deck is indeed under your feet and not above your head.'

There was a little forced laughter at that, and then silence.

'That's all for now,' the Captain said, 'just sit back and enjoy the ride.'

Sometime later, Jason and Kalli heard the engines rumble into life as the fission reactor heated the propellant into blazing vapour.

They felt themselves gain weight and their feet press onto the deck, instead of floating above it.

They made their way to the viewing area to find that most of the rest were already there. The Orbital Platform was visible, shining brightly in the unshaded sunlight, and beyond that was the home planet. The Platform drifted off to one side, and they were left looking at the planet Earth as slowly, slowly its entire circumference came into view.

It was a magnificent sight; it was the eastern hemisphere which was now visible, and Kalli could see the tremendous green and brown bulk of Africa laid out before her, with only a few wisps of cloud adorning it.

Above it was the Mediterranean and then Europe; where she had fought with wolves and found love.

But as usual, banks and curls of cloud hid it.

At the top and tail of the splendid disc were the great icecaps, reflecting the sun in almost blinding glory. Kalli could see that the northern cap reached down to nearly sixty-four degrees of latitude; but that would be its maximum extent; in this cycle at least.

She could stand it no longer.

She turned to Jason, tears winding their way down her cheeks.

'Oh, Jason! We're leaving behind everything! Everything we've ever known!'

He did not reply immediately because he was also crying.

\*\*\*

The journey did not seem long. Kalli was pleased to observe that some of the science of her grandmother's time had been retained. The vessel was protected by its own miniature magnetosphere, an invisible shield, which became increasingly vital as the Cytherean headed closer toward the sun's blinding photosphere, causing the rain of charged particles to grow to dangerous heights.

Venus grew brighter and brighter as they arced towards it. Soon it was bright enough to dazzle as a point source but a few eagle-eyed people, Kalli among them, could begin to see its disc.

And then one day it was no longer a point of light, or a barely discernible disc, but had become a world, a great ball of unbroken sulfurous-yellow cloud, streaked with dim bands of atmospheric turbulence. And close to that world, clearly in orbit around it, were objects that shone with the coruscant radiance of metal.

Kalli realised they must be huge, to be visible from their current distance.

Still, they swept silently on; still the planet grew and grew until it filled all their vision, and gradually the true nature of the orbiting structures was revealed. They could see that they were going to pass close to one of those immense structures.

It seemed to be bearing down on them with an inevitable collision as the consequence before Kalli realised that they had simply underestimated the size of the orbiting constructions, and it was still a very long way distant.

She could now see that it was a curving dish of at least a kilometre in diameter, and from the outward-facing side protruded at least a dozen mighty cylinders.

'What is it?' Jason said, shielding his eyes from the reflected sunlight.

Kalli searched through the voluminous stack of data that now resided in her subconscious. Then she had it.

'It's a laser array!' she breathed, 'a tremendous laser array!'

And then they were past it; below it.

The Captain's voice shook them out of their wonderment.

390

'Well everyone, I'm afraid this is the parting of the ways. The section of the craft in which you are sitting will now detach itself and continue its journey into the clouds on automatic pilot. In time it will return to rejoin the main part of the craft, but you will not be on it. So this is most definitely the parting of the ways! Bon voyage!'

Almost immediately there was a deep-throated roar as mighty metal components slipped past each other, then there was a sudden jolt and the view from the windows changed abruptly. The underside of the laser array rapidly shot upwards and was soon out of sight. Jason thought he had a brief glimpse of the major part of the Cytherea apparently rocketing up into a black sky, but he could not be sure.

As he and Kalli looked in the direction of travel, they could see faint yellowish tendrils of mist begin to rise from below; tendrils that soon became thicker; that became mighty anacondas of ochre cloud. And then without warning, they were in sulfurous obscurity as the outside world was transmuted into a yellow-brown wall of curling vapour. From outside came a strange ululation, as if they were passing through some resistant substance.

They were inside the clouds of Venus.

# Thirteen

As Fraschini looked out over the rolling yellow clouds, he hoped, as he had done so many times before, that they would break and yield a glimpse of the underlying land, but still this time, as so many times before, there was no sign of a tear or rift in that undulating mass of ochre obscurity.

He gave an unconscious shrug of disappointment but continued to gaze out over the mass of roiling clouds, unaware that De Vries had joined him.

Both men stood silent for some time, and when De Vries finally spoke, Fraschini gave a little start as he realised he was not alone.

'Still hoping for some change, something to see?' De Vries observed, in what was not really a question.

Fraschini shrugged. 'No harm in hoping.'

Both men fell silent again as they looked out over the slowly churning clouds.

In the brilliant sky, approaching the zenith, the last hope of humanity was glinting in the blaze of the fierce sun.

'What was that weird name you gave it?' De Vries asked, breaking the long pause.

Fraschini did not turn to look at his companion, and in the thick acid-streaked plexiglass his reflection was impassive.

'*Spes Nostra.*'

'Which means?'

Fraschini turned to De Vries, sighing as he did so..

'I've told you enough times. And it's not a weird name: it's a completely accurate, definite name.'

'OK, OK, calm down. I was just making conversation. I know you're under a lot of pressure, just take it easy. We all feel the same here.'

Fraschini gave a weak smile. 'Sorry. I know I'm jumpy, it's just that we're so close now, so damn close.'

De Vries gave his friend a quick pat on the shoulder.

392

'You're worried that we're leaving too many behind, aren't you?'

'Of course. But we can't go on rescuing them. It's too energy-intensive. We can't go on doing it. It's just; it's just...'

De Vries waited, silent, immobile.

'It's just what I'm condemning them to. So many of them, people just like you and me. They don't deserve it.'

'No-one deserves it, no-one could possible deserve it,' De Vries said slowly, and there was a great sadness behind his words. '*Spes Nostra*—well named. But the last cohort will be arriving soon. We must not show any despondency; we must give them hope.'

Fraschini remained silent for a while, and then, 'Hope. There must always be hope. Does the oak tree have hope when it drops an acorn to the forest floor? Hope that there will be life after its own death?'

De Vries turned back to the window, and the corrugated deck of slowly-churning cloud.

'You and I comprise that oak tree, Fraschini, and yes, we do have hope for the acorn we are about to send into the uncharted forest.'

Fraschini nodded his acceptance and said no more.

\*\*\*

The craft burst through the surface of the world-girdling mass of cloud. Kalli, Jason and all the others were eagerly waiting to discover what would be revealed now that they were free of that choking mass. On the forward-facing windows a fine mist of liquid had appeared; a mist that gradually congealed into oily droplets which ran slowly down the plexiglass.

'Sulfuric acid,' Kalli commented. She was no longer surprised when knowledge burst into her mind; she now just accepted such things as the way she was.

Jason wasn't listening. Instead, he pointed ahead of them and simply said, 'Look!'

393

Kalli looked. In the distance, seemingly hovering above the clouds, was a cluster of large spheres, linked together by transverse tubes. The orbs shone with a fierce intensity under the swollen sun, a sun that was fully forty percent wider than that seen from Earth. Beyond that cluster of spheres, almost touching the ochre horizon, was another cluster, and between them, a majestic airship was cruising.

'A cloud city!' Kalli breathed, 'so they did build it!'

Until that moment, she had had no recollection of ever having thought about cloud cities—but now she did.

The spheres grew rapidly as the detached portion of the Cytherea neared. Soon the travellers became aware of their gigantic scale as the scintillating points on their surfaces were revealed to be huge windows.

'It really is a city,' Jason said, with awe evident in his voice, 'a city in the clouds!'

'We must be about sixty kilometres above the surface,' Kalli said, speaking with authority on a subject she hadn't even considered a few minutes earlier, 'the atmospheric pressure and temperature are Earthlike at this height.'

'So we can breathe the air?'

Kalli shook her head. 'Not unless you can breathe carbon dioxide heavily infused with sulfuric acid.'

'Oh,' was Jason's only reply before he fell silent.

The city continued to grow in front of their entranced eyes until their vision could encompass only one sphere. A platform jutted out of its equator, and their transport settled gently onto it. Almost immediately a bellows-like tube extended itself and mated with their starboard side.

'Time to get off,' Jason said, a few seconds before the vessel's automatic voice said the same thing.

It took some time before all the evacuees had disembarked and Jason and Kalli were among the last.

The airlock closed smoothly behind them, and then the wall in front of them lifted itself to reveal a large enclosure, bounded on one side by a gigantic window. Through that window could be seen the swiftly diminishing airship as it continued its journey to the other cloud city.

And waiting for them were two men.

Neither was young. One was balding, the other with a shock of pure white hair.

The first man stepped forward. His face was both heavily wrinkled and heavily tanned. But his eyes were kind.

'Welcome my young friends to Venus Cloud City One. The first Venusian cloud city and we like to think the best.' He paused, as if expecting some reaction to that comment, but, receiving none, continued, 'I am Alberto Fraschini.' He turned, indicating the white-haired and dark-skinned man behind him, 'and this is Cornelius De Vries. And we have the honour, and also responsibility, of being the controllers of Venus City One. Welcome again. Now I will let my colleague say a few words.'

Fraschini stepped back slightly and De Vries took his place.

He pointed a remote-control device at a large monitor screen and it flashed into life, showing a shining dot, moving sedately against a black background.

'This is the craft that you are taking out of the Solar system. The *Spes Nostra.*'

There was a little buzz of discussion from the evacuees and a young woman at the front said, 'I don't know those words. Do they mean anything?'

'Yes. In an ancient language, now unfortunately dead. They mean "Our Hope". You may be thinking that's a rather maudlin concept, but it is meant in all seriousness. And not only is that craft our hope, it is also our last hope.'

There was another buzz of conversation, but De Vries put up a hand.

'Well, I think that's enough enigmatic comments for people who have only just arrived. We'll let you settle in, and after dinner, we'll fill in all the gaps and answer all your questions. Or at least, try to answer all your questions.'

Sometime later, the dinner of hydroponically grown proteins and carbohydrates was behind them, and Jason was standing in Kalli's room. His was an interior room and had no window, but Kalli's looked out over the rolling mass of sulfurous clouds. The cloud city moved faster than the mass of the planet, and the large sun was already setting as a great crimson ball in a tangerine and magenta sky. Near the blue-black zenith were filigree bands of frozen $CO_2$ cirrus. They both spent some time looking at that unearthly sunset until Jason said, 'So Venus was never more than a temporary stop, a way station.'

Kalli turned from the sunset to sit on the bed. 'Yes. That was obvious, really. Making Venus suitable for human habitation would be a titanic undertaking, even for a human race that was at the height of its powers. And certainly beyond the wounded fragment which remains. Seventy kilometres below us are rocks so hot they are almost glowing. It's an unimaginable Hell.'

'If it had been possible, it would have been much closer to home than what we are actually facing. It would be the same sun, the same constellations. Just the house next door.'

'There's no point being regretful about something that never could have happened. We are back to the original plan: escape to Alpha Centauri. But the hard way; through normal space instead of the shortcut that Baldwin could and should have given us. I don't know yet how long a standard journey will take, but it certainly won't be a single human lifetime.'

'No,' Jason said, with a tinge of sadness discolouring his speech, 'I guess not.'

Just then, Kalli's door alarm tinkled. She looked at her screen and saw it was Fraschini. She let him in.

'Oh,' he said, on entering, 'I assumed you'd be alone.'

'If you have anything to say to me,' Kalli said, 'then you can say it to Jason as well.'

Fraschini bowed slightly. 'Of course.'

He chose an armchair and sat down. He looked at Kalli.

'I wanted to tell you, Kalli, that De Vries and I know who you are. We know your family's story.'

Kalli looked instantly alert. 'You do?'

'Yes. We know of your grandparents, Idris Parry and Tamira

Adekola. We know what Elizabeth Baldwin was doing in Plato Base.'

Kalli leaned forward, looking strangely angry. 'Then why wasn't she stopped?'

Fraschini looked apologetic. 'I can understand your bitterness Kalli, but I am almost as remote from those terrible events as you are. The records are somewhat fragmentary due to the chaos that followed immediately after the initial disaster, but I can tell you this. The Council was not quite as supine as Baldwin thought. She had not bribed, blackmailed or seduced all of them. There was a group who she did not have in her pocket. They were moving against her, but she outwitted them. They thought it would take Baldwin several years to develop negative matter, but in fact she accomplished it in a few months. So she acted long before they were ready to entrap her.'

Kalli's disturbed expression did not soften. 'She didn't do that all by herself. She set up the equations and found solutions, but it was my grandmother who supplied the data for her to work with.'

Fraschini bowed his head slightly. 'I stand corrected. We didn't know that.'

Kalli's angry expression had changed so that an eager hunger was now the dominant emotion.

'But you know who it was that brought the black hole into the Solar system!'

'We weren't certain, but we have grounds for believing it was Baldwin herself who was the culprit. After all she was in charge and she didn't tend to rely on subordinates very much.'

Kalli rocked back on the bed, looking unseeingly at the ceiling.

'At last!' she breathed, 'at last!'

Fraschini looked at her for a few moments and then said, 'We don't know exactly what happened to Baldwin. We know she was in Greater New York just before Apophis fell on it and obliterated the city. Few records survive from that period. Can you shed any light on whether she died there?'

397

Kalli knew precisely what had happened to Baldwin, but all she said was, 'Yes. I can confirm she died in Greater New York.'

Fraschini nodded. 'Well, that's that then. I thought it only proper to let you know that we were aware of your background and were reasonably sure that the stories about your grandmother were untrue. Thank you for your time.' He stood up, ready to leave.

'Wait a minute!' Kalli said, 'you can't just leave it at that!'

'What do you mean?'

'The people in this room know the truth, but what about everybody else? What's left of the entire human race thinks my grandmother was guilty!'

'I have enough responsibilities and I'm afraid those people are not part of them. Is it not enough that the truth is known by those around you?'

'No it is not!' Kalli roared, 'you've known for God-knows how many years and done nothing!'

'What were we supposed to do?'

'What you will do!' Kalli snarled, her small frame shaking with the intensity of her passion, 'you will send out a radio transmission which will reach every part of the Solar system, which will reach Alpha Centauri and beyond, telling every sentient being in this galaxy, in every galaxy, that it was not Tamira Adekola but Elizabeth Baldwin who gave them the Doom of Stars!'

'I am not used to taking orders from young women,' Fraschini said coldly.

Kalli smiled. 'Yes, what you see is a young woman, one just finding her way in the big, bad world. But I am now much more than that. Much, much more. Within me, I carry the accumulated knowledge and wisdom of Idris Parry and Tamira Adekola; abilities and powers aborted by Baldwin. Day by day I can remember more of that store; access the depths of their understanding. Already I have thought of ways of combining their expertise to increase the chances of a successful journey. I am a match for Elizabeth Baldwin, and I will tell the whole

398

fucking universe what she was and what she did!'

'Why should we get involved in your personal disputes? What you ask will require a great expenditure of energy.'

'Have I not made myself clear, Fraschini? This is not the time for false modesty—I am the most critical person in this whole crew—my presence or absence may well determine whether this enterprise succeeds or fails. May I remind you that you have abundant solar energy? Or that you have access to plentiful raw materials from the poles of Mercury?

'Do I need to express myself in simpler terms?'

Fraschini's expression showed he was battling conflicting feelings.

Then he nodded. 'The sphere. We have been briefed on its capabilities. It is a pity it is no longer with us.'

Kalli shrugged. 'It served its purpose. One cannot depend upon the past forever. I take it that you agree to my requirements.'

Fraschini gave a smile, hesitant at first but then finally broad.

'Yes, of course, Boss. It shall be done.'

Jason, who had been transfixed by the interplay, also smiled. He turned to Kalli.

'And my orders, Boss?'

But now Kalli's expression was no longer fierce.

'Just one. Just be as you are—forever.'

He bowed.

'It shall be done.'

# Fourteen

There is not much more to relate.

The crew of the Spes Nostra spent a month on Cloud City One, learning everything about their craft that needed to be known. Jason showed such natural ability that he was chosen by secret ballot to be the Captain of the vessel.

Right at the beginning of their training, De Vries had explained the nature of their craft.

'The Spes Nostra, like the Nea Avgi, the Zhen He, the Resurgam and the Magellan, are lightsail craft, driven by lasers of hitherto unimaginable power. When its shield is fully operational, it will be five kilometres in diameter but only four point five microns thick. It required the development of a meshwear material composed of lithium-beryllium alloy for such structures to be created and prove strong and resistant enough for interstellar travel. It would have been much easier if we still had Elizabeth Baldwin's method for creating stable wormholes, but that knowledge was lost in the period of turmoil.'

'Given how dangerous that technology turned out to be, perhaps it's best it was lost,' someone at the front said.

De Vries raised his hands in a gesture of uncertainty. 'Perhaps. But your descendants will undoubtedly rediscover it someday.

'To continue: The lightsail will be given its initial impetus from the battery of orbiting laser complexes that you saw on the way in. Each unit will deliver twenty six Terawatts of power in a tightly focused beam.'

'And can you confirm the length of the journey?' said another crew member.

'Allowing for acceleration and deceleration, about two hundred and twenty years.'

'So I will die without seeing the Centauri system.'

'True. But if you stay here, you will also die without seeing the Centauri system. But this way your descendants should.'

*Baldwin, you have so much to answer for!* Kalli thought. But then she also thought, *If the Council hadn't been in the process of developing these cloud cities when the disaster struck, none of this would have been possible. There would be no Spes Nostra.*

Another crew member caught De Vries' attention.

'Is there no hope that the doom can be averted? Is it certain that the inner planets will be destroyed?'

De Vries looked down at the floor and it was quite some time before he raised his head again.

'There is no hope. Let me recapitulate what you have already been told: There are many planetary systems out in the galaxy where there is a giant planet which has migrated inward and now orbits very close to its star. In the process, it would have destroyed any terrestrial planets which were at habitable distances. For reasons not understood, our Solar system escaped that fate, which is how this system of planets was able to develop life and ultimately intelligence. But when the collapsar passed through the Solar system, it set up resonances which destabilised the planetary orbits from Jupiter inward. At first only the orbits of the Moon, Earth and Mars were badly affected. But before it was deflected it encountered the planet Jupiter itself. As a consequence, Jupiter's orbit is becoming more and more eccentric and will soon become chaotic. All our mathematical models agree on that. Once that amount of mass starts moving around it will do one of three things to all the inner planets: either collide with them, throw them out of the system or toss them into the sun.'

There was a grim silence. They had heard those repellent tidings before, but now that their departure was nearly upon them, the truth seemed more bitter, more poignant, more devastating.

De Vries continued: 'Already Jupiter is looming large in the skies of Earth and Venus. We calculate that in only a few years, Mars will be destroyed and shortly after, Earth will suffer one of the three fates I mentioned earlier. We can't be sure as yet which one it will be. Venus will not be long behind, as Jupiter's fall

401

accelerates.'

Kalli thought of the millions of innocent human beings trapped on Earth, fated to watch their sky become filled by the dreadful face of the giant planet, the Earth-destroyer.

It was unimaginable, unthinkable.

But true.

Soon the entire hall was filled with the sound of comfortless weeping.

Later, Fraschini asked for some time with Kalli.

She insisted that Jason be present.

Fraschini asked them to sit down in his room. Outside it was night. The grey cloud deck was black, as was the sky above it. But in that sky there was a terrible bright star, accompanied by four fainter ones.

The Earth-destroyer.

Fraschini spoke. 'As you know, the Spes Nostra will not be the first vessel we have sent out of the system. We started by sending crewless cargo ships to arrive at Alpha Centauri ahead of the crewed ships. You will need those supplies and materials to survive your first years in the system. Making it safe for humans will be a gargantuan task, much, much more difficult than it would have been if Baldwin had been a decent human being.

'But we cannot guarantee success. Interstellar travel by lightsail is incredibly hazardous. We lost contact with the Nea Avgi not long after it crossed the orbit of Sedna. We will not have time to finish the construction of the Phoenix. You may well be our last hope, but it is almost certain that you will die out there in the blackness beyond the heliopause, beyond the Oort Cloud, and our hope will come to nothing. To dust.'

But Kalli just shrugged and looked at him directly, steadfastly.

'You're an old man, Fraschini, and your thoughts are those of an old man. Ahead you see nothing but death and dissolution. Jason and I will not die in the interstellar void. We will escape the Doom of Stars. I, and through me Idris Parry and Tamira

Adekola, will ensure that outcome. We, and our fellows, and our descendants, will re-establish human society; a society which shall remember the great tragedy that befell its forebears. And old mistakes will not be repeated.'

Fraschini nodded and his lips made a wistful half-smile.

'Once again, I must accept the rebuke. I am indeed just as you describe me. Fortunately, people like me will not be making that journey. On behalf of all who have perished in innocent suffering, and those still to pass, I wish you well, and a calm and, who knows, perhaps prosperous voyage.'

Those were almost his last words to them.

\*\*\*

And so, finally, the day came. De Vries and Fraschini said goodbye and with the rest of Cloud City One began their preparation for the end of days. The crew were ferried up to the orbiting Spes Nostra; its mighty sail fully unfurled and ready to receive the blast of energetic photons which would begin to push it out of the Solar system, past the Earth-destroyer, faster and faster until it breached the heliopause and penetrated interstellar space itself, leaving to its terrible fate an entire planetary system in ruin.

Kalli looked at the control panel. There before her was the alert which showed that Fraschini had kept his word and the message revealing the true depth of Baldwin's crime was travelling out at the speed of light, into the far reaches of the galaxy.

The two women had never met, but somehow Kalli saw before her then the face of a radiant angel, surrounded by a lustrous cope of shining, golden hair.

In her reverie, she raised a fist to the vision.

*I've beaten you, Elizabeth Baldwin,* she thought, *finally, finally beaten you.*

Below her, the great laser complex, the last great achievement of Solar humanity, flashed into silent

403

incandescence, sending out titanic beams of a radiance otherwise unknown in the physical world; beams that crashed soundlessly onto the great sail of the Spes Nostra, transferring the momentum of their photons to the tremendous vessel.

It would be days before any appreciable velocity would be noticeable.

But then…

Jason was beside her. He reached for her hand, his arm long since wholly healed.

'The start of a journey,' he said, 'one we will never see the end of.'

She accepted his hand and held it tightly.

'There is only one journey that matters,' she said, 'the journey with you.'

And they kissed.

# Epilogue

The entity that had once been Tamira Adekola looked at her new surroundings as she fell towards the singularity.

As usual, Baldwin had been right: the negative matter had indeed prevented her from being ripped to subatomic particles by the fearsome gravitational potential of the black hole. And, the hole being a Reissner-Nordström-de Sitter collapsar, she had passed through both the Event horizon and the inner Cauchy horizon. She had penetrated them unharmed—but not unchanged.

As she had passed through that inner horizon she had seen an infinitely blueshifted point of light. She had known she was seeing a record of the total past history of the entire Universe, a Universe to which she was no longer causally connected.

'Goodbye Idris and Jahia,' she thought, 'never will I see you again. I hope you have good memories of me.'

Now she was also no longer causally connected to a transfinite number of possible futures.

She approached the central singularity. No longer a physical entity, she was heir to any one of those transfinite possibilities.

In her causally disconnected state, she saw the singularity and knew what it meant, how it existed, what its relationship to the rest of reality was.

The singularity repelled her and she was accelerated away.

Reality turned itself inside out and she was now flashing up through the horizons of a white hole.

In an instant she saw another infinitely blueshifted point of light: this time seeing all the possible future states of the Universe.

But none of these futures would be hers.

The white hole was not causally connected to her old universe, but it was to another.

As her physical form had been destroyed by the passage into the black hole, so a new physical form came into being as she was ejected from the white hole.

She looked at her new universe and saw that it was good.

There were no stars in this universe, no torrents of deadly radiation, no black gulfs of deadly emptiness.

But there was life and she could hear it calling to her, welcoming her.

And so the being that had once been Tamira Adekola ventured further into this new plane of existence to meet the unknown future.

———————

Other books by Martyn Rhys Vaughan published by Cambria.

*Quantum Exile*: ISBN 978-1-9161619-6-2
*The Cave of Shadows*: ISBN 978-1-9161619-9-3
*Hideous Night*: ISBN 978-1-8380752-2-4